Anonymous

The Journal of Negro History

Volume 6

Anonymous

The Journal of Negro History
Volume 6

ISBN/EAN: 9783337353124

Printed in Europe, USA, Canada, Australia, Japan

Cover: Foto ©Andreas Hilbeck / pixelio.de

More available books at **www.hansebooks.com**

THE JOURNAL
OF
NEGRO HISTORY

VOLUME VI

1921

CONTENTS

Vol VI—January, 1921—No. 1

Vol VI—April, 1921—No. 2

Vol VI—July, 1921—No. 3

VOL VI—OCTOBER, 1921—NO. 4

THE JOURNAL
OF
NEGRO HISTORY

VOL. VI—JANUARY, 1921—NO. 1

FIFTY YEARS OF NEGRO CITIZENSHIP AS QUALIFIED BY THE UNITED STATES SUPREME COURT

THE HISTORIC BACKGROUND

The citizenship of the Negro in this country is a fiction. The Constitution of the United States guarantees to him every right vouchsafed to any individual by the most liberal democracy on the face of the earth, but despite the unusual powers of the Federal Government this agent of the body politic has studiously evaded the duty of safeguarding the rights of the Negro. The Constitution confers upon Congress the power to declare war and make peace, to lay and collect taxes, duties, imposts, and excises; to coin money, to regulate commerce, and the like; and further empowers Congress "to make all laws which shall be necessary and proper for carrying into execution the foregoing powers and all other powers vested by this Constitution in the Government of the United States, or in any department or officer thereof." After the unsuccessful effort of Virginia and Kentucky, through their famous resolutions of 1798 drawn up by Jefferson and Madison to interpose State authority in preventing Congress from exercising its powers, the United States Government with Chief Justice John Marshall as the expounder of that document, soon brought the country around to the position of thinking that, although the Federal Government is one of enumerated powers, that government and not that of States is the judge of the extent of its powers and, "though limited in its powers, is supreme within its sphere of action."[1]

7

Marshall showed, too, that "there is no phrase in the instrument which, like the Articles of Confederation, excludes incidental or implied powers; and which requires that everything granted shall be expressly and minutely described."[2] Marshall insisted, moreover, "that the powers given to the government imply the ordinary means of execution," and "to imply the means necessary to an end is generally understood as implying any means, calculated to produce the end and not as being confined to those single means without which the end would be entirely unattainable."[3] He said: "Let the end be legitimate, let it be within the scope of the Constitution, and all means which are appropriate, which are plainly adapted to that end, which are not prohibited, but consist with the letter and the spirit of the Constitution, are constitutional."

Fortified thus, the Constitution became the rock upon which nationalism was built and by 1833 there were few persons who questioned the supremacy of the Federal Government, as did South Carolina with its threats of nullification. Because of the beginning of the intense slavery agitation not long thereafter, however, and the division of the Democratic party into a national and a proslavery group, the latter advocating State's rights to secure the perpetuation of slavery, there followed a reaction after the death of John Marshall in 1835, when the court abandoned to some extent the advanced position of nationalism of this great jurist and drifted toward the localism long since advocated by Judge Roane of Virginia.

In making the national government the patron of slavery, a new sort of nationalism as a defence of that institution developed thereafter, however, and culminated in the Dred Scott decision.[4] To justify the high-handed methods to protect the master's property right in the bondman, these jurists not only referred to the doctrines of Marshall already set forth above but relied also upon the decisions of Justice Storey, the nationalist surviving Chief Justice Marshall. They believed with Storey that a constitution of government founded by the people for themselves and their posterity and for objects of the most momentous nature—for perpetual union, for the establishment of justice, for the general welfare and for a perpetuation of the blessings of liberty— necessarily requires that every interpretation of its powers have a constant reference to those objects. No interpretation of the words in which those powers are granted can be a sound one which narrows down every ordinary import so as to defeat those objects.

In the decision of *Prigg* v. *Pennsylvania*, when the effort was to carry out the fugitive slave law,[5] the court, speaking through Justice Storey in 1842, believed that the clause of the Constitution conferring a right should not be so construed as to make it shadowy or unsubstantial or leave the citizen without the power adequate for its protection when another construction equally accordant with the words and the sense in which they were used would enforce and protect the right granted. The court believed that Congress is not restricted to legislation for the execution of its expressly granted powers; but for the protection of rights guaranteed by the Constitution, may employ such means not prohibited, as are necessary and proper, or such as are appropriate to attain the ends proposed. The court held, moreover, in *Prigg* v. *Pennsylvania*, that "the fundamental principle applicable to all cases of this sort, would seem to be, that when the end is required the means are given; and when the duty is enjoined, the ability to perform it is contemplated to exist on the part of the functionaries to whom it is entrusted." It required very little argument to expose the fallacy in supposing that the national government had ever meant to rely for the due fulfillment of its duties and the rights which it established, upon State legislation rather than upon that of the United States, and with greater reason, when one bears in mind that the execution of power which was to be the same throughout the nation could not be confided to any State which could not rightfully act beyond its own territorial limits. All of this power exercised in executing the Fugitive Slave Law of 1793 was implied, rather than such direct power as that later conferred upon Congress by the Thirteenth Amendment, which provided that Congress should have power to pass appropriate legislation to enforce it.

As the Supreme Court decided in the case of *Prigg* v. *Pennsylvania* that the officers of the State were not legally obligated to assist in the enforcement of the Fugitive Slave Law of 1793, Congress passed another and a more drastic measure in 1850 which, although unusually rigid in its terms, was enthusiastically supported by the Supreme Court in upholding the slavery regime. The Fugitive Slave Law of 1850 deprived the Negro suspect of the right of a trial by jury to determine the question of his freedom in a competent court of the State. The affidavit of the person claiming the Negro was sufficient evidence of ownership. This law made it the duty of marshals and of the United States courts to obey and execute all warrants and precepts issued under the provisions of this act. It imposed a penalty of a fine and imprisonment upon any person knowingly hindering the arrest of a fugitive or attempting to rescue one from custody or harboring one or aiding one to escape. The writ of habeas corpus was denied to the reclaimed Negro and the act was *ex post facto*. In short, the Fugitive Slave Law of 1850 committed the whole country to the task of the protection of slave property and made slavery a national matter with which every citizen in the country had to be concerned. In the interest of the property right of the master, moreover, the Supreme Court by the Dred Scott Decision[6] upheld this measure, feeling that there was in Congress adequate power expressly given and implied to enforce this regulation in spite of any local opposition that there might develop against the government acting upon individuals to carry out this police regulation. The Negro was not a citizen and in his non-political status could not sue in a Federal court, which for the same reason must disclaim jurisdiction in a case in which the Negro was a party.

In the decision of *Ableman* v. *Booth*[6a] the court in construing the provision for the return of slaves according to the Fugitive Slave Law of 1850 further recognized the master's right of property in his bondman, the right of assisting and recovering him regardless of any State law or regulation or local custom to the contrary whatsoever. This tribunal then believed that the right of the master to have his fugitive slave delivered up on the claim, being guaranteed by the Constitution, the implication was that the national government was clothed with proper authority and functions to enforce it. These were reversed during the Civil War by the nation rising in arms against the institution of slavery which it had economically outgrown and the court in the support of the Federal Government exercising its unusual powers in effecting the political and social upheaval resulting in the emancipation of the slaves, again became decidedly national in its decisions.

Out of Rebellion the Negro emerged a free man endowed by the State and Federal Government with all the privileges and immunities of a citizen in accordance with the will of the majority of the American people, as expressed in the Civil Rights Bill and in the ratification of the Thirteenth, Fourteenth and Fifteenth Amendments. A decidedly militant minority, however, willing to grant the Negro freedom of body but unwilling to grant him political or civil rights, bore it grievously that the race had been so suddenly elevated and soon thereafter organized a party of reaction to reduce the freedmen to the position of the free people of color, who before the Civil War had no rights but that of exemption from involuntary servitude. During the Reconstruction period when the Negroes figured conspicuously in the rebuilding of the Southern States they temporarily enjoyed the rights guaranteed them by the Constitution. As there set in a reaction against the support of the reconstructed governments as administered by corrupt southerners and interlopers, the support which the United States Government had given this first effort in America toward actual democracy was withdrawn and the undoing of the Negro as a citizen was easily effected throughout the South by general intimidation and organized mobs known as the Ku-Klux Klan.

One of the first rights denied the Negro by these successful reactionaries was the unrestricted use of common carriers. Standing upon its former record, however, the court had sufficient precedents to continue as the impartial interpreter of the laws guaranteeing all persons civil and political equality. In *New Jersey Steam Navigation Company* v. *Merchants Bank*[7] the court speaking through Justice Nelson took high ground in the defence of the free and unrestricted use of common carriers, a right frequently denied the Negroes after the Civil War. The court said that a common carrier is "in the exercise of a sort of public office and has public duties to perform from which he should not be permitted to exonerate himself without assent of the parties concerned." This doctrine was upheld in *Munn* v. *Illinois*[8] and in *Olcott* v. *Supervisors*[9] when it was decided that railroads are public highways established under the authority of the State for the public use; and that they are none the less public highways, because controlled and owned by private corporations; that it is a part of the function of government to make and maintain highways for the convenience of the public; that no matter who is agent or what is the agency, the function performed is *that of the State*; that although the owners may be private companies, they may be compelled to permit the public to use these works in the manner in which they can be used; "Upon these grounds alone," continues the opinion, "have courts sustained the investiture of railroad corporations with the States right of eminent domain, or the right of municipal corporations, under legislative authority, to assess, levy, and collect taxes to aid in the construction of railroads."[10] Jurists in this country and in England had also held that inasmuch as the innkeeper is engaged in a quasi public employment, the law gives him special privileges and he is charged with certain duties and responsibilities to the public. The public nature of his employment would then forbid him from discriminating against any person asking admission, on account of the race or color of that person.[11]

In the *Slaughter House Cases*[12] and *Strauder* v. *West Virginia*[13] the United States Supreme Court held that since slavery was the moving or principal cause of the adoption of the Thirteenth Amendment, and since that institution rested wholly upon the inferiority, as a race, of those held in bondage, their freedom necessarily involved immunity from, and protection against all discrimination against them, because of their race in respect of such civil rights as belong to freemen of other races. Congress, therefore, under its present express power to enforce that amendment by appropriate legislation, might enact laws to protect that people against deprivation, *because of their race*, of any civil rights granted to other freemen in the same States; and such legislation may be of a direct and primary character, operating upon States, their officers and agents, and also upon, at least, such individuals and corporations as exercise public functions and wield power and authority under the State.

The State was conceded the power to regulate rates, fares of passengers and freight, and upon these grounds it might regulate the entire management of railroads in matters affecting the convenience and safety of the public, such as regulating speed, compelling stops of prescribed length at stations and prohibiting discriminations and favoritisms. The position taken here is that these corporations are actual agents of the State and what the State permits them to do is an act of the State. The Thirteenth and Fourteenth Amendments made the Negro race a part of the public and entitled to share in the control and use of public utilities. Any restriction in the use of these utilities would deprive the race of its liberty; for "personal liberty consists," says Blackstone, "in the power of locomotion of changing situation, of removing one's person to whatever places one's own inclination may direct, without restraint, unless by due course of law."

In several decisions the court had held that the purpose of the Thirteenth and Fourteenth Amendments was to raise the Negro race from that condition of inferiority and servitude in which most of them had previously stood, into perfect equality of civil rights with all other persons within the jurisdiction of the United States. In *Strauder* v. *West Virginia*,[14] and *Neal* v. *Delaware*,[15] the court had taken the position that exemption from race discrimination is a right of a citizen of the United States. Negroes charged that members of their race had been excluded from a jury because of their color. The court was then of the opinion that such action contravened the Constitution and, as was held in the case of *Prigg* v. *Pennsylvania*, declared it essential to the national supremacy that the agent of the body politic should have the power to enforce and protect any right granted by the Constitution.

In *Ex Parte Virginia* the position was the same. In this case one Cole, a county judge, was charged by the laws of Virginia with the duty of selecting grand and petit jurors. The laws of that State did not permit him in the performance of that duty to make any distinction as to race. He was indicted in a Federal court under the act of 1875, for making such discriminations. The attorney-general of Virginia contended that the State had done its duty, and had not authorized or directed that county judge to do what he was charged with having done; that the State had not denied to the Negro race the equal protection of the laws; and that consequently the act of Cole must be deemed his individual act, in contravention of the will of the State. Plausible as this argument was, it failed to convince the court; and after emphasizing the fact that the Fourteenth Amendment had reference to the acts of the political body denominated a State, "by whatever instruments or in whatever modes that action may be taken" and that a State acts by its legislative, executive and judicial authorities, and can act in no other way, it said:

"The constitutional provision, therefore, must mean that no agency of the State, or of the officers or agents by whom its powers are exerted, shall deny to any person within its jurisdiction the equal protection of the laws. Whoever, by virtue of public position under a State government, deprives another of property, life, or liberty without due process of law, or denies or takes away the equal protection of the laws, violates the constitutional inhibitions; and, as he acts under the name and for the State, and is clothed with the State power, his act is that of the State. This must be so, or the constitutional prohibition has no meaning. Then the State has clothed one of its agents with power to annul or evade it. But the constitutional amendment was ordained for a purpose. It was to secure equal rights to all persons, and, to insure to all persons the enjoyment of such rights, power was given to Congress to enforce its provisions by appropriate legislation. Such legislation must act upon persons, not upon the abstract thing denominated as State but upon the persons who are the agents of the State, in the denial of the rights which were intended to be secured."[16]

The Supreme Court of the United States soon fell under reactionary influence and gave its judicial sanction to all repression necessary to establish permanently the reactionaries in the South and to deprive the Negroes of their political and civil rights. It will be interesting, therefore, to show exactly how far the United States Supreme Court, supposed to be an impartial tribunal and generally held in such high esteem and treated with such reverential fear, has been guilty of inconsistency and sophistry in its effort to support this autocracy in defiance of the well established principles of interpretation for construing the constitutions and laws of States and in utter disregard of the supremacy of Congress in the exercise of the powers granted the government by the Constitution of the United States.

THE RIGHT OF LOCOMOTION

In 1875 Congress passed a measure commonly known as the Civil Rights Bill, which was supplementary of other measures of the same sort, the first being enacted April 9, 1866.[17] and reenacted with some modifications in sections 16, 17, and 18 of the Enforcement Act passed August 31, 1870.[18] The intention of the statesmen advocating these measures was to secure to the freedmen the enjoyment of every right guaranteed all other citizens. The important sections of the Civil Rights Bill of 1875 follow:

Section 1. That all persons within the jurisdiction of the United States shall be entitled to the full and equal enjoyment of the accommodations, advantages, facilities, and privileges of inns, public conveyances on land or water, theatres, and other places of public amusement; subject only to the conditions and limitations established by law, and applicable alike to citizens of every race and color, regardless of any previous condition of servitude.

Section 2. That any person who shall violate the foregoing section by denying to any citizen, except for reasons by law applicable to citizens of every race and color, and regardless of any previous condition of servitude, the full enjoyment of any of the accommodations, advantages, facilities or privileges in said section enumerated, or by aiding or inciting such denial, shall for every such offense forfeit and pay the sum of five hundred dollars to the person aggrieved thereby, to be recovered in an action of debt, with full costs; and shall also, for every such offense be deemed guilty of a misdemeanor, and, upon conviction therefor, shall be fined not less than five hundred nor more than one thousand dollars, or shall be imprisoned not less than thirty days nor more than one year. *Provided*, That all persons may elect to sue for the penalties aforesaid, or to proceed under their rights at common law and by State statutes; and having so elected to proceed in the one mode or the other, their right to proceed in the other jurisdiction shall be barred: But this provision shall not apply to criminal proceedings, either under this act or the criminal law of any State: and provided further, That a judgment for the penalty in favor of the party aggrieved, or a judgment upon an indictment, shall be a bar to either prosecution respectively.

Although the Negroes by this measure were guaranteed the rights which were granted by the Constitution to every citizen of the United States, the members of the Supreme Court of the United States instead of upholding the laws of the nation in accordance with their oaths undertook to hedge around and to explain away the articles of the

Constitution in such a way as to legislate rather than interpret the laws according to the intent of the framers of the Constitution. Subjected to all sorts of discriminations at the polls, in the courts, in inns, in hotels, on street cars, and on railroads, Negroes had sued for redress of their grievances and the persons thus called upon to respond in the courts attacked the constitutionality of the Civil Rights Bill, and the War Amendments, contending that they encroached upon the police power of the States.

The first of these *Civil Rights Cases* were: *United States* v. *Stanley*, *United States* v. *Ryan*, *United States* v. *Nichols*, *United States* v. *Singleton*, and *Robinson and wife* v. *Memphis and Charleston R. R. Co.* Two of these cases, those against Stanley and Nichols, were indictments for denying to persons of color the accommodations of an inn or hotel; two of them, those against Ryan and Singleton, were, one on information, the other on indictments, for denying to individuals the privileges and accommodations of a theatre. The information against Ryan was for refusing a colored person a seat in the dress circle of McGuire's Theatre in San Francisco; and the indictment against Singleton was for denying to another person, whose color was not stated, the full enjoyment of the accommodation of the theatre known as the Grand Opera House in New York.

The argument to show the culpability of the State was that in becoming a business man or a corporation established by sanction of and protected by the State, such a person or persons discriminating against a citizen of color no longer acted in a private but in a public capacity and in so doing affected an interest in violation of the State by controlling, as in the case of slavery, an individual's power of locomotion. The Civil Rights Bill was appropriate legislation as defined by the Constitution to forbid any

18

action by private persons which "in the light of our history may reasonably be apprehended to tend, on account of its being incidental to quasi public occupations, to create an institution." The act of 1875 in prohibiting persons from violating the rights of other persons to the full and equal enjoyment of the accommodations of inns and public conveyances, for any reason turning merely upon the race or color of the latter, partook of the specific character of certain contemporaneous, solemn and effective action by the United States to which it was a sequel and is constitutional.

Giving the opinion of the court in Civil Rights Cases, [19] Mr. Justice Bradley said that the Fourteenth Amendment on which this act of 1875 rested for its authority, if it had any authority at all, does not invest Congress to legislate within the domain of State legislation or in State action of the kind referred to in the Civil Rights Act. He believed that the Fourteenth Amendment does not authorize Congress to create a code of municipal law for the regulation of private rights. He conceded that positive rights and privileges are secured by the Fourteenth Amendment but only by prohibition against State laws and State proceedings affecting those rights.[20] "Until some State law has passed," he said, "or some State action through its officers or agents has been taken, adverse to the rights of citizens sought to be protected by the Fourteenth Amendment, no legislation of the United States under said amendment, nor any proceeding under such legislation, can be called into activity; for the prohibitions of the amendment are against State laws and acts under State authority." Otherwise Congress would take the place of State legislatures and supersede them and regulate all private rights between man and man. Civil rights such as are guaranteed by the Constitution against State

19

aggression, thought Justice Bradley, cannot be impaired by the wrongful acts of individuals unsupported by State authority in the shape of laws, customs, or executive proceedings, for those are private wrongs.

Justice Bradley believed, moreover, that the Civil Rights Act could not be supported by the Thirteenth Amendment in that, unlike the Fourteenth Amendment, the Thirteenth Amendment is primary and direct in abolishing slavery. "When a man has emerged from slavery," said he, "and by the aid of beneficent legislation has shaken off the inseparable concomitants of that state there must be some stage in the progress of his elevation when he takes the rank of a mere citizen, ceases to be the special favorite of the laws, and when his rights as a citizen or a man, are to be protected in the ordinary modes by which other men's rights are protected." To eject a Negro from an inn or a hotel, to compel him to ride in a separate car, to deny him access and use of places maintained at public expense, according to Justice Bradley, do not constitute imposing upon the Negroes badges and incidents of slavery; for they are acts of individuals with which Congress, because of the limited powers of the Federal government, cannot have anything to do. The particular clause in the Civil Rights Act, so far as it operated on individuals in the several States was, therefore, held null and void, but the court held that it might apply to the District of Columbia and territories of the United States for which Congress might legislate directly. Since then the court has in the recent *Wright Case* declared null and void even that part which it formerly said might apply to territory governed directly by Congress, thus taking the position tantamount to reading into the laws of the United States and the laws of nations the segregation measures of a mediaeval ex-slaveholding commonwealth assisted by the nation in enforcing

20

obedience to its will beyond the three mile limit on the high seas.

Although conceding that the Thirteenth Amendment was direct and primary legislation, the court held that it had nothing to do with the guarantee against that race discrimination commonly referred to in the bills of complaint as the badges and incidents of slavery. The court found the Fourteenth Amendment negative rather than direct and primary because of one of its clauses providing that "no State shall make or enforce any law which shall abridge the privileges and immunities of citizens of the United States nor shall any State deprive any person of life, liberty and property without due process of law, nor deny to any person within its jurisdiction the equal protection of the laws." The court was too evasive or too stupid to observe that the first clause of this amendment was an affirmation to the effect that all persons born and naturalized in the United States and subject to the jurisdiction thereof are citizens of the United States and of the State wherein they reside. In other words, the court held that if there is one negative clause in a paragraph, the whole paragraph is a negation. Such sophistry deserves the condemnation of all fairminded people, when one must conclude that any person even without formal education, if he has heard the English language spoken and is of sound mind, would know better than to interpret a law so unreasonably.

In declaring this act unconstitutional the Supreme Court of the United States violated one of its own important principles of interpretation to the effect that this duty is such a delicate one, that the court in declaring a statute of Congress invalid must do so with caution, reluctance and hesitation and never until the duty becomes manifestly imperative. In the decision of *Fletcher* v. *Peck*,[21] the court said that whether the legislative department of the government has transcended the limits of its constitutional power is at all times a question of much delicacy, which seldom, if ever, is to be decided in the affirmative, in a doubtful case. The position between the Constitution and the law should be such that the judge feels a clear and strong conviction of their incompatibility with each other. In the *Sinking Fund Cases*[22] the court said: "When required in the regular course of judicial proceedings to declare an act of Congress void if not within the legislative power of the United States, this declaration should never be made except in a clear case. Every possible presumption is in favor of the validity of a statute, and this continues until the contrary is shown beyond a rational doubt. One branch of the government cannot encroach on the domain of another without danger. The safety of our institutions depends in no small degree on a strict observance of this salutary rule." And this is exactly what happened. The judiciary here assumed the function of the legislative department. Not even a casual reader on examining these laws and the Constitution can feel that the court in this case felt such a clear and strong conviction as to the invalidity of this constitutional legislation when that tribunal, as its records show, had under different circumstances before the Civil War held a doctrine decidedly to the contrary.

Mr. Justice Harlan, therefore, dissented. He considered the opinion of the court narrow, as the substance and spirit were sacrificed by a subtle and ingenious verbal criticism. Justice Harlan believed, "that it is not the words of the law but the internal sense of it that makes the law; the letter of the law is the body, the sense and reason of the law the soul." "Constitutional provisions adopted in the interest of liberty," said Justice Harlan, "and for the purpose of securing, through national legislation, if need be, rights inhering in a state of freedom, and belonging to American citizenship, have been so construed as to defeat the end the people desire to accomplish, which they attempted to accomplish, and which they supposed they had accomplished, by changes in their fundamental law."

The court, according to Justice Harlan, although he did not mean to say that the determination in this case should have been materially controlled by considerations of mere expediency or policy, had departed from the familiar rule requiring that the purpose of the law or Constitution and the objects to be accomplished by any grant are often the most important in reaching real intent just as the debates in the convention of 1787 and the discussions in the *Federalist* and in the ratifying conventions of the States have often been referred to as throwing important light on clauses in the Constitution seeming to show ambiguity. The debates on the war amendment, when they were proposed and ratified, were thoroughly expounded before the court in bringing before that tribunal the intention of the members of Congress, by which the court, according to a well established principle of interpretation, should have been influenced in construing the statute in question.

The court held that legislation for the enforcement of the Thirteenth Amendment is direct and primary "but to what specific ends may it be directed?" inquired Justice Harlan. The court "had uniformly held that national government has the power, whether expressly given or not, to secure and protect rights conferred or guaranteed by the Constitution."[23] Justice Harlan believed then that the doctrines should not be abandoned when the inquiry was not as to an implied power to protect the master's rights, but what Congress might, under powers expressly granted, do for the protection of freedom and the rights necessarily inhering in a state of freedom.

The Thirteenth Amendment, the court conceded, did more than prohibit slavery as an *institution*, resting upon distinctions of race, and upheld by positive law. The court admitted that it "established and decreed universal civil freedom throughout the United States." "But did the freedom thus established," inquired Justice Harlan, "involve more than exemption from actual slavery? Was nothing more intended than to forbid one man from owning another as property? Was it the purpose of the nation simply to destroy the institution and then remit the race, theretofore held in bondage, to the several States for such protection, in their civil rights, necessarily growing out of their freedom, as those States in their discretion might choose to provide? Were the States against whose protest the institution was destroyed to be left free, so far as national interference was concerned, to make or allow discriminations against that race, as such, in the enjoyment of those fundamental rights which by universal concession, inhere in a state of freedom?" Justice Harlan considered it indisputable that Congress in having power to abolish slavery could destroy the burdens and disabilities remaining as its badges and incidents which constitute its substance in visible form.

The court in its defense had taken as an illustration that the negative clause of the Fourteenth Amendment was not direct and primary, that although the States are prohibited from passing laws to impair the obligations of contracts this did not mean that Congress could legislate for the general enforcement of contracts throughout the States. Discomfitting his brethren on their own ground Harlan said: "A prohibition upon a State is not a *power* in *Congress or in the national government*. It is simply a *denial* of *power* to the State. The much talked of illustration of impairing the obligation of contracts, therefore, is not an example of power expressly conferred in contradistinction to that of this case and is not convincing for this would be a court matter, not a matter of Congress. The Fourteenth Amendment is the first case of conferring upon Congress affirmative power by *legislation to enforce* an express prohibition on the States. Judicial power was not specified but the power of Congress. The judicial power could have acted without such a clause. The Fourteenth Amendment is not merely a prohibition on State action. It made Negroes citizens of the United States and of the States. This is decidedly affirmative. This citizenship may be protected not only by the judicial branch of the government but by Congressional legislation of a primary or direct character. It is in the power of Congress to enforce the affirmative as well as the prohibitive provisions of this article. The acceptance of any doctrine to the contrary," continued Justice Harlan, "would lead to this anomalous result: that whereas prior to the amendments, Congress with the sanction of this court passed the most stringent laws—operating directly and primarily upon States and their officers and agents, as well as upon individuals—in vindication of slavery and the right of the master, it may not now, by legislation of a like primary and direct character, guard, protect, and secure the freedom established, and the most essential right of the citizenship granted, by the constitutional amendments."

It did not seem to Justice Harlan that the fact that, by the second clause of the first section of the Fourteenth Amendment, the States are expressly prohibited from making or enforcing laws abridging the rights and immunities of citizens of the United States, furnished any sufficient reason for upholding or maintaining that the amendment was intended to deny Congress the power, by general, primary, and direct legislation, of protecting citizens of the several States, being also citizens of the United States, against all discrimination, in respect of their rights as citizens, which is founded on "race, color, or previous condition of servitude." "Such an interpretation," thought he, "is plainly repugnant to its fifth section, conferring upon Congress power, by appropriate legislation, to enforce not merely the provisions containing prohibitions upon the States, but all of the provisions of the amendment, including the provisions, express and implied, in the first clause of the first section of the article granting citizenship." The prohibition of the State laws could have been negatived by judicial interpretation without the Fourteenth Amendment on the ground that they would have conflicted with the Constitution.

The court said the Fourteenth Amendment was not intended to enact a municipal code for the States. No one will gainsay this. This Amendment, moreover, is not altogether for the benefit of the Negro. It simply interferes with the local laws when they operate so as to discriminate against persons or permit agents of the States to discriminate against persons of any race on account of color or previous condition of servitude. Of what benefit was it if it did not do this? The constitutions of the several States had already secured all persons against deprivation of life, liberty or property otherwise than by due process of law, and in some form recognized the right of all persons to the equal protection of the laws. If this be the correct interpretation even, it does not follow that privileges which have been granted by the nation, may not be protected by primary legislation upon the part of Congress. Justice Harlan pointed out that it is for Congress not the judiciary, to say that legislation is appropriate, for that would be sheer usurpation of the functions of a coordinate department. Why should these rules of interpretation be abandoned in the case of maintaining the rights of the Negro guaranteed by the Constitution?

The Civil Rights Act of 1875 could have been maintained on the ground that it regulated interstate passenger traffic, as one of the cases, *Robinson and Wife* v. *Memphis and Charleston Railroad Company*, showed that Robinson a citizen of Mississippi had purchased a ticket entitling him to be carried from Grand Junction, Tennessee, to Lynchburg, Virginia. This case substantially presented the question of interstate commerce but the court reserved the question whether Congress in the exercise of its power to regulate commerce among the several States, might or might not pass a law regulating rights in public conveyances passing from one State to another. The court undertook to hide behind the fact that this specific act did not recite therein that it was enacted in pursuance of the power of Congress to regulate commerce. Justice Harlan, therefore, inquired: "Has it ever been held that the judiciary should overturn a statute, because the legislative department did not accurately recite therein the particular provision of the constitution authorizing its enactment?" On the whole, the contrary is the rule. It is sufficient to know that there is authority in the Constitution.

In this decision, too, there was the influence of the much paraded bugbear of social equality forced upon the whites. To use the inns, hotels, and parks, established by authority of the government and the places of amusement authorized as the necessary stimulus to progress, to buy a railroad ticket at the same window, ride in the same comfortable car on a limited train rather than incur the loss of time and suffer the inconvenience of inferior accommodations on a slow local train; to sleep and eat in a Pullman car so as to be refreshed for business on arriving at the end of a long journey, all of this was and is today dubbed by the reactionary courts social equality. Justice Harlan exposed this fallacy in saying: "The right, for instance, of a colored citizen to use the accommodations of a public highway, upon the same terms as are permitted to white citizens, is no more a social right than his right, under the law, to use the public streets of a city or a town, or a turnpike road, or a public market, or a post office, or his right to sit in a public building with others, of whatever race, for the purpose of hearing the political questions of the day discussed."

What did the Negro become when he was freed? What was he when, according to section 2 of Article IV of the Constitution, he became by virtue of the Fourteenth Amendment entitled to all privileges and immunities of citizens in the several States?[24] From what did the race become free? If Justice Bradley had been inconveniently segregated by common carriers, driven out of inns and hotels with the sanction of local law, and deprived by a mob of the opportunity to make a living, would he have considered himself a free citizen of this or any other country? "A colored citizen of Ohio or Indiana while in the jurisdiction of Tennessee," contended Justice Harlan, "is entitled to enjoy any privilege or immunity, fundamental in citizenship, which is given to citizens of the white race in the latter State. Citizenship in this country necessarily imports at least equality of civil rights among citizens of every race in the same State." In *United States* v. *Cruikshank*[25] it was held that rights of life and personal liberty are natural rights of man, and that "equality of the rights of citizens is a principle of republicanism."

INCONSISTENCY OF THE COURT

In the case of *Hall* v. *DeCuir*[26] the court reached an

28

important decision when an Act of Louisiana passed in 1869 to give passengers without regard to race or color equality of right in the accommodations of railroad or street cars, steamboats or other water crafts, stage coaches, omnibusses or other vehicles, was declared unconstitutional so far as it related to commerce between States.[27] Here a person of color had been discriminated against by a Mississippi River navigation company which was called to answer before a United States court for violating this act.

Giving the opinion of the court, Chief Justice Waite said: "We think it may be safely said that State legislation which seeks to impose a direct burden upon inter-state commerce, or to interfere directly with its freedom does encroach upon the exclusive power of Congress. The statute now under consideration in our opinion occupies that position." "Inaction by Congress," the court held, "is equivalent to a declaration that interstate commerce shall remain free and untrammelled." This meant that the carrier was "at liberty to adopt such reasonable rules and regulations for the disposition of passengers upon his boat, while pursuing her voyage within Louisiana or without, as seemed to him best for the interest of all concerned. The statute under which this suit is brought, as construed by the State court, seeks to take away from him that power so long as he is within Louisiana, and while recognizing to the fullest extent the principle which sustains a statute unless its unconstitutionality is clearly established, we think this statute to the extent that it requires those engaged in the transportation of passengers among the several States to carry colored persons in Louisiana in the same cabin with whites is unconstitutional and void. If the public good requires such legislation it must come from Congress and not from the States."

Justice Waite here expressed his fear as to the

delicate ground on which he was treading in saying: "The line which separates the powers of the States from this exclusive power of Congress is not always distinctly marked, and oftentimes it is not easy to determine on which side a particular case belongs. Judges not infrequently differ in their reasons for a decision in which they concur. Under such circumstances it would be a useless task to undertake to fix an arbitrary rule by which the line must in all cases be located. It is far better to leave a matter of such delicacy to be settled in each case upon a view of the particular rights involved." Thus the way was left clear to vary the principle of interpretation according to the color of the citizens whose rights might be involved.

In view of the subsequent decisions in separate car cases, moreover, the following portion of Justice Waite's opinion as to a clause in the law involved in the case of *Hall* v. *DeCuir* is unusually interesting. "It does not act," said he, "upon the business through the local instruments to be employed after coming within the State, from without or goes out from within. While it purports only to control the carrier when engaged within the State it must necessarily influence his conduct to some extent in the management of his business throughout his entire voyage. We confine our decision to the statute in its effect upon foreign and interstate commerce, expressing no opinion as to its validity in any other respect."[28]

With the rapid expansion of commerce in the United States and the consequent necessity for regulation both by the State and the United States, no power of Congress was more frequently questioned than that to regulate commerce and no litigant concerned in such constitutional questions easily escaped the consequences of the varying interpretation given this clause by the United States Supreme Court. The court, of course, accepted as a general principle that there are three spheres for the regulation of commerce, namely: that which a State cannot invade, that which the State may invade, when Congress has not interfered, and that which is reserved to the State in conformity with its police power. But as late as 1886 the nationalistic school found some encouragement in the decision of the *Wabash, St. Louis and Pacific Railway Company* v. *Illinois*[29] given by Justice Miller. He said: "Notwithstanding what is there said, that is, in the decisions of *Munn* v. *Illinois; C. B. and Q. R. R. Company* v. *Iowa*, and *Peik* v. *Chicago and N. W. R. R. Co.*,[30] this court held and asserted that it had never consciously held otherwise, that a statute of a State intended to regulate or to tax, or to impose any other restriction upon the transmission of persons or property or telegraphic messages, from one State to another, is not within the class of legislation which the States may enact in the absence of legislation by Congress; and that such statutes are void even as to the part of such transmission which may be within the State." Chief Justice Waite, and Justice Bradley and Justice Gray, however, dissented for various reasons.

In the *Louisville Railway Company* v. *Mississippi*,[31] however, in 1899, the court, evidently yielding to southern public opinion, reversed itself by the decision that an interstate carrier could not run a train through Mississippi without attaching thereto a separate car for Negroes and had the audacity to argue that this is not an interference with interstate commerce.[32] To show how inconsistent this interpretation was one should bear in mind that in *Hall* v. *DeCuir* the court had held that this was exactly what a State could not do in that the statute acted not upon business through local instruments to be employed after coming into the State, but directly

31

upon business as it comes into the State from without or goes out from within, although it purported only to control the carrier when engaged within the State. It necessarily influenced the conduct of the carrier to some extent in the management of his business throughout his entire voyage. "No carrier of passengers," said the court in *Hall* v. *DeCuir*, "can conduct his business with satisfaction to himself, or comfort to those employing him, if on one side of a State line his passengers, both white and colored, must be permitted to occupy the same cabin, and on the other to be kept separate. Uniformity in the regulation by which he is to be governed from one end to the other of his route is a necessity in his business, and to secure it, Congress, which is untrammelled by State lines, has been invested with exclusive legislative power of determining what such regulation should be."

Giving the opinion in the Mississippi case, however, Justice Brewer said: "It has been often held by this court that there is a commerce wholly within the State which is not subject to the constitutional provision and the distinctions between commerce among the States and the other class of commerce between citizens of a single State and conducted within its limits exclusively is one which has been fully recognized in this court, although it may not be always easy, where the lines of these classes approach each other, to distinguish between the one and the other."[33] He might have added some other comment to the effect that this court will not definitely draw the line of distinction between such classes of commerce since it desires to leave adequate room for evasion, because it had been unusually easy to find such a line in cases in which the rights of Negroes were concerned and such definite interpretation might interfere with the rights of white men. Justices Harlan and Bradley dissented on the grounds that the law imposed a burden upon an interstate carrier in that he would be fined if he did not attach an additional car for race discrimination, and that the opinion was repugnant to the principles set forth in that of *Hall* v. *DeCuir*.

The United States Supreme Court finally reached the position of following the decision of *Ex Parte Plessy* which justified the discrimination in railway cars on the grounds that it is not a badge of slavery contrary to the Thirteenth Amendment. This decision, in short, is: So long, at least, as the facilities or accommodations provided are substantially equal, statutes providing separate cars for the races do not abridge any privilege or immunity of citizens or otherwise contravene the Fourteenth Amendment of the United States Constitution. In such matters equality and not identity or community of accommodations is the extreme test of conformity to the requirements of the amendment. The regulation of domestic commerce is as exclusively a State function as the regulation of interstate commerce is a Federal function. The separate car law is an exercise of police power in the interest of public order, peace and comfort. It is a matter of legislative power and discretion with which Federal courts cannot interfere.

In *Hennington* v. *Georgia*,[34] it was later emphasized that it had been held that legislative enactments of the States, passed under the admitted police powers, and having a real relation to the domestic peace, order, health, and safety of their people, but which by their necessary operation, affect, to some extent, or for a limited time, the conduct of commerce among the States, are yet not invalid by force alone of the grant of power of Congress to regulate such commerce; and, if not obnoxious to some other constitutional provision or destructive of some right secured by the fundamental law, are to be respected

33

in the courts of the Union until they are superseded and displaced by some act of Congress passed in execution of power granted to it by the Constitution. Of course, there was no other provision to which such laws could be contrary after the Supreme Court had whittled away the war amendments.

In the case of *Plessy* v. *Ferguson*[35] the most inexcusable inconsistency of the court was shown when the persons of color aggrieved attacked the separate car law of Louisiana on the ground that it conflicted with the Fourteenth Amendment. Giving the opinion of the court, Justice Brown said: "So far, then, as a conflict with the Fourteenth Amendment is concerned, the case reduces itself to the question whether the statute of Louisiana is a reasonable regulation, and with respect to this there must necessarily be a large discretion on the part of the legislature. In determining the question of reasonableness it is at liberty to act with reference to the established usages, customs and traditions of the people, and with a view to the promotion of the public peace and good order. Gauged by this standard, we cannot say that a law which authorizes or even requires the separation of the two races in public conveyances is unreasonable, or more obnoxious to the Fourteenth Amendment than the acts of Congress requiring separate schools for colored children in the District of Columbia, the constitutionality of which does not seem to have been questioned or the corresponding acts of State legislatures."

Justice Harlan dissented, saying that he was of the opinion that the Statute of Louisiana is inconsistent with personal liberty of white and black in that State and hostile to both in the letter and spirit of the Constitution of the United States. Justice Harlan rightly contended that laws can have no regard to race according to the Constitution. If they do, they conflict with the rights of State and national citizenship and with personal liberty. The Thirteenth and Fourteenth Amendments removed race from our governmental system. But what has the court to do with the policy or expediency of legislation? "A statute may be valid, and yet upon grounds of public policy, may well be characterized as unreasonable." Accordingly Mr. Sedgwick, a distinguished authority, says: "The Courts have no other duty to perform than to execute the legislative will, without regard to their views as to the wisdom or justice of the particular enactment." "Statutes," said Justice Harlan, "must always have a reasonable construction. Sometimes they are to be construed strictly; sometimes, liberally, in order to carry out the legislative will. But, however construed, the intent of the legislature is to be respected."

The decisions in the cases of *M. K. and T. Railway* v. *Haber*[36] and *Crutcher* v. *Kentucky*,[37] are of some importance. In these cases the court reiterated the doctrine that the regulation of the enjoyment of the relative rights and the performance of the duties, of all persons within the jurisdiction of a State belong primarily to such a State under its reserved power to provide for the safety of all persons and property within its limits; and that even if the subject of such regulations be one that may be taken under the exclusive control of Congress, and be reached by national legislation, any action taken by the State upon that subject that does not directly interfere with rights secured by the Constitution of the United States or by some valid act of Congress, must be respected until Congress intervenes.[38] The court by this time, however, had all but held that the Constitution secured to the Negro no civil or political rights except that of exemption from involuntary servitude, and that law for the Negro is the will of the white man.

Further development of the doctrine as to the right of the State to deprive a Negro of citizenship is brought out in the *Lauder Case*.[39] The case was this: Lauder's wife purchased a first class ticket from Hopkinsville to Mayfield, both places within the State of Kentucky. She took her place in what was called the "ladies' coach" and was ejected therefrom by the conductor and assigned a seat in a smoking car, which was alleged to be small, badly ventilated, unclean and fitted with greatly inferior accommodations. This road ran from Evansville, Indiana, to Hopkinsville, Kentucky. It was held in the Court of Appeals that the decision of the United States Supreme Court in *Louisville, New Orleans and Railway* v. *Mississippi*[40] and *Plessy* v. *Ferguson*[41] was conclusive of the constitutionality of the act so far as the plaintiffs were concerned; and that the mere fact that the railroad extended to Evansville, in the State of Indiana, could in no wise render the statute in question invalid as to the duty of the railroad to respect it.

In the case of *Chesapeake and Ohio Railway Company* v. *Kentucky*,[42] this doctrine was carried to its logical conclusion. The question was whether a proper construction of the separate car law confines its operation to passengers whose journeys commence and end within the boundaries of the State or whether a reasonable interpretation of the act requires Negro passengers to be assigned to separate coaches when traveling from or to points in other States. In other such cases the Supreme Court of the United States had interpreted the local law as applying only to interstate commerce. The language of the first section of the Kentucky statute made it very clear that it applied to all carriers. The first section of the Kentucky law follows:

"Any railroad company or corporation, person or persons,

running or otherwise operation of railroad cars or coaches by steam or otherwise, in any railroad line or track within this State, and all railroad companies, person or persons, doing business in this State, whether upon lines or railroads owned in part or whole, or leased by them; and all railroad companies, person or persons, operating railroad lines that may hereafter be built under existing charters, or charters that may hereafter be granted in this State; and all foreign corporations, companies, person or persons, organized under charters granted, or that may be hereafter granted by any other State, who may be now, or may hereafter be engaged in running or operating any of the railroads of this State, whether in part or whole, are hereby required to furnish separate coaches or cars for travel or transportation of the white and colored passengers on their respective lines of railroad."

Any sane man can see that this law undertook to regulate interstate commerce. Justice Brown, however, tried to square the opinion with that of the Kentucky Supreme Court, upholding the law on the grounds that it was constitutional in as much as it applied only to intrastate passenger traffic, although the law plainly applies also to interstate traffic.

Speaking further for the court, Justice Brown said: "Indeed we are by no means satisfied that the Court of Appeals did not give the correct construction to this statute in limiting its operation to domestic commerce. It is scarcely courteous to impute to a legislature the enactment of a law which it knew to be unconstitutional and if it were well settled that a separate coach law was unconstitutional, as applied to interstate commerce, the law applying on its face to *all* passengers should be limited to such as the legislature were competent to deal with. The Court of Appeals has found such to be the intention of the General Assembly in this case, or at least, that if such were not its intention, the law may be supported as applying alone to domestic commerce. In thus holding the act to be severable it is laying down a principle of construction from which there is no appeal."

"While we do not deny the force of the railroad's argument in this connection, we cannot say that the General Assembly would not have enacted this law if it had supposed it applied only to domestic commerce; and if it were in doubt on that point, we should unhesitatingly defer to the opinion of the Court of Appeals, which held that it would give it that construction if the case called for it. In view of the language above quoted it would be unbecoming for us to say that the Court of Appeals would not construe the law as applicable to domestic commerce alone, and if it did, the case would fall directly within the *Mississippi Case*.[43] We, therefore, feel compelled to give it that construction ourselves and so construe it that there can be no doubt as to its constitutionality." Here we have a plain case of the United States Supreme Court declaring an act severable because thereby it could apparently justify as constitutional a measure depriving the Negroes of civil and political rights, whereas in some other cases it has held other acts not severable to reach the same end.

The court continued its reactionary course. In *Chiles* v. *Chesapeake and Ohio R. R. Company*[44] the court reiterated that "Congressional inaction is equivalent to a declaration that a carrier may, by its regulations, separate white and Negro interstate passengers. In *McCabe* v. *Atchinson, Topeka and Santa Fe Railway Company*,[45] Justice Hughes giving the opinion of the court, followed the *Plessy* v. *Ferguson* decision. He did not believe, moreover, "that the contention that an act though fair on its face may be so unequally and oppressively administered by the public authorities as to amount to an unconstitutional discrimination by the State itself, is applicable where it is the administration of the provisions of a separate coach law by carriers, which is claimed to produce the discrimination. The separate coach provisions of

Oklahoma[46] apply to transportation wholly intrastate in absence of a different construction by State courts and do not contravene the commerce clause of the Federal court. The court held, however, that so much of the Oklahoma separate coach law as permits carriers to provide sleeping cars, dining cars, and chair cars for white persons, and to provide no similar accommodations for Negroes, denies the latter the equal protection of the laws guaranteed by the Constitution.

The most recent case, that of the *South Covington and Cincinnati Street Railway, Plaintiff in error* v. *Commonwealth of Kentucky* shows another step in the direction of complete surrender to caste. This company was a Kentucky corporation, each of the termini of the railroad of which was in Kentucky. The complainant hoped to prevent the segregation of passengers carried from Ohio into Kentucky. The decision was that a Kentucky street railway may be required by statute of that State to furnish either separate cars or separate compartments in the same car for white and Negro passengers although its principal business is the carriage of passengers in interstate commerce between Cincinnati, Ohio, and Kentucky across the Ohio River. Such a requirement affects interstate commerce only incidentally, and does not subject it to unreasonable demands. In other words, this inconvenience to the carrier is not very much and the humiliation and burden which it entails upon persons of color thus segregated should not concern the court, although they are supposed to be citizens of the United States.

Justice Day dissented and Justices Van DeVanter and Putney concurred on the ground that the attachment of a different car upon the Kentucky side on so short a journey would burden interstate commerce as to cost and in the practical operation of the traffic. The provision for a separate compartment for the use of only interstate Negro passengers would lead to confusion and discrimination. The same interstate transportation would be subject to conflicting regulation in the two States in which it is conducted. They believed that it imposed an unreasonable burden and according to the dissentients was, therefore, void.

JUSTICE IN THE COURTS.

One of the most important constitutional rights denied the Negroes is that of justice in the courts. In as much as their former masters felt enraged against the freedmen because of their sudden release from bondage, they too often perpetrated upon the freedmen crimes for which the Negro had no redress in courts, for white persons constituted the accusers, the prosecutors, the judges, and the juries. Immediately following the Civil War, before the amendments of the Constitution enacted in the special behalf of the race were effected, Negroes were by the Black Codes deprived of all of the rights of citizens and nothing bore more grievously upon them than the deprivation of the right to serve on juries. Some States had special laws carrying out this prohibition. The first case of consequence requiring an interpretation of the State law to this effect was that of *Strauder* v. *West Virginia*,[47] already mentioned above. In this case the court took high constitutional ground. It was held that "a law of West Virginia limiting to white persons, twenty-one years of age and citizens of the State, the right to sit upon juries, was a discrimination which implied a legal inferiority in civil society, which lessened the security of the right of the colored race, and was a step toward reducing them to a condition of servility." The right of a man of color that, in the selection of jurors to pass upon his life, liberty, and property, there shall be no exclusion of his race and no discrimination against them because of color, was asserted in a number of cases, to wit: *Virginia* v. *Rives*,[48] *Neal* v. *Delaware*,[49] *Gibbons* v. *Kentucky*.[50]

In the case of *Bush* v. *The Commonwealth of Kentucky*[51] the Negro faced an additional difficulty in that the court held that wherein there was no specific law excluding persons from service upon juries because of their race or color, that the petitioner would have to show evidence to that effect. In the case of *Smith* v. *The State of Mississippi*[52] it was held that the omission or refusal of officers to include Negro citizens in the list from which jurors might be drawn is not, as to a Negro subsequently brought to trial, a denial of equal protection of laws. In the case of *Murray* v. *The State of Louisiana*[53] the decision was that the fact that a law confers on the jury commissioners judicial power in the selection of citizens for jury service, does not involve a conflict with the Fourteenth Amendment of the Constitution of the United States, although in the exercise of such power they might not select Negroes for jury service.

The case of *Williams* v. *Mississippi* was more interesting. The law of that State prescribed the qualifications of voters and of grand and petit juries and invested the administrative officers with a large discretion in determining what citizens have the necessary qualifications. As it appeared that in the use of their discretion they would exclude Negroes from such juries it was contended that the act of Mississippi was a violation of the Fourteenth Amendment. The court held, however, that the Mississippi law could not be held repugnant to the Fourteenth Amendment merely on a showing that the law might operate as a discrimination against the Negro race, in absence of proof of an actual discrimination in the case under consideration. This ground has often proved convenient for the Supreme Court of the United States in dodging the question whether or not the Negroes must be protected in the rights guaranteed them by the Constitution.

This case was decided in 1897 and two years later Mr. Justice Gray, giving the opinion of the court in the case of *Carter* v. *Texas*,[54] said that the exclusion of all persons of African race from a grand jury which finds an indictment against a Negro in a State court, when they are excluded solely because of their race or color denies him the equal protection of the laws in violation of the Fourteenth Amendment of the Constitution of the United States, whether such exclusion is done through the action of the legislature, through the courts, or through the executive or administrative officers of the State. This was substantially the position taken in the case of *Strauder* v. *West Virginia* twenty years earlier.

The Negroes received some encouragement, too, from the decision of *Rogers* v. *Alabama*.[55] It was held that there had been a denial of the equal protection of the laws by a ruling of a State court upon the motion to quash an indictment on account of the exclusion of Negroes from the grand jury list, which motion, though because of its being in two printed octavos, was struck from the files under the color of local practice for prolixity, contained an allegation that certain provisions of the newly adopted State constitution, claimed to have the effect of disfranchising Negroes because of their race, when such action worked as a consideration in the minds of the jury commissioners in reaching their decision. The court held in *Martin* v. *The State of Texas*, however, [56] that a discrimination against Negroes because of their race in the selection of grand or petit jurors as forbidden by the Fourteenth Amendment is not shown by written motion to quash, respectively, the indictment of the panel of petit jurors, charging such discrimination where no evidence was introduced to establish the facts stated in the omissions. It is not sufficient merely to prove that no persons of color were on the jury.

As certain States wished to make the government further secure in the elimination of Negroes from juries, after making the qualifications for voters unusually rigid so as to exclude persons of African descent, they easily established the same qualifications for jurors, to relieve persons of color also from that service. In the case of *Franklin* v. *South Carolina*[57] the court held that there was no discrimination against Negroes because of their race in the selection of the grand jury made by the laws of South Carolina,[58] giving the jury commissioner the right to select electors of good moral character such as they may deem qualified to serve as jurors, being persons of sound mind and free from all legal exceptions. A motion, therefore, to quash an indictment against a Negro for disqualification of the grand jurors who must be electors, because of a change in the State constitution of South Carolina respecting the qualifications of electors, did not violate the Act of Congress, June 25, 1868, and, therefore, did not present to the Supreme Court of the United States a question of a denial of Federal right where there is nothing in the record to show that the grand jury as actually impaneled contained any person who was not qualified as an elector under the earlier State constitution, which was, according to the allegation, so made up as to exclude Negroes on account of their color. The Supreme Court of the United States then took no account of the intent or the spirit of the law maker as this tribunal had been accustomed to do in cases of constitutional import and left upon the Negro the burden of performing the difficult task of showing that he had been discriminated against on account of his color when the discrimination could be easily effected without the possibility of his actually producing any evidence that on the face of itself could convince the court.

SUFFRAGE

As already mentioned above the Negroes during this period were struggling to retain the right of suffrage and, of course, were attacking in the courts those restrictions primarily directed toward the elimination of the Negroes from the electorate. The Supreme Court of the United States generally shrank from these cases by disclaiming jurisdiction. In *Ex Parte Siebold*, [59] *Ex Parte Yarborough*,[60] and *In re Coy*,[61] however, the general jurisdiction of Federal courts over matters involved in the election of national officers was affirmed. The court held that it had jurisdiction in the election case in *Wiley* v. *Sinkler*,[62] when there was brought an action to recover damages of an election board for wilfully rejecting a citizen's vote for a member of the House of Representatives. In *Swafford* v. *Templeton*[63] a suit was brought for damages for the alleged wrongful refusal by the defendants at an election of officers to permit the plaintiff to vote at a national election for a member of the House of Representatives. It was held that the court had jurisdiction.

From the Supreme Court of the United States, however, the Negroes received little encouragement, in as much as the right of suffrage, with its requirements of property ownership and the literacy test, could be withheld from the Negro without specifically discriminating against any one on account of race or color. In *Southy* v. *Virginia*, 181 U. S., Revised Statutes, of the United States, Cont. St. 1901, pages 37-42, providing that every person who prevents, hinders, controls or intimidates another

45

from exercising the right of suffrage, to whom that right is guaranteed by the Fifteenth Amendment of the Constitution of the United States, by means of bribery, etc., shall be punished, was held invalid as it was considered to be beyond the constitutional power of Congress to act in such a case except in that of race discrimination. If the discrimination is in a State or municipal election, however, Congress may intervene, if the discrimination is shown, but not until then.

In the case of *Giles* v. *Harris*[64] there was brought to the Supreme Court a bill in equity, complaining that Negroes qualified to vote for members of Congress had been refused on account of their color by virtue of the Alabama constitution, whereas white men were registered to vote at such an election. Relief was asked for on the basis of the Revised Statutes, Sec. 1979, praying that the Supreme Court should order that the petitioner be registered and declare null and void the special clause of the Alabama constitution. The court answered this petition with certain observations disclaiming jurisdiction largely for "want of merit in the averments which were made in the complaint as to the violation of Federal rights."

The court held that if the registrars acting at this election in Alabama had no authority under the new constitution, which the petitioner prayed that the court might declare null and void, they could not legally register the plaintiff. If they had authority, they were within their right to use their discretion. If this clause in the constitution should be struck down according to the prayer of the plaintiff, there would be no board to which the mandamus could be issued. The Supreme Court, therefore, held that no damage had been suffered because no refusal to register by a board constituted in defiance of the Federal Constitution could disqualify a legal voter otherwise entitled to exercising the electorate franchise, since this amounts to a decision upon an independent non-Federal ground sufficient to sustain the judgment without reference to the Federal question presented. It observed, moreover, that the bill imported that the great mass of the white population intended to keep the blacks from voting. To meet such an intent something more than ordering the plaintiff named to be inscribed upon the lists of 1902 would be needed.

Giving his dissenting opinion in this case, Justice Brewer showed that "although the statute and these decisions thus expressly limit the range of inquiry to the question of jurisdiction, it was held that there is a constitutional question shown in the pleadings. The certificate, therefore, might be ignored and the entire case presented to the court for consideration.... Hence every case coming up on a certificate of jurisdiction may be held to present a constitutional question and be open for full inquiry in respect to all matters involved." Brewer would not assent to the proposition that the case presented was not a strictly legal one and entitling a party to a judicial hearing and decision. "He is a citizen of Alabama entitled to vote. He wanted to vote at an election for a Representative in Congress. Without registration he could not, and registration was wrongfully denied him. That many others were thus treated does not deprive him of his right or deprive him of relief." Justice Harlan dissented also giving practically the same argument as that of Justice Brewer. He observed: "The court in effect says that although it may know that the record fails to show a case within the original cognizance of the Circuit Court, it may close its eyes to that fact, and review the case on its merit." In view of the adjudged cases, he could not agree that the failure of parties to raise a question of jurisdiction relieved this court of its duty to raise it upon its own motion.

There was thereafter presented a petition for modification of judgment and for a rehearing June 1, 1903. The court ordered the decree of affirmance changed adding these words: "So far as such decree orders that the petition be dismissed, but without prejudice to such further proceedings as the petitioner may be advised to make."

The case of *Giles* v. *Teasley*[65] was, to some extent, of the same sort. A Negro of Alabama who had previously been a voter and who had complied with the reasonable requirements of the board of registration, was refused the right to vote, for, as he alleged, no reason other than his race and color, the members of the board having been appointed and having acted under the provision of the State constitution of 1901. He sued the members of the board for damages and for such refusal in an action, and applied for a writ of mandamus to compel them to register him, alleging in both proceedings the denial of his rights under the Federal Constitution and that the provisions of the State Constitution were repugnant to the Fifteenth Amendment. The complaint had been dismissed on demurrer and the writ refused, the highest court of the State holding that if the provisions of the constitution were repugnant to the Fifteenth Amendment, they were void and that the board of registers appointed thereunder had no existence and no power to act and would not be liable for a refusal to register him, and could not be compelled by writ of mandamus to do so; that if the provisions were constitutional, the registrars had acted properly thereunder and their action was not reviewable by the courts.

"The right of the Supreme Court to review the decisions of the highest court of a State," said the national tribunal, "is even in cases involving the violations by the provisions of a State constitution of the Fifteenth Amendment, circumscribed by rules established by law, and in every case coming to the court on writ of error or appeal the question of jurisdiction must be answered whether propounded by the counsel or not. Where the State court decided the case for reasons independent of the Federal right claimed its action is not reviewable on writ of error by the United States Supreme Court." It was held that the writs of error to this court should be dismissed, as such decisions do not involve the adjudication against the plaintiff in error of a right claimed under the Federal Constitution but deny the relief demanded on grounds wholly independent thereof." In *Wiley* v. *Sinkler*, and *Swafford* v. *Templeton*, the registrars were legally averred to be qualified.[66]

In the Maryland case of *Pope* v. *Williams*[67] the court further explained its position. While the State cannot restrict suffrage on account of color, the privilege is not given by the Federal Constitution, nor does it spring from citizenship of the United States. While the right to vote for members of Congress is derived exclusively from the law of the State in which they are chosen but has its foundation in the laws and Constitution of the United States, the elector must be one entitled to vote under its statute. A law, therefore, requiring a declaration of intention to become citizens before registering as voters of all persons coming from without Maryland is not a violation of the Constitution.

In the case of *Guinn* v. *United States*[68] the court held that the literacy test was legal and not subject to revision but in this clause of the constitution that part of a section providing for literacy was closely connected with the so-called grandfather clause that the United States Supreme Court declared both unconstitutional as it did in the case also of *Myers* v. *Anderson*,[69] coming from Annapolis, Maryland, and in the case of *The United States* v. *Mosely*, from Oklahoma.[70] The clause referred to follows:

"No person shall be registered as an elector of this State or be allowed to vote in any election herein, unless he be able to read and write any section of the Constitution of the State of Oklahoma; but no person who was on January 1, 1866, or at any time prior thereto, entitled to vote under any form of government, or who at that time resided in some foreign nation, and no lineal descendant of such person, shall be denied the right to register and vote because of his inability to read and write sections of such constitution. Precinct election inspectors having in charge the registration of electors shall enforce the provisions of this section at the time of registration, provided registration be required. Should registration be dispensed with, the provisions of this section shall be enforced by the precinct officer when electors apply for ballots to vote."

The court held that this was a standard of voting which on its face was in substance but a revitalization of conditions which when they prevailed in the past had been destroyed by the self-operative force of the Thirteenth Amendment.

EDUCATIONAL PRIVILEGES

These suffrage laws left the Negroes in an untoward situation for the reason that there was little hope that, with the educational facilities afforded them, that they would soon be able to meet the same requirement of literacy as that which might not embarrass the whites offering themselves as jurors and electors. The States upheld in their action by the United States Supreme Court, had shifted from their shoulders the burden of the uplift of the Negro by the ingenious doctrine that equal accommodations did not mean identical accommodations and that the spirit and the letter of the law would be complied with by providing separate accommodations for Negroes. In the end, however, separate accommodations turned out to be in some cases no accommodations at all.

This was the situation as it was brought out in the case of *Cumming* v. *The Board of Education of Richmond County*.[71] It appeared that a tax for schools had been levied in this district. The Negroes objected to paying that portion of the tax which provided for the maintenance of a high school, the benefits of which they were denied, when there was no high school provided for them. The board of education of Richmond County had maintained a high school for Negroes but abolished it. The petitioner prayed, therefore, that an injunction be granted against the collection of such portion of the school tax as was used for the maintenance of said high school. The defendant set up the plea that it had not established a white high school, but had merely appropriated some money to assist a denominational high school for white children, saying "that it had to choose between maintaining the lower schools for a large number of Negroes and providing a high school for about sixty." The board of education, declared, moreover, that the establishment of a Negro high school was merely postponed.

The opinion of the court was that a decision by a State court, denying an injunction against the maintenance by a board of education of a high school for white children, while failing to maintain one for Negro children also, for the reason that the funds were not sufficient to maintain it in addition to needed primary schools for Negro children, does not constitute a denial to persons of color of the equal protection of the law or equal privileges of citizens of the United States. The court held that under the circumstances disclosed it could not say that this action of the State court was, within the meaning of the Fourteenth Amendment, a denial by the State to the plaintiffs and to those associated with them of the equal protection of the laws, or of any privileges belonging to them as citizens of the United States.

While the court admitted that the benefits and burdens of public taxation must be shared by citizens without discrimination against any class on account of their race, it held that the education of people in schools maintained by State taxation is a matter belonging to the respective States, and any interference on the part of Federal authority with the management of such schools cannot be justified except in case of a clear unmistakable disregard of rights secured by the supreme law of the land.

This is downright sophistry. To any sane man it could not but be evident that this was an "unmistakable disregard of rights secured by the Supreme law of the land." The school authorities had separated white and Negro children for purposes of education on account of race and had, moreover, refused to grant the Negro children the facilities equal to those of the white. The State, in the first place, in establishing separate schools on the basis of race, violated a right guaranteed the Negro race by the Constitution of the United States, and the board of education of Richmond County violated still another in failing to provide for the Negroes the same facilities for high school education as those furnished the whites while taxing all citizens without regard to race. It is true that the Federal Government cannot generally interfere in matters of police regulation of persons and property in the States but when the matter of race is introduced the national authority is thoroughly competent within the Constitution to restrain such local government or any group of persons so authorized by such government. It would have been unwise for the court to enjoin the collection of such a tax but it could have on the constitutional points raised in this case declared invalid laws separating the races for purposes of education.

The sophistry of the Supreme Court in seeking to

justify its refusal to maintain the rights of the Negro to education is still more evident from its opinion in the case of *Berea College* v. *The Commonwealth of Kentucky*, decided in 1908. Berea College was established in 1856 by a group of antislavery Kentucky mountaineers, led by John G. Fee, desiring to bring up their children in the love of free institutions. There were no Negro students prior to the Civil War but a few Negro soldiers were admitted on returning home from the front in their uniforms and members of the race were thereafter welcomed at Berea. In the course of time, however, this coeducation of the races became very distasteful to the State of Kentucky with its decided increase in race prejudice necessitating in their economy a thorough proscription of the Negro race. In 1904, therefore, the State of Kentucky enacted a law against persons and corporations maintaining schools for both white persons and Negroes.

Feeling that its charter was violated by this law and also that it infringed upon the rights guaranteed the Negro in the Constitution of the United States, Berea College attacked the validity of this measure in the inferior courts and finally in the Supreme Court of the United States. The plaintiff unanswerably contended that this Kentucky law abridged one's privileges and immunities, in violation of the Fourteenth Amendment of the Constitution of the United States, which was a limitation on the police power of the State when it brings in the matter of race. It further contended that the Constitution makes no distinction between races and that the Fourteenth Amendment is not only to protect Negroes but to protect white persons in the enjoyment of their rights. The plaintiff admitted that social equality could not be enforced by legislation but contended that voluntary social equality of persons cannot be constitutionally prohibited, unless it is shown that such is immoral, disorderly, or for some other reason so palpably injurious to the public welfare as to justify direct interference with the personal liberty of the citizens.

Evidently wishing to find some ground upon which it could base its opinion upholding the Supreme Court of Kentucky which had sustained this statute, the Supreme Court of the United States fell back upon various principles of interpretation. The court said it would not disturb the judgment of the State court resting on Federal or non-Federal grounds, if the latter was sufficient to sustain the decision in as much as the State court determines the extent of the limitations of powers conferred by the State on its corporations. It directed attention to the fact that a corporation is not entitled to all the immunities to which individuals are entitled and a State may withhold from its corporations privileges and powers of which it cannot constitutionally deprive individuals. A State statute limiting the powers of corporations and individuals may be constitutional as to the former, although unconstitutional as to the latter; and if separable it will not be held unconstitutional in the instance of a corporation unless it clearly appears that the legislature would not have enacted it as to corporations separately. "The same rule," continues the court, "which permits separable sections of a statute to be declared unconstitutional without rendering the entire statute void applies to separable provisions of a section of a statute. In coming to the assistance of the Supreme Court of Kentucky the national tribunal said the prohibition of Kentucky against persons and corporations maintaining schools for both white persons and Negroes is separable and, even if an unconstitutional restraint as to individuals, is not unconstitutional as to corporations, it being within the power of the State to determine the powers conferred upon its corporations.

The court conceded that the reserve power to alter, or amend charters is subject to reasonable limitations but insisted that the Kentucky law includes no alteration or amendment which defeats or substantially impairs the object of the grant of vested rights. The court then went almost out of its way to say that "a general statute which in effect alters or amends a charter is to be construed as an amendment for all even if not in terms so designated. The court conceded that a statute which permits the education of both whites and Negroes at the same time in different localities, although prohibiting their attendance in the same place, does not defeat the object of a grant to maintain the college for all persons and is not violative of the contract clause of the Federal Constitution, the State law having reserved the right to repeal, alter and amend charters.

Justice Harlan dissented. He referred to the fact that the court held also, in *Huntington* v. *Werthen*,[72] that if one provision of a statute be invalid the whole act will fall, where "it is evident the legislature would not have enacted one of them without the other." Harlan meant to say here that to construe this law as applying only to corporations and not to individuals would give it an interpretation that the legislature never had in mind. The intention of the State legislature was to prevent all coeducation of Negroes and whites whether it should be done by persons or corporations. The whole law, therefore, should fall. Justice Harlan conceded that a State reserved the right to repeal the charter but it was not repealed by this act. The statute did not purport even to amend the charter of any particular corporation but assumed to establish a certain rule applicable alike to all individuals, associations, or corporations that teach the white and black races together in the same institution. This decision of the United States

Supreme Court was then nothing more than "fine sophistry" to sanction an arbitrary invasion of the rights of liberty and property guaranteed by the Fourteenth Amendment.

Justice Harlan contended that if the giving of instruction is not a property right, it is one's liberty. Exposing the sophistry of the court he remarked that if the schools must be subjected to such segregation, why not also the Sabbath Schools and Churches? "If States can prohibit the coeducation of the whites and blacks it may prohibit the association of the Anglo-Saxons and Latins; of the Christians and the Jews. Have we become so inoculated with prejudice of race," continued Justice Harlan, "that an American government, professedly based on the principles of freedom, and charged with the protection of all citizens alike, can make distinctions between such citizens in the matter of their voluntary meeting for innocent purposes simply because of their respective races? Further if the lower court be right, then a State may make it a crime for white and colored persons to frequent the same market places, at the same time, or appear in an assembly of citizens convened to consider questions of a public or political nature in which all citizens without regard to race, are equally interested."

THE RIGHT TO LABOR

Although the Negro by these various decisions of the Supreme Court of the United States had been deprived of rights essential to freedom and citizenship in matters of voting, service upon juries, education, and the use of common carriers, there remained even another right which was to be infringed upon without the hope of any redress from the United States Supreme Court. This was the right to contract, to labor. Every honest man should live by his own labor and it is a well established principle of democratic government, that in the exercise of this right the individual should be free not only from interference on the part of the government but should enjoy protection from individuals subject to the government. Because of the development of race prejudice into a flame of bitter antagonism among the laboring men during the period of commercial expansion in the United States since the Reconstruction period, the country has been all but thoroughly organized through trades unions, so as to restrict the Negro to menial service by written constitutions in keeping with the caste which has so long figured conspicuously in American institutions.

Negroes sought redress in the courts and finally in the United States Supreme Court, the best case in evidence being that of *Hodges* v. *United States*.[/3] In this case came a complaint from certain Negroes in Arkansas laboring in the service of an employer according to a contract. Because of their color certain criminals in that community conspired to injure, oppress, threaten and intimidate them, resulting in the severance of their connection with this employer and the consequent economic loss resulting therefrom. The Negroes thus complaining brought this case to the United States Supreme Court contending that a remedy for this evil was to be found in the revised statutes of the United States Senate, Sections 1977, 1979, 5508, and 5510. These sections follow in the order of their importance:

> *Section 5508.* If two or more persons conspire to injure, oppress, threaten or intimidate any citizen in the free exercise or enjoyment of any right or privilege secured to him by the Constitution or laws of the United States, or because of his having so exercised the same; or if two or more persons go in disguise on the highway, or on the premises of another, with intent to hinder his free exercise or enjoyment of any right or privilege so secured, they shall be fined not more than five thousand dollars and imprisoned not more than ten years, and shall, moreover, be thereafter ineligible to any office, or place

of honor, profit or trust created by the Constitution or laws of the United States.

Other statutes referred to but not so vital were:

Section 1977. All persons within the jurisdiction of the United States shall have the same right in every State and Territory to make and enforce contracts, to sue the parties, give evidence, and to the full and equal benefit of all laws and proceedings for the security of persons and property as is enjoyed by white citizens, and shall be subject to like punishment, pains, penalties, taxes, licenses, and exactions of every kind, and to no other.

Section 1978. All citizens of the United States shall have the same right in every State and territory, as is enjoyed by white citizens thereof to inherit, purchase, lease, sell, hold, and convey real and personal property.

Section 1979. Every person who, under color of any statute, ordinance, regulation, custom, or usage, of any State or Territory, subjects, or causes to be subjected, any citizen of the United States or other persons within the jurisdiction thereof to the deprivation of any rights, privileges, or immunities, secured by the Constitution and laws, shall be liable to the party injured in an action at law, suit in equity, or other proper proceeding for redress.

Section 5510. Every person who, under color of any law, statute, ordinance, regulation, or custom, subjects or causes to be subjected, any inhabitant of any State or Territory to the deprivation of any right, privilege, or immunities, secured or protected by the Constitution and laws of the United States or to different punishments, pains or penalties, on account of such inhabitants being an alien, or by reason of his color, or race, than are prescribed for the punishment of citizens, shall be punished by a fine of not more than one thousand dollars or by imprisonment not more than one year, or by both.

The decision in this case was in substance that Congress cannot make it an offense against the United States for individuals to combine or conspire to prevent even by force, citizens of African descent, solely because of their race, from earning a living, although the right to earn one's living in all legal ways and to make lawful contracts in reference thereto is a vital point of freedom established by the Constitution. Section 5508 had been upheld in *Ex Parte*

58

Yarborough,[74] and in the case of *Logan* v. the *United States*[75] the court referred to this section as having been upheld in *Ex Parte Yarborough*. In *United States* v. *Reese*, moreover,[76] Justice Waite said in 1875, speaking for the court, "The rights and immunities created by or dependent upon the Constitution of the United States can be protected by Congress. The form and the manner of the protection may be such as Congress in the legitimate exercise of its legislative discretion shall provide. This may be varied to meet the necessities of the particular right to be protected."

"The whole scope and effect of this series of decisions," continued the court, "was that, while certain fundamental rights recognized and declared but not granted or created, in some of the amendments to the Constitution are thereby guaranteed only against violation or abridgement by the United States, or by the States, as the case may be, and cannot, therefore, be affirmatively enforced by Congress against unlawful causes of individuals; yet that every right created by, arising under, or dependent upon the Constitution of the United States may be protected and enforced by Congress by such means and in such manner as Congress in the exercise of the correlative duty of protection, or of the legislative powers conferred upon it by the Constitution, may in its discretion deem most eligible and best adopted to attain the object." This doctrine was sustained also by the decision in the case of *United States* v. *Waddell*,[77] and *Motes* v. *United States*.[78] Here it was emphatically stated that Congress might pass any law necessary or proper for carrying out any power conferred upon it by the Constitution.

The court here, however, evaded the real question as before, dodging behind the doctrine that while a State or the United States could not abridge the privileges and immunities of citizens, individuals or groups of individuals may do so and Congress has no power to interfere in such matters since these come within the police power of the State. In other words, the government cannot discriminate against the Negro itself, but it can establish agencies with power to do it. It is not surprising that Justice Harlan dissented, feeling as he had on former occasions that this decision permitted the States and groups of individuals supposedly subject to the government of those States to fasten upon the Negro badges or incidents of slavery in violation of the civil rights guaranteed him by the Thirteenth and Fourteenth Amendments. He believed that Congress had the right to pass any law to protect citizens in the enjoyment of any right granted him by Congress. The duty of the Federal government as Justice Harlan saw it was very clear in that the State had caused the race question to be injected therein and in such a case Congress always has power to act.

On the whole, however, the United States Supreme Court has not yet had the moral courage to face the issue in cases involving the constitutional rights of the Negro. Not a decision of that tribunal has yet set forth a straightforward opinion as to whether the States can enact one code of laws for the Negroes and another for the other elements of our population in spite of the fact that the Constitution of the United States prohibits such iniquitous legislation. In cases in which this question has been frankly put the court has wiggled out of it by some such declaration as that the case was improperly brought, that there were defects in the averments, or that the court lacked jurisdiction.

In the matter of jurisdiction the United States Supreme Court has been decidedly inconsistent. This tribunal at first followed the opinion of Chief Justice John Marshall in the case of *Osborn* v. *United States Bank*,[79] that "when a question to which the judicial power of the United States is extended by the Constitution forms an ingredient of the original cause it is in the power of Congress to give the Circuit Courts the jurisdiction of that cause, although other questions of fact or of law may be involved." Prior to the rise of the Negro to the status of so-called citizenship the court built upon this decision the prerogative of examining all judicial matters pertaining to the Federal Government until it made itself the sole arbiter in all important constitutional questions and became the bulwark of nationalism. After some reaction the court resumed that position in all of its decisions except those pertaining to the Negro; for in the recent commercial expansion of the country involving the litigation of unusually large property values, the United States Supreme Court has easily found grounds for jurisdiction where economic rights are concerned; but just as easily disclaims jurisdiction where human rights are involved in cases in which Negroes happen to be the complainants.

The fairminded man, the patriot of foresight, observes, therefore, with a feeling of disappointment this prostitution of an important department of the Federal Government to the use of the reactionary forces in the United States endeavoring to whittle away the essentials of the Constitution which guarantees to all persons in this country all the rights enjoyed under the most progressive democracy on earth. Since the Civil War the United States Supreme Court instead of performing the intended function of preserving the Constitution by democratic interpretation, has by its legislative decisions practically stricken therefrom so many of its liberal provisions and read into the Constitution so much caste and autocracy that discontent and radicalism have developed almost to the point of eruption.

C. G. Woodson

FOOTNOTES:

[1] *McCulloch* v. *Maryland*, 4 Wheaton, 416.

[2] *Ibid.*, 416.

[3] *Ibid.*, 416.

[4] *Dred Scott* v. *Sanford*, 19 Howard, 399.

[5] 16 Peters, 539, 612.

[6] *Dred Scott* v. *Sanford*, 19 Howard, 399.

[6a] 21 Howard, 506.

[7] 6 Howard, 344.

[8] 94 U.S., 113.

[9] 16 Wall., 678.

[10] This was held in *Township of Queensburg* v. *Culver* (19 Wall., 83), in *Township of Pine Grove* v. *Talcott* (19 Wall., 666), and in Massachusetts in *Worcester* v. *Western R. R. Corporation* (4 Met., 564).

[11] *Storey on Bailments*, Sec. 475-6, and *Rex* v. *Ivens*, 7 Carrington & Payne, 213; 32, E. C. L., 495.

[12] 16 Wall., 36.

[13] 100 U. S., 303.

[14] 100 U. S., 306.

[15] 103 U. S., 386.

[16] *Ex Parte Virginia*, 100 U. S., 346-7.

[17] 14 statutes, 27, Chapter 31.

[18] 16 statutes, 140, Chapter 114.

[19] 109 U. S., 1.

[20] *United States* v. *Cruikshank*, 92 U. S., 542; *Virginia* v. *Rives*, 100 U. S., 318; *Ex Parte Virginia*, 100 U. S., 339.

[21] 6 Cranch, 128.

[22] 99 U. S., 418.

[23] *United States* v. *Reese*, 92 U. S., 214; *Strauder* v. *West Virginia*, 100 U. S., 303.

[24] *Ward* v. *Maryland*, 12 Wall., 418; *Corfield* v. *Coryell*, 4 Washington, D. C., 371; *Paul* v. *Virginia*, 8 Wall., 168; *Slaughter-house cases*, *Ibid.*, 36.

[25] 92 U. S., 542.

[26] 95 U. S., 487.

[27] The Louisiana Act was:

> *Section—.* All persons engaged within this State in the business of common carriers of passengers, shall have the right to refuse to admit any person to their railroad cars, street cars, steamboats or other water-crafts, stage coaches, omnibusses, or other vehicles, or to expel any person therefrom after admission, when such persons shall, on demand, refuse or neglect to pay the customary fare, or when such person shall be of infamous character or shall be guilty, after admission to the conveyance of the carrier, of gross, vulgar, or disorderly conduct, or who shall commit any act tending to injure the business of the carrier, prescribed for the management of his business, after such rules and regulations shall have been made known: *Provided*, said rules and regulations make no discrimination on account of race or color, and shall have the right to refuse any person admission to such conveyance where there is not room or suitable accommodation; and, except in cases above enumerated, all persons engaged in the business of common carriers of passengers are forbidden to refuse admission to their conveyance, or to expel therefrom any person whomsoever.

> *Section 4.* For a violation of any provision of the first and second sections of this act, the party injured shall have right of action to recover any damage, exemplary as well as actual, which he may sustain, before any court of competent jurisdiction. Acts of 1869, page 77; Rev. Stat. 1870, page 93.

[28] Mr. Justice Clifford concurred in the judgment but went into details to justify the segregation whereas the opinion of the court merely tried to see whether the details conflicted with the power of Congress to regulate commerce.

64

[29] 118 W. S., 557.

[30] All of these are in 94 U. S.

[31] 133 U. S., 587.

[32] This was the law of Mississippi:

Sec. 1. "Be it enacted, That all railroads carrying passengers in this State (other than street railroads) shall provide equal, but separate accommodation for the white and colored races by providing two or more passenger cars for each passenger train, or by dividing the passenger cars by a partition, so as to secure separate accommodations."

Sec. 2. That the conductors of such passenger trains shall have power and are hereby required to assign each passenger to the car or the compartment of a car (when it is divided by a partition) used for the race to which said passenger belongs; and that, should any passenger refuse to occupy the car to which he or she is assigned by such conductor, said conductor shall have the power to refuse to carry such passenger on his train and neither he nor the railroad company shall be liable for any damages in any event in this State.

Sec. 3. That all railroad companies that shall refuse or neglect within sixty days after the approval of this act to comply with the requirements of section one of this act, shall be deemed guilty of a misdemeanor and shall upon conviction in a court of competent jurisdiction, be fined not more than five hundred dollars; and any conductor that shall neglect to, or refuse to carry out the provisions of this act, shall, upon conviction, be fined not less than twenty-five nor more than fifty dollars for each offense.

Sec. 4. That all acts and parts of acts in conflict with this act be, and the same are hereby repealed, and this act to take effect and be in force from and after passage. Acts of 1888, p. 48.

[33] 133 U. S., 592.

[34] 163 U. S., 317.

[35] *Ibid.*, 537.

[36] 169 U. S., 613, 645.

[37] 141 U. S., 61.

[38] In *Pa. R. R. Co.* v. *Hughes* (191 U. S., 489), Justice White says:

> "In the absence of Congressional legislation upon the subject an act of the Alabama legislature to require locomotive engineers to be examined and licensed by a board to be appointed by the governor for that purpose was sustained in *Smith* v. *Alabama*" (124 U. S., 465).

[39] 179 U. S., 393.

[40] 133 U. S., 587.

[41] 163 U. S., 537.

[42] 179 U. S., 388, 391.

[43] 133 U. S., 588.

[44] 218 U. S., 71.

[45] 235 U. S., 151.

[46] U. S., 18, 1907 Revised Statutes, 1910, Section 860, *et seq.*

[47] 100 U. S., 303.

[48] *Ibid.*, 313.

[49] 103 U. S., 370.

[50] 162 U. S., 565.

[51] 107 U. S., 110.

[52] 162 U. S., 592.

[53] 163 U. S., 101.

[54] 167 U. S., 442.

[55] 192 U. S., 226.

[56] 200 U. S., 316.

[57] 218 U. S., 161.

[58] Laws of South Carolina, 1902, page 1066, section 2.

[59] 100 U. S., 371.

[60] 110 U. S., 651.

[61] 127 U. S., 731.

[62] 179 U. S., 58.

[63] 185 U. S.

[64] 189 U. S., 475.

[65] 193 U. S., 146.

[66] The Constitution of Mississippi prescribing the qualifications for electors conferred upon the legislature the power to enact laws to carry those provisions into effect. Ability to read any section of the Constitution or to understand it when read was made a qualification necessary to a legal voter. Another provision made the qualifications for grand or petit jurors that they should be able to read and write. Upon the complaint of Negroes thus disabled the court held that these provisions do not on their face discriminate between white and Negro races and do not amount to a denial of the equal protection of the law secured by the Fourteenth Amendment of the Constitution. It had not been shown that their actual administration was evil, but that only evil was possible under them.

In Washington County, Mississippi, Williams had been indicted for murder by a grand jury composed of white men altogether. He moved that the indictment be quashed because the law by which the grand jury was established was unconstitutional. (*Williams* v. *Mississippi.*)

[67] 193 U. S., 621.

[68] 238 U. S., 347.

[69] *Ibid.*, 368.

[70] *Ibid.*, 763.

[71] 175 U. S., 528.

[72] 120 U. S., 102.

[73] 202 U. S., 1.

[74] 110 U. S., 651.

[75] 144 U. S., 236, 286, 293.

[76] 92 U. S., 214, 217.

[77] 110 U. S., 651.

[78] 178 U. S., 458, 462.

[79] 9 Wheaton, 738.

REMY OLLIER, MAURITIAN JOURNALIST AND PATRIOT[1]

It is of interest to the Negro to know the patriots of the race who have blazed the path of social progress in the various lands in which their lots have been cast. Not to all men is it given to be great as the world counts greatness. Each of us, however, may have a task which, if well done, may leave its impress upon the life of the community in which we live. These, although obscure, efforts of the talented and persevering are the monuments which silently mark the progress of the race. Remy Ollier was one of these obscure personalities; but yet, a man whose career made such contributions to the life of Mauritius that he is regarded by its people as one of the great figures in its political history. He was an educator, a journalist, a patriot, and in some respects a liberator of his people.

Mauritius is an island under British control situated in the Indian Ocean. It is 550 miles east of Madagascar, which lies off the east coast of Africa. Under the control of the French, it was known as Ile de France. It is mountainous in character and its scenery is most beautiful and picturesque. Its inhabitants may be divided into two main divisions: Europeans, chiefly French and British; and African and Asiatic peoples. French appears to be more commonly spoken than English, which accounts for the fact that the writings of Remy Ollier were in French.

The island was discovered by the Portuguese navigator, Mascarenhas in 1505. Until the sixteenth century the island remained under the control of Portugal. In 1598, the Dutch seized it and named it

"Mauritius" in honor of its stadholder, Count Maurice of Nassau. The Dutch built a fort there, introduced slaves and convicts, but they made no permanent settlements and, in 1710, it was abandoned. For a short time the island passed into the hands of the French East India Company, and later it became a crown colony. During the colonial wars between France and Great Britain, Mauritius was a source of much conflict. It was finally captured by the British in 1810; and by the Treaty of Paris in 1814, the British were definitely granted control of the island. Great Britain agreed, however, that the inhabitants should retain their own laws, customs, religion and language, all of which were of French origin.

In 1833 slavery was abolished in the British possessions. The Reformed Parliament forced by the denunciation of antislavery orators led by William Wilberforce, Thomas Clarkson, and Granville Sharp, enacted a bill providing that Negro slavery should gradually cease in the colonies, and that a compensation of £20,000,000 should be paid to the slaveholders. There were then enacted laws removing proscription and the Negroes were supposed to enjoy the same political rights as the whites; but the latter sought to make themselves the dominant element in Mauritius. In 1834 there were about 66,000 Negroes on the island, which ten years later had a population of 158,462.[2] Indian coolies were brought in to take the place of Negro slaves and many evils attended their introduction. The situation was then as it was later in the United States when the adjustment of freedmen to their new life was accompanied by painful experiences on the part of both freedmen and their former masters. The planters resented the presence of the freedmen and as far as possible their privileges were curtailed.[3] Militant agitators arose then among the Negroes demanding justice for the oppressed. Among these leaders thus promoting the march of the Negro population of Mauritius toward freedom were Adrien d'Epinay, whose prominence is attested by a monument to be erected in his memory, and Remy Ollier, who still lives in the hearts of his countrymen.

Remy Ollier was born at Grand Port on the island of Mauritius, October 16, 1816, six years after the conquest of the island by the English. He was the fourth child of Benoit Ollier, an artillery officer. His mother, J. Guillemeau, was a daughter of Dr. Guillemeau, a physician, and formerly a member of the Legislative Council of the island. When eight years of age, Ollier was sent to a private school taught by Captain Rault, a seaman who had served under Louis XVI. This work was supplemented by lessons every Saturday under the Reverend Father Rock, who was impressed with the boy's ability, and with the consent of his parents taught him the elements of English and Latin. Allowed to use the library of Mr. Rault, Ollier early became acquainted with the best literature. It is said that he had a very retentive memory and that he could repeat and write at will long passages from his favorite authors.

About 1832, an unexpected reverse in fortune reduced Ollier's father to abject poverty, and he died of a broken heart. Ollier, now scarcely sixteen, went to work as a clerk in a merchant's office; but his mother, thinking that his future in a clerkship was limited, secured him a place as an apprentice to a harness-maker. With a book in one hand and an awl in the other, Ollier prepared himself for his future career. Opportunities in the larger fields of life were closed to the Negro population as stated in the words of Ollier "that young men of the present generation could but become handicraftsmen. This is the only field open to us. But we must try to educate ourselves by all means; perseverance is the only key that opens the door to success. At whatever social rank man may be placed, education alone may confer upon him a superiority."

In 1833 there occurred an incident which proved to be a turning point in his life. Several members of the white population were charged with forming a conspiracy against British rule in the island. Rumor had it further that they had gathered arms and ammunition, that they expected to attack the British officials and restore the island to France. They were imprisoned and were denied the writ of habeas corpus. Young Ollier had developed a keen interest in politics and asked the permission of his employer to pay the men a visit. Later, he spent many of his working hours at the court trials to which he seemed irresistibly drawn. His employer wrote his mother stating that her son would never make a harness-maker; for he spent most of his time either in study when in the shop or at the courts when he should have been at work. His mother, whom he always loved, burned his books and reprimanded him for his conduct. For some time, he remained at the harness shop, but finally gave up the work in order to pursue the study he desired. Through his former friend, Mr. Rault, he obtained many books to replace the ones which he had lost by the hasty action of his mother.

By tutoring the children in the village of Petite Riviere and in the town of Port Louis, he managed to obtain a living. In 1837, he opened a private school in St. George street. It appears that this venture was not successful, for he soon accepted a position in a "boarding school conducted by Mr. Louis Barthelemy Raynaud, a white Mauritian Professor who did not scruple to teach the young generations of the white as well as of the colored population." When not engaged in tutoring at this school and the neighboring schools for young ladies, Ollier might be found devouring books on metaphysics, morals, criticism and politics. He was asked by several private institutions to give lessons in English, French and Geography; but while teaching others, he himself was studying with Mr. H. N. D. Beyts, who twice filled the post of officer administering the government. Ollier continued his work as a teacher until 1839. At the end of the school year, prizes were distributed, and he had the pleasure of presenting a prize to Miss Louis Sidonie Ferret whom he married in December, 1840.

About a year before his marriage, he bought the school from Mr. Raynaud, with the idea of enlarging it according to his own plans; but this project failed for some unknown reason. He then undertook a trip to India, which seems to have been successful. On his return, he entered business, opening two large stores. His associate did not agree with him in his business plans and the business was dissolved by legal process. He then resumed his position as a teacher in the boarding schools. In 1841, he and his wife opened a school in the western suburb of Port Louis where the Negro population could bring their children for a liberal education upon the payment of a moderate fee. This helped him for a time to solve some of his financial problems but finally failed.

Ollier remained an insatiable reader. He took an active part in a literary club in Port Louis, *Le Société d'Emulation Intellectuelle*, and this association helped greatly to increase his knowledge of the literary world. He read literature, history, travels, philosophy, politics and such authors as Lamennais, Montesquieu, Diderot, Rousseau, Voltaire, Adam Smith, Horace Say, Ricardo and the like. He read not only because of his love of reading but because he was ambitious to prepare himself for larger duties. The largest duty as he seemed to see it was the freedom of his people from insult and injustice, and the recognition of his people upon the same level as other Mauritians. Before the edict of emancipation, the Legislative Council on June 22, 1829, had granted the free population of color the same civil rights and privileges as other Mauritians possessed, but the local government had failed to carry out the enactment. Remy Ollier felt that this was a blot on the fair name of his country, as well as an affront to his people and longed to do his part in bringing about a change, which he believed could be effected by a newspaper.

An unusual incident translated into action his idea of founding a newspaper. Alexander Dumas had written a play entitled "Anthony," which is composed especially "to castigate morals by exposing vice in opposition to virtue." A contributor to one of the two papers, *Le Mauricien*, attacked the production of the play, and held up to ridicule the police authorities, who were supposed to be vested with censorial powers. He also criticized the author as a Negro glorifying adultery. The Negroes of the island became indignant and several answers were evoked. Remy Ollier presented a strong defense for Dumas. Another vigorous defense was prepared by Evénor Hitie, a writer of history. These articles were sent to the two papers of the island: *Le Cerneen* and *Le Mauricien*, both of which refused to publish them. An Englishman, Mr. Edward Baker, the owner of a printing plant, printed the two answers and circulated them in tract form.

The need of a newspaper became evident to the Negro population. In the time of Ollier, the press was used chiefly for political purposes rather than for the dissemination of information. Policies and parties were aided or hindered by the press, and this was its principal function. *Le Balance* had been the champion for the government and the rights of the weaker groups; but the editor, Mr. Berquin, was deported in 1833 because of utterances which were considered inimical to the policies of the colonial government. Since 1833, there had been no paper to champion the rights of the Negroes.

After the publication of the answers to the contributor of *Le Mauricien*, certain influential members of the Negro population, among whom was Remy Ollier, called to see Sir Lionel Smith, G.C.B., Baronet and Governor of the island of Mauritius. It is said that they were warmly received, and that he was astonished to learn that the Negroes, a majority of whom were "the equals of the whites by their stature, by their hearts and their intelligence," had no paper "to make known their wishes and their complaints." He advised his hearers to start a paper, and he promised to support their reasonable demands. But, dying in 1842, Sir Lionel Smith was unable to give any assistance to the new publication.

Through the assistance of Mr. Edward Baker, the printer, the paper *Le Sentinelle de Maurice* was started. The prospectus, written in French and in English appeared March 21, 1843, and on Saturday, April 8, the first number of the paper came from the press. It was a weekly publication with Ollier and Baker as the editors. The former wrote articles in French and the latter in English, the articles of each being admirably written. Each one in his own sphere spoke with great vehemence and elevation of mind for the cause of "liberty and justice." The paper was read with avidity by the middle and lower classes, and the Negroes soon regarded Ollier as their champion.

The first and most important fight which Ollier felt called upon to enter was the nomination by the Governor of members to the Legislative Council in June, 1843. Ollier noticed that no Negro member was nominated. The vacant seat was given to a white representative, Mr. Forster. Ollier observed "that although a white man whose heart is right and whose intentions are pure can represent the population of color," yet he considered the appointment "as an act that was unjust, impolitic, undemocratic and unconstitutional." He added in explanation that the act was unjust "because all the children of the mother-country, the white colonists especially, were already represented in the Council, except the men of color, whose number is twice that of other populations of the country; their destiny more illustrious, and the high state of their experience, their education, their intelligence and their morals are the same as with others; impolitic, because it discontents and disheartens the loyal and faithful British subjects and might alienate from the government the hearts of those who have invariably remained attached to it; undemocratic, and unconstitutional because the British constitution makes no exception of any person, and because it desires that all its subjects should have an equal part in its benefits."

In 1843, Ollier determined to have his paper appear three times a week, and for this purpose he bought the printing plant of *La Balance*, the paper which had been forced to suspend its publication ten years before. On the top of the first page of the paper, the royal arms of Great Britain were placed with the motto "Honi soit qui mal y pense! Dieut et mon droit!" He dedicated the paper to a strict vigilance over the abuse of power, "to redress the grievances of the weak and to encourage merit in all classes, creed or color." Those who now assisted him in the editorial work besides Mr. Baker, who edited the English page, were his wife, Emile Sandapa, and Emile Bouchet, a lawyer, who later defended Ollier when he was sued for libel. His editorials framed in animating language aroused his countrymen from their inaction and awakened in them new hopes and aspirations.

Ollier again attacked the government and the party in power, because no place was made for the Negro element in its civil service. In the first issue of *La Sentinelle*, he wrote, "From day to day the Maurician Press develops a system entirely dangerous and which seems to have this for a foundation—to discredit and debase English institutions and the English Government in the eyes of all. Here are the consequences of this system—the government believing that the opinions of the press are those of all the inhabitants of Maurice, has seen in us enemies rather than loyal and faithful subjects, whence this continual defiance which has driven up to now the people of color from all the public employment.... The organs of this country are all in accord in saying that the government of the United Kingdom is pernicious to us, that it long since desires and plans our ruin; and when our riches and our prosperity proclaim openly the falseness of these allegations, they wish that England, who makes possible this well-being for us, may not have a deep indignation against those who do not have even enough generosity to recognize the benefits of their mother-country.... As for us, our mission is to call all parties of our population to a united intelligence...." On October 22, 1844, he exclaimed, regarding racial distinctions: "Education levels everything. An erudite man in any class is equal to any other man having the same degree of education; he is a demi-god and is superior to kings, when the latter are immersed in the darkness of ignorance."

Ollier continued the attacks upon the government because of its discrimination against its citizens of color and yet he remained a lover of his country. Not only did he agitate through the columns of paper, but also through other available channels. In 1843, he drafted a petition to which many signatures were attached and sent it to Queen Victoria. This action has been called the death-blow to the monopoly of the local parliament by the white population. The petition was:

"May it please your Majesty,—On various occasions the British Throne has been approached by individual members or collective bodies of the Mauritius community in the exercise of that inestimable privilege of your Majesty's faithful subjects, the right of petition; but hitherto, never has any prayer of the great majority of your Majesty's loyal and attached subjects in this island been thus presented to your Majesty's attention.

"The colored classes of Mauritius, comprising a population of about 70,000, and including at least one third of the island's wealth and intelligence, although not deprived of any political right by the fundamental laws of the British realm, or by any act of Your Majesty's Parliament, actually enjoy but few privileges of British subjects; and can scarcely be said to have a political existence in the affairs of their native island.

"Your Majesty's petitioners will refer to the fact of no individual of the coloured classes having a seat in the Council of Government; notwithstanding that there are many in the island in every respect qualified by riches, talents, education, and moral character, to occupy a place in that assembly.

"Whilst therefore gratefully recognizing the equity and impartiality of the British laws and institutions, in which alone repose their best hopes for themselves and their children, your Majesty's petitioners humbly and reverently approach Your Imperial Throne with the prayer that, His Excellency the Governor of Mauritius may be authorized to call to his council one or more representatives of the people of colour in this island; or otherwise to grant to the country the privilege of electing its own representatives. Your Majesty's petitioners will only add the sincere declaration of their loyal and patriotic attachment to Your Majesty's person and Throne and Government; and your petitioners will ever pray."

In 1843, the editor of *Le Cerneen*, the oldest newspaper in the colony, was prosecuted, fined and imprisoned for publishing a defamatory article against the magistrate of Port Louis. Ollier had always advocated the freedom of the press, and he protested against the law which suppressed free speech, and against the persecution of a fellow-journalist, although the latter was his political enemy. Ollier's biographer adds: "Ollier indeed was an ardent lover and a good hater. This noble heart and comprehensive mind made him understand his duty toward men. He forgot enmity when fundamental principles were not adequately observed."

In 1844, there was established a rival newspaper, *l'Esprit Public*, to combat the policies of Remy Ollier. It was edited by Mr. Bruils, who had been educated in Europe as a lawyer. He began by finding fault with the style and grammatical form of Ollier's writing, but it is said that the subject-matter of his editorials could be rarely attacked. Ollier's writings were always hasty and he rarely took the time to polish them, while Bruil's style was more smooth and uniform. Ollier's style, however, was easy and original. He replied effectively to the invective of his enemies in prose and in verse. He seems to have had no difficulty in the composition of his sentences nor did he take the pains which would seem to be necessary for the average man to acquire the finished journalistic style. His motto was as he wrote a page "une feuille lue aujourd'hui, oubliée demain." Therefore, he gave his copies to the compositors without rereading them. Concerning the correctness of his writings, his biographer writes: "Like Carlyle, Shelly, Bossuet, Mirabeau and Moliere, the editor of *La Sentinelle* perpetrated many a small sin against the rules of grammar and certainly paid but a halting attention to the nice distinctions of punctuation. He very often did not know where to end a paragraph and begin another. On the whole, he is happily not obscure." His main effort was to state his idea and when he had made his statement, he was not as careful as he should have been regarding the construction of the statement. He consoled himself with the words, "Grammar is of man; the idea is of God."

His enemies, however, could not say that he was trying to overthrow the empire, for he was merely struggling for the liberty guaranteed by the empire. "In all the British Empire," said he, "there are no subjects more loyal than we. We are English today, we are not a conquered people, we are English people." He was convinced that if England would give the rights of Englishmen to the Mauritians, she would find them "as devoted as any children she could count in her bosom." He added, however, "We belong to England. Why do we not possess the institutions of England? If she wishes to make us love our nationality, to endow our island with that which makes for the glory of our mother-country; this, we shall not be able to know or appreciate if we are strangers to all that which makes it cherish its children and respect its people! At the sight of our institutions, in the presence of the happenings in Mauritius, advancements ruined, individual liberty violated, human life despised, one cannot believe that we belong to an English administration, and that we are a part of the most democratic people in the world."

It was agitation of this type which brought about what may be considered the definite contributions of Remy Ollier to Mauritian life: the creation of the Municipality, the Chambers of Commerce and Agriculture, the opening of credits to the Negroes by the Mauritian Commercial Bank, the reforms at the Royal College respecting the English Scholarships, and the employment of men of color in the departments of the government. His attacks upon capital punishment and barbarous prison treatment resulted in laws which mitigated the former harsh conditions, and his criticism of the banking institutions in the crisis of 1843 led to considerable reform in that quarter. His bitter attacks on political and social conditions made many enemies. One evening, he was waylaid by several assailants and given a whipping. He was imprisoned, but he wrote in prison as well as elsewhere.

His political activity was short, for in the early part of 1845, about two years after his appearance in journalism, he died at the early age of 28 years, after a short illness due to an inflammation of the intestines. Stoically he bore the bitter effects of his courageous utterances; and when death came to him after only a short period of endeavor, both in the interests of his own people, and also of the weaker classes of all groups, the success of his efforts had just begun to appear. The name of Remy Ollier in Mauritian history, therefore, symbolizes perseverance in the face of great obstacles, agitation as an instrument of social progress, patriotism as it relates to the island of Mauritius, and justice respecting all classes and races. In 1916, the centenary of his birth was celebrated in Port Louis. Then it was that the city and island demonstrated its love and gratitude for Ollier, because of the services which he rendered the colony in general and the population of color in particular. Remy Ollier was one of the unknown leaders in the cause of freedom.

CHARLES H. WESLEY

FOOTNOTES:

[1] This sketch is drawn largely from a pamphlet, presented to the Association for the study of Negro Life and History by the author A. F. Fokeer. The author states that he has not had access to all the material which he desired to use, for when he applied to the municipality for one of the books concerning Ollier, he received an answer stating "that books written by Mauritians, and published in the colony are by no means to be lent to anybody." Therefore, the source from which most of our information is secured is *A Biographical Sketch of the Life, Work and Character of Remy Ollier* by A. F. Fokeer, published by the General Printing and Stationery Cy. Ld., 23 Church Street, Mauritius. 1917.

[2] Earlier figures are not available.

[3] General information concerning the island may be obtained from the following: Martin, *The British Possessions in Africa*, Vol. IV.; Unienville, *Statistique de l'île Maurice et ses dépendances*; Epinay, *Renseignements pour servir à l'histoire de l'île de France*; Decotter, *Géographie de Maurice et de ses dépendances*; Chalmers, *A History of Currency in the British Colonies*; Anderson, *The Sugar Industry of Mauritius*; Keller, *Madagascar, Mauritius, and other East African Islands*; *The Mauritius Almanac*; *The Mauritius Civil Lists*; and *Annual Colonial Reports*.

A NEGRO COLONIZATION PROJECT IN MEXICO, 1895

The Negro question touched the relations of the United States and Mexico at several points. For instance, the escape of runaway slaves into Mexico where slavery was legally forbidden, was a factor in causing disturbances along the Rio Grande between 1850 and 1860.[1] Again, during the following decade when the colonization of the freedmen became a vital issue, there was at least one proposal to settle them on the border between the United States and Mexico. It was urged that a strip of land extending from the Rio Grande to the Colorado and westward to the mountains of New Mexico be set apart by the national government for this purpose. On January 11, 1864, Honorable James H. Lane of Kansas actually introduced a bill looking to this end, which received favorable consideration from the Committee on Territories, but so far as has been ascertained never came to a vote in Congress.[2]

In support of his proposal Lane urged, among other things, that the colonization of the Negroes on this frontier would prove beneficial to Mexico and tend to promote friendship between that country and the United States. "We can thus plant at the door of Mexico," he said, "four million good citizens, who can step in at any time, when invited, to strengthen the hands of that Republic."[3] In similar vein the territorial committee, of which Lane was chairman, declared: "It is desirable to cultivate friendly relations with the people of Mexico. It is known to us that among that people there are no prejudices against the black man, and that intermarriage is not prohibited either by law or custom.... It is confidently believed that the colony provided for in this bill, by intermarriage with the people of those Mexican States, and friendly intercourse with them, would so Americanize them as that they would be prepared and seek an annexation to our then glorious free republic."[4]

The project which is the subject of this paper had no official element motivating it, however. It was merely a private enterprise conducted for the profit of a Mexican land company and a member of the Negro race;[5] and not until the scheme had failed did the United States government take a hand. On December 11, 1894, H. Ellis,[6] a Negro, entered into a contract with the "Agricultural, Industrial, and Colonization Company of Tlahualilo, Limited," for the transportation from the United States by February 15, 1895, of one hundred colored families between the ages of twelve and fifty. The company obligated itself to pay the passage of the colonists provided it did not exceed $20, and after they were established upon the land, to furnish them agricultural implements, stock, seed, and housing quarters, as well as $6 monthly during the first three months, and thereafter a sum later to be agreed upon. Each family was to be given sixty acres for cultivation, forty for cotton, fifteen for corn, and five for a garden.[7] The company was to receive 40% of the yield of cotton and corn, the colonists 50%, and Ellis 10%. The colonists were to have two years in which to pay for their passage; but, of course, the money advanced for sustenance was to be paid from the first crop, except in the event of an extremely lean year. The entire produce of the garden was to go to the Negroes. Stores were to be established in the colony, the colonists were to have their cotton ginned at the gins of the company at the rate of $1.50 per bale, and the company was to be given preference on all the produce sold. The contract was to endure for a period of five years.[8]

Ellis set about immediately to fulfil his agreement. Going among the Negroes of Alabama and Georgia, he issued a rather extravagant circular representing his proposition as presenting the "greatest opportunity ever offered to the colored people of the United States to go to Mexico, ... the country of 'God and Liberty.'" He declared that the land of his company would easily produce a bale of cotton and from fifty to seventy-five bushels of corn per acre; spoke of irrigation facilities which made them independent of the rain, of "fine game, such as deer, bear, duck, and wild geese, and all manner of small game, as well as opossum," and of schools and churches to be constructed; and sought especially to impress upon their minds the fact that "the great Republic of Mexico extends to all of its citizens the same treatment—equal rights to all, special privileges to none."[9]

A number of Negroes were soon attracted by the project and early in February they were ready to set out. In fact, by the 6th a party had already arrived at the hacienda of the company, situated some thirty miles east of Mapimi, Durango, in a rather "wild and inaccessible place" several miles from a railway. On the 25th of the same month another group of colonists put in their appearance, making a total of about 816.

It is interesting to note the section from which the Negroes came, and the size and composition of the families which they brought. Twelve of the number came from Griffin, Georgia; all the rest were from one of seven towns in Alabama; namely, Tuscaloosa, Gadsen, Williams, Eutaw, Carter, Johns, and Birmingham. Of these towns Tuscaloosa furnished by far the greater number, while Eutaw, Gadsen, and Birmingham came next. Only a comparatively small number came from Williams, Carter, and Johns.

Instead of having some three or four members as apparently designed in the original contract, some of the families numbered six, eight, and even twelve; and the number of women and children was disproportionately large.

When the colonists arrived at the hacienda they found the ground covered with snow. They were crowded into small, leaky, adobe houses, without floors and with doors which could not be closed tightly. The remainder of the winter and the following spring proved unusually rainy and unpleasant; the food which they were given was probably of a somewhat inferior quality; and their tools were clumsy and dull. These factors possibly account for their homesickness and alleged indisposition to work. Moreover, the small number of able-bodied workingmen among them was disappointing to the colonization company. Naturally enough, mutual dissatisfaction led to quarrels and difficulties. As was to be expected, too, sickness soon visited the settlement, killing off large numbers and terrifying the rest. A sort of liver disease broke out among them in April causing several deaths, and this was followed early in July by the ravages of the smallpox.[10]

The first epidemic was sufficiently terrifying to cause some of the colonists to bolt their contract and attempt to return to the United States. When the smallpox broke out it proved to be too much for their sense of honor or any other restraining force. Those who were able began precipitously to desert the settlement for the United States, apparently giving no attention at all to the matter of sustenance for the journey. By the latter part of July all had left except about fifty of the most persistent and faithful who chose to stay by their crops.[11]

The sufferings of these colonists while at Tlahualilo and on their way to the Rio Grande furnished the press of the United States a sensational topic which it immediately seized upon. Indeed, the first report which reached the United States through official circles was itself sufficiently exaggerated to create excitement. On May 21, 1895, two fugitives from the colony arrived at Chihuahua City where they related stories of oppression and brutal cruelty. One of them reported that upon arriving at the colony the Negroes "found themselves in the worst form of bondage, with no hope of ever securing liberty," and that no letter informing friends of their condition and their suffering was ever permitted to reach the United States. He said he was one of a party of some fifty who had stolen away in the hope of making their escape. The other Negro declared that he was the sole survivor of a party of about forty which had likewise run away from the settlement, but had been overtaken and slain by a band of Mexican guards in the employment of the colonizing company. The consul of the United States at Chihuahua sent immediate notice of the affair to the State Department.[12]

E. C. Butler, chargé of the United States in Mexico, was immediately notified and directed to call upon the Mexican government to investigate the affair.[13] Meantime the consular officers of the United States began an investigation of their own which tended to convince them that the extravagant rumors regarding the cruelties perpetrated against the Negroes were totally unfounded. On June 24, the consul at Piedras Negras, Jesse W. Sparks, forwarded a report which he respectfully suggested should be given to the public "in order to contradict the terrible stories of murder and bad treatment of these Negroes ... and deter other Negroes who contemplate colonizing in Mexico." It was based upon a sworn statement made by the purported leader of the runaways, a deposition of another of the colonists, and information received through a traveller from New York City, who claimed to

87

have visited the colony, as well as through a civil engineer who was in the employment of the Mexican International Railroad. From the information furnished by these witnesses Sparks drew the conclusion that the Mexican colonization company had lived up to its contract, that the Negroes had not been cruelly treated while at the colony, and that the report concerning the murder of a portion of the band[14] attempting to escape was absolutely false. The Mexican soldiers alleged to have slain the Negroes were in fact a relief party sent out by the company which, being acquainted with the barren and desolate nature of the country which would have to be crossed in reaching the United States, surmised that the lives of the colonists were in danger.[15]

Those who left the settlement after the smallpox epidemic broke out really suffered severely from lack of food. Without money and without provisions, there would have been no alternative but starvation or highway robbery, if the consular agents of the United States had not come to the rescue. That they came and came effectively is evinced by the fact that very few of the colonists actually died of starvation. One hundred and twenty-five of the Negroes arrived at Mapimi about July 19 and sent a delegation from there to Torreón to appeal to the consul for aid.[16] The agent at this place wrote to the consul at Durango for advice and help, while at the same time he set about to raise funds by voluntary subscription. The consul at Durango responded immediately with financial aid and suggested that the Negroes seek employment; but the small number of the group which was able to work seemed disinclined to do so; and, to make matters worse, the smallpox continued its ravages and in a measure precluded the possibility of obtaining employment even if it had been desired.[17]

The consuls appealed at the same time to the

authorities at Washington who replied at first that there was no fund available for the relief of the destitute citizens. As early as July 26, however, General Bliss, who commanded the department of Texas, was ordered to send a physician to help look after the sick and to place 1500 rations into the hands of Consul Sparks at Piedras Negras; and the consul at Piedras Negras was directed, in case return to the colony was not "practicable or consistent with humane considerations," to endeavor to persuade the railroad companies to transport the Negroes to their homes under the promise of receiving remuneration as soon as Congress could be prevailed upon to make an appropriation for that purpose.[18]

Meantime, the demoralized colonists were leaving their crops and making their way first to Mapimi, and later to Torreón, where most of them caught the Mexican International to Eagle Pass. Here they were received in a quarantine encampment especially prepared for them and given clothes, provisions, and medical attention until the smallpox epidemic had been subdued. This required considerable time and the expense was by no means small. Finally, by September 26, those who had been taken into quarantine first were ready to leave, and on that date the Southern Pacific took aboard 167 of them destined for New Orleans, from which point they were to be transported by the Louisville and Nashville to Birmingham, Alabama. On October 4, another group boarded the train; on October 10, another; on October 22, still another; and on November 3, the last of the encampment left Eagle Pass. The last party reached New Orleans on the following day and perhaps arrived at Birmingham on the 5th.[19]

Thus ended the colonization scheme of Ellis and the Mexican land company. It had cost the United States Government more than twenty thousand dollars. It had cost the Tlahualilo Company about seven thousand. But the Negroes themselves had borne the greatest losses. Seventy or more of their number had found graves on the hacienda near Mapimi, 10 had died at Torreón, 8 while *en route* from that station to Eagle Pass, and 60 in the encampment there, making a total of about 148. Besides these, there were 250 not accounted for and half as many more scattered and possibly separated for years from their friends and relatives. Only 334 left Eagle Pass by train for their homes in Alabama, while the Louisville and Nashville records show that only 326 were taken aboard at New Orleans. What fate overtook the small number who chose to remain with their crops has not been ascertained.[20]

J. FRED RIPPY

UNIVERSITY OF CHICAGO

FOOTNOTES:

[1] For a brief discussion of these disorders see the present writer's "Border Troubles Along the Rio Grande, 1848-1860," in *The Southwestern Historical Quarterly*, XXIII, October, 1919, pp. 91-111.

[2] *Sen. Jour.*, 38 Cong., 1 Sess., p. 66, *passim*.

[3] *Cong. Globe*, 38 Cong., 1 Sess., p. 673.

[4] *Sen. Report* No. 8, 38 Cong., 1 Sess., p. 2.

[5] This seems to have been only one of some three or four such undertakings attempted at the time. See *House Doc.* No. 169, 54 Cong., 1 Sess., pp. 44-45.

[6] Elsewhere written W. H. Ellis.

[7] Ellis's contract promised more than this in case of larger families.

[8] For the contract between Ellis and the company see *House Doc.* No. 169, 54 Cong., 1 Sess., pp. 46-48; for that between Ellis and the colonists see *ibid.*, pp. 4-5. There are only a few minor differences in

the two.

[9] *Ibid.*, p. 59.

[10] Dwyer's Report, and enclosures, *ibid.*, pp. 42 ff.

[11] *Ibid.*, pp. 23, 36, 42.

[12] Burke to Uhl, May 28, 1895, and enclosure, *ibid.*, pp. 2-3.

[13] Olney to Butler, June 17, 1895, *ibid.*, p. 5.

[14] It appears that only one band had tried to escape prior to July 18 or 19.

[15] Sparks to Uhl, June 24, 1895, and enclosure, *ibid.*, pp. 6-11.

[16] *Ibid.*, pp. 12, 16.

[17] *Ibid.*, pp. 17-20.

[18] Sparks to Uhl, June 4, 1895, and enclosure, pp. 13-14.

[19] *Ibid.*, p. 65.

[20] Sparks to Uhl, June 24, 1895, and enclosure, pp. 42, 65-66.

President Cleveland, in his message of December 2, 1895, urged an appropriation for the reimbursements of the railroads, and on January 27, 1896, he sent a special message to Congress with reference to the matter. Richardson, *Messages and Papers*, IX, 634, 664.

An appropriation for urgent deficiencies which was passed on February 26, 1896, contained the following interesting item: "For the payment of the cost of transportation furnished by certain railway companies in connection with the failure of the scheme for the colonization of negroes in Mexico, necessitating their return to their homes in Alabama, ... five thousand and eighty-seven dollars and nine cents." 29 *U. S. Statutes at Large*, p. 18.

DOCUMENTS

JAMES MADISON'S ATTITUDE TOWARD THE NEGRO

Like most of the Revolutionary leaders, James Madison, moved by the social and political upheaval of that time thought seriously of the liberation of the slaves, largely for economic reasons. He believed that the country should depend as little as possible on the labor of slaves, knowing that their labor was not sufficiently skillful to furnish the basis for diversified industry. He considered slavery "the great evil under which the nation labors."[1] On another occasion he referred to it as a "portentous evil,"[2] and on still another "an evil, moral, political, and economic, a sad blot on our free country."[3] When, therefore, petitions for the abolition of slavery were presented to the legislature of Virginia, he did not frown upon the proposal as a mischievous agitation as did so many others. Madison looked forward to the eventual extermination of slavery through gradual methods of preparation for emancipation. Feeling that the thorough incorporation of the blacks into the community of whites would be prejudicial to the interests of the country, he had no other thought than that of deportation as a correlative of emancipation. Along with a number of others he discussed the proposal to set apart certain western public lands for the transplantation of the blacks from the slave holding States to free soil, but as the white man by his pioneering efforts so rapidly pushed the frontier to the west as to convince the country of the need of that territory for expansion, Madison soon receded from this position and advocated along with most of the leading men of his time the colonization of the Negroes in Africa.

Madison did not feel that there was any sure ground upon which Congress might participate in the emancipation and the colonization of the Negroes. He suggested that the constitution be amended. He even doubted that the Ordinance of 1787, enacted without authority, had the effect of the emancipation of the slaves and was finally of the opinion that the right of Congress to prohibit slavery in any territory during its territorial period, "depends on the clause in the constitution specially providing for the management of these subordinate establishments."[4] He was rather of the opinion that the restriction was not within the true scope of the constitution. Like Jefferson, therefore, during the later years of his life, Madison saw many difficulties in the way of abolishing slavery. He gave a sympathetic ear to the experiences of the Moravians, Hermonites, and the Shakers, but although he had to concede that slavery impaired the influence of the political example of the United States and was a blot on our republican character, he never became what we could call an abolitionist for the reason that he found it difficult to remove the Negroes from the country when freed. That being the case, he noted with some interest the increase of the slave population, the increase in voluntary emancipation, and the progress of the Colonization Society, to the presidency of which he was elected.[4]

To Robert Pleasants

Philadelphia, October 30, 1791

Sir,—The delay in acknowledging your letter of the 6th June last proceeded from the cause you conjectured. I did not receive it till a few days ago, when it was put into my hands by Mr. James Pemberton, along with your subsequent letter of the 8th August.

The petition relating to the Militia bill contains nothing that makes it improper for me to present it. I shall, therefore, readily comply with your desire on that subject. I am not satisfied that I am equally at liberty with respect to the other petition. Animadversions such as it contains, and which the authorized object of the petitioners did not require, on the slavery existing in our country, are supposed by the holders of that species of property to lessen the value by weakening the tenure of it. Those from whom I derive my public station are known by me to be greatly interested in that species of property, and to view the matter in that light. It would seem that I might be chargeable at least with want of candour, if not of fidelity, were I to make use of a situation in which their confidence has placed me to become a volunteer in giving a public wound, as they would deem it, to an interest on which they set so great a value. I am the less inclined to disregard this scruple as I am not sensible that the event of the petition would in the least depend on the circumstance of its being laid before the House by this or that person.

Such an application as that to our own Assembly, on which you ask my opinion, is a subject, in various respects, of great delicacy and importance. The consequences of every sort ought to be well weighed by those who would hazard it. From the view under which they present themselves to me, I cannot but consider the application as likely to do harm rather than good. It may be worth your own consideration whether it might not produce successful attempts to withdraw the privilege now allowed to individuals, of giving freedom to slaves. It would at least be likely to clog it with a condition that the person freed should be removed from the country; there being arguments of great force for such a regulation, and some would concur in it, who, in general, disapprove of the institution of slavery.

I thank you, sir, for the friendly sentiments you have expressed towards me, and am, with respect, your obt, humble servt.[5]

To Robert Walsh[6]

Montpellier, Mar. 2d, 1819.

Dr Sir,—I received some days ago your letter of Feby 15, in which you intimate your intention to vindicate our Country against misrepresentations propagated abroad, and your desire of information on the subject of negro slavery, of moral character, of religion, and of education in Virginia, as affected by the Revolution, and our public Institutions.

The general condition of slaves must be influenced by various causes. Among these are: 1. The ordinary price of food, on which the quality and quantity allowed them will more or less depend. This cause has operated much more unfavorably against them in some quarters than in Virginia. 2. The kinds of labour to be performed, of which the sugar and rice plantations

95

afford elsewhere, and not here, unfavorable examples. 3. The national spirit of their masters, which has been graduated by philosophic writers among the slaveholding Colonies of Europe. 4. The circumstance of conformity or difference in the physical characters of the two classes; such a difference cannot but have a material influence, and is common to all the slaveholding countries within the American hemisphere. Even in those where there are other than black slaves, as Indians and mixed breeds, there is a difference of colour not without its influence. 5. The proportion which the slaves bear to the free part of the community, and especially the greater or smaller numbers in which they belong to individuals.

This last is, perhaps, the most powerful of all the causes deteriorating the condition of the slave, and furnishes the best scale for determining the degree of its hardship.

In reference to the actual condition of slaves in Virginia, it may be confidently stated as better, beyond comparison, than it was before the Revolution. The improvement strikes every one who witnessed their former condition, and attends to their present. They are better fed, better clad, better lodged, and better treated in every respect; insomuch, that what was formerly deemed a moderate treatment, would now be a rigid one, and what formerly a rigid one, would now be denounced by the public feelings. With respect to the great article of food particularly, it is a common remark among those who have visited Europe, that it includes a much greater proportion of the animal ingredient than is attainable by the free labourers even in that quarter of the Globe. As the two great causes of the melioration in the lot of the slaves since the establishment of our Independence, I should set down: 1. The sensibility to human rights, and sympathy with human sufferings, excited and cherished by the discussions preceding, and the spirit of the Institutions growing out of that event. 2. The decreasing proportion which the slaves bear to the individual holders of them; a consequence of the abolition of entails and the rule of primogeniture; and of the equalizing tendency of parental affection unfettered from all prejudices, as well as from the restrictions of law.

With respect to the moral features of Virginia, it must be observed, that pictures which have been given of them are, to say the least, outrageous caricatures, even when taken from the state of society previous to the Revolution; and that so far as there was any ground or colour for them then, the same cannot be found for them now.

Omitting more minute or less obvious causes, tainting the habits and manners of the people under the Colonial Government, the following offer themselves: 1. The negro slavery chargeable in so great a degree on the very quarter which has furnished most of the libellers. It is well known that during the Colonial dependence of Virginia, repeated attempts were made to stop the importation of slaves, each of which attempts was successively defeated by the foreign negative on the laws, and that one of the first offsprings of independent republican legislation was an act of perpetual prohibition.

. . . .

With the exception of slavery, these demoralizing causes have ceased or are wearing out; and even that, as already noticed, has lost no small share of its former character. On the whole, the moral aspect of the State may, at present, be fairly said to bear no unfavorable comparison with the average standard of the other States. It certainly gives the lie to the foreign calumniators whom you propose to arraign.[7]

To Robert J. Evans (Author of the Pieces Published Under the Name of Benjamin Rush).

Montpellier, June 15, 1819.

Sir,—I have received your letter of the 3d instant, requesting such hints as may have occurred to me on the subject of an eventual extinguishment of slavery in the United States.

Not doubting the purity of your views, and relying on the discretion by which they will be regulated, I cannot refuse such a compliance as will, at least, manifest my respect for the object of your undertaking.

A general emancipation of slaves ought to be—1. Gradual. 2. Equitable, and satisfactory to the individual immediately concerned. 3. Consistent with the existing and durable prejudices of the nation.

That it ought, like remedies for other deep-rooted and widespread evils, to be gradual, is so obvious, that there seems to be no difference of opinion on that point.

To be equitable and satisfactory, the consent of both the master and the slave should be obtained. That of the master will require a provision in the plan for compensating a loss of what he held as property, guaranteed by the laws, and recognised by the Constitution. That of the slave, requires that his condition in a state of freedom be preferable, in his own estimation, to his actual one in a state of bondage.

To be consistent with existing and probably unalterable prejudices in the United States, the freed blacks ought to be permanently removed beyond the region occupied by, or allotted to, a white population. The objections to a thorough incorporation of the two people, are, with most of the whites,

97

insuperable; and are admitted by all of them to be very powerful. If the blacks, strongly marked as they are by physical and lasting peculiarities, be retained amid the whites, under the degrading privation of equal rights, political or social, they must be always dissatisfied with their condition, as a change only from one to another species of oppression; always secretly confederating against the ruling and privileged class; and always uncontrolled by some of the most cogent motives to moral and respectable conduct. The character of the free blacks even where their legal condition is least affected by their color, seems to put these truths beyond question. It is material, also, that the removal of the blacks to be a distance precluding the jealousies and hostilities to be apprehended from a neighboring people, stimulated by the contempt known to be entertained for their peculiar features; to say nothing of their vindictive recollections, or the predatory propensities which their state of society might foster. Nor is it fair, in estimating the danger of collisions with the whites, to charge it wholly on the side of the black. There would be reciprocal antipathies doubling the danger.

The colonizing plan on foot has, as far as it extends, a due regard to these requisites; with the additional object of bestowing new blessings, civil and religious, on the quarter of the Globe most in need of them. The Society proposes to transport to the African coast all free and freed blacks who may be willing to remove thither; to provide by fair means, and, it is understood, with a prospect of success, a suitable territory for their reception; and to initiate them into such an establishment as may gradually and indefinitely expand itself.

The experiment, under this view of it, merits encouragement from all who regard slavery as an evil, who wish to see it diminished and abolished by peaceable and just means, and who have themselves no better mode to propose. Those who have most doubted the success of the experiment must, at least, have wished to find themselves in an error.

But the views of the Society are limited to the case of blacks, already free, or who may be *gratuitously* emancipated. To provide a commensurate remedy for the evil, the plan must be extended to the great mass of blacks, and must embrace a fund sufficient to induce the master, as well as the slave, to concur in it. Without the concurrence of the master, the benefit will be very limited as it relates to the negroes, and essentially defective as it relates to the United States; and the concurrence of masters must, for the most part, be obtained by purchase.

Can it be hoped that voluntary contributions, however adequate to an auspicious commencement, will supply the sums necessary to such an enlargement of the remedy? May not another question be asked? Would it be reasonable to throw so great a burden on the individuals distinguished by their philanthropy and patriotism?

The object to be obtained, as an object of humanity, appeals alike to all; as a national object, it claims the interposition of the nation. It is the nation which is to reap the benefit. The nation, therefore, ought to bear the burden.

Must, then, the enormous sums required to pay for, to transport, and to establish in a foreign land, all the slaves in the United States, as their masters may be willing to part with them, be taxed on the good people of the United States, or be obtained by loans, swelling the public debt to a size pregnant with evils next in degree to those of slavery itself?

Happily, it is not necessary to answer this question by remarking, that if slavery, as a national evil, is to be abolished, and it be just that it be done at the national expense, the amount of the expense is not a paramount consideration. It is the peculiar fortune, or, rather, a providential blessing of the United States, to possess a resource commensurate to this great object, without taxes on the people, or even an increase of the public debt.

I allude to the vacant territory, the extent of which is so vast, and the vendible value of which is so well ascertained.

Supposing the number of slaves to be 1,500,000, and their price to average 400 dollars, the cost of the whole would be 600 millions of dollars. These estimates are probably beyond the fact; and from the number of slaves should be deducted; 1. Those whom their masters would not part with. 2. Those who may be gratuitously set free by their masters. 3. Those acquiring freedom under emancipating regulations of the States. 4. Those preferring slavery where they are to freedom in an African settlement. On the other hand, it is to be noted that the expense of removal and settlement is not included in the estimated sum; and that an increase of the slaves will be going on during the period required for the execution of the plan.

On the whole, the aggregate sum needed may be stated at about six hundred millions of dollars.

This will require 200 millions of acres, at three dollars per acre; or 300 millions at two dollars per acre; a quantity which, though great in itself, is perhaps not a third part of the disposable territory belonging to the United States. And to what object so good, so great, and so glorious, could that peculiar fund of wealth be appropriated? Whilst the sale of territory would, on one hand, be planting one desert with a free and civilized people, it would, on the other, be giving freedom to another people, and filling with them another desert. And if in any instance wrong has been done by our forefathers to people of one colour, by dispossessing them of their soil, what better atonement is now in our power than that of making what is rightfully acquired a source of justice and of blessings to a people of another colour?

As the revolution to be produced in the condition of the negroes must be gradual, it will suffice if the sale of territory keep pace with its progress. For a time, at least, the proceeds would be in advance. In this case, it might be best, after deducting the expense incident to the surveys and sales, to place the surplus in a situation where its increase might correspond with the natural increase of the unpurchased slaves. Should the proceeds at any time fall short of the calls for their application, anticipations might be made by temporary loans, to be discharged as the land should find a market.

But it is probable that for a considerable period the sales would exceed the calls. Masters would not be willing to strip their plantations and farms of their labourers so rapidly. The slaves themselves connected, as they generally are, by tender ties with others under other masters, would be kept from the list of emigrants by the want of the multiplied consents to be obtained. It is probable, indeed, that for a long time a certain portion of the proceeds might safely continue applicable to the discharge of the debts or to other purposes of the nation, or it might be most convenient, in the outset, to appropriate a certain proportion only of the income from sales to the object in view, leaving the residue otherwise applicable.

Should any plan similar to that I have sketched be deemed eligible in itself, no particular difficulty is foreseen from that portion of the nation, which, with a common interest in the vacant territory, has no interest in slave property. They are too just to wish that a partial sacrifice should be made for the general good, and too well aware that whatever may be the intrinsic character of that description of property, it is one known to the Constitution, and, as such could not be constitutionally taken away without just compensation. That part of the nation has, indeed, shewn a meritorious alacrity in promoting, by pecuniary contributions, the limited scheme for colonizing the blacks, and freeing the nation from the unfortunate stain on it, which justifies the belief that any enlargement of the scheme, if founded on just principles, would find among them its earliest and warmest patrons. It ought to have great weight that the vacant lands in question have, for the most part, been derived from grants of the States holding the slaves to be redeemed and removed by the sale of them.

It is evident, however, that in effectuating a general

emancipation of slaves in the mode which has been hinted, difficulties of other sorts would be encountered. The provision for ascertaining the joint consent of the masters and slaves; for guarding against unreasonable valuations of the latter; and for the discrimination of those not proper to be conveyed to a foreign residence, or who ought to remain a charge on masters in whose service they had been disabled or worn out, and for the annual transportation of such numbers, would require the mature deliberations of the national councils. The measure implies also, the practicability of procuring in Africa an enlargement of the district or districts for receiving the exiles sufficient for so great an augmentation of their numbers.

Perhaps the Legislative provision best adapted to the case would be an incorporation of the Colonizing Society, or the establishment of a similar one, with proper powers, under the appointment and superintendence of the National Executive.

In estimating the difficulties, however, incident to any plan of general emancipation, they ought to be brought into comparison with those inseparable from other plans, and be yielded to or not accordingly to the result of the comparison.

One difficulty presents itself which will probably attend every plan which is to go into effect under the Legislative provisions of the National Government. But whatever may be the effect of existing powers of Congress, the Constitution has pointed out the way in which it can be supplied. And it can hardly be doubted that the requisite powers might readily be procured for attaining the great object in question, in any mode whatever approved by the nation.

If these thoughts can be of any aid in your search of a remedy for the great evil under which the nation labors, you are very welcome to them.[8]

To Tench Coxe.

Montpelier, March 20, 1820.

I am glad to find you still sparing moments for subjects interesting to the public welfare. The remarks on the thorny one to which you refer in the "National Recorder," seem to present the best arrangement for the unfortunate part of our population whose case has enlisted the anxiety of so many benevolent minds, next to that which provides a foreign outlet and location for them. I have long thought that our vacant territory was the resource which, in some mode or other, was most applicable and adequate as a gradual cure for the portentous evil; without, however, being unaware that even that would encounter serious difficulties of different sorts.[9]

Montpelier, Nov. 25, 1820.

. . . .

The subject which ruffles the surface of public affairs most, at present, is furnished by the transmission of the "Territory" of Missouri from a state of nonage to a maturity for self-Government, and for a membership in the Union. Among the questions involved in it, the one most immediately interesting to humanity is the question whether a toleration or prohibition of slavery Westward of the Mississippi would most extend its evils. The human part of the argument against the prohibition turns on the position, that whilst the importation of slaves from abroad is precluded, a diffusion of those in the Country tends at once to meliorate their actual condition, and to facilitate their eventual emancipation. Unfortunately, the subject, which was settled at the last session of Congress by a mutual concession of the parties, is reproduced on the arena by a clause in the Constitution of Missouri, distinguishing between free persons of colour and white persons, and providing that the Legislature of the new State shall exclude from it the former. What will be the issue of the revived discussion is yet to be seen. The case opens the wider field, as the Constitution and laws of the different States are much at variance in the civic character giving to free persons of colour; those of most of the States, not excepting such as have abolished slavery, imposing various disqualifications, which degrade them from the rank and rights of white persons. All these perplexities develope more and more the dreadful fruitfulness of the original sin of the African trade.[10]

To F. Corbin

November 26, 1820.

. . . .

I do not mean to discuss the question how far *slavery* and *farming* are incompatible. Our opinions agree as to the evil, moral, political, and economical, of the former. I still think, notwithstanding, that under all the disadvantages of slave cultivation, much improvement in it is practicable. Proofs are annually taking place within my own sphere of observation; particularly where slaves are held in small numbers, by good masters and managers. As to the very wealthy proprietors, much less is to be said. But after all, (protesting against any inference of a disposition to undertake the evil of slavery,) is it certain that in giving to your wealth a new investment, you would be altogether freed from the cares and vexations incident to the shape it now has? If converted into paper, you already feel some of the contingencies belonging to it; if into commercial stock, look at the wrecks every where giving warning of the danger. If into large landed property, where there are no slaves, will you cultivate it yourself? Then beware of the difficulty of procuring faithful or complying labourers. Will you dispose of it in leases? Ask those who have made the experiment what sort of tenants are to be found where an ownership of the soil is so attainable. It has been said that America is a country for the poor, not for the rich. There would be more correctness in saying it is the country for both, where the latter have a relish for free government; but, proportionally, more for the former than for the latter.[11]

To General la Fayette.

1821.

.   .   .   .

The negro slavery is, as you justly complain, a sad blot on our free country, though a very ungracious subject of reproaches from the quarter which has been most lavish of them. No satisfactory plan has yet been devised for taking out the stain. If an asylum could be found in Africa, that would be the appropriate destination for the unhappy race among us. Some are sanguine that the efforts of an existing Colonization Society will accomplish such a provision; but a very partial success seems the most that can be expected. Some other region must, therefore, be found for them as they become free and willing to emigrate. The repugnance of the whites to their continuance among them is founded on prejudices, themselves founded on physical distinctions, which are not likely soon, if ever, to be eradicated. Even in States, Massachusetts for example, which displayed most sympathy with the people of colour on the Missouri question, prohibitions are taking place against their becoming residents. They are every where regarded as a nuisance, and must really be such as long as they are under the degradation which public sentiment inflicts on them. They are at the same time rapidly increasing from manumissions and from offspring, and of course lessening the general disproportion between the slaves and the whites. This tendency is favorable to the cause of a universal emancipation."[12]

To Dr. Morse

March 28, 1823

Queries.

1. Do the planters generally live on their own estates?

2. Does a planter with ten or fifteen slaves employ an overlooker, or does he overlook his slaves himself?

103

3. Obtain estimates of the culture of Sugar and Cotton, to show what difference it makes where the planter resides on his estate, or where he employs attorneys, overlookers, &c.

4. Is it a common or general practice to mortgage slave estates?

5. Are sales of slave estates very frequent under execution for debt and what proportion of the whole may be thus sold annually?

6. Does the Planter possess the power of selling the different branches of a family separate?

7. When the prices of produce, Cotton Sugar, &c., are high, do the Planters purchase, instead of raising, their corn and other provisions?

8. When the prices of produce are low, do they then raise their own corn and other provisions?

9. Do the negroes fare better when the Corn, &c., is raised upon their master's estate or when he buys it?

10. Do the tobacco planters in America ever buy their own Corn or other food, or do they always raise it?

11. If they always, or mostly, raise it, can any other reason be given for the differences of the system pursued by them and that pursued by the Sugar and Cotton planters than that cultivation of tobacco is less profitable than that of Cotton or Sugar?

12. Do any of the Planters manufacture the packages for their product, or the clothing for their negroes and if they do, are their negroes better clothed than when clothing is purchased?

13. Where, and by whom, is the Cotton bagging of the Brazils made? is it principally made by free men or slaves?

14. Is it the general system to employ the negroes in task work, or by the day?

15. How many hours are they generally at work in the former case? how many in the latter? Which system is generally preferred by the master? which by the slaves?

16. Is it common to allow them a certain portion of time instead of their allowance of provisions? In this case, how much is allowed? Where the slaves have the option, which do they generally choose? On which system do the slaves look the best, and acquire the most comforts?

17. Are there many small plantations where the owners

possess only a few slaves? What proportion of the whole may be supposed to be held in this way?

18. In such cases, are the slaves treated or almost considered a part of the family?

19. Do the slaves fare best when their situations and that of the master are brought nearest together?

20. In what state are the slaves as to religion or religious instruction?

21. Is it common for the slaves to be regularly married?

22. If a man forms an attachment to a woman on a different or distant plantation, is it the general practice for some accommodation to take place between the owners of the man and woman, so that they may live together?

23. In the United States of America, the slaves are found to increase at about the rate of 3 P cent. P annum. Does the same take place in other places? Give a census, if such is taken. Show what cause contributes to this increase, or what prevents it where it does not take place.

24. Obtain a variety of estimates from the Planters of the cost of bringing up a child, and at what age it becomes a clear gain to its owner.

25. Obtain information respecting the comparative cheapness of cultivation by slaves or by free men.

26. Is it common for the free blacks to labour in the field?

27. Where the labourers consist of free blacks and of white men, what are the relative prices of their labour when employed about the same work?

28. What is the proportion of free blacks and slaves?

29. Is it considered that the increase in the proportion of free blacks to slaves increases or diminishes the danger of insurrection?

30. Are the free blacks employed in the defence of the Country, and do they and the Creoles preclude the necessity of European troops?

31. Do the free blacks appear to consider themselves as more closely connected with the slaves or with the white population? and in cases of insurrection, with which have they generally taken part?

32. What is their general character with respect to industry and

105

order, as compared with that of the slaves?

33. Are there any instances of emancipation in particular estates, and what is the result?

34. Is there any general plan of emancipation in progress, and what?

35. What was the mode and progress of emancipation in those States in America where slavery has ceased to exist?

Hon. James Madison, Esq.

New Haven, Mar. 14, 1823.

Sir.—The foregoing was transmitted to me from a respectable correspondent in Liverpool, deeply engaged in the abolition of the slave trade, and the amelioration of the condition of slaves. If, sir, your leisure will allow you, and it is agreeable to you to furnish brief answers to these questions, you will, I conceive, essentially serve the cause of humanity, and gratify and oblige the Society above named, and, Sir, with high consideration and esteem, your most obt servt,

JED'H MORSE.

Answers

1. Yes.

2. Employs an overseer for that number of slaves, with few exceptions.

3. ——

4. Not uncommonly the land; sometimes the slaves; very rarely both together.

5. The common law, as in England, governs the relation between land and debts; slaves are often sold under execution for debt; the proportion to the whole cannot be great within a year, and varies, of course, with the amount of debt and the urgency of creditors.

6. Yes.

7-10. Instances are rare where the tobacco planters do not raise their own provisions.

11. The proper comparison, not between the culture of tobacco and that of sugar and cotton, but between each of these cultures and that of provisions. The tobacco planter finds it cheaper to make them a part of his crop than to buy them. The

cotton and sugar planters to buy them, where this is the case, than to raise them. The term, cheaper, embraces the comparative facility and certainty of procuring the supplies.

12. Generally best clothed when from the household manufactures, which are increasing.

14, 15. Slaves seldom employed in regular task work. They prefer it only when rewarded with the surplus time gained by their industry.

16. Not the practice to substitute an allowance of time for the allowance of provisions.

17. Very many, and increasing with the progressive subdivisions of property; the proportion cannot be stated.

18, 19. The fewer the slaves, and the fewer the holders of slaves, the greater the indulgence and familiarity. In districts composing (comprising?) large masses of slaves there is no difference in their condition, whether held in small or large numbers, beyond the difference in the dispositions of the owners, and the greater strictness of attention where the number is greater.

20. There is no general system of religious instruction. There are few spots where religious worship is not within reach, and to which they do not resort. Many are regular members of Congregations, chiefly Baptist; and some Preachers also, though rarely able to read.

21. Not common; but the instances are increasing.

22. The accommodation not unfrequent where the plantations are very distant. The slaves prefer wives on a different plantation, as affording occasions and pretexts for going abroad, and exempting them on holidays from a share of the little calls to which those at home are liable.

23. The remarkable increase of slaves, as shown by the census, results from the comparative defect of moral and prudential restraint on the sexual connexion; and from the absence, at the same time, of that counteracting licentiousness of intercourse, of which the worst examples are to be traced where the African trade, as in the West Indies, kept the number of females less than of the males.

24. The annual expense of food and raiment in rearing a child may be stated at about 8, 9, or 10 dollars; and the age at which it begins to be gainful to its owner about 9 or 10 years.

25. The practice here does not furnish data for a comparison of cheapness between these two modes of cultivation.

26. They are sometimes hired for field labour in time of harvest, and on other particular occasions.

27. The examples are too few to have established any such relative prices.

28. See the census.

29. Rather increases.

30. —————

31. More closely with the slaves, and more likely to side with them in a case of insurrection.

32. Generally idle and depraved; appearing to retain the bad qualities of the slaves, with whom they continue to associate, without acquiring any of the good ones of the whites, from whom (they) continued separated by prejudices against their colour, and other peculiarities.

33. There are occasional instances in the present legal condition of leaving the State.

34. None.

35. —————[13]

TO MISS FRANCES WRIGHT

MONTPELLIER, Sept. 1, 1825.

Dear Madam,—Your letter to Mrs. Madison, containing observations addressed to my attention also, came duly to hand, as you will learn from her, with a printed copy of your plan for the gradual abolition of slavery in the United States.

The magnitude of this evil among us is so deeply felt, and so universally acknowledged, that no merit could be greater than that of devising a satisfactory remedy for it. Unfortunately the task, not easy under other circumstances, is vastly augmented by the physical peculiarities[14] of those held in bondage, which preclude their incorporation with the white population; and by the blank in the general field of labour to be occasioned by their exile; a blank into which there would not be an influx of white labourers, successively taking the place of the exiles, and which, without such an influx, would have an effect distressing in prospect to the proprietors of the soil.

The remedy for the evil which you have planned is certainly recommended to favorable attention by the two characteristics: 1. That it requires the voluntary concurrence of the holders of the slaves, with or without pecuniary

108

compensation. 2. That it contemplates the removal of those emancipated, either to a foreign or distant region. And it will still further obviate objections, if the experimental establishments should avoid the neighborhood of settlements where there are slaves.

Supposing these conditions to be duly provided for, particularly the removal of the emancipated blacks, the remaining questions relate to the attitude and adequacy of the process by which the slaves are at the same time to earn the funds, entire or supplemental, required for their emancipation and removal; and to be sufficiently educated for a life of freedom and of social order.

With respect to a proper course of education, no serious difficulties present themselves. And as they are to continue in a state of bondage during the preparatory period, and to be within the jurisdiction of States recognizing ample authority over them, a competent discipline cannot be impracticable. The degree in which this discipline will enforce the needed labour, and in which a voluntary industry will supply the defect of compulsory labour, are vital points, on which it may not be safe to be very positive without some light from actual experiment.

Considering the probable composition of the labourers, and the known fact that, where the labour is compulsory the greater the number of labourers brought together (unless, indeed, where cooperation of many hands is rendered essential by a particular kind of work, or of machinery) the less are the proportional profits, it may be doubted whether the surplus from that source merely, beyond the support of the establishment would sufficiently accumulate in five, or even more years, for the objects in view. And candor obliges me to say that I am not satisfied either that the prospect of emancipation at a future day will sufficiently overcome the natural and habitual repugnance to labour, or that there is such an advantage of united over individual labour as is taken for granted.

In cases where portions of time have been allowed to slaves, as among the Spaniards, with a view to their working out their freedom, it is believed that but few have availed themselves of the opportunity by a voluntary industry; and such a result could be less relied on in a case where each individual would feel that the fruit of his exertions would be shared by others, whether equally or unequally making them, and that the exertions of others would equally avail him, notwithstanding a deficiency in his own. Skilful arrangements might palliate this tendency, but it would be difficult to counteract it effectually. [15]

The examples of the Moravians, the Harmonites, and the

Shakers, in which the united labours of many for a common object have been successful have, no doubt, an imposing character. But it must be recollected that in all these establishments there is a religious impulse in the members of a religious authority in the head, for which there will be no substitutes of equivalent efficacy in the emancipating establishment. The code of rules by which Mr. Rapp manages his conscientious and devoted flock, and enriches a common treasury, must be little applicable to the dissimilar assemblage in question. His experience may afford valuable aid in its general organization, and in the distribution and details of the work to be performed. But an efficient administration must, as is judiciously proposed, be in hands practically acquainted with the propensities and habits of the members of the new community.

With reference to this dissimilarity, and to the doubt as to the advantages of associated labour, it may deserve consideration whether the experiment would not be better commenced on a scale smaller than that assumed in the prospectus. A less expensive outfit would suffice; labourers in the proper proportions of sex and age would be more attainable; the necessary discipline and the direction of their labours could be more simple and manageable; and but little time would be lost; or, perhaps, time gained; as success, for which the chance would, according to my calculation, be increased, would give an encouraging aspect, to the plan, and probably suggest improvements better qualifying it for the larger scale proposed.

Such, Madam, are the general ideas suggested by your interesting communication. If they do not coincide with yours, and imply less of confidence than may be due to the plan you have formed, I hope you will not question either my admiration of the generous philanthropy which dictated it, or my sense of the special regard it evinces for the honor and welfare of our expanding, and, I trust, rising Republic.

As it is not certain what construction would be put on the view I have taken of the subject, I leave it with your discretion to withhold it altogether, or to disclose it within the limits you allude to; intimating only that it will be most agreeable to me, on all occasions, not to be brought before the public where there is no obvious call for it.

Writing to General Lafayette in 1826, Madison commented thus on the proposal of Miss Frances Wright for the uplift of Negroes.

You possess, notwithstanding your distance, better information concerning Miss Wright, and her experiment, than we do here.

We learn only that she has chosen for it a remote spot in the western part of Tennessee, and has commenced her enterprise; but with what prospects we know not. Her plan contemplated a provision for the expatriation of her Elèves, but without specifying it; from which I infer the difficulty felt in devising a satisfactory one. Could this part of the plan be ensured, the other essential part would come about of itself. Manumissions now more than keep pace with the outlets provided, and the increase of them is checked only by their remaining in the Country. This obstacle removed, and all others would yield to the emancipating disposition. To say nothing of partial modes, what would be more simple, with the requisite grant of power to Congress, than to purchase all female infants at their birth, leaving them in the service of the holder to a reasonable age, on condition of their receiving an elementary education? The annual number of female births may be stated at twenty thousand, and the cost at less than one hundred dollars each, at the most; a sum which would not be felt by the nation, and be even within the compass of State resources. But no such effort would be listened to, whilst the impression remains, and it seems to be indelible, that the two races cannot co-exist, both being free and equal. The great *sine qua non*, therefore, is some external asylum for the coloured race. In the mean time, the taunts to which this misfortune exposes us in Europe are the more to be deplored, because it impairs the influence of our political example; though they come with an ill grace from the quarter most lavish of them, the quarter which obtruded the evil, and which has but lately become a penitent, under suspicious appearances.[16]

To Joseph C. Cabell

Montpellier, January 5, 1829.

Dear Sir,—I have received yours of December 28, in which you wish me to say something of the agitated subject of the basis of representation in the contemplated convention for revising the State Constitution. In a case depending so much on local views and feelings, and perhaps on the opinions of leading individuals, and in which a mixture of compromises with abstract principles may be resorted to, your judgment, formed on the theatre affording the best means of information, must be more capable of aiding mine than mine yours.

What occurs to me is, that the great principle "that man cannot be justly bound by laws, in making which they have no share," consecrated as it is by our Revolution and the Bill of Rights, and sanctioned by examples around us, is so engraven on the public mind here, that it ought to have a preponderating influence in all questions involved in the mode of forming a convention, and in discharging the trust committed to it when

111

formed. It is said that west of the Blue Ridge the votes of non-freeholders are often connived at, the candidates finding it unpopular to object to them.

With respect to the slaves, they cannot be admitted *as persons* into the representation, and probably will not be allowed any claim as *a privileged* property. As the difficulty and disquietude on that subject arise mainly from the great inequality of slaves in the geographical division of the country, it is fortunate that the cause will abate as they become more diffused, which is already taking place; transfers of them from the quarters where they abound, to those where labourers are more wanted being a matter of course.

Is there, then, to be no constitutional provision for the rights of property, when added to the personal rights of the holders, against the will of a majority having little or no direct interest in the rights of property? If any such provision be attainable beyond the moral influence which property adds to political rights, it will be most secure and permanent if made by a convention chosen by a general suffrage, and more likely to be so made now than at a future stage of population. If made by a freehold convention in favour of freeholders, it would be less likely to be acquiesced in permanently.[17]

Feb. 1, 1830.

.　.　.　.　.　.　.　.　.

Your anticipation with regard to the slavery among us were the natural offspring of your just principles and laudable sympathies; but I am sorry to say that the occasion which led to them proved to be little fitted for the slightest interposition on that subject. A sensibility, morbid in the highest degree, was never more awakened among those who have the largest stake in that species of interest, and the most violent against any governmental movement in relation to it. The excitability at the moment, happened, also, to be not a little augmented by party questions between the South and the North, and the efforts used to make the circumstance common to the former a sympathetic bond of co-operation. I scarcely express myself too strongly in saying that any allusion in the Convention to the subject you have so much at heart would have been a spark to a mass of gunpowder. It is certain, nevertheless, that time, the great "Innovator," is not idle in its salutary preparations. The Colonization Society are becoming more and more one of its agents. Outlets for the freed blacks are alone wanted for a rapid erasure of the blot from our Republican character.[18]

To —— ——

June 28, 1831.

But the title in the people of the United States rests on a foundation too just and solid to be shaken by any technical or metaphysical arguments whatever. The known and acknowledged intentions of the parties at the time, with a prescriptive sanction of so many years consecrated by the intrinsic principles of equity, would overrule even the most explicit declarations and terms, as has been done without the aid of that principle in the slaves, who remain such in spite of the declarations that all men are born equally free.[19]

To Matthew Carey

Montpelier, July 7, 1831.

.　.　.　.　.　.　.　.　.

If the States cannot live together in harmony under the auspices of such a Government as exists, and in the midst of blessings such as have been the fruits of it, what is the prospect threatened by the abolition of a common Government, with all the rivalships, collisions and animosities inseparable from such an event? The entanglements and conflicts of commercial regulations, especially as affecting the inland and other non-importing States, and a protection of fugitive slaves substituted for the obligatory surrender of them, would, of themselves, quickly kindle the passions which are the forerunners of war.[20]

To R. R. Gurley, a promoter of colonization, Madison wrote the following December 28, 1831:

Dear Sir,—I received in due time your letter of the 21 ultimo, and with due sensibility to the subject of it. Such, however, has been the effect of a painful rheumatism on my general condition, as well as in disqualifying my fingers for the use of the pen, that I could not do justice "to the principles and measures of the Colonization Society, in all the great and various relations they sustain in our country and to Africa." If my views of them could have the value which your partiality supposes, I may observe, in brief, that the Society had always my good wishes, though with hopes of its success less sanguine than were entertained by others found to have been the better judges; and that I feel the greatest pleasure at the progress already made by the Society, and the encouragement to encounter the remaining difficulties afforded by the earlier and greater ones already overcome. Many circumstances at the present moment seem to concur in brightening the prospects of the Society, and cherishing the hope that the time will come when the *dreadful calamity which has so long afflicted our country, and filled so many with despair, will be gradually removed, and by means consistent with justice, peace, and the general satisfaction; thus giving to our country the full enjoyment of the blessings of liberty, and to the world the full benefit of its great example.* I have never considered the main difficulty of the great work as lying in the deficiency of emancipations, but in an inadequacy of asylums for such a growing mass of population, and in the great expense of removing it to its new home. The spirit of private maunmission, as the laws may permit and the exiles may consent, is increasing, and will increase, and there are sufficient indications that the public authorities in slaveholding States are looking forward to interpretations, in different forms, that must have a powerful effect.

With respect to the new abode for the emigrants, all agree that the choice made by the Society is rendered peculiarly appropriate by considerations which need not be repeated, and if other situations should not be found as eligible receptacles for a portion of them, the prospect in Africa seems to be expanding in a highly encouraging degree.

In contemplating the pecuniary resources needed for the removal of such a number to so great a distance, my thought and hopes have long been turned to the rich fund presented in the western lands of the nation, which will soon entirely cease to be under a pledge for another object. The great one in question is truly of a national character, and it is known that distinguished patriots not dwelling in slaveholding States have viewed the object in that light, and would be willing to let the national domain be a resource in effectuating it.

Should it be remarked that the States, although all may be interested in relieving our country from the coloured population, are not equally so, it is but fair to recollect that the sections most to be benefited are those whose cessions created the fund to be disposed of.

I am aware of the constitutional obstacle which has presented itself; but if the general will be reconciled to an application of the territorial fund to the removal of the coloured population, a grant to Congress of the necessary authority could be carried with little delay through the forms of the Constitution.

Sincerely wishing increasing success to the labours of the Society, I pray you to be assured of my esteem, and to accept my friendly salutations.[21]

To Thomas R. Drew

Montpellier, Feby 23, 1833

Dear Sir,—I received, in due time, your letter of the 15th ult. with copies of the two pamphlets; one on the "Restrictive System," the other on the "Slave Question."

The former I have not yet been able to look into, and in reading the latter with the proper attention I have been much retarded by many interruptions, as well as by the feebleness incident to my great age, increased as it is by the effects of an acute fever, preceded and followed by a chronic complaint under which I am still labouring. This explanation of the delay in acknowledging your favor will be an apology, also, for the brevity and generality of the answer. For the freedom of it, none, I am sure, will be required. In the views of the subject taken in the pamphlet, I have found much valuable and interesting information, with ample proof of the numerous obstacles to a removal of slavery from our country, and everything that could be offered in mitigation of its continuance; but I am obliged to say, that in not a few of the data from which you reason, and in the conclusion to which you are led, I cannot concur.

I am aware of the impracticability of an immediate or early execution of any plan that combines deportation with emancipation, and of the inadmissibility of emancipation without deportation. But I have yielded to the expediency of

115

attempting a gradual remedy, by providing for the double operation.

If emancipation was the sole object, the extinguishment of slavery would be easy, cheap, and complete. The purchase by the public of all female children, at their birth, leaving them in bondage till it would defray the charge of rearing them, would, within a limited period, be a radical resort.

With the condition of deportation it has appeared to me, that the great difficulty does not lie either in the expense of emancipation, or in the expense or the means of deportation, but in the attainment—1, of the requisite asylums; 2, the consent of the individuals to be removed; 3, the labour for the vacuum to be created.

With regard to the expense—1, much will be saved by voluntary emancipations, increasing under the influence of example, and the prospect of bettering the lot of the slaves; 2, much may be expected in gifts and legacies from the opulent, the philanthropic, and the conscientious; 3, more still from legislative grants by the States, of which encouraging examples and indications have already appeared; 4, nor is there any room for despair of aid from the indirect or direct proceeds of the public lands held in trust by Congress. With a sufficiency of pecuniary means, the facility of providing a naval transportation of the exiles is shewn by the present amount of our tonnage and the promptitude with which it can be enlarged; by the number of emigrants brought from Europe to N. America within the last year, and by the greater number of slaves which have been, within single years, brought from the coast of Africa across the Atlantic.

In the attainment of adequate asylums, the difficulty, though it may be considerable, is far from being discouraging. Africa is justly the favorite choice of the patrons of colonization; and the prospect there is flattering—1, in the territory already acquired; 2, in the extent of coast yet to be explored, and which may be equally convenient; 3, the adjacent interior into which the littoral settlements can be expanded under the auspices of physical affinities between the new comers and the natives, and of the moral superiorities of the former; 4, the great inland regions now ascertained to be accessible by navigable waters, and opening new fields for colonizing enterprises.

But Africa, though the primary, is not the sole asylum within contemplation; an auxiliary one presents itself in the islands adjoining this continent, where the coloured population is already dominant, and where the wheel of revolution may from time to time produce the like result.

Nor ought another contingent receptable for emancipated slaves to be altogether overlooked. It exists within the territory under the control of the United States, and is not too distant to be out of reach, whilst sufficiently distant to avoid, for an indefinite period, the collisions to be apprehended from the vicinity of people distinguished from each other by physical as well as other characteristics.

The consent of the individuals is another pre-requisite in the plan of removal. At present there is a known repugnance in those already in a state of freedom to leave their native homes, and among the slaves there is an almost universal preference of their present condition to freedom in a distant and unknown land. But in both classes, particularly that of the slaves, the prejudices arise from a distrust of the favorable accounts coming to them through white channels. By degrees truth will find its way to them from sources in which they will confide, and their aversion to removal may be overcome as fast as the means of effectuating it shall accrue.

The difficulty of replacing the labour withdrawn by a removal of the slaves, seems to be urged as of itself an insuperable objection to the attempt. The answer to it is—1, that notwithstanding the emigrations of the whites, there will be an annual and by degrees an increasing surplus of the remaining mass; 2, that there will be an attraction of whites from without, increasing with the demand, and, as the population elsewhere will be yielding a surplus to be attracted; 3, that as the culture of tobacco declines with the contraction of the space within which it is profitable and still more from the successful competition in the West, and as the farming system takes the place of planting, a portion of labour can be spared without impairing the requisite stock; 4, that although the process must be slow, be attended with much inconvenience, and be not even certain in its result, is it not preferable to a torpid acquiescence in a perpetuation of slavery, or an extinguishment of it by convulsions more disastrous in their character and consequences than slavery itself?

In my estimate of the experiment instituted by the Colonization Society, I may indulge too much my wishes and hopes, to be safe from errors. But a partial success will have its virtue, and an entire failure will leave behind a consciousness of the laudable intentions with which relief from the greatest of our calamities was attempted in the only mode presenting a chance of effecting it.

I hope I shall be pardoned for remarking, that in accounting for the depressed condition of Virginia, you seem to allow too little to the existence of slavery, ascribe too much to the tariff laws, and not to have sufficiently taken into view the effect of the rapid settlement of the Western and Southwestern country.

117

Previous to the Revolution, when, of these causes, slavery alone was in operation, the face of Virginia was, in every feature of improvement and prosperity, a contrast to the Colonies where slavery did not exist, or in a degree only, not worthy of notice. Again, during the period of the tariff laws prior to the latter state of them, the pressure was little, if at all, regarded as a source of the general suffering. And whatever may be the degree in which the extravagant augmentation of the Tariff may have contributed to the depression, the extent of this cannot be explained by the extent of the cause. The great and adequate cause of the evil is the cause last mentioned, if that be indeed an evil which improves the condition of our migrating citizens, and adds more to the growth and prosperity of the whole than it subtracts from a part of the community.

Nothing is more certain than that the actual and prospective depression of Virginia is to be referred to the fall in the value of her landed property, and in that of the staple products of the land. And it is not less certain that the fall in both cases is the inevitable effect of the redundancy in the market of land and of its products. The vast amount of fertile land offered at 125 cents per acre in the West and S. West could not fail to have the effect already experienced, of reducing the land here to half its value; and when the labour that will here produce one hogshead of tobacco and ten barrels of flour will there produce two hhd and twenty barrels, now so cheaply transportable to the destined outlets, a like effect on these articles must necessarily ensue. Already more tobacco is sent to New Orleans than is exported from Virginia to foreign markets; whilst the article of flour, exceeding for the most part the demand for it, is in a course of rapid increase from new sources as boundless as they are productive. The great staples of Virginia have but a limited market, which is easily glutted. They have in fact sunk more in price, and have a more threatening prospect, than the more southern staples of cotton and rice. The case is believed to be the same with her landed property. That it is so with her slaves is proved by the purchases made here for the market there.

The reflections suggested by this aspect of things will be more appropriate in your hands than in mine. They are also beyond the tether of my subject, which I fear I have already overstrained. I hasten, therefore, to conclude, with a tender of the high respect and cordial regards which I pray you to accept.[22]

To Henry Clay

June, 1833.

It is painful to observe the unceasing efforts to alarm the South by imputations against the North of unconstitutional designs on the subject of the slaves. You are right, I have no doubt, in believing that no such intermeddling disposition exists in the body of our Northern brethren. Their good faith is sufficiently guarantied by the interest they have as merchants, as ship-owners, and as manufacturers, in preserving a union with the slaveholding States. On the other hand, what *madness* in the South to look for greater safety in disunion. It would be worse than jumping out of the frying-pan into the fire; it would be jumping into the fire for fear of the frying-pan. The danger from the alarm is, that the pride and resentment exerted by them may be an overmatch for the dictates of prudence, and favor the project of a Southern Convention, insidiously revived, as promising, by its councils, the best securities against grievances of every sort from the North.[23]

FOOTNOTES:

[1] *Letters and other Writings of James Madison*, III, 138.

[2] *Ibid.*, 170.

[3] *Ibid.*, 239.

[4] *Letters and other Writings of James Madison*, III, 168.

[5] *Letters and other Writings of James Madison*, I, 542-543.

[6] *Ibid.*, III, 121.

[7] *Letters and other Writings of James Madison*, III, 122-124.

[8] *Letters and other Writings of James Madison*, III, 133-138.

[9] *Ibid.*, III, 170.

[10] *Letters and other Writings of James Madison*, III, 190.

[11] *Letters and other Writings of James Madison*, III, 193-194.

[12] *Letters and other Writings of James Madison*, III, 239, 240.

[13] *Letters and other Writings of James Madison*, III, 310-315.

[14] These peculiarities, it would seem, are not of

equal force in the South American States, owing, in part, perhaps, to a former degradation, produced by colonial vassalage; but principally to the lesser contrast of colours. The difference is not striking between that of many of the Spanish and Portuguese Creoles and that of many of the mixed breed.—J. M.

[15] *Letters and other Writings of James Madison*, III, 495-498.

[16] *Letters and other Writings of James Madison*, III, 541-542.

[17] *Letters and other Writings of James Madison*, III, 2-3.

[18] *Letters and other Writings of James Madison*, IV, 60.

[19] *Ibid.*, IV, 188.

[20] *Letters and other Writings of James Madison*, IV, 192.

[21] *Letters and other Writings of James Madison*, IV, 213-214.

[22] *Letters and other Writings of James Madison*, IV, 274-279.

[23] *Letters and other Writings of James Madison*, IV, 301.

ADVICE GIVEN NEGROES A CENTURY AGO

The following addresses to the free people of color, taken from the *Minutes of the American Convention of Abolition Societies* active in this country during the first fifty years of the republic of the United States, show the method employed by these early friends of the Negroes to effect their social uplift while this organization was working for the abolition of the slave trade and the destruction of slavery. The advice to the Negroes as to how they should conduct themselves is very interesting. After 1820 the American Convention of Abolition Societies paid less attention to such advice to the people of color and concerned itself primarily with appeals to others in their behalf. The free Negro made so much moral progress during the period that they ceased to be a cause of anxiety.

To The

FREE AFRICANS AND OTHER FREE PEOPLE OF COLOR

IN THE

UNITED STATES.

THE Convention of Deputies from the Abolition Societies in the United States, assembled at Philadelphia, have undertaken to address you upon subjects highly interesting to your prosperity.

They wish to see you act worthily of the rank you have acquired as freemen, and thereby to do credit to yourselves, and to justify the friends and advocates of your color in the eyes of the world.

As the result of our united reflections, we have concluded to call your attention to the following articles of Advice. We trust, they are dictated by the purest regard for your welfare, for we view you as Friends and Brethren.

In the first place. We earnestly recommend to you, a regular attention to the important duty of public worship; by which means you will evince gratitude to your CREATOR, and, at the same time, promote knowledge, union, friendship, and proper conduct amongst yourselves.

Secondly,

Secondly, We advise such of you, as have not been taught reading, writing, and the first principles of arithmetic, to acquire them as early as possible. Carefully attend to the instruction of your children in the same simple and useful branches of education. Cause them, likewise, early and frequently to read the holy Scriptures. They contain, among other great discoveries, the precious record of the original equality of mankind, and of the obligations of universal justice and benevolence, which are derived from the relation of the human race to each other in a COMMON FATHER.

Thirdly, Teach your children useful trades, or to labor with their hands in cultivating the earth. These employments are favorable to health and virtue. In the choice of masters, who are to instruct them in the above branches of business, prefer those who will work with them; by this means they will acquire habits of industry, and be better preserved from vice, than if they worked alone, or under the eye of persons less interested in their welfare. In forming contracts, for yourselves or children, with masters, it may be useful to consult such persons as are capable of giving you the best advice, who are known to be your friends, in order to prevent advantages being taken of your ignorance of the laws and customs of our country.

Fourthly, Be diligent in your respective callings, and faithful in all the relations you bear in society, whether as husbands, wives, fathers, children or hired servants. Be just in all your dealings. Be simple in your dress and furniture, and frugal in your family expenses. Thus you will act like Christians as well as freemen, and, by these means, you will provide for the distress and wants of sickness and old age.

Fifthly, Refrain from the use of spirituous liquors. The experience of many thousands of the citizens of the United States has proved, that these liquors are not necessary to lessen the fatigue of labor, nor to obviate the extremes of heat or cold; much less are they necessary to add to the innocent pleasures of society.

Sixthly, Avoid frolicking, and amusements which lead to expense and idleness; they beget habits of dissipation and vice, and thus expose you to deserved reproach amongst your white neighbors.

Seventhly, We wish to impress upon your minds the normal and religious necessity of having your marriages legally performed; also to have exact registers preserved of all the births and deaths which occur in your respective families.

Eighthly, Endeavour to lay up as much as possible of your earnings for the benefit of your children, in case you should die before they are able to maintain themselves—your money will be safest and most beneficial when laid out in lots, houses or small farms.

Ninthly, We recommend to you, at all times and upon all occasions, to behave yourselves to all persons in a civil and respectful manner, by which you may prevent contention and remove every just occasion of complaint. We beseech you to reflect, it is by your good conduct alone, that you can refute the objections which have been made against you as rational and moral creatures, and remove many of the difficulties, which have occurred in the general emancipation of such of your brethren as are yet in bondage.

With hearts anxious for your welfare, we commend you to the guidance and protection of that BEING who is able to keep you from all evil, and who is the common Father and Friend of the whole family of mankind.[1]

The Convention of Delegates from the Abolition Societies in the United States, having again assembled for the purpose of promoting your happiness, consider it their duty, once more to call your attention to the advice which was addressed to you by the Convention of last year; and which we subjoin to the present address, in order that you may at one view be able to profit by these collected advices of your sincerest friends. The oftner we review that advice, the more we are impressed with its importance, and the more anxious we are to urge your strict and faithful observance of it. We shall only add thereto, at present, one other request, and that is, that you would avoid gaming in all its varied forms—the ruinous and miserable consequences of this most pernicious evil, are so notorious, and so generally acknowledged, that we cannot too forcibly endeavour to guard you against it. It subjects you to the control of the most degrading passions, and too generally leads to the loss of fortune, reputation, and of every good principle.

We can with peculiar satisfaction inform you, that schools and places of worship have been established, and that they are well attended by people of your color, in New-York, New-Jersey, Pennsylvania, Maryland, Virginia, and other places; and we are happy to find, that many of you have evinced, by your prudent and moral conduct, that you are not unworthy of the freedom you enjoy.

Go on in these paths of virtue:—By persevering in them you will justify the solicitude and labors of your friends in your behalf, and furnish an additional argument for the emancipation of such of your brethren as are yet in bondage in the United States and in other parts of the world.[2]

The American Convention for promoting the Abolition of Slavery and improving the Condition of the African Race, believe it proper to address you, on subjects highly interesting to your well being.

You can have no doubt but that our views are disinterested, and we therefore think ourselves entitled to your attention, whilst we speak of matters in which you are greatly concerned.

As you are free men, we wish you to place a proper estimate on your privileges, and to act in a manner becoming your character; that, by your worthy conduct, you may destroy the prejudices which some persons entertain against you, and relieve your friends from the censures which they incur in consequence of your errors; we beseech you, reflect seriously and endeavor to remove these reproaches; and it is our earnest and affectionate advice, that you remember your great and good Creator, who has placed you in this life, in order that you may, by acting well your part here, be qualified for everlasting happiness hereafter—Can you expect that happiness, if instead of attending places of divine worship, there to pray for his holy aid, you spend the Sabbath, as well as much of the other parts of your time, in rolicking, drinking, or other evil practices, which destroy your own comfort, give cause of offense to your neighbours, and above all greatly displease that all-seeing God, before whom you must appear to give an account for all your conduct? Let us prevail upon you to refrain from the use of spirituous liquors, which have occasioned misery to thousands—from gaming, a vice which will bring poverty upon your families, and from frolicking and amusements, which lead to idleness and expence; these habits of dissipation, can in no wise add to your comfort. Be industrious, diligent in your business, frugal in your expences, and endeavour to lay up part of your earnings against a time of need. Some of you can read, such know the advantages of it; you who cannot, strive to acquire that knowledge.—Surely this knowledge is an object of great importance, were it only for the opportunity it affords of becoming acquainted with that best of books, the Bible. The holy Scriptures of the old and new testament, contain invaluable treasures of instruction, and of comfort. It would give us much satisfaction, could we oftener see them in the hands of those who are able to read them, and that an increasing anxiety to become possessed of their contents, and to profit by their precepts, might be more and more observable among you.

Very much depends upon the right education of your children, endeavour to have them brought up to labour, and taught to read and write; early place them apprentice with suitable masters, and whether they be tradesmen or farmers, be always particularly careful to prefer such, as by their example, will encourage them in industry and sobriety.

In all your dealings be just and honest, give no cause of offence to any, and if any dispute, either among yourselves, or with others, should unhappily arise, in which you find difficulty, apply to such persons in your neighborhoods as you know to be your friends, and able to give you advice and assistance. Be assured you will find this practice contributes much more to your peace and interest, than the settling of your differences at law.

Be careful to observe your marriage covenants, remembering that those who violate them, will fall under the displeasure of the Almighty. We wish also to impress your minds, the necessity of having your marriage ceremonies legally performed, and that the births and deaths in your respective families, be carefully registered. In the words of an address heretofore made, we recommend you at all times, and upon all occasions, to behave yourselves in a civil and respectful manner, by which you may prevent contention and remove many causes of complaint: we beseech you to reflect, that you may, by your good conduct, refute the objections which have been made against you as rational and moral creatures and lessen many of the difficulties which now occur in the emancipation of such of your brethren, as are yet in bondage.

In all your communications with those of your brethren who remain in slavery, we desire you unceasingly to impress them with the necessity of contentment with their situations, submission to their masters, and fidelity to their interests—that they be not merely eye-servants, but carefully perform the labours assigned them, and manage everything intrusted to their care, with as much faithfulness as if it were their own. By this conduct they will excite in their masters, a disposition to treat them with humanity and gentleness, and to increase the number of their privileges and comforts; and contribute to the peace of their own minds.

Console them with the reflection, that unmixed happiness in a future life, will be the portion of all good men, whatever may have been their lot here below.[3]

To the free Blacks and other free people of colour in the United States

The American Convention for promoting the Abolition of Slavery, and improving the Condition of the African Race, having again assembled for the purpose of advancing your best interest, and the welfare of your offspring; deem it expedient, once more to address you as children of one Almighty Parent, and members of the same extended family. The objects we have so long, and so assiduously pursued, are highly interesting to society at large, and infinitely important to you in particular.... For their attainment, we therefore claim your zealous and uniform co-operation. This demand we make with much confidence, as we are persuaded many of you have already verified, in your own experience, the propriety of former recommendations. You have found that industry and economy have procured for you, independence; that temperance has greatly promoted, if not absolutely secured to you, health; and that the cultivation of the faculties of the mind, has enlarged the capacity for discharging your various

125

duties, and for enjoying the numerous benefits you have received. On the contrary, you have seen that idleness, gambling, and dissipation, have uniformly produced poverty and disgrace; that intemperance has generally been the parent of loathsome disease, and the cause of premature death; and that the consequences of ignorance are too frequently, contention and loss. Trusting then, that we can with confidence appeal to your own experience, for a test of the truth of precepts so often inculcated, we beseech you with anxious and tender solicitude to bear them constantly in remembrance, and, with a steady zeal, put them in practice. We are well aware that human nature is frail, and prone to depart from the strait path of rectitude. On this weakness let us not however rely for a justification of our deviations, but rather let it operate as an inducement to double our diligence and increase our caution. Then while we are conscious of having honestly and earnestly endeavored to discharge the duties we owe to our Maker and to each other, we can look with more confidence to our great Creator for pardon of our past transgressions and strength to preserve us from a repetition of them.

In our observations thus far we have chiefly endeavoured to convince you, that on your own conduct depends your prosperity and happiness, but be assured the consequences do not rest there. The greater portion of your brethren still remains in bondage. One great obstacle to their release, it is in your power and it is eminently your duty to remove; the enemies of your liberty have loudly and constantly asserted that you are not qualified to enjoy it, that your proneness to dissipation, your inattention to your particular concerns, and your disregard of the interests of each other, will ever produce your own wretchedness and lasting mischief to those among whom you dwell: in what degree the imputations may be just we leave to your own candour to decide; but we cannot leave the subject without conjuring you to remove, by the utmost circumspection of conduct, the causes that have been and continue to be urged against you; and thereby contribute your part towards the liberation of such of your fellow men as yet remain in the shackles of slavery.

The education of your offspring is a subject of lasting importance, and has obtained a large portion of our attention and care. In this too we call upon you for your aid; many of you have been favoured to acquire a comfortable portion of property, and are consequently enabled to contribute in some measure to the means of educating your offspring. While you thus benefit your own, you will also confer a favor on the children of those who are indigent; in as much as there will remain a large proportion of other funds to be applied to their improvement.

Having thus fully communicated our sentiments on subjects the most important to your present and eternal welfare, we beg you to give them your close attention, and sincerely wish you that happiness which is consistent with the will of an all-wise and protecting Providence.[4]

The American Convention composed of Delegates from several Abolition and Manumission Societies in the United States, being assembled in Philadelphia, for the purpose of promoting the great cause of emancipation, and for the melioration of the condition and the general improvement of the descendants of the African race; have deemed it their duty to address you, on some subjects intimately connected with your future welfare and prosperity. They perform this duty the more willingly, from a conviction that such counsel and advice as they may communicate, will be received and listened to with attention, from the circumstance of its proceeding from those who have long had your best interests at heart.

Vain will be the desire on the part of the friends of abolition, to behold their labours crowned with success, unless those colourd people who have obtained their freedom, should evince by their morality and orderly deportment, that they are deserving the rank and station which they have obtained in society: unavailing will be the most strenuous exertions of humane philanthropists in your behalf, if you should not be found to second their endeavours, by a course of conduct corresponding with the expectations and the wishes of your friends.

We intreat you therefore by the ties which bind us together as children of one common Creator;—by the obligation imposed upon us, as joint objects of redeeming love; as heirs alike with us, of the rewards and benedictions which rest upon all who perform the religious and social obligations of life with fidelity; —by the sacred duties which you owe to yourselves, and to the Author of your existence; seriously to consider the great responsibility which rests upon you as Freemen, so to order and regulate your conduct and deportment in the world and amongst men, that your example may exhibit a standing refutation of the charge, that you are unworthy of freedom. And let us impress it upon YOU, whose opportunities of information have been greater than the generality of your colour, to use the influence which your superior knowledge may have given you among your brethren, to dissuade *them* from the commission and practice of those vices which degrade and disgrace them in the eyes of mankind; particularly let it be your constant endeavour to repress among them dram drinking, frequenting of tippling shops and places of diversion, idleness and dissipation of every description, and to promote and encourage as much as possible, habits of sobriety, industry and economy, punctual attendance on places of religious worship, particularly on the day appointed for rest from labour, and for the exercises of devotion; avoiding noisy and disorderly conduct on those days, as well as at other times; and to demean themselves peaceably and respectfully, towards all those with whom they have intercourse. This will do more, towards advancing your cause in the earth, than the labours of your friends can effect in your behalf.

The great work of emancipation is not to be accomplished in a day;—it must be the result of time, of long and continued exertions: it is for you to show by an orderly and worthy deportment that you are deserving of the rank which you have attained. Endeavour as much as possible to use economy in your expences, so that you may be enabled to save from your earnings, something for the education of your children, and for your support in time of sickness, and in old age: and let all those who by attending to this admonition, have acquired means, send their children to school as soon as they are old enough, where their morals will be an object of attention, as well as their improvement in school learning; and when they arrive at a suitable age, let it be your especial care to have them instructed in some mechanical art suited to their capacities, or in agricultural pursuits; by which they may afterwards be enabled to support themselves and a family. Encourage, also, those among you who are qualified as teachers of schools, and when you are of ability to pay, never send your children to free-schools; this may be considered as robbing the poor, of the opportunities which were intended for them alone.

Keep out of all contentions and law-suits with each other; by which your valuable time, which should be spent in useful occupations, is grievously misapplied, your money wasted, and your character in the world, is unhappily injured and degraded: —it is a mortifying sight to your friends, to see the coloured people bringing each other before the civil officers and in courts of justice for trifling causes of contention, which by exercising an amiable and forbearing disposition might be easily settled, without going to law, and spending their time and money, in useless disputations.

Be faithful to the obligations of the marriage covenant. Be diligent in your respective callings, so that you may not disappoint the expectations of those who have confided in you, and in the capacity of domestics or hired servants, shew yourselves faith-ful; remembering that no situation in life is disgraceful in itself, but that upon your own conduct, will depend the estimation in which you will be held by others; and if you perform your duty with fidelity, you will be respected and

128

esteemed. Be just in all your dealings, and strictly punctual in the performance of all your promises; so shall you gain the approbation and the confidence of your white neighbours, and justify the conduct of those who have laboured for your emancipation.

Let an especial attention be had to keep a regular record of your marriages, and of the births of your children, by which their ages may at any time be legally established;—this will be of essential service to you in placing them out as apprentices and prevent impositions being practised upon you. Finally—be sober; be watchful over every part of your conduct, keeping constantly in view, that the freedom of many thousands of your colour, who still remain in slavery, will be hastened and promoted by your leading a life of virtue and sobriety.[5]

FOOTNOTES:

[1] American Convention Abolition Societies. Minutes, 1796, pp. 12, 14.

[2] American Convention of Abolition Societies, Minutes of, 1797, pp. 16 and 17.

[3] American Convention Abolition Societies, Minutes, 1804, pp. 30-33.

[4] Minutes of Proceedings of Tenth American Convention for promoting the Abolition of Slavery, 1805, pp. 36-39.

[5] Minutes of the American Convention Abolition Societies, 1818. Pages 43 and 47.

SOME UNDISTINGUISHED NEGROES

Juan Bautista Cesar

A few years ago a bookseller handed me a book of MSS. papers for classification. I noted that they belonged to some military court or the archives of a Spanish Audiencia having jurisdiction in New Spain. Most of them had something to do with Texas when it was part of Mexico and belonged to the kingdom of Spain. These papers were of the highest historical value in so far as Texas was concerned. My curiosity was aroused by the original transcript of a court martial called upon to judge the transgressions of the Anglo-Americans, as they were called in those days. From these papers Philip Nolan, around whom a halo of false patriotism still lingers, was nothing more or less in the judgment of the court martial than a horse thief. It was the practice of Nolan, Bean, Fero and others to make periodical incursions across the State and stampede home, domestic, and wild horses for their mutual benefit. On this occasion the Spaniards were prepared for the malefactors and when surrounded in their provisional fort they refused at first to surrender, but the killing of Nolan put an end to all resistance and Elias Bean, David Fero and the Negro Cesar were put in St. Charles jail to await the slow machinery of the Spanish courts. Bean and Fero attempted to escape from the jail. One of these patriots became intimate with the jailer's wife and his intercepted notes showed him a depraved specimen of humanity. Among the papers examined was a deposition of Nolan's slave known in the histories of Texas by the name of Cesar, under the Spanish correct form he takes the proper name of Juan

Bautista Cesar, a native of Grenada, when the island belonged to France. He was a professed Christian belonging to the Roman Catholic faith. So that during the dawn of the incipient difficulties surrounding Texas, therefore, when becoming part of the United States, there figured a Negro the tool of his master, in common with Nolan and others, reputed horse thieves, the patriots whose depredations were as annoying to the Mexicans in 1804 as Villa's bandit incursions (during 1914-20) are reprehensible to Americans.

The manuscript follows:

Juan Bautista Cesar.

En el referido Presidio de San Carlos en el mismo dia, mes y año arriba citado el nominado Sr. Capitán hizo comparacer ante si al Interprete José Jesús de los Santos y al Negro Juan Bautista, conocido con el nombre de Cesar á quienes juramento en debida forma ante mí el Escribano y bajo lo cual prometió el primero traducir fielmente lo que declara et expresáda Juan Bautista y este decir verdad en lo que supiere y fuere preguntado y siendo por su Nombre, y Patria y Religión. Dijo que se llama Juan Bautista Cesar, que es natural de las islas Francesas que llaman la Granada y que es Católico Apostolico Romano.

Preguntado si sabe porqué está preso: dijo. Que sabe se haya preso por haber acompañado á su amo Dn. Felipe Nolan en la entrada que hizo á la Provincia de Texas.

Preguntado si no ha habido algun noevo motivo para que la prision se le agrave; Dijo que no sabe si habia habido algun motivo para tenerlo en el calabozo en donde ahora existe privandolo del alivio que ántes disfrutaba de tener todo el Presidio por Cárcel.

Preguntado que es lo que sabe de la fuga que intentaron hacer los Anglo-Americanos compañeros de Nolan. Dijo; Que la fuga si la intentaron los, Anglo Americanos se la han ocultado al declarante pues jámas le han comunicado cosa alguna relativa á ella y antes bien ha observado que cuando hablan entre sí los expresados Anglo-Americanos y el declarante se presenta, luega callan y solo continuan hablando cosas diferentes: que el diá que pusieron al que declara en el calabozo en union de Elias Bean y David Fero oyo el declarante que David pregunto a Elias que si habia escrito alguna carta á Chihuahua y respondiendole Elias que si, le contestó David ya verás como por eso nos ponen en el calabozo y te apostara una oreja que es asi; que nada mas has oido ni visto nunca sobre la fuga de que se trata: Que el declarante desde que se murió su amo Nolan siempre ha sido mirado con desprecio por los Anglo-Americanos compañeros de aquel y por lo mismo le ha quadrado mas alojarse siempre con los Españoles como se verificó cuando lo pusieron en el calabozo que dormia con tres de los Españoles.

Preguntado si sabe o ha oíds que lesl Anglo-Americanos tuviesen prevenidas Armas y municiones de boca y guerra para meditar su fuga intentarla: Dijo que nada sabe sobre lo que contiene la Pregunta, no ha oido cosa alguna sobre el particular.

Preguntado si tiene algo mas que declarar sobre el particular: Dijo que no tiene mas que declarar sobre el particular y que lo dicho es la verdad a cargo del juramento que lleva hecho en que se afirmó y ratificó despues de enterado por el Interprete de lo que contiene esta su declarencion y por no saber escribir pusieron ambos la señar de cruz firmando dicho señor y el presente Escribano.

(Firmado) Texada   X   X   Ante mi Jose Cano

Provincia de la Nueve Vizcaya Año de 1804. Diligencias practicadas de órden del Sr. Comandants General en la Fuga que intentaron hacer los Anglo-Americanos. Comisionado el Capiten Dn Antonio Garcia de Texada.

ARTHUR A. SCHOMBURG.

A BENEVOLENT SLAVEHOLDER OF COLOR

John Barry Meachum, a free man of color, became prominent as pastor of the African Baptist Church at St. Louis. Meachum was born a slave, but obtained his liberty by his own industry. By his hard earnings he purchased his father, a slave, and Baptist preacher in Virginia. He was then a resident of Kentucky, where he married a slave, and where he professed religion.

Soon thereafter his wife's master removed to Missouri, and Meachum followed her, arriving at St. Louis, with three dollars, in 1815. Being a carpenter and a cooper, he soon obtained employment, purchased his wife and children, commenced preaching, and was ordained in 1825. During subsequent years he purchased, including adults and children, about twenty slaves, but he never sold them again. His method was to place them in service, encourage them to form habits of industry and economy, and when they had paid for themselves, he set them free. In 1835 he built a steamboat, which he provided with a library, and from which he excluded the use and sale of intoxicating drinks. He was then worth about $25,000.

He was not less enterprising in religious matters. The church of which he was pastor, consisted of about 220 members of whom 200 were slaves. A large Sabbath school, a temperance society, a deep-toned missionary spirit, good order and correct habits among the slave population in the city, strict and regular discipline in the church, were among the fruits of his arduous, persevering labor.[1]

FOOTNOTES:

[1] *The Liberator*, December, 10, 1836.

BOOK REVIEWS

The Republic of Liberia. By R. C. F. MAUGHAN, F.R.G.S. and F.Z.S., etc., H. B. M., Consul-General at Monrovia. New York, Charles Scribner's Sons, 1919. Pp. 299. Price $6.50.

This work is a general description of the Negro Republic, with its history, commerce, agriculture, flora, fauna, and present methods of administration. The book contains several maps and thirty-seven illustrations. The more interesting topics as to history and administration appear first and those of the statistically scientific and commercial order come nearer to the end.

The book was written in 1918 before the United States took sufficient interest in the republic to bring about certain epoch-making changes. The United States has since offered the country a loan of five million dollars and with the approval of Great Britain and France and with the request of the Liberian Government has consented to become the sole adviser in Liberian affairs. Since then Hon. C. D. B. King, who became President of Liberia in January 1920, has participated in the world's peace conference and visited Europe and America, where the heads of nations have assured him of deeper interest in Liberia than they have heretofore manifested.

This book was written from a point of view decidedly different from that of most writers on Liberia, whose tone is that of "gentle melancholy," descanting "upon the country and the people to whom it belongs as with a pen dipped in sighs." Instead of criticising he has in most cases merely described. Where criticisms have crept in they have been given in a spirit of sympathetic friendship. He finds in the country, therefore, much to admire and praise and an economic situation "which will assuredly bid fair, when normal conditions shall have returned to us once more, to attain to a measure of gratifying expansion and progress." He believes that Liberia will then be in a position "of having her feet placed firmly upon the ladder which should bring her in time to great heights. The author concedes that the rung which Liberia has already reached is not a high one perhaps, "but the way before her seems plain and unmistakable." He believes that the present guidance from the outside guarantees these most sanguine expectations in as much as the foreigners controlling the financial policy of the little republic are hard-working men who have already set the house somewhat in order. This, supplemented by a liberal policy of internal improvements, will result in the prosperity of the whole land.

In discussing this phase of the administration of Liberian affairs, the author does not bring out any particular resentment on the part of the natives as to foreign interference. The native officials welcome helpful advice and when not given they sometimes seek it. The author himself came into contact with a number of functionaries who frankly asked him to tell them what he thought of their methods. Except so far as such foreign guidance may bring financial relief, however, it is doubtful that these natives so easily yield to this sort of domination; for many Liberians are to-day endeavoring to get rid of the American loan which they fear may lead to conquest like that in Haiti. On the whole, however, this work comes nearer to the true portraiture of the Liberian situation than most volumes in this field.

The United States in Our Own Times, 1865-1920. By PAUL HAWORTH, Ph.D. New York, Charles Scribner's Sons, 1920. Pp. vii, 563.

The publication of this volume is justified by the author on the ground that in as much as an important object of history study is to enable one to understand the present, greater emphasis than hitherto must be laid on the period since the Civil War. Hoping then to supply the need of students who desire to know our own country in our own times the author has directed his attention to the problems of the new day, to social and industrial questions which have attained importance since the Civil War, and which, as the author views it, served as a break between these two distinct periods in our history.

Briefly stated, the author covers a little better than usually the field in which many others have recently written. There appears the aftermath of the Rebellion, then the drama of Reconstruction followed by national development making possible a new era, the changing order, the revival of the Democratic Party, hard times, free silver, troubles with Spain, imperialism, Roosevelt and the Panama Canal, the New West, Progressivism, the "New Freedom," "Watchful Waiting," the World War, and the Peace Conference. The book is well illustrated with useful maps showing the West in 1876, the Cuba and Porto Rican campaigns, the Philippines, Mexico, West Indies, and Central America, the percentage of foreign-born whites in the total population in 1910, the percentage of Negroes in the total population in 1910, the Western Front in 1918, and the United States in 1920.

Discussing thus a period during which the most important problems before the American people has been how to segregate the Negroes within the law, the author touched here and there the so-called Negro question. While Dr. Haworth has not shown all of the breadth of mind expected in an historian he has been much more liberal than the pseudo-historians who endeavor merely to justify the proscription of the freedmen on the basis of so-called racial inferiority. Dr. Haworth does occasionally mention a Negro as having said or done something worthy of notice. In the average Reconstruction history there is no personal mention of the Negro except for the purpose to condemn him and to advise him how to make himself acceptable to his so-called superiors.

In his last chapter which he calls "A Golden Age in History" he says some things which we do not find in the works of the would-be historians of this period. On page 509 he writes: "A historian ought not to suppress uncomfortable facts, and it is undeniable that the treatment of the Negroes forms a blot on America's fair name. In parts of the South they are kept in a state of practical serfdom; in all cities they are herded into unsanitary districts; they are denied equal opportunities for advancement; and not infrequently they are maltreated and murdered by brutal mobs. It is true that individual Negroes, by fiendish assaults on white women, now and then rouse men to frenzy, but statistics show that only about a fifth of the lynchings of Negroes are because of the 'usual crime.' Burning at the stake is never justifiable under any circumstance, and it is undeniable that in race riots scenes of horror have been enacted that are a disgrace to American civilization. Such scenes are sadly out of place in a nation that proclaims itself the special champion of liberty and justice and which enlists in a crusade 'to make the world safe for democracy.'"

———

The American Colonization Society, 1817-1840. By

EARLY LEE FOX, Ph.D., Professor of History in Randolph-Macon College. Baltimore. The John Hopkins Press, 1919. Pp. viii, 231.

This is another study made under the direction of the Johns Hopkins University faculty of Historical and Political Science and like many others of this order lies in the field of southern history and is written from the ex parte point of view. It does not cover the whole history of the American Colonization Society but restricts itself to that period when it was largely a southern enterprise primarily interested in getting rid of the Negro. Throughout the story there is too much effort to evade eloquent facts, too much effort to excuse the sins of the South by showing that the North itself was once slaveholding and slavetrading. On the whole, however, the author has in the use of such valuable material as the manuscripts and especially the letters of the American Colonization Society brought to light significant facts which the historian will be glad to use more advantageously.

After a brief introduction the book treats of the free Negro and the slave. Then comes the chapter on the organization, purpose, and early record of the Society. Attention is next directed to the conflict between the colonizationists and the abolitionists. Colonization is afterward discussed in connection with emancipation and finally with the African slave trade. Throughout the whole treatise there is a defense of the "lofty" motives of the men who labored so hard for the expatriation of the Negroes. As the author sees it, although the Society did not send many Negroes to Africa, it was after all a success; for it had a bearing on the emancipation of slaves, and on the suppression of the African slave trade. Abolitionists, attacking this undertaking based upon national sentiment, were endangering the union by their propaganda founded upon sectional sentiment.

Colonization, therefore, was just because it was "born out of a desire to unite the North and the South in the settlement of the Negro problem." The purpose of the treatise then is to (page 127) "set forth the true aims of orthodox Colonizationists, or from another point to demonstrate that their aims were as sincerely expressed as sound policy would admit, and that, where motives were concealed, they were concealed in order to secure the freedom of the slaves."

Written from this point of view the dissertation becomes too much of a polemic to be accepted as a scientific treatise. Too much space is devoted to the task of unifying the widely different views of the colonizationists, too much effort is made to contrast the methods of the colonizationists with those of the abolitionists. The author does not seem to realize or at least fails to admit that the abolitionists were radical reformers seeking to eradicate the cause of social disease whereas the colonizationists were merely treating the symptoms of the malady in undertaking the impossible task of transplanting a whole race.

The general argument of the author in favor of the beneficence of colonization is not convincing. There is no authority for the contention that colonization promoted emancipation when the records show that the majority of slaveholders who supported it had in mind the expatriation of the free Negroes who among the bondmen were a living testimony against slavery. To say that colonization might check the slave trade by establishing one small colony in Africa is about as unsound, contended some free Negroes in 1831, as to argue that "a watchman in the city of Boston would prevent thievery in New York; or that the custom house officers there would prevent goods being smuggled into any other part of the United States." It is an insult to the intelligence of men who have seriously considered history to say that colonization was so built upon national sentiment as to have a direct bearing on the preservation of the Union when the colonizationists differed widely among themselves in the very beginning and finally divided just as the abolitionists, who at one time had also a national standing, in that most anti-slavery societies were once found in the South. Until Negro history, therefore, has been removed from the hands of those using it to whitewash their ancestors the world must still lack knowledge as to how the progress of mankind has been influenced by the Negro.

———

The Voice of the Negro. By ROBERT T. KERLIN, Professor of English at the Virginia Military Institute. New York, E. P. Dutton and Company, 1920. Pp. xii, 188.

The purpose of this book may best be expressed in the words of the author himself, when he says, in the preface: "The following work is a compilation from the colored press of America for the four months [July 1st to November 1st, 1919] immediately succeeding the Washington riot. It is designed to show the Negro's reaction to that and like events following, and to the World War and the discussion of the Treaty. It may, in the Editor's estimation, be regarded as a primary document in promoting a knowledge of the Negro, his point of view, his way of thinking upon race relations, his grievances, his aspirations, his demands." A book of such purport, especially when coming from the pen of a white man, must attract attention, and if the newspapers and periodicals from which the various extracts are chosen may be called truly representative, as in this case they are, the compiler has performed a distinct service in the field of American History.

141

Professor Kerlin has culled his clippings from eighty current Negro periodicals, published from Massachusetts to Georgia, and ranging from the startlingly radical to the most hide-bound conservative type. He has used only articles written by Negroes in Negro publications, has sorted them and grouped them under ten heads, entitled respectively: The Colored Press, The New Era, The Negro's Reaction to the World War, The Negro's Grievances and Demands, Riots, Lynchings, The South and the Negro, The Negro and Labor Unionism and Bolshevism, Negro Progress, and The Lyric Cry,— a remarkable assortment of first-hand information concerning Negro thought with regard to each topic.

Professor Kerlin makes no attempt to interpret the material of his book; he merely presents it. It is for him who reads also to read between the lines. It is doubtless impossible to choose any one expression that will accurately represent Negro thought as caught in these pages, yet four lines of poetry included in the book will serve as well as any:

> "We would be manly—proving well our
> worth,
> Then would not cringe to any *god* on
> earth.
>
> .   .   .   .
>
> "We would be peaceful, Father,—but
> when we must,
> Help us to thunder hard the blow
> that's just!"

This is the Voice of the Negro which Professor Kerlin intimates cannot go unheeded.

The book might have been made more useful by the addition of an alphabetical and topical index of the

142

periodicals used.

D. A. Lane.

———————————————

NOTES

The following account of the centenary celebration of St. Philip's Episcopal Church from the *New York World* of November 14, 1920, will be interesting to all persons interested in Negro history:

"The Right Rev. Charles Sumner Burch, D.D., Bishop of New York, and the Right Rev. Henry Beard Delany, D.D., Suffragan Bishop of North Carolina, will participate in the centennial celebration at St. Philip's Church, No. 212 West 134th Street, the Rev. H. C. Bishop, rector, which will begin to-day.

"One hundred years ago Nov. 14 St. Philip's Church was incorporated under the laws of the State of New York. The event is significant, for it antedated the Civil War by forty-one years and the Emancipation Proclamation of Abraham Lincoln by forty-five years. It is not only, nor primarily, an ecclesiastical event, but a political and social one as well, inasmuch as this act of Legislature recognized and confirmed the citizenship of the petitioners, showing that these colored Episcopalians were an integral part of the body politic.

"It was in 1809, under the leadership of Mr. McCoombs, a lay reader, that a mission for colored people was opened in a school room on the corner of Frankfort and William Streets, where they remained until 1812, and after the death of Mr. McCoombs removed to a room in Cliff Street with Peter Williams, Jr., a colored man, as lay reader, where they remained five years, moving from there to a school room on Rose Street.

"In 1819 three lots were obtained on the west side of

Collect, now Centre Street, and upon this site a wooden building was erected at a cost of $5,000. It was consecrated by Bishop John Henry Hobart, July 19, 1819, and was named St. Philip's Church. After its incorporation in 1820 Mr. Williams, who had been ordained to the Deaconate in October, was appointed minister in charge, Dec. 24, 1821, the building was destroyed by fire, but was rebuilt the following year of brick at a cost of $8,000.

"Mr. Williams was advanced to the priesthood in 1827, and became the first rector of the church. He died in 1840. In 1853 the parish was received into union with the Convention of the Diocese of New York. At that time the church was at No. 305 Mulberry Street, and the Rev. William Morris LL.D., rector of Trinity School, was the officiating minister.

"The parish was without a rector from 1840 to 1872, when the Rev. William J. Alston, trained at Kenyon College, Gambier, O., was called to the rectorship. He continued in office until 1874, and there was a vacancy until 1875, when the Rev. Joseph J. Atwell, a native of Barbados, British West Indies, was elected rector. His death in 1882 again left the office vacant until 1886, when the present incumbent, the Rev. Hutchens C. Bishop, was elected.

"During Mr. Atwell's incumbency the Parish House for Aged Women was founded. The long years of vacancy retarded the growth of the parish so that in 1885 there were but 284 communicants after a group existence of seventy-six years.

"In 1886 the congregation made another journey, locating at No. 161 West 125th Street, where it remained until 1910, when, following the migration northward, lots running from 133d to 134th Street were obtained and a commodious church and parish house were erected. The growth of the parish since that time has been phenomenal. There are now over 2,500 communicants and not room enough in the parish house to accommodate the various activities.

"At the present time St. Philip's may be said to be the only church in the neighborhood in any way equipped to serve the colored people of the community. Churchmen point out that if there is one place in Manhattan where there should be buildings adapted for indoor recreation and entertainment for the young colored people, it is that particular part of the city. They claim there should be day nurseries, gymnasiums, beneficial societies and forums for the discussion of industrial problems, where employer and employee might meet and each present his side.

"The centennial celebration will extend over a week. Bishop Burch will preach at the special thanksgiving service to-day at 11 o'clock, while Bishop Delany and one of the two negro Bishops in the Episcopal Church will make an address at the evening service.

"There will be an historical pageant to-morrow night. A public meeting with the pastors of St. Mark's, Olivet, Mother, A. M. E. Zion, St. Cyprian, George Foster Peabody and James Weldon Johnson as the speakers will take place Tuesday night. Following this meeting there will be a reception and parish supper in the basement of the church. Wednesday night is set apart for a praise service, when the Rev. Dr. Manning, Dr. Stires, Dr. Grant and Dr. Bragg will deliver addresses.

"The newly organized Provincial Conference of Church Workers Among Colored People will hold its sessions Thursday and Friday, when representative ministers and lay workers will participate. The conference will be addressed Friday night by Dr. Harry T. Ward of Union Theological Seminary and Dr. Robert Russa Moton, Principal of Tuskegee Institute."

146

PROCEEDINGS OF THE ANNUAL MEETING, WASHINGTON, D. C., NOVEMBER 18, AND 19, 1920.

The annual meeting of the Association for the Study of Negro Life and History was called to order by Dr. C. G. Woodson, the Director of Research and Editor of the *Journal of Negro History*. After a few preliminary remarks, President John W. Davis of the West Virginia Collegiate Institute was asked to open the meeting by the invocation of divine blessing. Professor William Hansberry of Straight College was introduced to deliver a lecture on the Ancient and Mediaeval Culture of the People of Yorubuland. This was a most informing disquisition on the achievements of these people prior to the time when they came into contact with the so-called more advanced Asiatic and European races. On the whole, Professor Hansberry made a strong argument in behalf of the contention that the culture of these people was indigenous and that brought into comparison with that of the ancient Greek and Roman it does not materially suffer.

Mr. A. O. Stafford, the principal of the Lincoln School of Washington, D. C., then read a very illuminating and informing paper on African folk lore. He discussed briefly the various authorities producing works in this field and indicated sources of information which have not yet been explored. He then made a general survey of African folk lore, showing how the Negro mind from the very earliest periods of African history exhibited independent thought and philosophical tendency.

At the conclusion of these addresses there followed a general discussion in which participated Principal D. S.

S. Goodloe of the Maryland State Normal and Industrial School, Mr. John W. Cromwell, President of the American Negro Academy, Mr. Monroe N. Work, Director of Research and Records, Tuskegee Institute, and President John W. Davis of the West Virginia Collegiate Institute.

At two o'clock the Association held a business session. The general routine of business was followed. There being no unfinished business or reports of special committees, the Association heard the reports of the officers of last year. The Director read his report and the report of the Secretary-Treasurer was presented by his assistant, Miss A. H. Smith. They follow:

THE REPORT OF THE DIRECTOR

During the year 1919-1920 the Association has made steady progress in spite of the difficulties resulting from the increasing cost of labor and supplies. There has been some difficulty in raising additional funds adequate to the needs of the Association and for this reason the organization is now suffering from a deficit of about $2500. Persons of means, however, have from time to time volunteered so as to give sufficient relief to keep the work going. Efforts are now being made to remove this deficit in the near future through the increase in the contributions annually received and gifts from other friends who will be asked to make sacrifices for the cause.

The study of Negro history has not extended by leaps and bounds but the progress of the work is in every way encouraging. The number of subscribers to the JOURNAL OF NEGRO HISTORY has not increased because of the necessity to double the subscription price in keeping with the demands of high prices, but the influence of the work has considerably expanded. This magazine is now being used as collateral reading in most of the leading white and Negro institutions of the country and the number of classes thus engaged are increasing every year. There is also a healthy public opinion in favor of prosecuting the study of Negro history more vigorously. Almost any book setting forth facts as to what the Negro has thought and felt and done now has considerable demand among persons in this country and abroad. While this Association does not claim credit for all which has been accomplished in this field, it has certainly given a decided

149

stimulus to the work.

It will be interesting to report, moreover, the number of institutions closely cooperating with the Association in prosecuting the study of the Negro. Among these may be mentioned special classes in this work at Howard University, conducted by the Director himself last year, and at the West Virginia Collegiate Institute, where he is now engaged. In Lincoln Institute, Missouri, considerable good has been accomplished among students even of a high school grade, whereas at the State Normal and Industrial Institute at Frankfort, Kentucky, the work has interested a larger number of more advanced students. Institutions like Straight College, Fisk, Atlanta, Morehouse, Wilberforce, and Lincoln are laying a good foundation in this field.

REPORT OF THE SECRETARY-TREASURER.

The Association for the Study of Negro Life and History, Incorporated, Washington, D. C.

Gentlemen: I hereby submit to you a report of the amount of money received and expended by the Association for the Study of Negro Life and History, Incorporated, from September 30, 1919 to September 30, 1920, inclusive:

```
Receipts                          Expenditures


Subscriptions               $ 778.32   Printing  and
Stationery     $2,733.54
Memberships                   160.00    Petty  Cash
Expenses         551.26
Contributions               3,331.00    Rent   and
Light            250.30
News  Agents                   69.47   Stenographic
Service          901.80
Advertisements                264.05   Miscellaneous
Expenses         269.98
Books                          19.63    Total
Expenditures   $4,706.88
Rent                           15.00   Balance September
30, 1920.    48.86

_____                            _____

Total             Receipts,                     Sept.
30,                            $4,755.74
1919, to Sept. 30,
1920                $4,637.47
Balance Sept. 30, 1919    118.27
                                       _____
```

150

$4,755.74

Respectfully submitted,
ALETHE H. SMITH
Assist. to the Secretary-Treasurer.

After a brief discussion these reports were accepted and approved. The Association then spent some time in discussing the advisability of holding annual meetings at strategic points and there prevailed a motion to the effect that the Executive Council be requested to hold the next annual meeting of the Association in Atlanta, Georgia. The meeting adjourned after electing the following as officers: Robert E. Park, President, Jesse E. Moorland, Secretary-Treasurer, Carter G. Woodson, Director of Research and Editor; who with Julius Rosenwald, George Foster Peabody, James H. Dillard, John R. Hawkins, Emmett J. Scott, William G. Willcox, Bishop John Hurst, Albert Bushnell Hart, Thomas Jesse Jones, A. L. Jackson, Moorfield Storey, and Bishop R. E. Jones, were made members of the Executive Council.

At the evening session at the John Wesley A. M. E. Z. Church, the Association was addressed by three men of distinction. The first speaker was Professor Kelly Miller of Howard University who briefly discussed the Limits of Philanthropy in Negro Education, endeavoring to show that helpful as has been the program of the whites to educate the Negroes, their work must be a failure, if it does not ultimately result in equipping the Negro to take over his own school systems that the direction, hitherto in the hands of whites, may be dispensed with.

Professor Robert T. Kerlin of the Virginia Military Institute, having misunderstood his place on the program appeared at this meeting and, as one of the persons scheduled to address the session did not present himself, he was permitted to speak. His discourse was an extensive discussion of the role played by poetry in the civilization of a people and how the Negro poet is rendering his race and the country service in singing of his woes and clamoring for a new opportunity.

The meeting was closed with an address by Mr. Oswald Garrison Villard, the Editor of the *Nation*, discussing the subject, The Economic Bases of the Race Question. His discourse was a political and sociological treatise based upon facts of history and economics to show the hopelessness of a program to right the wrongs of the Negroes unless that program has its foundation in things economic, in as much as the present day situation offers no hope that politics will play any particular part in the solution. All three speakers made a very favorable impression upon the audience and so enlightened it by the masterful array of facts presenting their point of view as to make this one of the most interesting sessions ever held by the Association.

The first session of the second day consisted of a conference on the Negro in America. In the absence of Dr. R. E. Park, Dr. C. G. Woodson spent most of the time discussing the achievements in the writing of history of the Negro in America, especially in the United States. He discussed the various motives actuating persons to enter this field, showing that in most cases these were propagandists and for that reason a non-partisan and unbiased history of the Negro has not yet been written. He then discussed the possibility of producing interesting, comprehensive and valuable works by the proper use of the various materials. These materials, however, contended he, would have to be given scientific treatment that the whole truth might be extracted therefrom. He then showed the possibility of error in accepting as evidence the opinions of the proslavery element about the antislavery element, the opinions of the abolitionists about the colonizationists and vice versa. These will have to be scientifically examined and after all the actual facts of Negro history must be determined from such sources as letters, diaries, books of travel, and unconscious evidence in the current publications of the times.

At the conclusion of the address remarks were made by Mr. A. H. Grimke, Mr. T. C. Williams, Mr. G. C. Wilkinson, Mr. A. C. Newman, Professor A. H. Locke, Professor Walter Dyson, and Professor William L. Hansberry. Professor Hansberry discussed for a few minutes the value of the sources in African history making his talk very illuminating and instructive.

The afternoon was devoted to a meeting of the Executive Council to which the public was not invited but in the evening a large number of members and friends of the cause attended the session, at the John Wesley A. M. E. Z. Church. The speakers of the occasion were Mr. Charles E. Russell of Washington, D. C., and Professor Albert Bushnell Hart of Harvard University. Mr. Russell discussed the *Negro's Right to Justice* taking the record of the Negro as a worthy one and the fallacy of discrimination against him in the midst of the struggle for democracy. The address was both illuminating and convincing. Then followed the address of Professor Hart on *Free Men by Choice*. He endeavored to show that no person is actually free. That all elements of the population and all classes are more or less restricted. This discussion was both legal and historical, presenting in its various ramifications the social order in the country and the legislation underlying the same. He finally brought out the important fact that although the institution of slavery imprisoned the body of the Negroes, it could not control their minds.

THE JOURNAL
OF
NEGRO HISTORY

Vol. VI—April, 1921—No. 2

MAKING WEST VIRGINIA A FREE STATE

THE HISTORIC BACKGROUND

In 1763 the Peace of Paris definitely fixed the boundaries of Virginia, giving as its western line, the Mississippi River from the Ohio River to the Lake of Woods.[1] As time and settlement progressed, the other colonies, growing fearful of Virginia's commanding position, protested against her retention of this vast territory. Finally, in 1784, Virginia ceded to the Congress of the Confederation all lands lying north and west of the Ohio River. She wanted it stipulated, however, that the territory between the Ohio River and the Allegheny Mountains comprising what is now West Virginia should remain forever hers. Although the Congress did not make this stipulation, for the reason that Virginia was unable to show title; Virginia was, nevertheless, permitted to retain possession of the said territory.[2]

"The surface of Virginia of that day is divided into two unequally inclined planes and a centrally located valley. The eastern plane is subdivided into the Piedmont and the Tidewater; the western into the Allegheny Highlands, the Cumberland Plateau, and the Ohio Valley section; the area between was designated the Valley." The eastern part of the State abounds in rich fertile soil, well adapted to agriculture, while the western portion, especially the trans-Allegheny region possesses in large quantities such natural resources as bituminous coal, building stone, natural gas and petroleum.[3] The "Valley," a part of the great Appalachian range of valleys, is a depressed surface, several hundred feet below the top of the Blue Ridge

156

Mountains on the one side, and the Alleghenies on the other. It is the dividing line of the two sections of the State then known as eastern and western Virginia.

The earlier settlements west of the mountains were made by the more adventurous persons of the east, who had no property or other ties to attach them to the soil whence they came. At a later date, a more substantial class, Germans and Scotch-Irish Presbyterians, made settlements in this western country. They brought few slaves with them but engaged in agriculture. A new type of people from the free States to the north and west, next, came to Western Virginia.[4]

Slavery did not become a flourishing institution there, and in the decades between the years of 1840 and 1860, the demand for slave labor in the Gulf States caused the bulk of the slave population to go to that market. The commercial and industrial interests developed there found their outlets west and north. There was little intercourse of any kind and practically no commerce with Eastern Virginia. No railroad connected the west with the east. Burning political differences manifested themselves, and these, with the lack of commercial and social intercourse already noted, accentuated strife between the two sections, [5] as was manifested in every State constitutional convention held prior to the Civil War.

The Constitutional Convention of 1829 at Richmond was one of the most important conventions in the history of the Virginia dissension. The transmontane people, the people of the Valley and some of those of the Piedmont were arrayed against the aristocratic land owners of the Tidewater, demanding a greater share in the government of the Commonwealth. The leading issues before the convention were: (1) the question of extension of suffrage, (2) a more

157

equitable basis of representation in the legislature, and (3) the question of taxation as a minor problem.

The right of suffrage was then conditioned upon the ownership of land. The law regulating this matter had remained the same since 1776, except that the number of acres of improved land, the possession of which entitled one to vote, had been reduced from 50 to 25.[6] Thus all those persons who were not attached to land or who did not possess land in sufficient quantities were denied the ballot. The west, whose white population, in 1829, was 319,516, argued and fought for citizen-suffrage, while the east, whose white population was 362,745 at this time, representing a fifteen per cent increase since 1790, as compared with one of 150 per cent for the west, opposed this measure.[7]

The question of the reapportionment of representation was one of the greatest importance. Here again, just as suffrage was based upon the ownership of land, representation was based upon interests. In 1828 the House of Delegates consisted of two hundred and fourteen members; the Senate of twenty-four." Of these numbers the transmontane country had but eighty delegates and nine senators. [8] This section, then proposed that the basis of apportionment should be the white population. The cismontane people opposed this, since any change in this direction would tend to place too much political power in the hands of the westerners.

After a discussion on the white and mixed bases proposals, which lasted three weeks, the convention finally turned to a consideration of the various plans of compromise. Mr. Gordon, of Albemarle County, presented a plan which was finally accepted with slight modifications. He ignored completely the basis question and attempted an equitable distribution of representation. "It provided for a Senate of twenty-four, of which ten would come from the West; and a House of one hundred and twenty; of which twenty-six would come from the trans-Allegheny, twenty-four from the Valley, thirty-seven from the Piedmont and thirty-three from the Tidewater."[9] Incidentally this plan was quite acceptable to the populous counties of the Piedmont foothills and the Valley, for it tended to increase their representation.

As a constitutional basis for future reapportionments of representation, the following provision was made a part of the constitution:

"That the General Assembly, after the year of 1841 and at intervals of not less than ten years, shall have authority, two-thirds of each House concurring, to make re-apportionments of Delegates and Senators throughout the Commonwealth, so that the number of Delegates shall not at any time exceed one hundred and fifty, nor of Senators thirty-six."[10]

The question of taxation was one of some importance. Prior to 1829, the west had drawn annually for administrative purposes more than it had contributed to the treasury. Real estate values in the west were low because of the lack of speculative spirit there, and, consequently, taxes were not collected in great amounts. The west now desired (1) greater revenues to construct roads and canals and to maintain free schools and (2) the power to tax the slave property of the east. There were at this time east of the Blue Ridge Mountains 397,000 Negro slaves subject to taxation and nearly 50,000 in the west. The slave property contributed one-third of the revenue of the State. The east, therefore, determined not to give to the west the desired power to tax her property.[11]

Although the question of reapportionment of representation, the question of taxation and the suffrage question were among the foremost considerations of the Convention, the underlying and

159

basic cause of all this strife was the slavery issue.[12] Those who advocated and supported the institution of slavery were loath to surrender to the people of the west any of the power and privileges that they possessed. Some of Eastern Virginia and a great majority of the people in Western Virginia were opposed to slavery. They believed still in the principles advocated by the fathers of the country as set by George Mason, who, while deploring the institution, had formerly said: "Slavery discourages arts and manufactures. The poor despise labor when performed by slaves. They prevent the immigration of whites, who really enrich and strengthen a country. They produce the most pernicious effect on manners. Every master of slaves is born a petty tyrant. They bring the judgment of Heaven on a country. By an inevitable chain of causes and effects, Providence punishes national sins by national calamities."[13]

A memorial presented to the convention in October in 1829, said that Virginia was in a state of "moral and political retrogression" and proceeded to specify:

"That the causes heretofore frequently assigned are the true ones we do not believe.... We humbly suggest our belief that the slavery that exists and which with gigantic strides is gaining ground among us, is, in truth, the great efficient cause of the multiplied evils we deplore. We cannot conceive that there is any other cause sufficiently operative to paralyze the energies of a people so magnanimous, to neutralize the blessings of Providence included in the gift of a land so happy in its soil, its climate, its minerals and its waters; and to annul the manifold advantages of our republican system and geographical position. If Virginia has already fallen from her high estate, and if we have assigned a true cause for her fall, it is with the utmost anxiety that we look to the future to the fatal termination of the scene. As we value our domestic happiness, as our hearts yearn for the prosperity of our offspring, as we pray for the guardian care of the Almighty over our Country— we earnestly inquire what shall be done to avert the impending ruin. The efficient cause of our calamities is vigorously increasing in magnitude and potency, while we wake and while we sleep."[14]

The able men in the convention saw that no permanent agreement could be reached between the two sections until the basic cause of the whole conflict had been settled. The power of the big planters, however, was too great and there was made no constitutional provision having the purpose to abolish slavery. The Convention of 1829-30, therefore, settled nothing. A compromise was effected on the question of re-apportionment of representation; a constitutional provision set forth a program of future apportionments; but the permanent settlement of this and other important questions was left for the Convention of 1850.

The Assembly of 1831-32 was the scene of an intense debate on the issue of slavery. Because of a turn of events, a more definite cleavage had come between the east and the west. The domestic slave trade, improved methods of agriculture, internal improvements, better means of communication, the consequent increase of capital which helped to restore the impoverished lands and to bring into use the uncultivated areas of the east, brought about in that section a marked revival of interest in the economic possibilities of slavery.[15] The west took a step in the opposite direction.

It must be remembered, however, that there were but few abolitionists of the extreme type in the western sections of Virginia. The responsible leaders in this movement against slavery were not concerned with any moral or religious theories on the subject, but rather, were acting because of their conviction that slavery was an economic evil. These men saw that the States to the north and west of them had outstripped them in the race for material prosperity. They saw, too, the gradual but unrelenting impoverishment of the east. They concluded, therefore, that their lack of prosperity was due to

161

their proximity to the slave-holding section of the State. The belief became current that the natural resources of the west would attract capital and population, if the objectional slaves were removed. In consequence, therefore, they favored a gradual emancipation and deportation of the slaves.[16]

Numerous petitions, memorials and resolutions found their way to the Assembly. These may be divided into three classes: (1) those asking for the removal of free Negroes from the State; (2) those seeking to amend the Federal Constitution with a view to giving Congress power to appropriate money with which to purchase slaves and transport them and the free Negroes from the United States; and (3) those urging the State to devise some scheme for gradual emancipation.[17] The first class of petitions came principally from the large slave-holding sections of the State; the second and third classes came from those sections of the State in which slaves were not numerous.

It was evident that this Assembly must take a definite position with reference to the question of the abolishment of slavery. Accordingly, therefore, a number of these resolutions concerning slavery were referred to a select committee composed of twenty-one members, sixteen of whom were from counties east of the Blue Ridge. After three days of conference, during which fiery discussions and motions were rampant in the legislature, the committee reported to the effect that "it is inexpedient for the present to make any legislative enactment for the abolition of slavery."[18] Mr. Preston, of Montgomery, moved immediately to amend the report by substituting therefor: "It is expedient at this time to adopt some legislative enactment for the abolition of slavery."[19] The amendment was defeated by a vote of seventy-three

162

to fifty-eight. Mr. Bryce, of Goochland County, thereupon, proposed to amend the report of the select committee, already herein noted, by prefixing the following preamble: "Profoundly sensible of the great evils arising from the condition of the Colored population of the Commonwealth; induced by humanity as well as policy to an immediate effort for the removal, in the first place as well as those who are now free as of such as may hereafter become free, believing that this effort, while it is in just accordance with the sentiment of the community on the subject, will absorb all our present means; and that a further action for the removal of the slaves, should await a more definite development of public opinion."[20] This preamble was adopted, despite tremendous opposition of the pro-slavery men.

The discussion of 1832 was followed by a decided reaction against the proposal for the abolition of slavery. Professor Thomas R. Dew, of William and Mary College, crystallized the pro-slavery sentiment in a masterful essay entitled: *A Review of the Debates in the Virginia Legislature of 1831-32*. This essay dealt with the theoretical and practical aspects of slavery in all countries and especially with the rise and development of Negro slavery in America. It pointed out the difficulties attendant upon the deportation of the free black and slave populations, and the danger to society of their emancipation without deportation. It ridiculed the idea of a successful slave uprising under the conditions then obtaining, and held that the whole discussion of so momentous a question by young and inexperienced legislators was entirely out of order.[21] The forceful argument of Professor Dew was met by one from Jesse Burton Harrison, whose essay was entitled: "A Review of the Speech of Thomas Marshall in the Virginia Assembly of 1831-32." Mr. Harrison's arguments to prove that Negro slavery in Virginia was an economic evil appeared to be merely a reiteration of the arguments of Marshall. [22] Former President Madison also replied briefly to Dew. His essay set forth that Dew had held too cheaply the presence of Negro slavery and emigration and ascribed too much importance to the influence of the tariff laws.[23]

By far the most important sectional issue in Virginia during the period 1834 to 1850 was that arising out of a movement for a united slave-holding South. The Virginia Congressmen had voted as a body against the "Wilmot Proviso," the abolition of the domestic slave trade and the abolition of slavery in the District of Columbia. In spite of these facts, leading citizens of Western Virginia were trying to devise ways and means whereby to rid that portion of the State of Negro slavery. Dr. Henry Ruffner, Henry McDowell Moore and John Letcher were prominent among those who proposed a plan whereby the gradual emancipation of all slaves in the State west of the Blue Ridge Mountains would be effected. The plan was first debated in the Franklin Society at Lexington in 1847. Later it appeared as a pamphlet entitled *An Address to the People of West Virginia by a Slaveholder of West Virginia*. This pamphlet proposed to show that slavery was opposed to the public welfare and that it might be gradually abolished without results detrimental to the rights and interests of the slave holders. It contained elaborate comparisons between the slave-holding States and those not holding slaves, to the disadvantage of the former, in tending to prove that slavery was an economic evil.[24]

Dr. Ruffner, later speaking of the movement, said: "No one so far as I can remember took the abolitionist ground that slave holding was a sin and ought to be abolished. With us, it was merely a question of expediency and was argued with special reference to

164

the interests of West Virginia." Speaking of the reception of the pamphlet in Western Virginia, he said that the editors in the Valley, doubting the success of the scheme, hesitated to endorse his efforts; but that west of the Alleghenies it met with a most encouraging reception.[25]

There began during the two decades from 1830 to 1850 a period of internal improvements because of a rapid increase in the population and wealth of Western Virginia. The construction of turnpikes and local railroads in the trans-Allegheny country and the projection of other improvements attracted there immigrants, and served also to interest speculation in its cheap lands and natural resources. English and eastern capitalists purchased large tracts of land and sold them in small parcels to settlers who occupied them.[26] Capitalists from the Middle West and New England States established small manufactories there, and immigrants coming thither chose between working therein and becoming farmers or teachers. A considerable German population was numbered among these immigrants. The census of 1850 showed an excess of 90,372 white population in the West over that in the East. The lands in the transmontane country had risen to a value of only fifteen million dollars less than the cash value of the lands east of the Blue Ridge.[27]

It is significant that the improvements during this period had tended, altogether, to connect the commercial interests of Western Virginia more definitely with those of the Free States to the north and west. Not a single railroad connected the western part of the State with the Tidewater. The proceeds of bond issues floated to promote internal improvements in the State had not been used to effect commercial ties between the two sections of the State, nor had any considerable portion thereof been used to improve the western districts. On the other hand, the interest of the people at the foot hills of the Piedmont had become more definitely aligned with those of the other eastern sections of the State. The chief grievance of the former had been remedied by the compromise convention of 1829-30, which gave them a larger representation in the House of Delegates. Likewise, the pursuit of intensive agriculture in the Valley had led to the introduction of many slaves there, thus tending to create a bond of interest between this region and the slave-holding east. In the Constitutional Convention of 1850, therefore, the people of the transmontane country found themselves arrayed against the three other sections of the State.[28]

It has been herein noted that the Convention of 1829-30 settled nothing. A compromise had been effected which relieved somewhat the tension that existed over the matter of representation. The constitutional provision that gave to the Assembly the power, after 1841 and thereafter at intervals of not less than ten years, and under prescribed conditions, to make re-apportionments of representation had never been availed of. In view of its phenomenal growth in wealth and population, the west keenly resented this failure to act on the part of the Assembly of 1841-42.[29] The questions, therefore, that confronted the Convention of 1829-30 were again brought forward in 1850.

The Convention of 1850 met at Richmond in October, but shortly adjourned until January 6, 1851. In February the question of the basis of representation was taken up. The Committee appointed to determine the proper basis could reach no agreement; thereupon, many plans were submitted by delegates from each section of the State. The western delegates proposed that the House of Delegates should consist

166

of one hundred and fifty-six members, should be elected biennially, and that the Senate should consist of fifty members chosen for four years; both Houses should be elected upon the suffrage basis; and in 1862 and every ten years thereafter, a re-apportionment should be made on that basis. The eastern delegates proposed a House of Delegates of one hundred and fifty-six members and a Senate of thirty-six; both Houses should be elected on the mixed basis and re-apportionments should be made on that basis in 1855 and every ten years thereafter.[30]

Neither of these plans was adopted. Consequently various plans of compromise were brought forward. Botts, of Richmond, and George W. Summers, of Kanawha, were among those who suggested propositions. On the motion of Mr. Martin, of Henry County, it was decided that a committee of eight, four from each section, be elected by the convention to provide a compromise. On the fifteenth day of May, this committee reported in favor of a House of Delegates of one hundred and fifty members; eighty-two from the west and sixty-eight from the east; and a Senate of fifty; thirty from the east and twenty from the west. It provided further for a re-apportionment in 1865 and for submitting both the mixed and suffrage bases to the people should the Assembly, at that time, fail to agree.[31] The plan was rejected. Following the failure of several other compromise plans, Chilton presented with modifications the report of the committee of eight.[32] This report provided that the numbers therein indicated for each house remain unchanged; but should the legislature of 1865 fail to re-apportion representation, the governor would be "required to submit to the vote of the people four propositions, namely; (1) the suffrage basis, (2) the mixed basis, (3) the white population basis, and (4) the taxation

167

basis." This plan was carried in committee of the whole and later, with slight modifications, was adopted by the Convention.

The question of suffrage was settled amicably since the delegates from neither section opposed an extension thereof. The privilege of the ballot, therefore, was extended to "Every white male citizen of the commonwealth of the age of twenty-one years";[33] paupers and others usually excepted, not to be included.

The question of taxation was one of the important issues to be settled. The eastern delegates opposed the white basis of representation, chiefly through the fear that westerners would use their newly gained political power to tax slave property to secure funds for internal improvements.[34] The eastern members insisted, therefore, that all property taxes should be ad valorem and that no one species should be taxed higher than another. They were unwilling, too, that Negro slaves under twelve years of age should be taxed at all. It was finally provided that an ad valorem tax be placed on all property according to its value, but that Negro slaves under twelve years of age be exempt and slaves twelve years and over be taxed per capita at not more than the tax on land worth three hundred dollars.[35] The inhabitants of the west never became reconciled to this discriminating arrangement and it was especially irritating during the years immediately preceding the war,[36] when the price of slaves often ranged from sixteen hundred to eighteen hundred dollars.[37]

In this Convention the men of the west were less bent upon obtaining a constitutional provision declaring for the gradual emancipation of slaves than they were in 1829-30. Their efforts were directed towards shifting the political balance of power from east to west, whereby this purpose might be accomplished with less difficulty.[38] In this they were not successful. Likewise the east was dissatisfied over the apportionment of representation and the west did not want to accept the principle of taxation.[39] The question of the extension of suffrage was the only leading issue settled. This convention, like that of 1829-30, was essentially a compromise convention; for no permanent settlement of the great problems could be effected with the State virtually half slave and half free.

The Virginia policy during the period of 1850 to 1861 was influenced largely by the nation-wide idea that the question of slavery could be settled only by civil strife. Accordingly the Virginia politicians, and especially Governor Wise[40] during his term of office, were at great pains to connect Eastern Virginia in thought and in purpose with the slave-holding South. This was a period of great internal improvements in Virginia. The State incurred a bonded debt of thirty-six million dollars. Many of the loans constituting this debt were used to promote and facilitate the building of railroads and canals. The railroads in question, almost without exception, tended to connect Eastern Virginia socially, industrially and commercially with her neighbors to the south. On the other hand, the only large railroad of Western Virginia, the Baltimore and Ohio, was constantly discriminated against at Richmond[41] and in every session of the legislature restrictions were aimed at its activities. It is significant that the hostility to railroad facilities for the Northwest persisted down to the beginning of the Civil War.[42]

While Western Virginia was denied railroad facilities out of deference to southern and slave-holding interests, liberal appropriations were made for the building of turnpike roads in that territory.[43] This consideration tended to some extent to alleviate the feeling of dissatisfaction. The fact remained, however, that Western Virginia had become one in thought and in purpose with the people of Pennsylvania and Ohio, and she was influenced considerably by her intercourse with Baltimore. It was to these places that she had easy access. It followed, therefore, that in 1861 when Eastern Virginia seceded from the Union and went with the slave-holding States of the South, the western part of the State had little choice save to remain loyal to the Union.

170

SECESSION AND ITS RESULTS

In 1860 there were in all Virginia 498,887 slaves, of whom 12,771 were in the forty-eight counties originally constituting the State of West Virginia.[44] With an overwhelming majority of all the slaves in the State located in the East, the people of this section were, naturally enough, profoundly interested in the events then occurring in other pro-slavery commonwealths. Influenced by the secession of six States from the Union and their subsequent formation of the Confederate States of America, Governor Letcher issued a proclamation convening the General Assembly in extra session on the seventh day of January, 1861.[45]

According to the act of the Assembly, a state convention was assembled at Richmond on the thirteenth day of February. Forty-seven of the one hundred and fifty-two delegates present represented counties now included in the State of West Virginia. [46] On the sixteenth of April the Convention met in secret session and the chairman of the Committee on Federal Relations appointed early in February reported a measure entitled "An Ordinance to Repeal the Ratification of the Constitution of the United States." [47] The ordinance recited the reasons for the repeal of the ratification of the Federal Constitution, dissolved the union between Virginia and the other States, asserted the complete sovereignty of the State of Virginia, released her citizens from responsibility to the Federal Constitution, noted the date upon which and provided the conditions under which the said ordinance would become effective. It was adopted the next day by a vote of eighty-eight to fifty-five. Immediate steps were then taken to form an alliance with the Confederate States,[48] the same being effected on the twenty-fifth day of April. Meanwhile some of the delegates from Western

171

Virginia withdrew from the Convention.

When news of the action taken by the Richmond convention reached Northwestern Virginia a storm of protest arose. A vast majority of the citizens of this region were not in accord with the action of the State in seceding to the Confederacy. They were determined, therefore, that the part of the State known as the trans-Allegheny region should be saved to the Union. Resolutions emanating from the meetings held in the several counties joined with the press to denounce the action taken by the aforesaid convention. The Clarksburg[49] meeting, assembled for this purpose on the twenty-second of April, sounded the call for united action and proposed that a convention composed of the twenty-seven counties of Western Virginia should assemble at Wheeling on the thirteenth of May.

The May Convention assembled at the time and place indicated and proceeded straightway to the business of the hour. The permanent President, John W. Moss, of Wood county, outlined the purpose of the Convention.[50] His remarks were followed by a resolution of Mr. Tarr, of Brooke County, to the effect that "a Committee, to be known as the Committee on Federal and State Relations and to comprise one member from each County, be appointed by the President to consider all resolutions of the body looking to action by the Convention."[51] Significant among the numerous resolutions presented was one by John S. Carlile calling for a new Virginia,[52] but the sense of the Convention was that such action was premature.

Out of the maze of resolutions offered, the committee finally made its report. Among other provisions, the report recommended that in the event of the ratification, by vote, of the Ordinance of Secession, the counties there represented and all others

172

disposed to co-operate with them, should appoint delegates on the fourth day of June to meet in general convention on the eleventh day of June at such place as thereinafter provided, with a view to devising such measures and taking such action as the people they represent might demand.[53] It was further recommended that a central committee be appointed to attend to all matters connected with the objects of the convention, to assemble it at their discretion and to prepare an address to the people of Virginia in conformity with the resolution there made.[54]

The passage, on the twenty-third day of May, of the Ordinance of Secession, necessitated the meeting of the second convention. It assembled on the eleventh of June at Wheeling. Upon the effecting of a permanent organization, Mr. Dorsey, of Monongalia, offered a resolution to the effect that immediate steps be taken to form a new State from the counties represented.[55] Mr. Carlile endeavored to show a lack of wisdom in such a course, saying: "Let us organize a legislature, swearing allegiance to the Federal Government, and let that legislature be recognized by the government of the United States as the legislature of the State of Virginia."[56] He urged that under that condition they would be under the protecting care of the Federal Government and would be in position to effect a constitutional separation from Virginia. His judgment prevailed.

The important acts of this Convention were: (1) the Declaration of Rights of the People of Virginia and its adoption;[57] (2) the adoption of an Ordinance for the Reorganization of the State[58] and (3) the election of State Officers.[59] The Convention then adjourned.

On the sixth of August, the adjourned Convention reassembled, as provided, at Wheeling. The principal work of this convention was the adoption of an ordinance to provide for the formation of a new State out of a portion of the State of Virginia.[60] It provided also for an election to be held on the twenty-fourth of October (1) to ratify the ordinance there adopted and (2) to select delegates to a convention to frame a constitution for the new State, in case a majority of the voters should decide in favor of formation. The vote at this election was 18,408 for ratification and 481 for rejection. Accordingly, upon certification of the same to the governor, he issued his proclamation, calling the delegates elected to a constitutional convention to meet in Wheeling on the twenty-sixth of November.[61]

The Constitutional Convention met at the scheduled time in the United States Court room at Wheeling.[62] Thirty-four delegates of the forty chosen were present. No time was lost in effecting a permanent organization of the Convention, in order that the momentous problems to be solved might be brought before that august body. Not the least important one of these questions was that of the disposal of slavery. The questions of the hour were these: Was the new State to be a free or a slave State? Would the Union admit another slave State?

It was on the fourteenth day of the Convention that Robert Hagar, a Methodist preacher from Boone county, offered a resolution to the effect that the convention inquire into the propriety of making the new State free, by incorporating into the Constitution a clause for gradual emancipation.[63] A counter proposal was offered on the same day by Mr. Brown, an ardent pro-slavery advocate, from Kanawha. His resolution asserted that it was "unwise and impolitic to introduce the question of slavery into the Convention."[64] Despite the fact that the organic law of the new State was then being framed, this pro-slavery champion deplored any attempt of the body

174

to discuss or decide upon the question of slavery, the most vital question of economic policy with which the people would be concerned. There were present, however, other men who were determined to champion the cause of freedom.

On the sixteenth day of the convention the courageous Mr. Gordon Battelle, a delegate from Ohio county, offered for reference the following proposition:[65]

(1) "No slave shall be brought into the State for permanent residence after the adoption of this constitution.

(2) "The legislature shall have full power to make such just and humane provisions as may be needful for the better regulation and security of the marriage and family relations between slaves, for their proper instruction, and for the gradual and equitable removal of slaves from the State.

(3) "On and after the fourth day of July 18—, slavery or involuntary servitude, except for crime, shall cease within the limits of this State."

On the twenty-seventh day of January, Mr. Battelle offered the following:[66]

(1) "No slave shall be brought into the state for permanent residence after the adoption of this constitution.

(2) "All children born of slave parents in this state on and after the fourth day of July 1865 shall be free; and the Legislature may provide by general law for the apprenticeship of such children during their minority and for their subsequent colonization."

It is obvious that the first set of propositions provided for the total abolition of slavery, the date undetermined; whereas the second, while providing for the freedom of the children, born of slave parents on and after a specified date, condemned to perpetual slavery all other persons who prior to that date were slaves.

In line with the proposals of Mr. Battelle was the pertinent and clear-sighted editorial of *The Wheeling*

175

Intelligencer under date of December ninth, 1861. It said: "We have endeavored to show how entirely adverse to the best interests of Western Virginia it would be for the present convention to adjourn without first engrafting a free State provision on our constitution in shape of a three, five or ten years emancipation clause. We should esteem it far better that the Convention had never assembled than that it should omit to take action of this character.... Congress would hesitate long before it will consent to the subdivision of a slave State simply that two slave States may be made out of it. The evil which has so nearly destroyed not only Western Virginia, but the whole country, will find that its tug-of-war is yet to come, when it has run the gauntlet of our Convention and our Legislature. We believe that when it reaches Congress, it will reach its hitherto and that it will never pass. It will avail very little for this convention to remain in debate on this subject for a month at a heavy expense and consummate a work which will only last end in a defeat and entail upon its framers the cold distrust of the only friends they have in the world. The loyal masses of the free States who are fighting the great battle of Constitutional freedom, who are endeavoring to stay the absorbing and consuming demands of slavery upon this continent, will never consent that in the very midst of them it shall burst out, in a new place, with the extraordinary demands that its present representation of a state in their Senate shall be doubled.... We say then to the members of our convention that before you waste your time and money on a constitution you look to its probable fate."[67]

That this prophetic message from the *Intelligencer* reflected the opinion of the people of Western Virginia and the state of mind of the Congress, was clearly shown by subsequent events. On the nineteenth day of the Convention an adroit attempt was made to have West Virginia become a slave State.[68] Thomas Harrison, of Harrison county, offered a resolution providing that the making of a new constitution be dispensed with for the present, and that the Virginia Constitution be referred to a Committee of Five with instructions to modify it to suit the needs of the proposed new State. Significant among the provisions of the Virginia Constitution was one altered at the Richmond Secession Convention to the effect that the General Assembly should have power to prohibit the future emancipation of slaves. By its provisions, therefore, the slave could never become free during his residence in the State. On motion of Mr. Van Winkle, the Convention voted that action on the resolution be indefinitely postponed.[69]

Battelle, persistent in his efforts to make some provision in reference to the freedom of the slaves, decided to submit emancipation to the people. Accordingly, therefore, on the twelfth of February, 1862, he offered the following:[70]

(1) "Resolved. That at the same time when this Constitution is submitted to the qualified voters of the proposed new state to be voted for or against, an additional section to article——, in the words following: 'No slave shall be brought or free person of color come into this state for permanent residence after this constitution goes into operation, and all children, born of slave mothers after the year 1870 shall be free, the males at the age of twenty-eight years, and the females at the age of eighteen years; and the children of such females shall be free at birth'. Shall be separately submitted to the qualified voters of the proposed new state for their adoption or rejection, and if the majority of the votes cast for and against said additional section are in favor of its adoption, it shall be made a part of article—of this constitution and not otherwise."

(2) "Resolved that the committee on schedule be and they are hereby instructed to report the necessary provisions for carrying the foregoing resolution into effect."

Mr. Sinsel moved that the resolutions be made the order of the next morning at ten o'clock; Mr. Hall, of Marion county, moved to amend the motion to the effect that it be laid on the table. Mr. Battelle deplored the application of the gag rule. The question not being a debatable one, the vote was taken. By a majority of one vote of the forty-seven cast, the resolutions were indefinitely laid on the table.[71]

On the thirteenth day of February, after the disposition of other important business, Mr. Pomeroy, of Hancock county, suggested that the questions raised by the resolutions offered the day before by Mr. Battelle might be compromised, either by adopting one of the propositions already presented, or by referring the whole matter to a representative committee of conference. Many members of the convention shared the views of Mr. Pomeroy and so stated their convictions to the body. Indeed they favored the settlement of the question then and there, without reference to a committee. Mr. Hall, of Marion, was of the opinion that its reference to a committee might carry abroad the idea that a division existed there; that that which was done, was accomplished only through a committee of compromise. Mr. Hervey was convinced that the new State must be a free State and therefore desired to vote the proposition as it stood, without the committee. Mr. Dille was of the opinion that there would be no objection to a constitutional provision forbidding the entrance into the State for permanent residence, of free Negroes or slaves, after the adoption of the Constitution. Mr. Brown, of Kanawha, sustained the view of Mr. Dille. Mr. Pomeroy made a motion to the effect that the first clause of Mr. Battelle's resolution be acted upon by the body. Mr. Battelle favored the reference of the question to a committee, thus opposing a vote that morning because he had assured a colleague of the opposite side that the question would not be brought up that morning and he wanted that all the proponents and opponents of the measure be present at the taking of the vote.

Mr. Stewart, of Doddridge, the gentleman to whom Mr. Battelle referred, having just entered, stated that he understood the motion before the House to be a compromise measure that would settle the question. Thereupon, Mr. Battelle served notice that while he would support the pending motion, he had entered into no compromise. It was his plan, therefore, to prosecute the case before the public forum. The question was put and it was agreed with one dissenting vote that there should be incorporated into the Constitution the first clause of Mr. Battelle's resolution; namely: "No slave shall be brought or free person of color come into this State for permanent residence after this constitution goes into effect."[72]

On the third day of April the vote on the question of the adoption of the constitution was taken; 18,862 votes were cast for adoption and 514 for rejection. A significant incident to the general election was the informal vote taken, at the suggestion of *The Wheeling Intelligencer*, on Mr. Battelle's emancipation proposition which had been rejected by the Convention. Despite the irregular and unauthorized manner in which this was done, by the several counties holding such extra election, the count showed that six thousand votes were cast for emancipation and six hundred against.[73] It is not improbable, therefore, that the constitution would have been adopted without difficulty had the emancipation clause been included. The politicians and not the people were on the wrong side of the issue.

Pursuant to the call of the Governor, the general assembly met in its second extra session on the sixth of May.[74] On the thirteenth day of the same month it passed "An Act giving the assent of the Legislature of Virginia to the Formation of and Erection of a New State within the jurisdiction of this State."[75]

Everything was now in readiness for the presentation of documents and credentials to Congress, by the proposed new State, in support of its application for admission into the Union.

Prior to this Mr. Battelle, in pursuance of his earnest efforts to make the proposed new State free, had prepared a masterly address on the subject of the emancipation of the slaves, to be delivered in convention to his colleagues. The sense of the convention was such that the courageous gentleman was unable to engage its attention for that purpose. Accordingly, therefore, he had printed in pamphlet form the address that he intended to deliver, and distributed it throughout the counties of Northwestern Virginia. Among the salient points therein set forth the following are noteworthy: first, that since the institution of slavery as it existed within the bounds of Western Virginia was the mere creature of law, the law was competent to remove it; and that, therefore, it was fairly and properly a subject for the consideration of those in convention assembled; second, that the gradual emancipation of the slaves was both fundamental and vital to the success of the new State, and in consequence thereof the question should be settled in the organic law. Mr. Battelle discussed the question from two points of view, that of principle, and that of expediency. It was developed that the principle of slavery was wrong and that the system, therefore, should be abolished. "While discrimination must be made between the system and the acts of individuals, the former," he said, "is always bad, is always inconsistent with the obvious requirements of either justice or morals."[76]

Considering the proposition in the light of expediency, the question was asked: "What do the best interests of the people of West Virginia require from the persons assembled to frame the organic law?" In reply thereto there was developed the theme that labor was fundamental to the material prosperity of the commonwealth; that slave labor and free had always been and would doubtless always be unharmonious and inconsistent in purpose. Since slave labor, it was pointed out, was competent to perform only the crudest work and most menial tasks, it followed that free labor was indispensable to the material progress of the new State. "Slave labor," Battelle said, "drove out free labor and tended to make all labor undignified and despised. It should, therefore, be dispensed with." In reply to the assertion that since the system was destined to die a quick and certain death no action on the part of the State was necessary, Mr. Battelle urged that "if that be true, it furnished an additional reason for the incorporation into the constitution of a provision terminating slavery." "Such action would be but just to all parties—to both the proponents and the opponents of the present system." The argument closed with an exposition, first, on slavery as the fundamental cause of the then current distress in Virginia and in the nation; and second, on the propriety of such an act at that particular time. This argument doubtless had an unexpected effect in preparing the minds of the people of the State for the acceptance of the plan of gradual emancipation, the condition on which West Virginia was finally admitted.[77]

SLAVERY AND THE ADMISSION OF WEST VIRGINIA

Waitman T. Willey, a member of the Senate from Virginia, having obtained the permission of that body to do so, presented on May 29th a certified original of the constitution together with a copy of an Act of the General Assembly of Virginia, of May 13, 1862, under the Restored Government, giving its permission for the formation of a new State within the commonwealth of Virginia. He presented at the same

181

time the memorial of the General Assembly requesting Congress to admit the State of West Virginia into the Union. Following the receipt of these documents they were referred to the Committee on Territories, of which B. F. Wade, of Ohio, was the Chairman.[78]

On the twenty-third of June Senate Bill No. 365 providing for "the admission of the State of West Virginia into the Union" was reported, read and passed to a second reading.[79] On the twenty-sixth day of June, on motion of Mr. Wade, the bill was taken up for immediate consideration in a committee of the whole. The bill proposed to admit West Virginia into the Union on equal footing with the original States in all respects whatever, subject, among other conditions, to the following: "That the convention thereinafter provided for shall in the constitution to be framed by it, make provision that from and after the fourth day of July, 1863, the children of all slaves born within the limits of the said State shall be free." [80]

Following the action noted, Mr. Sumner, Senator from Massachusetts, quoted that provision of the bill relating to the emancipation of slaves and raised the following objections, namely: (1) that by the passage of the bill a new slave State would be admitted into the Union and (2) that the existing generation of slaves would remain such throughout the course of their lives. He was unalterably opposed to the measure so long as it contained these features; and he, therefore, sought to remove them by means of the same policy that Jefferson applied to the territories of the Northwest. Accordingly, he offered an amendment to the effect "that the convention hereinafter provided for, in the Constitution to be framed by it, make provision that from and after the fourth day of July, 1863, within the limits of said State, there shall be neither slavery nor involuntary servitude otherwise than in the punishment of crime, whereof the party shall be duly convicted."[81] A vote on the amendment was requested and ordered but not then taken.

Dissatisfied with the purport of the proposed amendment, Senator Willey expressed his intention to amend the same; whereupon the presiding officer of the Senate proposed that he offer an amendment to the bill rather than to the proposed amendment of Senator Sumner. In the meanwhile, Mr. Hale, of New Hampshire, a member of the committee that framed the bill, affirmed his intention to sustain it. His remarks were suspended by order of the chair for the purpose of considering another matter which had priority to the one then being discussed.

On the motion of Senator Willey the bill was again considered on the first day of July, the question pending being the amendment of Mr. Sumner.[82] In support thereof, Mr. Sumner asserted that from statistics of Mr. Willey it appeared that twelve thousand bondsmen in Western Virginia were doomed to continue as such for the remainder of their lives, and that consequently the Senate must, for a generation, be afflicted with two additional slave-holding members. He quoted from Webster's speech of December 22, 1845, on the admission of Texas into the Union and rested his case on its arguments. Briefly stated, Mr. Webster opposed the admission of other States into the Union as slave States, and at the same time granting to them the inequalities arising from the mode of apportioning representation to Congress, as granted by the Constitution to the original slave-holding States. He held that the free States have the right to demand the abolition of slavery by a commonwealth seeking admission with a slave-holding constitution.[83]

During the continuation of the debate, Mr. Hale asserted that Mr. Webster abandoned the position just attributed to him when in 1850 he voted against any restrictions upon any territory coming into the Union with a slave-holding constitution and when he voted exclusively against applying the "Wilmot Proviso" to these States. Mr. Hale added tersely that since Congress had consistently admitted States with slave-holding constitutions providing for perpetual slavery, it would be the merest folly to refuse to admit the first State whose constitution provided for gradual emancipation.[84]

A new issue was injected into the debate when Mr. Collamer, of Vermont, while reviewing what is implied in being a sovereign State and a State in the Union, argued that the imposition by Congress of any condition precedent to the entrance, whether or not that condition be the abolition of slavery, is an unwarranted interference with the internal affairs of that State. Under such circumstances the proposed new State would not come into the Union on equal footing with other States. He did not wish, however, to be understood as saying that he would not vote against a State desiring to come in as a perpetual slave-holding State; but he failed to see the wisdom or justice in making the abolition of slavery a condition precedent to entrance. On the other hand, he saw no difference, in principle, between the provision in the bill as reported and the amendment offered by Mr. Sumner, since both of them failed to reflect the will of the Convention that framed the State's constitution.[85]

Thereupon Mr. Willey announced that he would offer the following amendment: "That after the fourth day of July, 1863, the children born of slave mothers within the limits of the said State shall be free, and that no law shall be passed by the said State by which any citizen of either of the States of this Union shall be excluded from the enjoyment of the privileges and immunities to which such citizen is entitled under the Constitution of the United States; provided that the convention that ordained the constitution aforesaid, to be reconvened in the manner prescribed in the schedule thereto annexed, shall by a solemn public ordinance declare the assent of the said State to the said fundamental condition, and shall transmit to the President of the United States on or before the 15th of November, 1862, an authentic copy of the said ordinance; upon receipt whereof the President by proclamation shall announce the fact; whereupon and without any further procedure on the part of Congress the admission of the said State into the Union shall be considered as complete."[86]

Throughout the debate that followed there were found many supporters of the program of gradual emancipation for the proposed new State. Chairman Wade, of the Committee of Territories, made thereupon the following important remarks: (1) that the proposed new State had voluntarily fixed the marks of extermination of the institution of slavery; (2) that the principal men of the commonwealth had told him that the first legislature to convene would do away with the whole institution, as fast as the nature of the case would permit; (3) that he believed the efforts of West Virginia were constitutional; (4) that it was just and expedient to admit her; (5) that he did not favor the inclusion in the commonwealth of the pro-slavery counties of the Valley; (6) that he did not want a provision saying that a person born one day should be a slave forever, and that one born the next day should be free; and finally (7) that he would like to see an amendment, providing that "all children who, at the time this constitution takes effect, are fifteen or sixteen years of age, shall be free upon arriving at the age of twenty-one or thirty-five years," i.e., a provision for gradual emancipation that will enable some of those born before as well as all of

185

those born July fourth, 1863, to obtain their freedom.
[87]

Mr. Fessenden, of Maine, prefacing his remarks with the statement that he had not examined the question, proceeded to make the following observations: (1) that he wished to be assured that the State could be admitted constitutionally; (2) that considering the position of the State, the feeling of the people about the matter, the small number of slaves there at the present time, he believed it not only the duty, but the entire right of the body (Congress) to prescribe before the State comes in that she shall put herself in a proper and irreversible position on the subject of the gradual abolition of slavery; (3) that when a definite and fixed date is given for the termination of slavery, the State becomes in point of fact a free State; (4) that he was glad to know (according to Mr. Wade) that the people of West Virginia concurred in opinion with the principles sponsored by himself; and (5) that the interests of the State itself and those of all of the States in the Union demanded an irreversible agreement on the whole matter.[88] Further consideration of the bill was then postponed.

Shortly after an unsuccessful attempt on the part of Mr. Willey to have the consideration of the bill continue,[89] it was brought up again on the fourteenth of July by Senator Wade. The pending question was the amendment of Mr. Sumner. The vote was taken and the amendment was rejected.[90] Mr. Willey then offered the amendment already herein noted. He was followed by Mr. Wade, who, expecting the State to be admitted, if at all, under the amendment of Mr. Willey, moved to amend the amendment by inserting at the proper place the words: "And that all slaves within the State who shall at the aforesaid time be under twenty-one years, shall be free when they arrive at the age of twenty-one

186

years."[91] Despite the anti-slavery principle here involved, Mr. Wade was convinced that some provision was necessary to facilitate the running of the bill in the Senate and in the House. He thought, too, that the harshness and abruptness of the bill would be thereby smoothed down, softened and rendered harmonious.[92]

It was no easy task, however, that the Senator from Ohio had essayed to accomplish. His proposal brought from Mr. Willey the personal conviction of the man. Mr. Willey preferred that the State be admitted under the constitution precisely as submitted by the people. That not being possible, he wished that his amendment (which was not to his personal tastes) be carried. He deplored the situation that would follow should the amendment of Mr. Wade be passed. He pointed out: (1) that the majority of slaves were in counties contiguous to what would be the borders of the old State of Virginia; (2) that many of them ranged in age from one to twenty-one years; (3) that when they should arrive at a convenient age for sale, they would be silently transferred across the border into Kentucky or Virginia or the further South, if needs be, and there sold into the cotton fields of the South or the tobacco plantations of the East, where slavery was admittedly at its worst; (4) that many of the slaves were females, the offspring of whom would be free, were the mothers allowed to remain in the State, but upon the passage of the amendment even those would be doomed to the perpetual slavery of the far South. Replying to an inquiry made by Mr. Lane, of Kansas, as to whether or not public sentiment would condone such action, he asked if public sentiment would be likely to influence those slave owners who lived in territory contiguous to Virginia. The loyalty and fidelity of West Virginia should, in Mr. Willey's opinion, guarantee the safe manner in which the commonwealth would handle the question. Never before in similar situations, he argued, had slaves *in esse* been freed; freedom extended only to those unborn at the passage of the constitution or to those born on or after a date therein designated.[93]

Again joining issue with Senator Willey, Mr. Lane pointed out that the same situation arose in Kansas when in February, 1856, the people adopted a constitution providing for the emancipation of the slaves on the fourth of the following July. The slaves, however, handled the situation. They told their masters that since they should become free after the date designated, they would not permit themselves to be taken out of the State prior to that date.[94] Mr. Lane did not doubt the capacity to do likewise on the part of the slaves then being considered.

An interesting spectacle presented itself when the two Senators from Virginia engaged in spirited debate. Mr. Carlile desired that the State be admitted under the terms of the constitution framed at Wheeling, the alternative being that the people of the State should have the new terms submitted to them for approval. He believed that Mr. Willey's amendment was incomplete as it stood, and that an amendment in conformity with the one presented by Mr. Wade was necessary, providing, of course, that it was the sense of the Senate to admit the State only upon conditions. He took issue with Mr. Willey's assertion that the passage of Mr. Wade's amendment would be followed by a wholesale delivery of slaves to purchasers further South.[95] In the meanwhile Mr. Wade's amendment was agreed to.

Mr. Carlile now began overtly his campaign of obstruction and opposition to the admission of the State into the Union. He offered as an amendment to that of his colleague to be inserted at the end of the sixteenth line, the following words: "After the said

188

ordinance shall be submitted to the vote of the people in the said State of West Virginia and be ratified by the vote of the majority of the people thereof." The sinister motive underlying his proposal was clearly perceived and ably met by Mr. Willey. He opposed the measure: first, because of the unusual requirement of the majority vote of the people, and, second, because of the new convention that would be required to assent to the fundamental proposition, and the consequent new election and additional costs to the people. The constitutional convention, he argued, was still in existence, was still a legal body, and that, therefore, there was no sufficient reason for the reference of the matter beyond the jurisdiction thereof.[96]

Dissatisfied but not discouraged, Mr. Carlile explained away the objection to the words "majority of the people." He maintained, however, that the changes contemplated would affect the fundamental law and that they should, therefore, be ratified by the people subsequent to being assented to by the Convention. It was, he argued, a departure from and in derogation of the customs and ideas of Virginia to change the organic law without first submitting the proposed new law to the people. Setting forth more clearly his position on the whole matter Carlile said: "Supposing —as I suppose, I will see when I move this test amendment, which I shall, to this proposition—that the Senate is unwilling to admit us without conditions, I shall vote against any bill, if it is pressed, exacting conditions, for the purpose of going home to my people asking them to assemble a Convention between this and the first Monday in December, and act upon the suggestion which we have received here from the Senate, if they desire to do so and come here with a constitution that will enable Congress, without such arbitrary stretch of power to admit us at once without delay."[97]

189

It was evident that Carlile was committed to a proslavery program and that his plan, if adopted, would result in the indefinite postponement of the admission of the new State. His colleague, therefore, with an apparently sincere effort to meet the wishes of the Senate and to satisfy the objections of Mr. Carlile, read the bill which was presented in the House by Mr. Brown, of Virginia. At the same time he announced that that bill, if agreeable to the Committee and to his colleagues, would be acceptable to him as a compromise.[98] This assented to, Mr. Willey withdrew his original amendment and offered the Brown bill as a substitute for the whole bill, striking out all after the word "whereas" in the preamble and substituting this measure in lieu of the Committee's bill.[99] The bill as finally presented follows:

"Section 1. That the State of West Virginia be and is hereby declared to be one of the United States of America, and admitted into the Union on an equal footing with the original States in all respects, whatever, and until the next general census shall be entitled to three members in the House of Representatives of the United States: Provided always that this act shall not take effect until after the proclamation of the President of the United States hereinafter provided for.

"Section 2. It being represented to Congress that since the Convention of the 26th of November, 1861, that framed and proposed the Constitution, for the said State of West Virginia, the people thereof have expressed a wish to change the seventh section of the eleventh article of the said Constitution by striking out the same and inserting the following in its place, namely, 'The children of slaves born within the limits of this State after the fourth day of July, 1863, shall be free, and no slave shall be permitted to come into the State for permanent residence therein.' Therefore be it enacted, that whenever the people of West Virginia shall, through their said convention, and by a vote to be taken at an election to be held within the limits of the State at such time as the Convention may provide, make and ratify the change aforesaid and properly certify the same under the hand of the President of the Convention, it shall be lawful for the President of the United States to issue the proclamation stating the fact and thereupon this act shall take effect and be in force from and after sixty days from the date of said proclamation."[100]

It will be observed that the terms of the amendment made no provision for the subsequent freedom of those slaves *in esse*. It was the sense of the committee of the whole, expressed in its action on Mr. Wade's amendment, that a specified class of slaves *in esse* should be given their freedom upon their arrival at a designated age. In conformity with this view, Mr. Lane, of Kansas moved to amend the second section by inserting after the word *free* the following: "And that all slaves within the State who shall at the time aforesaid be under ten years of age shall become free when they arrive at the age of twenty-one years, and all slaves over ten years and under twenty-one years of age, shall become free when they arrive at the age of twenty-five years."[101] This amendment was accepted.

After the passage of the above amendment, Mr. Carlile, persistent in his policy of opposing admission, proposed to amend Mr. Willey's last proposition. His amendment was to the effect that the proposed new State be admitted without conditions. In speaking thereupon, Mr. Willey affirmed that this amendment conformed to his personal views, but that as a matter of good faith and honor he was precluded from espousing its cause.[102] The amendment was

191

rejected.

Following the report of the bill to the Senate and the concurrence of the latter in the compromise amendment of Mr. Willey as amended by Mr. Lane, Mr. Sumner advised that he had proposed to offer to the Senate his amendment lately rejected in Committee. Referring to this proposal, Mr. Lane asserted his assurance that the insertion of the provision in question would cause the bill to fail before the House of Representatives and to merit the disapproval of the people of West Virginia. He urged, therefore, that it would be the better policy to vote for the bill as already amended and to endure slavery in the State for another generation, if need be. Despite the conformity of this view with those of a majority of his colleagues, Mr. Sumner, though declining to offer the amendment, stated his irrevocable opposition to the admission of another slave State, even though the term of slavery be for but twenty-one years. He considered it his duty, therefore, to vote against the measure as it then stood.[103]

The engrossment of the bill for a third reading found its opponents still unweary in their efforts to obstruct or defeat its passage. Senator Trumbull, of Illinois, summed up his opposition to the bill in two objections, namely: (1) since all persons over twenty-one years of age were thereby doomed to perpetual slavery, the new State would be in theory and in practice a slave State; and (2) he failed to see the necessity for or wisdom in dividing any of the old States until the situation could be seen as a whole. He let it be known, however, that this statement should not be construed to commit him to the position of opposing the admission of a slave State under all circumstances whatever. In conformity with his conviction, he moved that all consideration of the bill be postponed until the first Monday of December next. The Senator from Illinois was ably supported by Mr. Carlile, who, failing in his last attempt to amend the bill to the effect that the State should come in without conditions, affirmed his opposition to any proceedings whereby the organic law of a State is framed by Congress and asserted that he would support the Trumbull motion at the risk of misconstruction.[104]

Those Senators who favored the immediate passage of the bill were not unprepared for the most determined attacks of its opponents. Mr. Howard, of Michigan, requested of the Senators from Virginia, whether the Wheeling Legislature had taken any action on the "Joint Resolution passed by Congress suggesting that the so-called border slave States take some action in reference to the final emancipation of their slaves." Replying thereto, Mr. Willey asserted that the Legislature was entirely favorable to a program involving final emancipation. He took occasion, moreover, to add that "his colleague, Mr. Carlile, was misrepresenting the attitude of the legislature that sent him there in interposing the objection that was calculated to thwart the whole movement."[105]

Agreeing with the remarks of Mr. Willey, Mr. Wade, while opposing the motion of Senator Trumbull, explained that Mr. Carlile had penned all the bills and drawn them up; that he was the hardest worker and the most cheerful of them all, that he was the most forceful among them in pressing his views upon the Committee. "Whence," asked he, "came this change of heart? For indeed his conversion was greater than that of St. Paul." "Now," said Mr. Wade, "is the time for West Virginia to be admitted into the Union." "Let us not postpone the action for the next session, but let us reject the motion of the gentleman from Illinois and pass the bill."[106]

Continuing the debate, Mr. Ten Eyck affirmed the legality and the expediency of admitting the new State. His arguments were substantially as follows: (1) that the legal question, that is, the right of the legislature to give assent to the division of the State, was settled when the Senate accepted as members the two men appointed by the said legislature; (2) as a matter of policy he urged that the people of Western Virginia should not be forced to run the risk of having the whole State, because of the collapse of the rebellion, repeal the act of the legislature and thereby continue a domination of tyranny over them. The vote was taken and the motion to postpone was rejected.[107]

The final objection prior to the passage of the bill, came from Mr. Powell, of Kentucky. Asserting, in substance, that since ten of the forty-eight counties to be included in West Virginia were unrepresented in the Convention and in the Legislature, and since less than one-fourth of the people gave their consent to the formation of a new State, he held that there was no constitutional right to act. He was, therefore, unalterably opposed to the admission of the new State. Unswerved from his position, by the assurances of Mr. Willey, that (1) the absence of ten thousand men under arms, and (2) the foregone conclusion that separation would be effected jointly accounted for the small number of nearly nineteen thousand votes, Mr. Powell called for the yeas and nays. The motion was put and the bill to admit was passed.[108]

Even the passage of the bill did not cause Mr. Carlile's opposition to cease. Determined in his efforts to make a final plea for the slave-holding interests, he introduced Senate Bill No. 531[109] supplemental to the act for the admission of West Virginia into the Union and for other purposes. This bill sought, of

194

course, to make effective his plan that the whole work of the Constitutional Convention be reenacted. The bill was reported with amendments and adversely from the Judiciary Committee, whereupon Mr. Carlile sought to have it considered in the Senate. This effort, like his previous ones, was wholly unsuccessful.[110]

While this battle was in progress in the Senate the House also was considering the question. The debate in the Senate on the admission of the proposed new State of West Virginia into the Union hinged largely upon the consideration of the question of slavery. Was the new State to be admitted as a slave State, providing for gradual emancipation? Was it to be admitted on a program of immediate emancipation, or was it to come in with no conditions relating to the disposition of this all-absorbing matter? These were the questions to be determined. They were not altogether the chief considerations in the House.

On the twenty-fifth day of June, 1862, Mr. Brown, of Virginia, by unanimous consent, introduced before the House a bill for the "Admission of West Virginia into the Union and for other purposes." After the first and second readings it was referred to the Committee on Territories.[111] On the sixteenth of July the bill as passed by the Senate was read a first and second time. Mr. Bingham demanded previous question on the passage of the bill; whereupon Mr. Segar, representing a district in Eastern Virginia, objected to a third reading and moved that the bill be laid on the table. On a call for the vote the motion was defeated. On the motion of Roscoe Conkling the consideration of the bill was postponed until the second Tuesday in December, 1862.[112]

The bill came up again for consideration in the House at the time designated, December 9, 1862. Mr. Conway, of Kansas, obtaining the floor through the courtesy of Mr. Bingham, remarked that he had no objection to the erection of a new State in Western Virginia; that he understood that the inhabitants were thoroughly loyal; that they were opposed to slavery; and that they would make a powerful and prosperous State. Despite these considerations, he was not prepared to adhere to the program of admission. He objected, therefore, that the application had not come up in the proper constitutional form. The commonwealth was not organized into a territorial form of government, and so, said he, no enabling act could be passed. The constitutional provision that no State may be divided without the assent of the legislature thereof was not, in his opinion, adhered to. He questioned the legitimacy of the so-called "Restored Government of Virginia" after a part of the State had seceded from the Union.[113] It was his contention that the failure of the State government caused the sovereignty of the State to accrue to the Federal Government. Any application for admission into the Union, on the part of West Virginia, should proceed on this theory.[114]

Replying to these arguments, Mr. Brown, of Virginia, claimed constitutional regularity of procedure in forming the new State and in seeking to have it admitted into the Union. He referred to the case of Kentucky as a precedent, attempting thereby to show the competency of Congress to admit a State formed within the jurisdiction of another. He pointed out that the Senate, the House, the Executive Department of the United States Government and a State Court in Ohio had, all, by their several acts and relationships with the Wheeling Legislature recognized it to be the legal legislature of Virginia. Discussing the original powers of the people, Mr. Brown asserted "that the principle was laid down in the Declaration of Independence that the legislative powers of the people cannot be annihilated; that when the

196

functionaries to whom they are entrusted become incapable of exercising them, they revert to the people, who have the right to exercise them in their primitive and original capacity." "When, therefore, the government of old Virginia capitulated to the Confederacy," said he, "the loyal people of Western Virginia acted in accordance with the directing principle of the Declaration of Independence."[115]

Conforming to the opinion of Mr. Brown, Mr. Colfax urged the admission of the proposed new State, "because in their constitution, the people provided for the ultimate extinction of slavery."[116] Among other speakers urging the admission of the new State were Edwards, Blair, Stevens, and Bingham. Edwards asserted that the two questions presented had to do with (1) the constitutional power of Congress to admit the State and (2) the question of expediency. Blair, while urging the admission of the new State, took occasion to inform Mr. Crittenden, of Kentucky, that the people of the proposed new State of West Virginia had bound themselves to pay a just proportion of the public debt owed by the State of Virginia, prior to the passage of the Ordinance of Secession. Thaddeus Stevens held that the act of the legislature of Virginia assenting to the division of the State was invalid as such, but that West Virginia might be admitted under the absolute power that the laws of war give to Congress under such circumstances. "The Union," he said, "can never be restored under the Constitution as it was," and with his consent, it could never be restored with slavery to be protected by it. He was in favor of admitting West Virginia because he "found in her constitution a provision which would make her a free state."[117]

Perhaps no man in the House opposed more vigorously the admission of the State under the bill being considered than did Mr. Segar. According to his point of view, the people of the proposed new State had made a pro-slavery constitution; they had retained their former slave status, merely prohibiting the coming in for permanent residence of additional slaves and free Negroes. The bill presented here, he argued, requires them to strike out the provision that they have seen fit to make with reference to slavery; Congress has made for them a constitution of fast emancipation, one of virtual anti-slavery variety. "This," said he, "is nothing less than a flagrant departure from the doctrine that the States may of right manage their domestic affairs and fashion their institutions as they will."[118] During the course of his remarks, he found occasion to deny the constitutionality of the legislature, by whose authority he held his seat in Congress.

Concluding the debate, Mr. Bingham, who had advocated the admission of the State throughout the course of its consideration by the House, summed up in succinct form, first, the positions taken by the preceding speakers; and second, citations and arguments to show the constitutionality of the proceedings. Continuing, he urged the expediency of admission; he asserted that the chief objection to admission on the part of most of the gentlemen opposed was that, thereby, a new slave State would be admitted into the Union; and finally he trusted that the bill would pass, because his confidence in the people of Western Virginia had convinced him that they would not only ratify the provision for gradual emancipation, but would avail themselves of the opportunity afforded by the President's proclamation to bring about the immediate or ultimate emancipation of every slave within the State. On motion, the roll was called and the bill was passed by a vote of 96 to 55.[119]

On the twenty-third day of December, President

198

Lincoln requested the written opinion of the members of his cabinet on the Act for the admission of West Virginia into the Union, first, as[120] to its constitutionality and second, as to its expediency. Of the six members who replied, Messrs. Seward, Chase and Stanton decided that the measure was both constitutional and expedient; whereas Welles, Blair and Bates decided that it was neither constitutional nor expedient.[121] In the meanwhile, Governor Pierpont of the Restored Government of Virginia sent to the President a message urging upon him the absolute and complete necessity for his assent to the measure.[122]

The decision of the President was awaited with anxiety. Without underestimating the importance attaching to the opinions of his advisors, it was evident that Mr. Lincoln's opinion was all-important. Characteristic of the President, and despite the wealth of opinion and advice at his command, he found his own reasons for concluding that the act was both constitutional and expedient. Not the least important one among these reasons was the fact that "the admission of the new State would turn just that much slave soil to free."[123]

After the signing of the bill by the President and in conformity with the requirements of the amended constitution, the constitutional convention reassembled for the purpose of approving the gradual emancipation amendment inserted by Congress. Completing its work in a session of eight days, the Convention adjourned on the twentieth day of February. On the twenty-sixth day of March the people adopted the amendment; 27,749 voted for ratification and 572 for rejection. Certification of the election results was made to Governor Pierpont, who forthwith communicated the fact to the President of the United States. On the twentieth day of April,

President Lincoln issued his proclamation relating to the admission of the State of West Virginia into the Union, the same to take effect sixty days from date thereof. Accordingly, therefore, on the twentieth day of June, 1863, the commonwealth of West Virginia formally entered into the Union as a State, the first one to do so with a constitution providing for the gradual emancipation of any class of slaves within the limits of its territory.[124]

ALRUTHEUS A. TAYLOR.

FOOTNOTES:

[1] Hall, *The Rending of Virginia*, 13.

[2] *Ibid.*, 13.

[3] Ambler, *Sectionalism in Virginia*, 1776-1861, 1-3.

[4] Hall, *The Rending of Virginia*, 30.

[5] *Ibid.*, 30.

[6] Ambler, *Sectionalism in Virginia*, 1776-1861, 137.

[7] Hall, *The Rending of Virginia*, 42.

[8] Ambler, *Sectionalism in Virginia*, 1776-1861, 137.

[9] Ambler, *Sectionalism in Virginia*, 1776-1861.

[10] *Ibid.*, 169.

[11] *Ibid.*, 140, 141.

[12] Hall, *The Rending of Virginia*, 38.

[13] *Ibid.*, 47.

[14] Hall, *The Rending of Virginia*, 45.

[15] Ambler, *Sectionalism in Virginia*, 187.

[16] Ambler, *Sectionalism in Virginia*, 186.

[17] *Ibid.*, 189.

[18] *Ibid.*, 192.

[19] *Ibid.*, 1776-1861, 192.

[20] Ambler, *Sectionalism in Virginia*, 200.

[21] *Ibid.*, 201.

[22] Ambler, *Sectionalism in Virginia*, 202.

[23] *Ibid.*, 202.

[24] *Ibid.*, 244.

[25] Ambler, *Sectionalism in Virginia*, 245.

[26] *Ibid.*, 1776-1861, 251.

[27] *Ibid.*, 251-252.

[28] Ambler, *Sectionalism in Virginia*, 253.

[29] *Ibid.*, 253.

[30] Ambler, *Sectionalism in Virginia*, 262.

[31] *Ibid.*, 264.

[32] *Ibid.*, 265.

[33] *Ibid.*, 1776-1861, 266.

[34] Ambler, *Sectionalism in Virginia*, 266.

[35] *Ibid.*, 267.

[36] *Ibid.*, 268.

[37] Hall, *The Rending of Virginia*, 62.

[38] Ambler, *Sectionalism in Virginia*, 1776-1861, 269.

[39] *Ibid.*, 269.

[40] Ambler, *Sectionalism in Virginia*, 311.

[41] Hall, *The Rending of Va.*, 60.

[42] *Ibid.*, 61.

[43] Ambler, *Sectionalism in Va.*, 1776-1861, 301.

[44] Hall, *The Rending of Va.*, 60.

[45] Lewis, *How W. Va. Was Made*, 8.

[46] *Ibid.*, 10.

[47] *Ibid.*, 14.

[48] *Ibid.*, 19.

[49] Lewis, *How W. Va. Was Made*, 63.

[50] *Ibid.*, 41.

[51] *Ibid.*, 45.

[52] *Ibid.*, 48.

[53] Lewis, *How W. Va. Was Made*, 63.

[54] *Ibid.*, 64.

[55] *Ibid.*, 83.

[56] *Ibid.*, 108.

[57] *Ibid.*, 86.

[58] *Ibid.*, 92.

[59] *Ibid.*, 139.

[60] Lewis, *How W. Va. Was Made*, 284.

[61] *Ibid.*, 318.

[62] *Ibid.*, 318.

[63] Hall, *The Rending of Va.*, 396.

[64] *Ibid.*, 396.

[65] Hall, *The Rending of Va.*, 416.

[66] *Ibid.*, 416.

[67] Hall, *The Rending of Virginia*, 417.

[68] *Ibid.*, 418.

[69] Hall, *The Rending of Va.*, 418.

[70] *Ibid.*, 419.

[71] Hall, *The Rending of Virginia*, 421.

[72] Hall, *The Rending of Virginia*, 421-429.

[73] *Ibid.*, 439.

[74] Lewis, *How W. Va. Was Made*, 322.

[75] *Ibid.*, 323.

[76] Hall, *Rending of Va.*, p. 440.

[77] Hall, *The Rending of Virginia*, 440-456.

[78] Lewis, *How W. Va. Was Made*, 325.

[79] *Congressional Globe*, Pt. 3, 2nd Session, 37th Congress, 1861-62, 2864.

[80] *Ibid.*, Pt. 4 and App. 2nd Session, 37th Congress, 1861-62, 2941.

[81] *Ibid.*, Pt. 4 and App. 37th Cong., 2nd Session, 1861-62, 2941.

[82] *Congressional Globe*, 2942.

[83] *Ibid.*, 3034.

[84] *Ibid.*, 3034.

[85] *Congressional Globe*, 3035.

[86] *Ibid.*, 3036.

[87] *Congressional Globe*, Pt. 4 and App. 2nd Session of 37th Congress, 1861-62, 3038.

[88] *Congressional Globe*, 3038.

[89] *Ibid.*, 3134-3135.

[90] *Ibid.*, 3308.

[91] *Ibid.*, 3308.

[92] *Ibid.*, 3308.

[93] *Congressional Globe*, Pt. 4 and App. 2nd Session, 37th Cong., 1861-62, 3308.

[94] *Ibid.*, 3309.

[95] *Congressional Globe*, 3309.

[96] *Ibid.*, 3310.

[97] *Congressional Globe*, 3311.

[98] *Ibid.*, Pt. 4 and App. 2nd Sess., 37th Cong., 1861-62, 3314.

[99] *Ibid.*, 3315.

[100] *Congressional Globe*, 3316.

[101] *Congressional Globe*, 3316.

[102] *Ibid.*, 3316.

[103] *Ibid.*, 3316.

[104] *Congressional Globe*, Pt. 4 and App. 2nd Session, 37th Cong., 1861-62, 3317.

[105] *Ibid.*, 3317-3320.

[106] *Congressional Globe*, 3317-3320.

[107] *Ibid.*, 3320.

[108] *Ibid.*, 3320.

[109] *Congressional Globe*, Pt. 2, 3rd Session, 37th Cong., 1862-63, 952.

[110] *Ibid.*, 1302.

[111] *Ibid.*, Pt. 4 and App. 2nd Session, 37th Cong., 1861-62, 2933.

[112] *Congressional Globe*, 3397.

[113] *Ibid.*, Pt. 1, 3rd Session, 37th Cong., 37.

[114] Hall, *The Rending of Va.*, 474.

[115] Hall, *The Rending of Virginia*, 475.

[116] *Cong. Globe*, Pt. 1, 3rd Session, 37th Congress, 43.

[117] *Congressional Globe*, 47-57.

[118] *Ibid.*, 54.

[119] *Congressional Globe*, Pt. 1, 3rd Session, 37th Cong., 1862-63, 58.

[120] Hall, *The Rending of Virginia*, 485.

[121] *Ibid.*, 490-494.

[122] *Ibid.*, 488.

[123] *Ibid.*, 496.

[124] Lewis, *How W. Va. Was Made*, 330-334.

CANADIAN NEGROES AND THE JOHN BROWN RAID

Canada and Canadians were intimately connected with the most dramatic incident in the slavery struggle prior to the opening of the Civil War, the attack of John Brown and his men on the federal arsenal at Harper's Ferry, Virginia, on the night of Sunday, October 16, 1859. The blow that Brown struck at slavery in this attack had been planned on broad lines in Canada more than a year before at a convention held in Chatham, Ontario, May 8-10, 1858. In calling this convention in Canada, Brown doubtless had two objects in view: to escape observation and to interest the Canadian Negroes in his plans for freeing their enslaved race on a scale never before dreamed of and in a manner altogether new. It was Brown's idea to gather a band of determined and resourceful men, to plant them somewhere in the Appalachian mountains near slave territory and from their mountain fastness to run off the slaves, ever extending the area of operations and eventually settling the Negroes in the territory that they had long tilled for others. He believed that operations of this kind would soon demoralize slavery in the South and he counted upon getting enough help from Canada to give the initial impetus.

What went on at Chatham in May, 1858, is fairly definitely known. Brown came to Chatham on April 30 and sent out invitations to what he termed "a quiet convention ... of true friends of freedom," requesting attendance on May 10. The sessions were held on May 8th and 10th, Saturday and Monday, and were attended by twelve white men and thirty-three Negroes. William C. Munroe, a colored preacher, acted as chairman. Brown himself made the opening and principal speech of the convention, outlining plans for carrying on a guerilla warfare against the whites, which would free the slaves, who might afterwards be settled in the more mountainous districts. He expected that many of the free Negroes in the Northern States would flock to his standard, that slaves in the South would do the same, and that some of the free Negroes in Canada would also accompany him.

The main business before the convention was the adoption of a constitution for the government of Brown's black followers in the carrying out of his weird plan of forcible emancipation. Copies of the constitution were printed after the close of the Chatham gathering and furnished evidence against Brown and his companions when their plans came to ground and they were tried in the courts of Virginia. Brown himself was elected commander-in-chief, J. H. Kagi was named secretary of war, George B. Gill, secretary of the treasury, Owen Brown, one of his sons, treasurer, Richard Realf, secretary of state, and Alfred M. Ellsworth and Osborn Anderson, colored, were named members of Congress.

It was more than a year before Brown could proceed to the execution of his plan. Delays of various kinds had upset his original plans, but early in June, 1859, he went to Harper's Ferry with three companions and rented a farm near that town. Others joined them at intervals until at the time of their raid he had eighteen followers, four of whom were Negroes. The story of the attack and its failure need not be told here. It is sufficient to say that when the fighting ended on Tuesday morning, October 18, John Brown himself was wounded and a prisoner; ten of his party, including two of his sons, were dead, and the others were fugitives from justice. Brown was given a preliminary examination on October 25th and on the following day was brought to trial at Charlestown. Public sentiment in Virginia undoubtedly called for a speedy trial, but there was evidence of panicky feeling in the speed with which John Brown was rushed to punishment. On Monday, October 31, the jury, after 45 minutes' deliberation, returned a verdict of guilty of treason, conspiracy with slaves to rebel and murder in the first degree. On November 2nd, sentence was pronounced, that Brown should be hanged on December 2nd. As the trap dropped under him that day, Col. Preston, who commanded the military escort, pronounced the words: "So perish all such enemies of Virginia. All such enemies of the Union. All such foes of the human race." That was the unanimous sentiment of Virginia. But in the North Longfellow wrote in his journal: "This will be a great date in our history; the date of a new revolution, quite as much needed as the old one."[1] And Thoreau declared: "Some 1800 years ago Christ was crucified; this morning, perchance, Captain Brown was hung. These are the two ends of a chain that is not without its links."[2]

John Brown's raid on Harper's Ferry made a profound impression in Canada. Although the Chatham convention had been secret there were some Canadians who knew that Brown was meditating a bold stroke and could see at once the connection between Chatham and Harper's Ferry. The raid was reported in detail in the Canadian press and widely commented upon editorially. In a leading article extending over more than one column of its issue of November 4, 1859, *The Globe*, of Toronto, points out that the execution of Brown will but serve to make him remembered as "a brave man who perilled property, family, life itself, for an alien race." His death, continued the editor, would make the raid valueless as political capital for the South, which might expect other Browns to arise. References in this article to the Chatham convention indicate that George Brown, editor of *The Globe*, knew what had been going on in Canada in May, 1858. Three weeks later, *The Globe*, with fine discernment, declared that if the tension between north and south continued, civil war would be inevitable and "no force that the south can raise can hold the slaves if the north wills that they be free."[3] On the day of Brown's execution *The Globe* said: "His death will aid in awakening the north to that earnest spirit which can alone bring the south to understand its true position," and added that it was a "rare sight to witness the ascent of this fine spirit out of the money-hunting, cotton-worshipping American world."[4] Once again, with insight into American affairs it predicted that "if a Republican president is elected next year, nothing short of a dissolution of the union will satisfy them" (the cotton States).

The special interest taken by *The Globe* in American affairs and its sane comment on the developments in the slavery struggle were due to George Brown's understanding of the situation, resulting from his residence for a time under the stars and stripes before coming to Canada. The feeling of the public in Toronto over the execution of John Brown was shown by the large memorial service held in St. Lawrence Hall on Dec. 11, 1859, at which the chief speaker was Rev. Thomas M. Kinnaird, who had himself attended the Chatham convention.[5] In his address Mr. Kinnaird referred to a talk he had had with Brown, in which the latter said that he intended to do something definite for the liberation of the slaves or perish in the attempt. The collection that was taken up at this meeting was forwarded to Mrs. Brown. At Montreal a great mass meeting was held in St. Bonaventure Hall, attended by over one thousand people, at which resolutions of sympathy were passed. Among those on the platform at this meeting were L. H. Holton, afterwards a member of the Brown-Dorion and Macdonald-Dorion administrations, and John Dougall, founder of *The Montreal Witness*. At Chatham and other places in the western part of the province similar meetings were held.

The slave-holding States were by no means blind to the amount of support and encouragement that was coming from Canada for the abolitionists.[6] They were quite aware that Canada itself had an active abolitionist group. They probably had heard of the Chatham convention; they knew of it, at least, as soon as the raid was over. In his message to the legislature of Virginia immediately after the Harper's Ferry incident Governor Wise made direct reference to the anti-slavery activity in Canada. "This was no result of ordinary crimes," he declared. "... It was an extraordinary and actual invasion, by a sectional organization, specially upon slaveholders and upon their property in negro slaves.... A provisional government was attempted in a British province, by our own countrymen, united to us in the faith of confederacy, combined with Canadians, to invade the slave-holding states ... for the purpose of stirring up universal insurrection of slaves throughout the whole south."[7]

Speaking further of what he conceived to be the spirit of the North he said: "It has organized in Canada and traversed and corresponded thence to New Orleans and from Boston to Iowa. It has established spies everywhere, and has secret agents in the heart of every slave state, and has secret associations and 'underground railroads' in every free state."[8]

Speaking on December 22, 1859, to a gathering of medical students who had left Philadelphia, Governor Wise is quoted as saying: "With God's help we will drive all the disunionists together back into Canada. Let the compact of fanaticism and intolerance be confined to British soil."[9] *The New York Herald* quoted Governor Wise as calling upon the President to notify the British Government that Canada should no longer be allowed, by affording an asylum to fugitive slaves, to foster disunion and dissension in the United States. Wise even seems to have had the idea that the President might be bullied into provoking trouble with Great Britain over this question. "The war shall be carried into Canada," he said in one of his outbursts.[10]

Sympathy for the South was shown in the comment of a part of the Tory press in Canada, *The Leader* declaring that Brown's attack on Harper's Ferry was an "insane raid" and predicting that the South would sacrifice the union before submitting to such spoliation.[11] The viewpoint of *The Leader* and its readers may be further illustrated by its declaration that the election campaign of 1860 was dominated by a "small section of ultra-abolitionists who make anti-slavery the beginning, middle and end of their creed." As for Lincoln he was characterized as "a mediocre man and a fourth-rate lawyer,"[12] but then some of the prominent American newspapers made quite as mistaken an estimate of Lincoln at that time.

The collapse of John Brown's great adventure at Harper's Ferry furnished complete proof to the South of Canada's relation to that event. The seizure of his papers and all that they told, the evidence at the trial at Charlestown and the evidence secured by the Senatorial Committee which investigated the affair, all confirmed the suspicion that in the British provinces to the north there was extensive plotting against the slavery system. The Senatorial Committee declared in its findings that the proceedings at Chatham had had as their object "to subvert the government of one or more of the States, and, of course, to that extent the government of the United States."[13] Questions were

211

asked of the witnesses before the investigating committee which showed that in the minds of the members of that committee there was a distinctly Canadian end to the Harper's Ferry tragedy.[14] Their suspicions may have been further confirmed by the fact that Brown's New England confederates, Sanborn, Stearns and Howe, all fled to Canada immediately after the raid.

In the actual events at Harper's Ferry the assistance given by Canada was small. Of the men who marched out with Brown on that fateful October night only one could in any way be described as a Canadian. This was Osborn Perry Anderson, a Negro born free in Pennsylvania. He was working as a printer in Chatham at the time of the convention and threw in his lot with Brown. He was one of those who escaped at Harper's Ferry. He later wrote an account of the affair, served during the latter part of the Civil War in the northern army and died at Washington in 1871. He is described by Hinton as "well educated, a man of natural dignity, modest, simple in character and manners."[15]

There naturally arises the question, why was the aid given John Brown by the Canadian Negroes so meagre? That Brown had counted on considerable help in his enterprise from the men who joined with him in drafting the "provisional constitution" is certain. John Edwin Cook, one of Brown's close associates, declared in his confession made after Harper's Ferry, that "men and money had both been promised from Chatham and other parts of Canada."[16] Yet, apart from Anderson, a Negro, only one other Canadian of either color seems to have had any share in the raid. Dr. Alexander Milton Ross went to Richmond, Virginia, before the blow was struck, as he had promised Brown he would do, and was there when word came of its unhappy ending. Brown evidently counted on Ross being able to keep him in touch with developments at the capital of Virginia.

Chatham had been chosen as the place of meeting with special reference to the effect it might have on the large Negro population resident in the immediate vicinity. There were more Negroes within fifty miles of Chatham than in any other section of Canadian territory and among them were men of intelligence, education and daring, some of them experienced in slave raiding. Brown was justified in expecting help from them. There is also evidence that among the Negroes themselves there existed a secret organization, known under various names, having as its object to assist fugitives and resist their masters. Help from this organization was also expected.[17] Hinton says that Brown "never expected any more aid from them than that which would give a good impetus."[18] John Brown himself is quoted by Realf, one of his associates, as saying that he expected aid from the Negroes generally, both in Canada and the United States,[19] but it must be remembered that his plans called for quality rather than quantity of assistance. A few daring men, planted in the mountains of Virginia, would have accomplished his initial purpose better than a thousand.

The real reason why the Canadian Negroes failed to respond in the summer of 1860 when Brown's men were gathering near the boundary line of slavery seems to be that too great a delay followed after the Chatham convention. The convention was held on May 8 and 10, 1858; but Brown did not attack Harper's Ferry until the night of October 16, 1859, nearly a year and a half later. The zeal for action that manifested itself in May, 1858, had cooled off by October, 1859, the magnetic influence of Brown himself had been withdrawn, and the Negroes had entered into new engagements. Frank B. Sanborn says he understood from Brown that he hoped to

213

strike about the middle of May of 1858, that is about a week after the convention or as soon as his forces could gather at the required point.[20] The delay was caused by the partial exposure of Brown's plans to Senator Henry Wilson by Hugh Forbes, who had been close to Brown. Panic seized Brown's chief white supporters in New England, the men who financed his various operations, and they decided that the plans must be changed. Brown was much discouraged by their decision, but being dependent upon them for support in his work he submitted and went west to Kansas. Among his exploits there was the running off of more than a dozen slaves whom he landed safely at Windsor, Canada.

There was some effort made in the early summer of 1859 to enlist the support of the Canadian Negroes, [21] the mission being in charge of John Brown, Jr., who was assisted by Rev. J. W. Loguen, a well-known Negro preacher and anti-slavery worker. Together they visited Hamilton, St. Catharines, Chatham, London, Buxton and Windsor, helping also to organize branches of the League of Liberty among the Negroes. The letters of John Brown, Jr., show that there was little enthusiasm for the cause, which, indeed, could only have been presented in an indefinite way. There was more interest at Chatham than elsewhere, as might be expected, but even there it was not sufficiently substantial to bring the men that were needed. Against this rather dismal picture should be placed some evidence that there were a few Canadians on the way South when the end came.[22]

FRED LANDON.

214

FOOTNOTES:

[1] Longfellow, *Life of Longfellow*, vol. II, p. 347.

[2] Thoreau, *A Plea for Capt. John Brown, read at Concord, October 30, 1859*.

[3] *Toronto Weekly Globe*, Nov. 25, 1859.

[4] *Ibid.*, Dec. 9, 1859, and Dec. 16, 1859.

[5] *Toronto Weekly Globe*, Dec. 12, 1859.

[6] "There is no country in the world so much hated by slaveholders as Canada," Ward, *Autobiography of a Fugitive Negro*, London, 1855, p. 158.

[7] *Journal of the Senate of Virginia*, 1859, see pp. 9-25.

[8] *The Toronto Weekly Globe* of Dec. 6, 1859, reported Governor Wise as saying: "One most irritating feature of this predatory war is that it has its seat in the British provinces which furnish asylum for our fugitives and send them and their hired outlaws upon us from depots and rendezvous in the bordering states."

[9] *Toronto Weekly Globe*, Dec. 28, 1859.

[10] *Toronto Weekly Globe*, Dec. 28, 1859.

[11] *Ibid.*, Dec. 23, 1859.

[12] *Ibid.*, July 20, 1860.

[13] *Harper's Ferry Invasion, Report of Senatorial Committee*, pp. 2 and 7.

[14] *Harper's Ferry Invasion, Report of Senatorial Committee*, p. 99.

[15] Hinton, *John Brown and His Men*, pp. 504-507.

[16] *Ibid.*, appendix, p. 704. See also report of Senatorial Committee, p. 97.

[17] Hinton, *John Brown and His Men*, pp. 171-172.

[18] *Ibid.*, p. 175.

[19] *Report of Senatorial Committee*, p. 97.

[20] Sanborn, *Life and Letters of John Brown*, pp. 457-8.

[21] Sanborn, *Life and Letters of John Brown*, pp. 536-538, 547.

[22] Hinton, *John Brown and His Men*, pp. 261-263.

THE NEGRO AND THE SPANISH PIONEER IN THE NEW WORLD

Negro slaves probably made their first appearance in the New World in 1502. Those who came in the beginning were Christians and personal servants of masters who had acquired them in Spain, but soon afterwards, thanks to the influence of the religious order of *Predicatores* and of the more famous Las Casas, they began to be introduced directly from Africa, in order that the sufferings of the Indians who were dying out under the Spanish system of forced labor might be alleviated.[1] By the close of the second decade of the sixteenth century no inconsiderable number had been brought over, and a perusal of the early accounts of the exploits of the *Conquistadores* will reveal the fact that the Negro participated in the exploration and occupation of nearly every important region from New Mexico to Chile. As personal attendants of the Spanish Pioneers, as burden-bearers and drudges connected with exploration and the founding of colonies, they played an indispensable though inconspicuous rôle in one of the greatest achievements which history records. Such accounts of their service as have been preserved are, for the most part, accidental: only when he performed an act of unusual heroism or connected himself with a strange or humorous occurrence was the Negro's name placed alongside of that of his Spanish master where it is destined to remain for all time.

When Balboa set out from Darién on the tour of exploration which resulted in the discovery of the South Sea, at least one Negro, Nufio de Olano, was numbered in his party. Three years later, when the timbers for the four boats with which he intended to explore the Pacific had been prepared, thirty Negroes were among those who carried them piece by piece over mountain and jungle from Acla to San Miguel. Moreover, when Balboa's successor constructed the first highway from ocean to ocean he made use of Negro labor along with that of the Indian.[2]

Hernán Cortés carried with him from Cuba not only Indian servants but Negro slaves who helped to drag along the artillery which he used to strike mortal terror into the Indians of Mexico. There has been preserved a list of those who set out on this famous expedition, and among the names are those of two Negroes, one of whom Saco claims to have been the first to sow and reap small grain in Mexico. Moreover, two Negroes were among the company sent out by Velásquez in 1520 to punish Cortés for his insubordination. One of these has the unenviable distinction of having introduced smallpox among the Mexican Indians. The other, who seems to have observed the fight between the men of the agent of Velásquez (Narváez) from the safe and comfortable distance of a neighboring tree, has, because of some witty and flattering remarks which he made to Cortés, received the honor of a paragraph in the *Decades* of Herrera.[3]

It is not definitely known whether Pedro de Alvarado, one of the bravest and most gallant lieutenants of Cortés, carried Negroes with him into Guatemala in 1523, but it is certain that eleven years later, when his ambition and love of gain led him to fit out that ill-fated expedition to Quito, he saw fit to include in the company two hundred black slaves, most of whom perished while making their way through the blinding snows of the Andes.[4]

It is certain, moreover, that several Negroes were along with the *Conquistadores* of Perú and Chile. The contract of Francisco Pizarro permitted him to introduce fifty Negroes into Perú free of duty; and even before this, Negroes had accompanied those who had spied out the land. In 1525, when Diego de Almagro effected a landing near the port of Quemado, on the west coast of South America, and attempted to penetrate the adjacent country, he encountered rather severe opposition from the Indians of the section. During the resulting skirmish one of his eyes was crushed by a dart and he was saved from captivity and death only by the valiant succor of his Negro slave. A year later, the debarkation of a Spaniard and his slave at Tumbez resulted in an amusing occurrence which once more gave the Negro a few brief sentences in the *Decades*. Astonished at the color of his face, the natives of the region had him wash time after time in order to see if the black would disappear; and the Negro, true to his good nature and love of a joke, complied willingly while he grinned so as to display his pearly white teeth.[5]

Several Negroes assisted the Yanaconas Indians in carrying the baggage of Diego de Almagro and Rodrigo Orgoñez during their perilous journey along the frozen Andes from Cuzco to Chile; and many of them perished on the way.[6] Moreover, upon at least one occasion the forces of the great conqueror of Chile, Pedro Valdivia himself, would probably have been destroyed, had it not been for the cool-headed alertness of Captain Gonzalo de los Rios and a Negro who managed to procure the saddle-horses of the Spaniards as soon as they saw a band of Indians dart from their hiding places.[7]

Numerous African slaves were along with the Spanish pioneers in Venezuela. Ortal, Sedeño, and Heredia each had permission to introduce one hundred Negroes to build fortresses and search for mines; and in 1537, when the licentiate Vadillo came to Cartagena to hold the residencia of Heredia, he brought down a large number who later accompanied him on the luckless excursions which he undertook apparently in the hope of finding the mines of Perú.[8]

But of all the members of the colored race who accompanied the Spaniards upon their explorations in the New World, it may be doubted whether any played so conspicuous a part as did Estevánico, or Estévan, an Arabian black from Azamor, in Morocco, and the slave of Andrés Dorantes de Carrança. He was a member and one of the survivors of the ill-fated expedition of Pánfilo de Narváez which went to pieces somewhere on the southern coast of the United States, (1528). For six years he was a captive and slave among the Indians of Texas where, in company with others of the expedition who had escaped with their lives, he effected miraculous cures. He was one of the three companions of Cabeza de Vaca on his historic journey across the continent from the Gulf of Mexico to Culiacán. From Culiacán he accompanied De Vaca and his companions to Mexico City, where he was honored by being made the slave of the viceroy, Antonio de Mendoza.

Surely these were rare and noteworthy experiences for a member of the black race, but still greater things awaited Estévan. He was destined ere he met his tragic fate to accompany the expedition which resulted in the discovery of New Mexico and Arizona. The party which, besides the Negro, consisted of three Spaniards—Fray Marcos de Niza, a lay brother, and Fray Onorato—and several Pima Indians, set out from Culiacán on March 7, 1539. They were in search of the famed Seven Cities.

After proceeding northward several days, Fray Marcos decided to rest while he dispatched the Negro to reconnoiter. He directed Estévan to advance to the north several leagues, and in case he discovered indications of a rich and populous country, to return in person or await his coming, sending back, by some of the Pimas who were to accompany him, a cross the size of which should be in proportion to the importance of the information gained. Four days passed, and then the messengers of Estévan returned bearing a cross "as high as a man" and the news that the Negro had discovered "the greatest thing in the world." Fray Marcos hastened to follow in the footsteps of Estévan hoping to overtake him soon, but his efforts were vain. The dusky adventurer could not resist the temptation to proceed and win for himself the honor of conquering the rich country.

This country concerning which such glowing reports had reached Estévan was none other than the land of the Pueblo Indians. His procedure after separating from Fray Marcos is thus narrated by a contemporary, though not an eyewitness:

"After Estevan had left the friars, he thought he could get all the reputation and honor himself, and that if he should discover these settlements with such famous high houses, alone, he would be considered bold and courageous. So he proceeded with the people who had followed him, and attempted to cross the wilderness which lies between the country he had passed through and Cibola, ... [He] reached Cibola loaded with the large quantity of turquoises they [the Indians along the route] had given him and some beautiful women whom the Indians who followed him and carried his things were taking with them and had given him. These had followed him from all the settlements he had passed, believing that under his protection they could traverse the whole world without any danger. But as the people in this country were more intelligent than those who followed Estevan, they lodged him in a little hut they had outside their village, and the older men and governors heard his story and took steps to find out the reason he had come to that country. The account which the Negro gave them of two white men who were following him, sent by a great lord, who knew about the things in the sky, and how these were coming to instruct them in divine matters, made them think that he must be a spy or a guide from some nations who wished to come and conquer them, because it seemed to them unreasonable to say that the people were white in the country from which he came and that he was sent by them, he being black. Besides these other reasons, they thought it was hard of him to ask them for turquoises and women, and so they decided to kill him. They did this, but they did not kill any of those who went with him...."[9]

From this and other contemporary sources, Lowery[10] has constructed a more complete and lively picture of Estévan's last days. Lowery says that "he travelled with savage magnificence, gaily dressed with bells and feathers fastened about his arms and legs. He carried with him a gourd decorated with bells and two feathers, one white and the other red. This gourd he sent before him by messengers as a symbol of authority and to command obedience, as he had seen successfully done in the western part of Texas, when in company with Cabeza de Vaca.... As soon as they had delivered the gourd to the chief [of the pueblo] and he had observed the bells he became very angry," and ordered Estévan and his party to depart at once. But the Negro was persistent. He and his retinue lodged just outside the walls of the Pueblo of Hawaikuh. Early the next morning they were attacked by a large band of warriors from the Pueblo and Estévan was killed while attempting to make his escape.

There has been preserved among the legends of the Zuñi Pueblos of New Mexico one which apparently dates back to the coming of Estévan, the Black Mexican from the south. The scene of his death is placed at Kiakima, and the single Black Mexican has been magnified into many, but the legend is nevertheless interesting and significant.

"It is to be believed that a long time ago, when roofs lay over the walls of Kya-ki-me, when smoke hung over the housetops, and the ladder rounds were still unbroken in Kya-ki-me, then the Black Mexicans came from their abodes in Everlasting Summerland. One day, unexpectedly, out of Hemlock Cañon they came, and descended to Kya-ki-me. But when they said they would enter the covered way, it seems that our ancients looked not gently at them; for with these Black Mexicans came many Indians of So-no-li, as they call it now, ... who were enemies of our ancients. Therefore, these our ancients, being always bad-tempered, and quick to anger, made fools of themselves after their fashion, rushing into their town and out of their town, shouting, skipping and shooting with their sling-stones and arrows and tossing their war-clubs. Then the Indians of So-no-li set up a great howl, and thus they and our ancients did much ill to one another. Then and thus was killed by our ancients, right where the stone stands down by the arroyo of Kya-ki-me, one of the Black Mexicans, a large man, with chilli lips [*i.e.*, lips swollen from eating chilli peppers], and some of the Indians they killed, catching others. Then the rest ran away, chased by our grandfathers, and went back toward their country in the Land of Everlasting Summer...." [11]

J. FRED RIPPY.

FOOTNOTES:

[1] José Antonio Saco, *Historia de la Esclavitud ...* (Barcelona, 1879), IV, 57 ff.

[2] Saco, *op. cit.*, IV, 74, 75, 178; Gonzalo Fernandez de Oviedo, *Historia General ...* tom. 3, lib. 29, cap. 3.

[3] Dec. 2, lib. 10, cap. 4; Bernal Diaz del Castillo, *Conquista de Nueva-Espana*, cap. 124.

[4] Herrera, dec. 5, lib. 5, cap. 7-9.

[5] Dec. 3, lib. 10, cap. 5.

[6] Herrera, *op. cit.*, dec. 5, lib. 10, cap. 1, 2, y 3.

[7] Saco, *op. cit.* IV, 166.

[8] *Ibid.*, IV, 170.

[9] Pedro de Casteñeda, "Account of the Expedition to Cibola which took place in the year 1540 ...," translated in *Spanish Explorers in the Southern United States* (J. F. Jameson, ed.), pp. 289-290.

[10] *Spanish Settlements in the United States*, 1513-1561, pp. 278-280.

[11] Quoted in Lowery, *op. cit.*, pp. 281-282.

THE ECONOMIC CONDITION OF THE NEGROES OF NEW YORK PRIOR TO 1861

The institution of slavery existed in the State of New York until 1827. The number of slaves had increased from 6,000 slaves in 1700 to 21,000 in 1790.[1] Moved by the struggle for the rights of man, the legislature of New York passed in 1799 an act of emancipation, providing that all children born of slave parents after July 4 ensuing should be free and subject to apprenticeship in the case of males until the age of 28, and of the females until the age of 25, while the exportation of slaves was forbidden. By the process of emancipation all slaves were liberated in 1827. Thenceforth, birth on the soil of New York was a guaranty of freedom and slaves from other States fled to New York as an asylum.[2] As a result of these efforts at gradual emancipation, there were more than 10,000 free Negroes in New York City in 1800.

We are to inquire here as to exactly what was the economic condition of these Negroes. What of their wealth, their means and methods of living well and wisely? With gradual emancipation and the cessation of the sale of slaves the Negroes became economically unimportant to the whites.[3] They were employed as servants, laborers, sailors and mechanics.[4] It was reported to the American Convention of Abolition Societies in 1797, however, "that a degree of decorum and industry prevailed among them much to their honor and advantage." This report further said that "Many in the town and country were freeholders, several worth from $300 to $1,300. Various associations among the free blacks for mutual support, benefit and improvement had been established. One of these had a lot for a burying ground and the site of a church worth fifteen hundred dollars. All were in a state of progressive improvement."[6] Still another part of the report made by these delegates stated that "on the whole they exhibited an example of successful industry highly honorable to themselves, gratifying to their parents, encouraging to patrons and consoling to humanity."[7] Again, in 1803, the New York delegates reported that the "increase of the number of freeholders among the free blacks is an evidence of the progress of industry, sobriety, and economy, and strengthens the hope that they will gradually emerge from their degraded condition to usefulness and respectability."[8]

Further evidence of the economic improvement of free Negroes during this period is evidenced by a significant appeal made by the members of the American Convention of Abolition Societies to the Free Negroes of New York in 1805. "The education of your offspring," said these friends of the Negroes, "is a subject of lasting importance and has obtained a large portion of your attention and care. In this, too, we call upon you for your aid; many of you have been favored to acquire a comfortable portion of property and are consequently enabled to contribute in some measure to the means of educating your offspring."[9] In response to this appeal, the society of free people of color was established in 1812 to maintain a Free Orphan School in New York City and employed two teachers; and there were three other schools which they supported with their tuition fees, while those who were not sufficiently well circumstanced to educate their children sent them to the African Free Schools maintained by the New York Manumission Society.[10]

These African Free Schools were conducted in such a way as to have a direct bearing on the economic improvement of the Negroes. In 1818 the New York Mission Society informed the American Convention of Abolition Societies that the former had devised a plan of extending their care to certain children of color who had completed their course of instruction in the New York African Free Schools "in putting them at some useful trade or employment." These friends of the race in New York said that it had long been a regret that Negro children "educated at their schools had been suffered after leaving it to waste their time in idleness, thereby incurring those vicious habits which were calculated to render their previous education worse than useless." To remedy this evil they appointed an Indenturing Committee, whose duty was to provide places for these children and put them at a trade or some other employment when they had completed their education. The Committee took special care that the persons with whom children might be placed should be those of good character and while on the one hand they insisted that the children demean themselves with sobriety they extended their guardian care to them so that they might not "become subjects of oppression and tyranny." This Indenturing Committee in reaching its decision as to the sort of occupations to which the children could be apprenticed expressed a decided preference for agricultural pursuits, being persuaded that an occupation of this nature was far more conducive to the moral improvement of these Negroes than the pursuits of the city under the most favorable circumstances. This plan upon being presented to the parents and guardians of these children was favorably received, but it does not appear that a large number of them thereafter participated in agriculture.[11]

The activity of the girls who had received instruction in household economics in free schools showed progress in another direction. They formed a society under the name of the African Dorcas Association for the purpose of procuring and making garments for the destitute. The boys, too, contributed their share to this progress, taking up such trades as sail makers, tire-workers, tailors, carpenters and blacksmiths.

Such reports[12] represent the condition of the free Negroes of New York before slavery was completely abolished. This change in the status of the Negroes then, and the evolving industrial system effected a change in the economic condition of the Negro throughout the city.[13]

It must be remembered in this connection, however, that these Negroes experienced difficulties on account of their color either in obtaining a thorough knowledge of the trades or, after they had obtained it, in finding employment in the best shops. White and black laborers at first worked together in the same room and at the same machine. But soon prejudice developed. It was made more intense by the immigration into this country of a large number of poor Germans and Irish, who came to our shores because of the disturbed conditions of Europe. Their superior training and experience enabled them to get positions in most of the trades. Most northern men, moreover, still objected to granting Negroes economic equality. When the supply of labor exceeded the demand, the free Negroes, unable to compete with these foreigners, were driven not only from the respectable positions, but also from the menial pursuits. Measures to restrict to the whites employment in higher pursuits were proposed and where they were not actually made laws, public opinion, to that effect, accomplished practically the same result. This reversal of the position of labor, however, did not take place without a struggle, for there soon arose ill-feeling which culminated in the riots between 1830 and 1840.[14]

In spite of this condition, Arthur Tappan, Gerrit Smith and William Lloyd Garrison reported to the Second American Convention for the Improvement of the Free People of Color that "by perseverance, the youth of color could succeed in procuring profitable situations. [15] To these benefactors, however, it was soon evident that Negroes had to be trained for the competition with white laborers or be doomed to follow menial employment. In accordance with this Gerrit Smith established in 1834 a school in Peterboro, for the purpose of training Negro youths under the manual labor system.[16] With such training, he believed, free Negroes would gain a livelihood, send their children to school, and gradually accumulate money. He hoped that many of them would make progress to the extent of possessing property valued at $250, which amount would enable citizens of color[17] to vote in the State of New York.

Hoping to put an end to economic poverty among these Negroes, Gerrit Smith devised a scheme for the distribution of 3,000 parcels of land of 40 or 60 acres each among the unfortunate blacks then handicapped in this untoward situation in New York City. From a list of names furnished him by Rev. Charles B. Ray, Rev. Theodore F. Wright and Dr. J. McCune Smith, three prominent Negroes in New York City, Gerrit Smith apportioned this land among the Negro colonists in the counties of Franklin, Essex, Hamilton, Fulton, Oneida, Delaware, Madison, and Ulster. On account of the intractability of the soil, however, the harshness of the climate, and, in a great measure, the inefficiency of the settlers, the enterprise was a failure and offered no relief to the economic condition of the Negroes in this city.

It will be interesting to note the observations of a promoter of colonization on the condition of Negroes in New York City at this time. While his statements must be taken with some reservation they, nevertheless, contain a truth which must be taken into account. Hoping to induce Negroes to accept colonization in Africa, he endeavored to show that they could not finally succeed in the struggle in competition with the white laborers and would be crowded out of the higher pursuits of labor. He referred to the fact that a few years prior to 1846 there was a vast body of colored laborers in New York but that at that time they could not be seen. The writer inquired as to "who may find a dray or a cart or a hack driven by a colored man?" "Where are the vast majority of colored people in the city?" "None," said he, "can deny that they are sunken much lower than they were a few years ago and are compelled to pursue none but the meanest avocations."

The gentleman making these observations tried to emphasize this striking contrast by calling attention to the fact that New York was a place that had a great deal of compassion for the slave while it was neglecting to take into account the awful condition of the free Negroes, in spite of the fact that the process of their depression had been going on at the same time that the abolitionists in New York were working for the emancipation of the slave. Although these friends of the Negroes and the Negroes themselves had during these years been boldly asserting their rights and demanding to be elevated, they had been losing ground, sinking into meaner occupations and less lucrative employments. He believed that the day was not far when every desirable business in the city would be entirely monopolized by the whites because of the rapid influx of foreigners who had to labor or serve and knew how to toil to advantage, to the extent that they could make their labor more valuable than that of the people of color.[18]

In things economic, however, the free Negroes of New

York made considerable improvement after 1845; a decided improvement in this respect was noted by 1851. So evident was this progress that the colonizationists who had repeatedly referred to the poverty of the Negroes and the prejudice against them in the laboring world as a reason why they should migrate to Africa, thereafter ceased to say very much about their poverty, shifting their complaint rather to social proscription. In 1851 a contributor to *The African Repository*, the organ of the American Colonization Society, discussed the situation of the 48,000 free Negroes of New York. Directing his attention to the 14,000 living in the metropolis, the editor said that the condition of 4,000 of them approached that of comfort; 1,000 of the number having substantial wealth, or that one out of every ten was in a pleasant and enviable social condition. As this pessimist was compelled to concede that this was not a bad showing for an oppressed people he goes off on another line, saying: "Everywhere the Negro, whatever his wealth or education or talents, is excluded from social equality and social freedom."[19]

There were many instances of individual enterprise, however, but these often meant little since Negroes had such a little knowledge of business that white persons often defrauded them out of what they accumulated. Sojourner Truth accumulated more than enough money to supply her wants, but lost some of it by depositing it in a bank without taking account of the sum which she deposited and without asking for the interest when she drew her money from the bank. [20] One Pierson persuaded her to take her money out of the bank and invest it in a common fund which he was raising to be drawn upon by all needy and faithful free Negroes.[21] Her savings, therefore, served to increase this fund, which instead of relieving the economic condition of many needy free Negroes enriched this white impostor.

231

As evidences of this unusual progress of the Negroes there are many instances of persons who gained wealth in spite of the various handicaps. Many of the caterers and restaurant keepers of high order of New York were Negroes, the most popular of whom being Thomas Downing, the keeper of a restaurant under what is now the Drexel Building, near the corner of Wall and Broad streets, New York City.[22] Abner H. Frances and James Garrett, were formerly extensive clothiers of Buffalo, New York, doing business to the amount of $60,000 annually. They continued their enterprise successfully for years, their credit being good for any amount of money they needed. They failed in business in 1849 but thereafter adjusted the claims against them.[23] Henry Scott and Company, of New York City, engaged in the pickling business, principally confined to supplying vessels.[24] Edward V. Clark, another business man of New York, had a jewelry establishment requiring much capital. His name had, moreover, a respectable standing even among the dealers of Wall Street.[25] Mr. Huston kept for years an intelligence office in New York. He was succeeded by Philip A. Bell, an excellent business man. Concerning it, Austin Steward reported in his book entitled "*The Condition of the Colored People*" that "his business is very extensive, being sought from all points of the city by the first people of the community.[26]

Many other names may be mentioned. William H. Topp was one of the leading merchant tailors of Albany, New York. Starting in the world without aid he educated and qualified himself for business.[27] In Penyan, Messrs. William Platt and Joseph C. Cassey were said to be carrying on an extensive trade in lumber.[28]

Situated in the midst of a rapidly developing country the enterprises of these free Negroes increased in importance every year. This was especially true of the drug stores of Dr. James McCune Smith, on Broadway, a Negro physician, who was practicing in New York City during the thirties, and of the establishment of Dr. Philip White, on Frankfort street. Many Negroes accumulated considerable wealth. Edward Bidwell successfully operated during the period of 1827-40 two stores on the main street of New York City, hoarding considerable money. Austin Steward, still another instance of New York City, made "handsome profits" from the sale of spirituous liquors. At one time he said that no further exertion was necessary on his part to enjoy life, or to better his economic condition. Finally, William Smith, a shrewd sailor of New York, managed to accumulate considerable wealth.

The statistics of the census of 1850 give further evidences of this general progress. Of the 50,000 free people of color in the State of New York over 15 years of age in 1850, sixty were clerks, doctors and lawyers and about 55 were merchants and teachers.[29] There were, moreover:

2 apprentices	3 barkeepers	4 bakers
1 blacksmith	122 barbers	21 boarding house keepers
28 boatmen	33 butchers	8 cigar makers
12 carpenters	39 carmen	95 cooks
107 coachmen	2 confectioners	1 gunsmith
24 farmers	7 gardeners	3 merchants
2 hatters	11 ink makers	1144 laborers
3 jewelers	21 ministers	4 painters
24 musicians	434 mariners	2 mechanics
15 marketmen	4 printers	23 tailors
44 stewards	808 servants	23 shoemakers

```
12 sextons            8 teachers
                    207 engaged in other
                        occupations
```

Many Negroes used wisely the money which they obtained from these businesses. Out of a free population of 50,000 Negroes, 5,447, or about one in ten was in school during this period. In a pamphlet entitled the *Present Condition of Free People of Color* published by James Freeman Clarke in 1859, the author stated that they were no less neat in person and attire than their white neighbors.[30] One year during the period from 1850 to 1860 Negroes of New York City invested in business carried on by themselves $775,000; in businesses of Brooklyn $76,000. That same year these free Negroes purchased real estate in New York worth $733,000, and in Brooklyn $276,000.[31]

With complete freedom in New York, free Negroes made more efforts to improve their condition. There were established several newspapers which served not only to present their cause to the public but also as economic factors. First of these must be mentioned a publication called *Freedom's Journal* or *The Rights of All*. This paper, edited by James B. Russworm, the first Negro college graduate in the United States, and Rev. Samuel F. Cornish, was established in March, 1827.[32] Another journal, styled *The Weekly Advocate*, changing its name later to *The Colored American*, appeared in New York, March 4, 1837. The editor was Philip A. Bell. Later Charles Bennett Ray became one of the proprietors and editors. Finally, mention must be made of such journals of this period as *The Elevator*, of Albany, edited by Stephen Myers; *The Genius of Freedom*, by David Ruggles; *People's Press*, by Thomas Hamilton; and *North Star*, by Frederick Douglass. Concerning the last named publication, it was generally said that it was conducted on a higher plane than any of the

others and that it was among the first newspapers of
the country.

ARNETT G. LINDSAY.

FOOTNOTES:

[1] Census of New York before 1790:

Year	Number
1664	"very few"
1678	"very few"
1698 King's County,	293.
1703, 5 counties about N. Y. City	1,301.
1712, 5 counties about N. Y. City	1,775.
1723	6,171
1731	7,231
1746	9,717
1774	21,717
1790	21,324
1800	20,903
1810	15,017
1820	10,088
1830	75
1840	4

NEW YORK CITY SLAVES.

1703	801
1712	960
1731	1,571
1737	1,719
1746	2,444

Morgan, *Slavery in New York*, page 38.

[2] *New York Emancipation Law—African Repository,*

236

Vol. 31, page 155.

[3] *Half a Man*, M. W. Ovington, page 69.

[4] *American Convention of Abolition Societies, 1797*, p. 39.

[5] *Ibid.*, p. 31.

[6] *Ibid.*, p. 39.

[7] *Ibid.*, p. 30.

[8] *Ibid.*, 1803, p. 7.

[9] *American Convention of Abolition Societies, 1805*, p. 38.

[10] *Ibid.*, 1812, p. 7.

[11] *American Convention of Abolition Societies, 1812*, p. 14.

[12] Inspectors of the New York African Free Schools reported to *The Commercial Advertiser*, May 12, 1824, that "we never beheld a white school of the same age in which without exception there was more order, neatness of dress, and cleanliness of person."

[13] *Ibid.*

[14] *Journal of Negro History*, Vol. III, p. 354.

[15] Woodson, *Education of the Negro Prior to 1861*, p. 286.

[16] *Journal of Negro History*, Vol. III.

[17] *Hurd's Law of Freedom-Bondage*, p. 81.

[18] *African Repository*, September, 1846, p. 278.

[19] *Ibid.*, 1851, p. 263.

[20] *Narrative of Sojourner Truth*, p. 99.

[21] *Ibid.*, p. 99.

[22] Martin Delaney, *Condition of Colored People*, p. 139.

[23] *Ibid.*, p. 102.

[24] *Ibid.*, p. 106.

[25] Austin Steward, *Condition of Colored People*, p.

237

102.

[26] *Ibid.*, p. 102.

[27] Austin Steward, *Condition of Colored People*, p. 102.

[28] *Ibid.*, p. 132.

[29] *Seventh Census of the United States.*

[30] J. F. Clarke, *Present Condition of People of Color*, p. 14.

[31] *Ibid.*

[32] *Afro-American Press*, p. 27.

DOCUMENTS

THE APPEAL OF THE AMERICAN
CONVENTION OF ABOLITION SOCIETIES

The student of the so-called Negro problem of today may find it profitable to study the methods of persons thus concerned more than a century ago. What their plans were, what machinery they constructed for carrying them out, and the hopes they had for ultimate success, will furnish much material for reflection for social workers. There is published below, therefore, a number of the annual appeals of the American Convention of Abolition Societies to the various branches, setting forth the annual review of the work, the general survey of results obtained and the ways and means to carry it forward to a successful completion.

TO THE ANTISLAVERY GROUPS

To the   *Society for
promoting the abolition of Slavery, Ec.*

It is with peculiar pleasure we inform you, that the Convention of Delegates, from most of the Abolition Societies formed in the United States, met in this city, have, with much unanimity, gone through the business which came before them. The advantages to be derived from this meeting are so evident, that we have agreed earnestly to recommend to you, that a similar meeting be annually convened, until the great object of our association—the liberty of our fellowmen—shall be fully and equivocally established.

To obtain this important end, we conceive that it is proper, constantly to have in view the necessity of using our utmost and unremitting endeavors to abolish slavery, and to protect and meliorate the condition of the enslaved, and of the emancipated. The irresistible, though silent progress of the principles of true philosophy, will do much for us; but, placed in

239

a situation well adapted to promote these principles, it surely becomes us to improve every occasion of forwarding the great designs of our institutions. For this purpose, we think it proper to request you to unite with us, in the most strenuous exertions, to effect a compliance with the laws in favour of emancipation; and, where these laws are deficient, respectful applications to the State-Legislatures should not be discontinued, however unsuccessful they may prove.—Let us remember, for our consolation and encouragement in these cases, that, although interest and prejudice may oppose, yet the fundamental principles of our government, as well as the progressive and rapid influence of reason and religion, are in our favour—and let us never be discouraged by a fear of the event, from performing any task of duty, when clearly pointed out; for it is an undoubted truth—that no good effort can ever be entirely lost.

While contemplating the great principles of our associations, we cannot refrain from recommending to your attention the propriety of using your endeavours to form, as circumstances may require, Abolition Societies in your own, and in the neighboring States; as, for want of the concurrence of others, the good intentions and efforts of many an honest and zealous individual are often defeated.

But, while we wish to draw your attention to these objects, there is another which we cannot pass over. We are all too much accustomed to the reproaches of the enemies of our cause, on the subject of the ignorance and crimes of the Blacks, not to wish that they were ill-founded. And though, to us, it is sufficiently apparent that this ignorance, and these crimes, are owing to the degrading state of slavery; yet, may we not, with confidence, attempt to do away the reproach?— Let us use our endeavours to have the children of the emancipated, and even of the enslaved Africans, instructed in common literature—in the principles of virtue and religion, and in those mechanic arts which will keep them most constantly employed, and, of course, will less subject them to idleness and debauchery; and thus prepare them for becoming good citizens of the United States: a privilege and elevation to which we look forward with pleasure, and which we believe can be best merited by habits of industry and virtue.

We shall transmit you an exact copy of our proceedings, with the different memorials and addresses which to us have appeared necessary at this time; and would recommend to you the propriety of giving full powers to the Delegates who are to meet in the year 1795; believing that the business of that Convention will be rendered more easy and more extensively useful, if you send, by your Representatives, certified copies of the constitution and laws of your *Society*, and of all the laws existing in your state concerning slavery, with such facts

240

relative to this business, as may ascertain the respective situation of slavery, and of the Blacks in general.

To the   Society for
           promoting the abolition of Slavery, &c.

The Delegates, from the several Abolition Societies in the United States, convened in this city, express to you, with great satisfaction, the pleasure they have experienced from the punctual attendance of the persons, delegated to this Convention, and that harmony with which they have deliberated on the several matters that have been presented to them, at this time, for their consideration. The benefits which may flow from a continuance of this general meeting, by aiding the principal design of its institution—the universal emancipation of the wretched Africans who are yet in bondage, appear to us so many and important, that we are induced to recommend to you, to send Delegates to a similar Convention, which we propose to be holden, in this city, on the first day of January, in the year one thousand, seven hundred and ninety-six.

We have thought it proper to request your further attention to that part of the address of the former Convention, which relates to the procurement of certified copies of the laws of your state respecting slavery; and that you would send, to the next Convention, exact copies of all such laws as are now in force, and of such as have been repealed. Convinced that an historical review of the various acts and provisions of the Legislatures of the several states, relating to slavery, from the periods of their respective settlements to the present time, by tracing the progress of the system to African slavery in this country, and its successive change in the different governments of the Union, would throw much light on the objects of our enquiry and attention, and enable us to determine, how far the cause of justice and humanity has advanced among us, and how soon we may reasonably expect to see it triumphant;—we recommend to you, to take such measures as you may think conducive to that purpose, for procuring materials for the work now proposed, and assisting its publication; and to communicate, to the ensuing Convention, what progress you shall have made toward perfecting the plan here offered for your consideration and care.

Believing that an acquaintance with the names of the officers of the several Abolition Societies, would facilitate that friendly correspondence which ought always to be preserved between our various associations, we request that you would send, to the next, and to every future Convention, an accurate list of all

241

the officers of your Society, for the time being, with the number of members of which it consists. And it would assist that Convention in ascertaining the existing state of slavery in the United States, if you were to forward to them an exact account of the persons who have been liberated by the agency of your Society, and of those who may be considered as signal instances of the relief that you have afforded; and, also, a statement of the number of free blacks in your state, their property, employments, and moral conduct.

As a knowledge of what has been done, and of that success which has attended the efforts of humanity, will cherish the hope of benevolence, and stimulate to further exertion, we trust that you will be of opinion with us, that it would be highly useful to procure correct reports of all such trials, and decisions of courts of judicature, respecting slavery, a knowledge of which may be subservient to the cause of abolition, and to transmit them to the next, or to any future Convention.

It cannot have escaped your observation, how many persons there are who continue the hateful practice of enslaving their fellow men, and who acquiesce in the sophistry of the advocates of that practice, merely from want of reflection, and from an habitual attention to their own immediate interest. If to such were often applied the force of reason, and the persuasion of eloquence, they might be awakened to a sense of their injustice, and be startled with horror at the enormity of their conduct. To produce so desirable a change in sentiment, as well as practice, we recommend to you the instituting of annual, or other periodical, discourses, or orations, to be delivered in public, on the subject of slavery, and means of its abolition.

We cannot forbear expressing to you our earnest desire, that you will continue, without ceasing, to endeavour, by every method in your power which can promise any success, to procure, either an absolute repeal of all the laws in your state, which countenance slavery, or such an amelioration of them as will gradually produce an entire abolition. Yet, even should that greater end be happily attained, it cannot put a period to the necessity of further labor. The education of the emancipated, the noblest and most arduous task which we have to perform, will require all our wisdom and virtue, and the constant exercise of the greatest skill and discretion. When we have broken his chains, and restored the African to the enjoyment of his rights, the great work of justice and benevolence is not accomplished—The new born citizen must receive that instruction, and those powerful impressions of moral and religious truth, which will render him capable and desirous of fulfilling the various duties he owes to himself and to his country. By educating some in the higher branches of science, and all in the useful parts of learning, and in the precepts of religion and morality, we shall not only do away with the reproach and calumny so unjustly lavished upon us, but confound the enemies of truth, by evincing that the unhappy sons of Africa, in spite of the degrading influence of slavery, are in no wise inferior to the more fortunate inhabitants of Europe and America.

As a mean of effectuating, in some degree, a design so virtuous and laudable, we recommend to you to appoint a committee, annually, or for any other more convenient period, to execute such plans, for the improvement of the condition and moral character of the free blacks in your state, as you may think best adapted to your particular situation.

By a decree of the National Convention of France, all the blacks and people of color, within the territories of the French republic, are declared free, and entitled to an equal participation of the rights of citizens of France. We have been informed that many persons, of the above description, notwithstanding the decree in their favor, have been brought from the West-India islands, by emigrants, into the United States, and are now held as slaves,—We suggest to you the propriety, as well as the necessity, of making enquiry into the subject, and of effecting their liberation, so far as may be found consistent with the laws of your state.[2]

To the   *Society for promoting*
the Abolition of Slavery, &c.

The Delegates from the several Abolition Societies in the United States inform you, that, agreeably to the recommendation of the Convention of last year, they met in this city on the first instant, and have, with much harmony and satisfaction, gone through the business which came before them. They have the pleasure to assure you, that every successive meeting evinces the importance of that union and concert which are so happily established among the several Societies, in pursuing the great object of their association.

But, although the exertions of this delegated Body have been hitherto attended, as we hope, with considerable success— Although we are persuaded that no small progress may be marked in the great business of emancipation; yet much remains to be done; as long as *seven hundred thousand* of our Fellow Creatures, in the United States, continue in a state of bondage, there appears a pressing necessity for the continuance of our efforts; that we should keep our attention fixed upon the subject, and stand ready to improve every favorable opportunity that may occur, to forward the

243

interesting cause in which we are engaged. We are therefore induced to continue the recommendation heretofore made, that a similar meeting be annually held; and as convening at the present season is attended with inconveniences, we propose, that the next Convention, should assemble in this city, on the first Wednesday of May, in the year 1797.

It gives us pleasure to learn, from various reports which were laid before us, that most of the recommendations made by the former Conventions, had received a considerable degree of attention, from the several societies to whom they were addressed. But, as they have not been uniformly and perfectly complied with, permit us to repeat the request, *so far as the same may be applicable to your society*, that you transmit to the next Convention, certified copies of all such laws, in any wise respecting slavery, as are now in force, as have been repealed, or may hereafter be enacted—Correct lists of the officers of your society, for the time being, and also the names of all your members, and their places of abode—An account of the proceedings of your society, in relieving Africans and others unlawfully held in bondage—A statement of the condition of the blacks, both bond and free, in your state, with respect to the property of the free, and the employment and moral conduct of all—Reports of such trials and decisions of the Courts of Judicature, relative to Africans, as may have taken place—An account of the endeavors which have been used to obtain a repeal or amelioration of the laws respecting slavery— information concerning what has been done, in pursuance of the recommendation of the last Convention, to establish periodical discourses on the subject of slavery, and the means of its abolition—And finally, a report of the progress you have made in extending to Africans the benefits of education. And we further request, that whatever communications may be made to the next, or to any future Convention, in consequence of the above recommendations, be presented in the form of regular written reports, noticing in what manner and degree you have carried them into effect, and how far your efforts have been ineffectual. By this means there will be exhibited such a view of the state of each Society, as that the several reports may be entered on the minutes of the Convention, who will thereby be better enabled to decide on the propriety of making public such parts of these communications as may be best adapted to advance the cause of truth and humanity.

And as very important advantages have, in several instances, resulted from accurate registers being kept, by persons appointed for that purpose by certain of the Abolition Societies in the United States, of such manumissions as have taken place; we do earnestly recommend, should you not already have entered into this regulation, that you make it hereafter an object of diligent attention. Such records may, in various ways, subserve the cause of emancipation.

We learn, that the proposal made by the last Convention, respecting the blacks, and people of color, who have emigrated from the West Indies, and now reside in the United States, has, in many instances, given rise to difficulty; in order to remove which, we have been induced to transmit to you the following extract from the twelfth article of the Consular Convention between France and the United States; which by designating the proper tribunals to whom application, in such cases, is to be made, will, we trust, be found sufficient, in future, to direct your proceedings in this business, *viz.*

"That all differences and suits between French citizens in the United States, and between American citizens in the dominions of France, shall be determined by the respective Consuls and Vice Consuls either by a reference to arbitrators, or by a summary judgment, and without costs; and that no officer of the country, civil or military, shall interfere therein, or take any part whatever in the matter."

When we contemplate the odious nature and the immense magnitude of the evil which you have associated to oppose, and the inestimable importance of the objects which you are seeking to obtain, we cannot forbear to urge unremitted exertions, in pursuing the great ends before you. We are persuaded you will not neglect any just means in your power, which may tend to advance, either directly, or indirectly, the cause of equal liberty;—And it gives us pleasure also to express our persuasion, that, in this pursuit, much is still in your power. Although you cannot control Legislatures; and though, when you plead the cause of humanity, they will not, at all times, listen to you; yet there are other means to be used, perhaps, more effectual—You can do much, by directing your efforts to the conviction of individuals—by diffusing proper publications amongst them, and by presenting the evils of slavery in various forms to their minds.[3]

The following was inserted in the Address to the Pennsylvania Abolition Society.

And as precise information, on this subject, cannot be too generally diffused, we request you to collect all possible intelligence relative to such blacks and people of color in the United States as are made Citizens of the French Republic, by the decree of the National Convention, of the sixteenth Pluviose, second year of the republic, and transmit the same to all the other Abolition Societies in the United States.

Nor can we suppose, it would be an effort altogether ineffectual in favor of liberty, were its friends, throughout the United States, in all cases where it is practicable, to display a marked preference of such commodities, as are of the culture or manufacture of freemen, to those which are cultivated or manufactured by slaves—In this way, every individual may discountenance oppression, and bear testimony against a practice, which is still suffered to remain the disgrace of our land.

We have thought proper to address the free Africans and other free people of color in the United States, on various subjects, which we believe nearly to concern their interest and happiness. We have directed copies of this address to be transmitted to you and request you to distribute the same, in your State, in such manner as you may judge best calculated to promote its design.

We cannot conclude, without calling your attention, in a particular manner, to the necessity of appointing such of your members to represent you in the Convention, as will be punctually attentive to the duties of their appointment. We are sorry to observe, that there is some ground of complaint, on this subject; but we trust, that, in future, such a full representation will appear, as will give encreasing encouragement, energy and success to our united endeavors in the great cause of human happiness.

Copies of our proceedings will be laid before you; from which we hope, you will derive satisfaction, and perceive the importance of the several objects which we have recommended to your attention.[4]

To the   _Society for promoting the_
                        Abolition of Slavery.

To inform you of our proceedings; to solicit your further advice and assistance; and to request your special attention to the original object of our meetings, we now address you.

We have, as formerly, gone through our business with harmony and satisfaction; the peculiar objects, thereof will appear from our minutes, herewith transmitted; and we can truly add, that the important advantages evidently arising from such a collection of information and exchange of sentiment are too obvious, not to unite us in the recommendation, that a similar Convention of delegates from the different abolition societies, be held in this city on the first day of June, 1798.

The non-compliance of several societies with this proposal for some years past, induces us to believe that some obstacles may exist, which possibly might be removed; we therefore request, that where it is not agreed to send delegates, such societies would favor the Convention, in writing, with their determination and the causes of it. This better enables the Convention to judge of the most proper mode of proceeding in future.

A table, containing the requisitions of this and the former Conventions, and how far they have hitherto been complied with by each society, will shew the propriety and necessity of fulfilling these requisitions; which, after being thus pointed out need not now be further insisted on.

When we consider the extensive influence of education on society, we think a due attention to the instruction of the blacks and people of color of every description cannot be too forcibly impressed. This will apply not merely to what is called school learning, but essentially consists in inculcating the sound principles of morality and religion as well as habits of temperance and industry. From a continued regard to the welfare of this much injured and much oppressed people, we have again addressed them on such points as we judged would be most beneficial; but it will in a great degree rest with you to circulate and enforce the advice recommended: and we may add, that, as the evils which must necessarily result from their being retained in a state of ignorance are incalculable, so it is, in our opinion, the greatest and perhaps the only important service we can render to them and to our country, to disseminate learning and morality amongst them, thus raising them gradually and safely to that level, to which they must, in the course of time, inevitably attain.

The different Conventions have from year to year, endeavoured to procure from the Abolition Societies, every kind of information which may illustrate the history of slavery in the United States; we now repeat their request, with a view to the formation of a history of this important subject.

From the general accounts received, as well as from our own observations we are induced strongly to recommend, that where several Abolition Societies exist in one state, they would, if possible, form a general plan of union or confederation, so as, on all important occasions, to act in concert.

You are already well informed of the act of Congress of March twenty-second, 1794, prohibiting the citizens of the United States from supplying foreign nations with slaves; you will also most probably have heard that this wise and humane law has been too frequently violated by our citizens; in consequence of which the Abolition Societies of Pennsylvania, New-York and Providence, have severally commenced prosecutions against divers persons and vessels, engaged in this abominable traffic; the first named society has been successful in the two prosecutions they undertook in the District Court of Pennsylvania and of the United States of America. The vessels have been condemned, and actions are pending against the masters and owners in the Circuit Court of the United States in and for the Pennsylvania district of the middle circuit. There is good ground to believe that the other societies will meet with equal success.

Besides the information mutually given by the societies to each other as occasions may require, to assist them in checking such clandestine practices, we believe it would be highly useful to forward every particular that comes to your knowledge on this subject, to the next Convention, who may make a very important use of it.

The difficulties which have continually occurred respecting the blacks and people of color, who have for several years past emigrated from the French West-Indies into the United States, have engaged the attention of this and the preceding Conventions. To remove these difficulties, we transmit you a certified copy of an authenticated decree of the National Convention of France, of the sixteenth Pluviose, second year of the Republic; (February fifth, 1794,) which has been lately received by the Pennsylvania Abolition Society. With this decree, since fully confirmed by the French constitution of 1795, we believe you will have it in your power to afford every legal and effectual assistance to these unfortunate people.

There yet remains a subject which, though often urged, still continues to demand our serious attention; we allude to the most proper means of extending the principles of just and equal liberty amongst mankind: and as we profess to assume no other powers than those of persuasion and convincement, founded on the unerring basis of truth and justice, we wish you duly to advert to the magnitude of the cause in which we are engaged, to persevere with patience and fortitude in your applications to legislative bodies and courts of justice, for the relief of our unfortunate African brethren, and to continue to enlighten the public mind, by spreading as much as possible, all kind of useful information on the subject: that thus we may, in every form, and on every occasion, be ready to plead the cause of the oppressed, in the language of persuasion and of truth. And then we shall have done our duty; and then we may, in humble confidence, look up for the blessing and protection of the great Father of all, *whose ways are just and equal, and who hath made of one blood all nations of men.*[5]

To the   *Society for promoting the*
                        Abolition of Slavery, &c.

248

THE Convention of delegates from the Abolition Societies established in different parts of the United States, assembled at Philadelphia, congratulate their constituents on the general progress of their objects since last meeting, and on the union of sentiment, and harmony of deliberation, which has prevailed in all their proceedings.

The assembling in Convention, at proper intervals, has produced so many advantages in combining the views and operations of the friends of emancipation throughout the United States, that we are persuaded you will unite with us in opinion, that it is expedient that another Convention of delegates from the several Abolition Societies, be held in this city on the first Wednesday of June, in the year one thousand eight hundred.

The alteration in the period of meeting we have adopted under a consideration of the peculiar situation of our country, and the state of the objects which have hitherto occupied our attention; but, we earnestly request, that a general representation, and a punctual attendance, may take place at the time recommended.

Although, from the reports of such of the Societies as have sent delegates to this Convention, we have observed, with encouragement and pleasure, the perseverance that is used, and the progress that is made, in the great work for which we have associated; yet, we cannot help noticing, with regret, the absence of many of our members, and the total omission of several of the Societies to appoint Representatives, or to comply with the request of the last Convention, that, where it was not agreed to send delegates, such determination and the cause of it might be reported to the Convention in writing. To those societies, therefore, which have failed in this respect, we are induced earnestly to repeat the request, and to urge their particular attention thereto.

By some of the Societies the general requisitions of former Conventions, have not yet been answered or complied with, and by others only in part. An accurate table of these requisitions, and the manner in which each Society had complied with them, was made out by the last Convention and forwarded to the different Abolition Societies. By a reference thereto, and to the report of the committee of this Convention, to whom the several communications were referred, which is included in the copy of our proceedings herewith transmitted to you, you will observe what yet remains to be done; and we hope you will be able to make complete returns to the succeeding Convention, together with such other information as may appear to you to be useful towards the important purpose of forming a history of the progress and state of slavery in the United States.

Too much cannot be said on the necessity of a constant attention to the subject of education. To prepare the minds of our unfortunate African brethren for that condition of freedom and rank in society to which they must, sooner or later, arrive —to disseminate among them useful instruction on moral and religious subjects, and to use our utmost endeavours to have schools established, for the purpose of teaching them to read and write, ought, we conceive, to be the primary object of all the Abolition Societies. We also think it of importance, at this particular period, to impress upon the minds of those who are in bondage, the propriety of a quiet submission to the injunctions of their masters, assuring them that by such conduct they will be likely to experience not only the advantages of better treatment in their present situation, but also cause, perhaps, even their possessors to perceive the injustice that is attached to the principles of slavery.

Firmly persuaded that considerable benefit has already resulted from inculcating friendly advice to this oppressed people, and believing that the sentiments contained in the addresses of the former Conventions to the free blacks and other people of color in the United States cannot be too frequently repeated and enforced, we recommend to the consideration of the Societies, the propriety of a republication of those addresses by each society, and such communication and distribution thereof as may be best calculated to promote a beneficial effect.

The Convention having been informed, that vessels are fitted out with cargoes for certain of the West Indian Islands, parts of which cargoes are their disposed of, and, with the proceeds, slaves are purchased and carried to other of the said Islands, and sold; also that other vessels are loaded with rum, for certain ports in Africa, with the proceeds of which, we have reason to believe, the natives are purchased and afterwards conveyed and sold as slaves in the West Indies. We recommend a strict enquiry to be made into the conduct of persons thus offending against the dictates of humanity and the honor and interest of our country, that proper measures, to punish and prevent such nefarious and disgraceful practices, may be adopted.

We have thought it expedient to confine our attention at present, principally to carrying into effect the measures heretofore advised. Let us, however, whilst prudent and cautious, continue to be firm and sincere. Let us embrace every opportunity which may offer for ameliorating the condition of slaves so far as the laws, under which we severally act, will permit us to proceed. Let us do nothing which may justly draw forth the censure of our country, but act, in all things, with that moderation and propriety which have heretofore distinguished the Abolition Societies.

250

We confidently trust, that when the storms, by which the world is at present agitated, shall have subsided, the light of truth will break through the dark gloom of oppression—cruelty and injustice will not only hear, but obey, the voice of reason and religion; and in these United States the practice of the people will be conformable to their declaration—"That all men are born equally free, and have an unalienable right to Liberty."[6]

To   *Society, &c.*

The Convention of delegates, from the different Abolition Societies established in the United States, feel a pleasure in informing you, that their deliberations have been conducted with much harmony and satisfaction to themselves.

They, however, deeply regret, that so few of the Societies have been induced to send Representatives to the Convention.

The great and good work of restoring liberty to the captive, and fitting him to fill that station in the scale of being, from which he has been forced by the domineering spirit of power and usurpation, may be considered as little more than begun. How many thousands of miserable wretches yet languish in slavery, in these United States, to whom the light of morn, which should awaken all nature alike to harmony and joy, affords, perhaps, no other consolation save the solitary certainty, that one day more is taken from the long period of their sufferings—This is not all—In vain do you liberate the Africans, while you neglect to furnish him with the means of properly providing for himself, and of becoming an useful member of the community. This subject alone opens an extensive field for active benevolence, and justly demands the exercise of a large portion of the talents and labours of the friends of emancipation.

To effect these desirable objects, so importunately called for by every sentiment of a feeling heart, union and concentration of energy appear to be indispensable. The societies should never be found in the pursuit of incongruous measures, but act in concert; and this cannot, perhaps be better accomplished than by a free and liberal interchange of information, whence useful knowledge should diverge to each society, communicating life, energy, and consistency to the whole.

The advantages resulting from this institution may be known by past experience; but as an additional instance of the good effects flowing from it, we refer you to the addresses forwarded this year to the Convention, and printed in the minutes; in which you will perceive, and especially in the one from New York, much valuable matter. That society mentions a species of kidnapping, which to the disgrace of humanity, has been carried on in that city in a manner at once evincing the barefaced hardiness of its perpetrators, and the wicked and cunning arts practiced, by the enemies of freedom, on an oppressed people. There is good reason to believe, that similar practices are secretly pursued in other parts of the Union. We therefore earnestly press your vigilant attention to the subject, in order that if any other persons should be engaged in this nefarious traffic, they may be made to suffer that exposure and punishment which the enormity of the crime so richly merits.

Fully impressed with the magnitude of the object, and the benefits to be derived from it, we cannot forbear strongly to recommend, that another Convention be held in this city on the first Wednesday in June, in the year 1801. And, in order to insure permanency, and its consequent advantages to this establishment, we submit to your consideration, the expediency of delegating to your Representatives, the power of aiding in the formation of a Constitution, for the government of future Conventions.

The case mentioned by the Virginia society, held at Richmond, from which it seems evident that a small sum of money, beyond what their funds are calculated to bear, might restore a considerable number of persons to liberty, who were unlawfully taken from their state into Georgia, and there sold as slaves, has called forth the sympathy of this Convention; and forcibly suggests the propriety of enabling the next Convention, by the voluntary contributions of the different societies, to grant some pecuniary aid to similar and other proper objects. Much good might be done in this way; and perhaps some societies, who are capable, may be found willing promptly to bestow a portion of their funds to the Virginia society, to enable them more effectually to prosecute this particular claim, it is also to be presumed, that some of the Societies, especially in the eastern states, where slavery no longer exists, might render their benevolent exertions more extensively useful, by suitable and timely grants to others, who are less wealthy, and have much to do.

You have embarked in an excellent cause—go on and prosper, —until liberty, like the light of Heaven, or the air we breathe, shall, however, men may be diversified by color, shape of habit, become the equal inheritance of all.[7]

To the   *Society for promoting*
              the Abolition of Slavery.

THE seventh Convention of Delegates from the several

252

Abolition Societies in the United States, now address you on the subject of their appointment. The concord and reciprocity of sentiment which have attended our proceedings will, we trust, have a happy influence on the cause in which we are engaged, and aid in advancing the great interests of humanity and freedom.

The work which we have undertaken is not a light and trivial nature. It is, on the contrary, one of the utmost magnitude and importance. To remove the foul blot which now stains our country, to break the chains with which so many of our degraded fellow creatures are fettered, and to qualify them for the station for which a beneficent Creator designed them, are labours requiring the vigorous endeavours of every friend to mankind throughout the world. We, therefore, earnestly entreat that the cause may not be suffered to slumber in your hands, but that every favorable opportunity may be *eagerly* embraced of promoting the work of gradual emancipation.

The subject of the education of the blacks has claimed a share of our consideration. It is an object of so much interest that we cannot too often bring it to view. To adopt the language of the Convention of 1795, "when we have restored the African to the enjoyment of his rights, the great Work of justice and benevolence is not accomplished—The new born citizen must receive that instruction and those powerful impressions of moral and religious truth which will render him capable and desirous of fulfilling the various duties he owes to himself and to his country." On this point we particularly refer you to the sentiments so forcibly expressed in the addresses of preceding conventions, and we strenuously urge a strict compliance with the recommendations therein contained.

The great increase of the practice of kidnapping in defiance of every principle of moral and legal obligation, induces us pressingly to recommend the most earnest endeavours to root out the enormous evil. In this instance there will be less to combat than on the general principle; the slave holders themselves being interested in preventing this addition to the many calamities inflicted on the unfortunate blacks.

With feelings of sorrow and regret, we learn that the horrid trade to Africa for slaves is still continued by many of our fellow citizens. The hearts of those who can contemplate this subject without emotion must indeed be destitute of every sentiment of tenderness. It seems scarcely possible that men accustomed to the enjoyment of liberty, and partaking of the blessings of a free government should so far disregard the rights of humanity as to engage in so diabolical a commerce. The fact however, incredible as it may seem, certainly exists and to a very alarming extent, particularly in the eastern states; we wish to arouse your zeal on the occasion and to

253

incite your diligence and activity in carrying into rigorous execution the laws of the states and of the general government against such atrocious offenders.

The several Societies having expressed themselves favorable to the adoption of a constitution for the government of future conventions, we have made it a subject of our deliberations and being of opinion that the measure would be attended with considerable advantages we have agreed on a plan which we shall forward to you. The provisions of this instrument you will observe are of as general a nature as its objects would admit, and we hope it will prove acceptable to our constituents. If its present form should be approved you will be aware of the necessity of its speedy ratification. From the difficulty of framing a work of this kind, and accommodating it to the wishes and sentiments of every individual, it is hoped that verbal criticisms and alterations of an unimportant nature will be avoided; this point however, we submit to your prudent consideration and decision. Should you think proper to adopt it we request your aid in establishing the contemplated fund.

As numerous misrepresentations of the views of our institutions have gone abroad, and as the unhappy attempt at insurrection on the part of some of the blacks in the southern states, has been called in aid of these misrepresentations by the enemies of liberty, and lessened the activity of some of its friends, we have judged it prudent to publish an address to our fellow citizens, copies whereof will be transmitted to you; you will observe from a perusal of its contents that its object is also to bear our testimony, and produce individual exertion against the abominable practice of kidnapping and the cruel trade to Africa, which, as before observed, still disgrace our country. We anticipate the satisfaction of your approval of this measure, and invite your assistance by every means in your power, in giving it general circulation.

We have had our attention drawn to a subject, believed by our predecessors to be of considerable importance to the work of emancipation; the project of forming a history of slavery in the United States. With a view of forwarding this design, we have appointed a committee to examine and arrange the various papers and documents heretofore received by the several Conventions; to prepare an analysis of their contents, and to report the same with such other information as they may be enabled to obtain, to the ensuing Convention. We request you to examine the minutes and addresses heretofore transmitted, for the purpose of ascertaining how far the requisitions of former Conventions have been complied with on your part, and if my information connected with the object in view remains to be afforded, a benefit will arise from its speedy communication to the committee, and if individuals friendly to the cause, be possessed of any important documents relating to this subject, the committee will no doubt make a proper use of any information with which they may be favored.[8]

To the   *Society for Promoting the*
                          Abolition of Slavery.

It is with lively satisfaction that the eighth Convention of Delegates from different Abolition Societies in the United States, embrace the opportunity of addressing you on the interesting cause, which thus continues to claim our persevering attention, the ultimate success whereof, will, we confidently hope, yield an ample reward for all our labours.

Various and important, in our opinion, are the benefits resulting from thus meeting in annual Conventions. For though we are not invested with legislative influence, yet the opportunity, by this means afforded, for a free interchange of sentiments and communion of feelings, gives energy to action and animation to those who, from multiplied difficulties, are almost ready to relinquish the pursuit.

We have with the united consent of our constituents, fully ratified the Constitution which was presented for your consideration, and have appointed officers for the ensuing year.

This organization of the body, will, we earnestly hope, induce your renewed attention to the nomination of Delegates to the next Convention, and we urge the necessity of your deputing those, whom you have reason to believe, may be willing to devote an adequate portion of their time and attention to a compliance with the objects of their appointment; we request also in an especial manner that you will not fail, regularly to forward written communications from your societies.

Several societies have instructed their representatives to pay certain sums towards the formation of a general fund, from which, if it continues to accumulate, as we hope, it will, much good may be expected to our common cause, particularly in furnishing aid to those societies who are deficient in pecuniary resources.

In the promotion of the laudable purposes to which this fund may be thus applied, we trust our friends in several of the Eastern States, whose domestic exertions have become almost unnecessary by the disappearance of slavery from amongst them, will feel a lively interest;—we, therefore, earnestly solicit their peculiar attention to the subject, persuaded they will feel, in a consciousness of having done well, and in a view of the useful result of their beneficence, an ample reward. We are aware of the varied difficulty and opposition that attend the interference of some societies in this benevolent undertaking. But we sincerely hope they may not be overcome by any discouragements, and we request that they may continue to meet at regular periods, to preserve the form of their association, embracing every opportunity that may occur for useful exertions.

As the general establishment of a legislative plan, for the gradual abolition of slavery throughout the United States, is a desideratum highly interesting to humanity, we cannot but press all those societies which exist in states, where no such legal provisions are in force, to make every proper exertion, in promoting the enaction of a law to this effect.

Much has been said by former Conventions on the subject of schools, and the vast importance of cultivating the minds and the morals of the blacks; no doubt difficulties of various kinds arise in many places to the attainment of this essential point, yet the happy effects abundantly conspicuous in divers neighbourhoods, on a persevering attention to this object, furnish great encouragement to unrelaxed exertion, and we sincerely hope that you may not diminish in zeal, for the promotion of this benevolent, this consistent work. We learn with particular pleasure, that the state of Schools for the African race, is, in several places, flourishing and progressive; and that in others, much good has been done therein, by the laudable and disinterested demand the acknowledgment of our unfeigned approbation.

We perceive, with emotions of horror and regret, that the diabolical practice of kidnapping, notwithstanding the vigilance of societies and recommendations of former Conventions, prevails in many places to a lamentable extent. We are also informed that a new species of this wicked outrage on the feelings of humanity is pursued by the perpetrators taking advantage of the provisions of the fugitive act to lay unfounded claims on the blacks and thus, under colour of the law, to drag them into slavery. We recommend you to urge every suitable means to procure such modifications of your laws as they may need to fit them for holding out efficient and prompt restraints against those wicked proceedings, and for bringing the offenders to exemplary punishment.

We are informed by the reports from New-Jersey, that a new society has been established at Trenton, forming a constituent branch of the general society of that state. This has afforded us peculiar satisfaction; it promises to be materially useful to the cause, and we recommend the example as worthy of your special notice, and so far as you deem it practicable of your example.

In one of the societies from which we have had communications, a standing committee has been appointed, who are charged with the selection and publication of such extracts, essays and fugitive pieces relative to slavery, as they apprehend may give currency to the subject and revive in the minds of our fellow citizens, from time to time a few reflections on the condition of those who still wear the galling chains, deprived of one of the dearest privileges of our nature. We highly approve of this mode of circulating a knowledge of the subject, and recommend it to the imitation of all, who are not in a similar practice.

The committee appointed by the last Constitution to arrange the papers and documents relative to the formation of a history of slavery in the United States, and to produce an analysis of their contents, produced a report, from which we have judged it right to nominate three of our members in Philadelphia to engage some suitable literary character to undertake the work, and to have it published under the care, and superintendence of the committee; should you be in possession of any documents or other important information on the subject, we request you will forward them free of expense and with all convenient dispatch to the said committee, in order that they may be used as circumstances may render necessary.

The circuitous trade to Africa we have reason to believe, still continues to be carried on, particularly from many ports in the Eastern States, and although several of the attempts which have been made to punish infractions of the laws of the United States on this subject, have not resulted in the wished for event, nevertheless, we invite your vigilant and persevering opposition to this disgraceful traffic, and attention to the discovery and prosecution of the offenders, and we are willing to hope that though a partial perversion of the public sentiment, and the cupidity of interested individuals, may for a time, present considerable discouragement, yet that the virtuous exertions of the friends of the human race, will at last be blessed with the merited success.

To conclude, fellow labourers, we believe the magnitude of the work in which we are engaged is by no means lessened, and that the alarming and direful consequences attendant in various quarters, on this unchristian and inhuman usurpation of power, call for our united vigilance, and redoubled exertions, in contributing our share towards the eradication of this evil so portentous to our land.[9]

To the   *Society for Promoting the*
                          Abolition of Slavery.

We have received, with cordial satisfaction, the addresses to this Convention from the societies in New-York, New-Jersey, Pennsylvania, and Delaware.

This interchange of opinion and information, between the Convention and its constituents, is as the vital current of the body, flowing from part to part, and communicating genial warmth, and health, and vigour, to every portion of the system.

Our satisfaction would have been much increased, could we have acknowledged the receipt of communications and delegations from several societies which were represented in former Conventions, but from whom we have now to direct intelligence; and had some of the addresses which have now no direct intelligence contained more detailed information.

Impressed with a sense of the interesting nature of the subject, we cannot but call your renewed attention to the education of the blacks. The schools are represented as being, in some parts, in a flourishing condition; while in others it is to be feared, little or nothing has been done towards their establishment and support. We recommend to such societies as have it not in their power, from the scantiness of their funds and other circumstances, to employ regular tutors, to form associations of their members, or other well disposed individuals, to instruct the people of colour in the most simple and useful branches of education; especially on the first day of the week—a day too often devoted to dissipation. It is also of importance that their religious and moral education should keep pace with their knowledge of letters, or much permanent good will not be accomplished. They should be taught to fear and venerate the Deity; to respect the laws of the country, and in all things to act as becomes men escaped from bondage, and on whose good conduct must, in some measure, depend the liberation of their brethren, and the kind of treatment of such as remain in slavery. We believe it would be profitable occasionally to convene them, in order to afford suitable opportunities to impress their minds with these truths.

As much good may be expected to result from the establishment of a fund, to be at the disposal of the Convention, we hope the laudable example set by some of the societies, in their donations for that purpose, will be followed by wealthy individuals, and by other societies who are in a capacity to afford it.

A person of established literary reputation has been engaged to write a history of the rise, progress, and present state of slavery in the United States; and some advancement has been made in the work—As a great variety of information on this subject will be necessary, to enable the author to compose a

258

correct and ample history, you are requested to collect and forward, without delay all such essays and facts, relative to the design, as may be in your power.

At the same time that we invite a vigilant and constant attention, in the friends of the blacks, to prevent as far as their power extends, the infraction of the laws of the country in favour of emancipation, we confidently trust that due care will be observed to select men to the several offices of the societies, who have their zeal tempered with prudence and knowledge; for we are sensible, that for want of sound discretion on the part of some well-meaning but over-zealous individuals, the views and conduct of the body at large, have been grossly misunderstood; the cause has suffered undeserved reproach in the minds of some of our fellow citizens, and heavy expenses have been incurred in the unfavorable termination of suits undertaken without sufficient evidence, and with too much precipitation.

Being persuaded that no favourable opportunity should be lost for impressing the public mind with the iniquity of slavery, and the varied vices and evils, which are incident to it, in all their forms and consequences, we entreat such of you as have not chosen Standing Committees, charged with the publication of extracts and fugitive pieces, on this very interesting subject, to adopt the measure. Its utility has been fully proven by experience, which is the best of wisdom. To those societies who have derived advantage from the practice, we recommend a diligent and habitual attention to the subject.

We observe, with much sensibility and regret, that the inhuman and wicked practice of kidnapping, still prevails in our country, and that several cases of it have occurred since the meeting of the last Convention. Was there no other object to claim the ardent sympathy, and the active opposition of our associated brethren, than this alone, it would of itself be sufficiently interesting and momentous to justify an union of all our powers, and a vigorous combination of all our efforts, to resist this single enormity, this cruel and savage violation of the rights of our fellow-men. We request that you will, in your succeeding communications to the Convention, furnish accurate accounts of the several cases which may come under your notice, and that you will detail with precision, such of them as may be attended with particular circumstances of atrocity. The perpetrators should be known and exposed to public odium. Their names whenever detected, should be circulated throughout the continent, through the medium of the public prints; and no offender, who can be brought to punishment, should be suffered to escape the just penalty of his transgressions.

The discouragements which prevail among the friends and

259

advocates of the African race, especially to the southward, have excited the anxious concern of the Convention. While we have nine hundred thousand slaves in our country—while we have the strongest evidence that new importations will take place—while the abominable practice of kidnapping exists to an alarming and most sorrowful extent—while we have reason to believe that hundreds of vessels sail annually from our shores to traffic in the blood of our fellow-men—and while we feel, acknowledge, and deplore, that the cause of emancipation has many strenuous, powerful, and unwearied opponents in every quarter of the union—Can this be the time to remit our effort? and to abandon that standard under which, with the favour and protection of Providence, so many thousands have been rescued from the yoke of bondage, and restored to the enjoyment of their natural rights? Not so brethren—Be not disheartened—Let us rather redouble our diligence to help forward the great and good work in which we have engaged; resting our hopes of ultimate success, on our honest and disinterested endeavours, and on the justice of our cause.[10]

To the   *Society for promoting the Abolition of Slavery.*

THIS Convention has the pleasure of acknowledging the reception of addresses from the Societies of New York, New Jersey, Pennsylvania, and Delaware; and of a communication from the Society of Rhode Island. A free interchange of sentiments between the different societies, through the medium of the Convention, we consider as a matter of primary importance. By such communications, the Convention becomes the central fountain, into which the opinions, and experience of the different societies are received, and from whence the united knowledge may be transmitted to the individual branches. We therefore recommend, to each society, a continuation of the practice, and we earnestly entreat them to comply with our request of last year, by furnishing us with "more detailed information," not only respecting the moral, literary, and legal condition of slaves, and other persons of colour, within their districts, but also with minute accounts of every attempt at kidnapping, mentioning the names of the parties concerned in the business. Such information will open to us an extensive view of slavery and its attendant evils, as they exist within the whole circle of our societies, and enable us to labour with greater certainty and more effect, for the performance of the solemn duties which are imposed on us.

We perceive, with sincere and deep regret, that some societies have not yet made much progress in the establishment of schools for the literary and moral improvement of the people of colour. We cannot withhold the expression of our anxiety on this subject.... We consider it a matter of high moment, involving the most interesting and affecting consequences. Shall we, by lukewarmness or neglect, give the enemies of our institutions the triumph of reproaching us with indifference.... With a want of that virtue ... that inflexible spirit of perseverance, without which the tree we have nourished, and hoped to bring to maturity, may erect its barren and useless branches before us, a gloomy monument of our indolence? With what reproaches, and difficulties, and dangers, have our societies heretofore contended! with a courage and temperance, which could have been maintained only in a great and good cause; we have withstood all the rude onsets of the enemies of rational liberty, and, under the protection of a wise Providence, we have, step by step, moved forward, subduing by the eloquent voice of reason and humanity, the oppressors of the weeping Africans, until we have seen the fetters fall from thousands, and beheld those, who had been reduced to the condition of beasts of burthen, rising from the earth with the privileges and rights of men! Shall we now desert them? after teaching them that they belong to the rank of man, shall we refuse to employ our time and talents in preparing their minds for the enjoyment of those pleasures, and the practice of those virtues which belong to their species? We have hitherto been their friends; if we now desert them, to whom shall they apply for help? Their fate, as it regards human aid, rests chiefly with us. Let us try the strength of our virtue.... Let us decide, by a vote in our societies, whether we will continue our parental care over them, or leave them friendless and abandoned to their own weakness and ignorance. This vote will proclaim to the world the sincerity of our views, and the integrity of our hearts. If we are weary of well-doing, we shall forsake them; but if our breasts still glow with benevolence, we shall decide, with one voice, in their favour. Before we determine the important question, it will be well for us to recollect that no good deed passes unrewarded. Every individual sacrifice, to humanity and virtue, will be placed to our credit in the records of our lives.

The Convention have been informed, by one society, that "not being able to raise funds for the payment of a tutor, they have appointed a committee, of ten members, who maintained a school during the last summer and autumn, on the First-day afternoon of each week, for the moral and literary education of people of colour," and that they propose re-commencing the business early next summer. This conduct merits and receives our approbation, and we regard it as highly worthy the attention of societies in similar circumstances.... We exhort them to "go and do likewise."

In the cities of New York and Philadelphia, the schools appear to be in a flourishing condition; in some of them persons of colour are employed as teachers, and where such persons, properly qualified, can be procured, the Convention believes the employment of them will be attended with peculiar advantages.... It will contribute to kindle a spirit of emulation in their brethren. In some places there are persons of colour whose pecuniary circumstances would allow them to give something towards the support of schools, for their own class, and we think it proper and just, that their aid should be solicited.

Several societies have informed us that benefit has arisen from their meetings with the coloured people. We therefore, recommend that each society select a committee, of suitable members, whose duty it shall be to assemble the free persons of colour, as often as they shall judge it useful, and communicate to them such advice and instruction, as they shall think necessary; and that the committee report, in writing, the result of their opinions respecting the conference, to the next succeeding meeting of their society.

The Convention of last year, recommended to each society, the appointment of a committee for the purpose of publishing extracts, and essays, shewing the impolicy, and injustice of slavery; but we observe, with regret, this subject has not received that serious and diligent attention to which it was entitled. No abolition society can be ignorant that there are yet many thousands of persons, within the United States, who are opposed, on what they esteem grounds of justice and policy, to African liberty. Many remain under the erroneous notion, that the blacks are a class of beings not merely inferior to, but absolutely a species different from the whites, and that they are intended, by nature, only for the degradations and sufferings of slavery. There was a time when the people of all our states, and members of every religious sect, were overshadowed by the darkness of this error, and, in consequence of their erroneous opinions, practised legal violations of the rights of humanity. The pen, and the tongue of reason and truth have convinced thousands of the falsity of those opinions, and such instruments should not be permitted to rest in idleness, until truth and humanity obtain a complete and universal triumph.

We lament the continued necessity, of inviting your attention to the clandestine commerce, which, in defiance of our state and national laws, is still carried on to the coast of Africa. Information has been received that artful men, with the secrecy of midnight robbers, have contrived means of loading their vessels for Africa, and obtaining cargoes of slaves, and vending them in the West Indies, without subjecting themselves to such detection as would lead to legal punishment. Let us keep a watchful eye on all persons of this class, and endeavour to deter them from the perpetration of such cruel offences, by the only argument of which they are susceptible, the fear of the just punishment of the laws of their country.

This address will be accompanied by a number of copies of our advice to the free people of colour. We leave it to your discretion, to distribute them, together with such parts of our former advices, as you shall judge expedient.

Finally, brethren, we beseech you by the rights of humanity ... by the pleadings of mercy ... by the great and interesting cause which we have espoused, that you suffer nothing to discourage you in your useful labours, ... but that you persevere in your good works of justice and benevolence, with a temperate and firm spirit until your task, by the aid of Providence, shall be accomplished.[11]

To

WE the American Convention of Delegates for promoting the Abolition of Slavery, feeling the importance of the business which you have committed to our deliberation, deem it our duty to address you, and to communicate some of the subjects which have claimed our particular attention.

We learn that in some parts of the United States, there are yet men so lost to all honourable feelings, so deeply depraved as to violate those laws of their country which were intended to protect the rights of free persons of colour. Those who have any knowledge of the heart of man, his selfish attachments, and the firm grasp with which he seizes and holds all that he calls his own, cannot be surprized at the reluctance which individuals evince, in resigning their claims to those people of colour who are legally their slaves: but at this period when the rights of man are so well understood, in a country where the highest degree of civil liberty is enjoyed by the white citizens, it appears astonishing that the kidnapper should be permitted to carry on his depredations; that his audacious encroachments on the rights and happiness of the suffering people of colour should, for a moment, be tolerated. We hope our feelings on this subject, will not be considered as the offspring of misguided zeal. Every one in whose heart the pulse of benevolence beats, whose sentiments are not degraded beneath the dignity of man *must feel* on this occasion; he must be sensible of the deep crime which the kidnapper commits against the laws of his country, and the violent nature of his trespass on the dearest rights of humanity. The man of colour whom our country has declared *free*; around whose liberty the law has thrown its protecting arms, in defiance of the voice of that country and that law, is torn from his family by the midnight robber, and transported to the mournful regions of perpetual slavery, while his wife and his little ones are left to struggle alone, in poverty, for the bread of mere existence. This is a melancholy but a faithful picture of the miseries occasioned by the detestable kidnapper. Let us exert our best faculties for the purpose of eradicating such evils. Those societies who form the line of demarcation between the states in which slavery has been partially or totally abolished, and those in which it is unconditionally maintained, are particularly and earnestly requested to use all their vigilance for the detection of kidnappers and the suppression of those crimes. We do not mean to say that any deficiency, in proper zeal, has been manifested by those societies, we rather wish to speak the language of encouragement.

We observe with satisfaction the continued care, of several societies, in the great task of education. We hope there is not a single member of any one of our societies who does not perceive the importance of it. To make men happy in themselves and useful to society it is not necessary that they be taught the abstruse sciences, but it is indispensibly requisite that they be qualified to form a correct estimate of those powers, and to exercise those faculties which the Great Creator of man has been pleased to intrust to their care. The Abolition Societies may be regarded as the paternal protectors and friends of the people of colour. They have undertaken that task, and it is their duty to persevere in their labours, to hold out to the end in their good work. Although liberty be a blessing, when we obtain the freedom of the slave our work is not completed. It then becomes our peculiar charge to endeavour to teach the enfranchised man how to value, and how to employ the privileges which have fallen to his lot. This noble task is rapidly progressing in some societies, and we seriously and affectionately invite others to imitate their benevolent efforts. Lancaster's plan of instruction seems admirably adapted for the communication of the rudiments of literature, we hope there are, in all our societies, some individuals whose condition of life will allow them leisure, and whose virtue will animate them to persevering efforts in the blessed task of instructing the forlorn, and in some places, we may say almost friendless people of colour. Let them be taught to read and they will be introduced to a knowledge of the scriptures, those sacred repositories of moral and divine truth; let them be taught the elementary branches of arithmetic which will prepare them for the common concerns of life.

We rejoice with you that our national Government has had the wisdom and humanity, to embrace the first constitutional opportunity afforded, to pass a law which entirely prohibits our citizens from foreign traffic in human flesh. We hope our hearts are not without sentiments of sincere gratitude to the great disposer of events for that signal blessing. But we have to sympathize with nearly a million of human beings who are subject to the bonds of slavery within the United States, we have yet to mourn over this dishonour of our country. The progress of truth, or correct opinion of right has accomplished great ends, but much remains to be done. Domestic slavery is a national crime; a crime which is calculated to excite in the man of upright sentiments, serious and awful apprehensions of the final consequences of its continuance. It is our duty to employ the pen and the press for the dissemination of such arguments as shall convince our countrymen of the injustice and impolicy of such slavery. The man whose mind is clouded by prejudice, while his heart is hardened by selfish considerations, must have truth frequently repeated, and presented under various aspects, before his errors can be corrected, his prejudices subdued, and the noble feelings of philanthropy excited in his breast. This is a constant, an arduous, but not a hopeless duty. We therefore recommend the frequent publication of extracts from celebrated works, or original essays, tending to establish the justice and policy of gradual and general emancipation.

One society has informed us that a committee of its members held a satisfactory conference with the blacks and other people of colour. We think such conferences, under the direction of discreet men, may have a beneficial influence on the minds of the blacks, we again recommend the subject to your attention. In such meetings the advice of former Conventions may be renewed, and, we think, the necessity of legal marriages, honesty in their dealings, and the importance of religious instruction should be impressively urged upon them.

We learn that Thomas Clarkson's history of the abolition of the slave trade, which has been reprinted in Philadelphia, is now published for the emolument of its author. When we consider the value of this work to the cause of emancipation, the indefatigable zeal of that powerful and benevolent advocate for the rights of the Africans, and his great expense in the performance of his labours, we think ourselves bound in duty, to contribute our aid for the general circulation of his interesting history. We therefore earnestly recommend that work to your patronage, and we hope you will cheerfully employ such means, as you may think effectual for promoting its sale.[12]

To the   Society for promoting the abolition.

IN discharging the customary duty of addressing you, we have great satisfaction in stating, that the business of the Convention has been conducted, throughout, with the utmost cordiality.

We cannot, however, forbear the expression of our sincere regret, that so few societies have been represented in this Convention. When we contemplate the interesting magnitude of the cause in which we have unitedly and voluntarily embarked—when we consider the solid and obvious advantages, which have hitherto been derived, to the friends of humanity, from a free and personal interchange of opinion and from unison of action, we confidently trust that trifling impediments will not be suffered to interpose in the fulfilment of our duty. We therefore, in that freedom which becomes the advocates of truth and justice, do most earnestly and affectionately recommend a more zealous attention to this important point, in order that the succeeding Convention may be more fully attended. Much has been accomplished, but, when we remember that it has been officially announced by the late census that nearly twelve hundred thousand of our fellow beings remain in a state of abject bondage in our deluded country, it surely will not, cannot be denied, that much, very much, remains yet to be done. You have put your hands to the plough—look not back till ye shall have accomplished the end. You have commenced the wrestling, cease not your hold till ye shall have obtained the prize.

While against the oppressor, we plead the cause of the oppressed—While we invite the unhappy slave to a patient and Christian submission to his condition—and urge on his legalized master a humane exercise of his power—While we feel ourselves bound, by all honourable and lawful means, to protect those whom the laws have enfranchised, from being again dragged into slavery—let us not forget how much depends on the careful instruction of all who are free. Without this our labour will be but very partially accomplished. This great object, so important to ourselves, as members of those who are the subjects of our care; and the Convention have learned, with heart-felt satisfaction, that it is proposed, by the people of colour in New York, to raise a fund among themselves, for the instruction of their orphan children. This circumstance, while it proves an honourable testimony to the persevering zeal of the New-York Manumission Society, reflects great credit on the blacks themselves; and we hope the example will not be without beneficial effects elsewhere. Could such of these people as have it in their power, be persuaded to apply a part of their surplus earnings to the establishment of similar funds, instead, as is unhappily the case in too many instances, of spending their money in courses which prove injurious to their health and morals, not only their race, but the community at large, would from such meritorious efforts speedily reap the most unequivocal advantages.

It appears that, in defiance of the laws already provided to interdict the inhuman practice, and notwithstanding the enormity of the offence in itself, men are yet found, so lost to justice and the tender feeling of humanity, as to be guilty of carrying free blacks from some of the states, and selling them as slaves in others. We, therefore, recommend renewed vigilance to detect and prosecute these hardened transgressors—and that, whenever the laws are found to be defective, or insufficient to the correction of the evil, application be made, to the constituted authorities, for such amendments, and alterations as may be necessary and effectual; that our country may be purged of this most grievous iniquity.

The Pennsylvania Society accompanied their address to the Convention with some very interesting documents, which were transmitted to them by the African Institution in London, part of which it is proposed to publish in the form of an appendix to our printed minutes, in order that the information which it contains may be more generally diffused. The Convention have not, at this time, deemed it necessary or expedient, to take any further order on this subject. Were the laws of the general government, in relation to the slave trade, duly and faithfully executed, it is believed they would put an end to this inhuman traffic, which, to the disgrace of some of our citizens, it is but too evident they have been carrying on under the protection and cover of foreign flags. We invite you to a careful perusal of these documents. They contain the evidence of a mass of iniquity, the development of which cannot but excite the indignation of every feeling mind.

You will perceive, by the minutes of our proceedings, that the friends of humanity have gained an accession to their cause in the establishment of an Abolition Society in Kentucky. We trust their labours will be blessed with success, and that this dawn of light will burst into a more perfect day on our brethren of the southern states, casting its cheering and benign influence alike on all; that the ensanguined lash of the task master, and the cries of the slave, may no longer appal the ear and sicken the heart, in this boasted land of mercy and equal rights.[13]

The Committee appointed to draft an address to the several Abolition, Manumission, &c. Societies in the United States—reported an essay, which was read, considered by paragraphs, and adopted, as follows:—

To the various Societies instituted to promote the Abolition of Slavery in the United States, or to protect the rights and improve the condition of the People of Color.

The American Convention of delegates from Societies, associated in various parts of our country, to promote the abolition of slavery and improve the condition of the African race, convened in Philadelphia, having harmoniously transacted its important concerns, address you at this time with increased interest for the success of the cause they have espoused; firmly relying on the Divine Being for a blessing on their feeble efforts to promote the cause of justice and mercy.

The communications forwarded to the Convention at this time, fully evince that the cause of emancipation continues to advance, and that even in the strongholds of slavery the friends of the oppressed slave are fast increasing in numbers. Our fellow citizens of the south and west are becoming more and more awakened to a sense of the evil, injustice, and impolicy of slavery; and we firmly trust that those who have engaged in the benevolent work of "restoring liberty to the captive, and to let the oppressed go free," will not look back with discouragement at the long period this cruelty has prevailed, but continue to press forward with increased energy to the goal they have set before them, the complete and final abolition of slavery within the United States. To promote this desirable object we know of no measures more efficient than the formation of anti-slavery associations, particularly in situations where the evils of slavery prevail; for experience has fully proved that a combination of effort has often effected that which individual exertion has attempted in vain. The dissemination of useful works and tracts on the subject of slavery, cannot but have a powerful effect in enlightening the public mind on this awfully interesting subject. The Convention would particularly recommend the following works to your special attention—viz: Clarkson's Abolition of the Slave Trade, abridged by Evan Lewis; Clarkson's Thoughts on Slavery; Laws of the State of Pennsylvania, passed 1780; Tract on Slavery, published by the Tract Association of Friends in Philadelphia; Hodgson's Letter to J. B. Say, on the comparative productiveness of Free and Slave Labor; and a work now preparing for publication in this city, entitled, A Sketch of the Laws in relation to Slavery in the United States, by George M. Stroud. They also recommend that each Anti-Slavery Society subscribe, and promote subscriptions among their members and others, for the Genius of Universal Emancipation, edited by Benjamin Lundy, of Baltimore; and to the African Observer, a periodical work published in Philadelphia, by Enoch Lewis; and the Freedom's Journal, a weekly paper published at New York, by John B. Russwurm, a person of color. All these works we believe are well conducted, and will be powerful aids to the cause of liberty and justice.

As an incipient step to the abolition of slavery, we earnestly recommend that immediate application be made to the Legislature of states where slavery exists, to prohibit the sale of slaves out of the state. The traffic which is thus carried on from state to state, is fruitful of evil consequences, not only depraving the minds of those engaged in it, but producing the most cruel separations of near connexions, and depriving its victims of almost every incentive to conjugal fidelity or correctness of conduct. Perhaps next in importance in meliorating the condition of the slaves, is the adoption of regulations for their religious instruction, and the education of their children.

The condition of the free people of color in the United States has claimed our attention, and we earnestly recommend to the several societies, not only to use their endeavors to protect them in their just rights, but to use every means in their power to elevate them in the scale of society, by affording them and their children the means of literary instruction. And as the first day of the week is too frequently spent by them in dissipation, we would suggest the formation of associations wherever practicable, for the establishment of first day or Sunday schools for their benefit, as well as schools on the other days of the week. The degraded condition of this class of men ought to call forth our regret and sympathy; being precluded from pursuing the lucrative employments of life, it is much to be desired that more of them than have heretofore been permitted may be instructed in handicraft trades, and employed in manufactures.

You will observe, by our minutes, that the Convention has again addressed Congress, on the important subject of the abolition of slavery in the District of Columbia, and the restriction of the further introduction of slaves into the Territory of Florida; and we hope our application will be supported by addresses from other bodies of our constituents. The Convention believes that if the advocates of freedom persevere in endeavoring to enlighten the public mind on this all important subject, that the time is not far distant when a triumph will be obtained over the strong prejudice and delusion which has so long continued, and the cause of justice and humanity will finally prevail.

The Convention fervently desires that all who have put their hands to this great work may really deserve the epithet of "Saints," which in irony has been reproachfully cast upon them; and by their energy, prudence, and moderation, convince their opponents they have been mistaken in their characters and conduct. And we confidently hope that the blessing of that Almighty Being, who equally regards the bond and the free, will crown your righteous labor with success.[14]

To the various Anti-Slavery Societies in the United States.

The American Convention, for promoting the abolition of slavery, and improving the condition of the African race, feeling desirous to encourage every measure that may have a tendency to aid this deeply injured people, and to relieve our country from the many evils inseparably connected with the system of individual oppression, take the liberty to address you upon the present occasion. And in the performance of this task, we are particularly solicitous to draw your attention to the subject of the abolition of slavery in the District of Columbia—a subject which we view as highly important, especially at the present moment, and deserving your most serious consideration.

When we reflect that the government of this District emanates from the Congress of the United States—that the power to regulate its political and municipal concerns is solely vested in

270

that body—that the people of every State must share the honor or opprobrium attending the course of conduct pursued by the authorities in the administration of its local government —and that the whole Union must be measurably responsible for the consequence resulting therefrom—when we take this view of the subject, we ought not for a moment to hesitate in appealing to the friends of humanity in every section of the country, and urging them to use all lawful and just means, within their reach, to limit, and finally to eradicate the demoralizing and corrupting system of slavery, which is yet upheld and tolerated there.

We will not enter into a minute detail of the many advantages that would result to the nation, either morally or politically, from the abolition of slavery, in the District aforesaid.—But we feel it an imperious duty to state, that in our opinion it would be attended with the most salutary effects on other portions of the Union, the *influence* of which would be incalculable. Under the present regulations, that distinguished spot on which is erected the sacred Fane of republican Freedom, is not only polluted by the galling shackle and the iron rod of oppression, but is absolutely converted into a great depository for the purchase and sale of human beings. The demoralizing effect which this must produce on the minds of many who become familiarized with it, and the odium which it attaches to us, in the estimation of enlightened foreigners, many of whom are constant witnesses thereof, must inevitably sap the foundation of our free institutions, and degrade our national character in the eyes of the world. This, we conceive, (to say nothing of the injustice of slavery and its concomitants,) should be a sufficient incentive to action—a sufficient inducement to labor in the holy cause of emancipation.

We are aware that it has been asserted, even on the floor of Congress, that we should wait until the people of that District themselves demand the abolition of the system of slavery. This doctrine we conceive to be fallacious. *The people there are not exclusively responsible for the national disgrace and criminality attending it.* The United States government, and of course, the people in every section of the Union, must bear the odium and meet the consequences:—and if so, it follows, that they have a perfect right to avert the same, by such just and legal means as their wisdom may point out, and their judgment select. But a portion of the people of that District *are* now demanding the eradication of the evil in question. Societies for the abolition of slavery have been organized among them; and they have protested against the continuance of the cruel and disgraceful practice. Let, then, the voice of their brethren elsewhere, be heard in unison with theirs. Let a strong appeal be made to the justice of the nation, that the constituted authorities may be induced to take up the subject, and bestow upon it that care which its importance imperiously requires.

271

To facilitate the accomplishment of this purpose, we would advise and recommend, that petitions and memorials be circulated by all the anti-slavery societies in each of the States and territories, for the signature of the citizens at large, and that they be forwarded to Congress by the Representatives, with instructions to lay them before that body, at an early day.

The Committee appointed to consider on and report what measures, &c. made the following report.

To the American Convention for promoting the Abolition of Slavery, &c.

The Committee appointed "to consider of and report what measures are necessary to be taken to promote the Abolition of the Domestic Slave Trade, and to protect free persons of color from being kidnapped, and whether any regulations might be adopted to prevent their being carried off in steam boats, stages, and coasting vessels," Report, that although in their opinion the intimate connexion existing between the Domestic Slave Trade and the system of slavery generally, precludes the expectation of applying a very efficient check to the one, except by a reduction of the other, yet they indulge the hope that the united influence of the several Abolition and Anti-Slavery Societies throughout the Union, directed to memorializing Congress, might procure some wholesome restraint upon a traffick fraught with such aggravated evil, and productive of such complicated misery.

In relation to the other subject submitted to them, viz. "the protection of free persons of color against kidnappers," the Committee are of opinion that the existing laws appear to be amply sufficient, if properly executed. They have, therefore, no other measures to recommend than the less obtrusive, but persevering exertions, of the several associations now formed, and which may be hereafter instituted, in the different sections of our country.

On behalf of the Committee,

DAVID SCHOLFIELD, *Chairman*.[15]

To the Abolition, Manumission, and Anti-Slavery Societies in the United States of America.

FELLOW LABORERS.—In reviewing the labors of the several Anti-Slavery Societies in the United States, there is much to cheer and gratify us. In looking over the different sections of our extended country, we find the cause of truth and humanity has slowly, but regularly advanced, in the minds of our fellow citizens generally. And we think nothing remains but perseverance in presenting the subject of slavery in its native deformity and its hideous aspect, to convince its advocates of their error, and to overcome all the opposition which can be arrayed against us. We are satisfied that to the perseverance of its advocates alone, we are indebted in a considerable degree for the change of opinion in the Northern, Middle, and some of the Western States: and we sincerely hope that a similar change will be ultimately made in the southern sections of our county. Let us never relax in our exertions to promote the emancipation, and meliorate the condition of slaves, till every human being in these United States shall equally enjoy, all the blessings of our free Institutions. How can we feel apathy or indifference while we can almost see from the windows of the room in which we are now deliberating, a receptacle for slaves, in which they are thrust, manacled and bound, all ready to ship by their avaricious owner in the first vessel whose master or owners are as hard hearted and unprincipled as himself! Yes! A dungeon, the horrors of which has called forth deep emotions of regret from all who are permitted to see the misery and wretchedness of its inmates, and particularly the tears and great agitation of a benevolent aged stranger, who, in visiting this country, which has always professed "That all men are by nature, and of right ought to be free," was surprised and shocked to find in the precincts of one of the most professedly enlightened and patriotic cities in the Union, a storehouse of human flesh!

Slavery in whatever point of light considered, is a revolting subject, repugnant to the best feelings of our nature, as inconsistent with the rights and happiness of man. We therefore, urge the respective Societies to renewed exertions, in behalf of our colored population, and to petition Congress to abolish Slavery in the District of Columbia, and also to prevent its further extension in the territories of the United States.

Deeply injured as they have been by the whites, the colored people certainly claim from us some degree of retributive justice; we would, therefore, at this time particularly and earnestly recommend to the renewed attention of all the Abolition, Manumission and Anti-Slavery Societies in this country, the all-important subject of giving the colored children literary instruction, and placing them as apprentices to useful trades.

For, unquestionably, the most efficient means of promoting the moral improvement of this degraded portion of the human family is the institution of schools. And it must be obvious to every thinking mind, that a portion of education will be absolutely necessary to prepare the slave for the enjoyment of freedom; and such has been the happy influence of it on the scholars in the New York African Free School, that the Trustees

273

in that city, state, that no scholar who has been regularly educated in their school, has ever been convicted of crime in any of their courts of justice. We have no doubt that if similar means were used in other places, the like happy result would be obtained. And it is equally certain, that facts like these do more to obliterate idle prejudice than all abstract reasoning on the subject.

The Convention have been highly pleased at this time by the exhibition of some handsome specimens of the skill and talent of some of the boys in the African school under the charge of *Charles C. Andrews*, in New York; creditable alike to the Teacher and the scholar. For a more particular description of these articles, we refer to page 20 of the minutes of this Convention.

We again call your attention to the following extract from our Address last year, particularly applicable to the present subject.

"As an incipient step to the Abolition of Slavery, we earnestly recommend, that immediate application be made to the Legislatures of States where Slavery exists, to prohibit the sale of slaves out of the state. The traffic which is thus carried on from state to state, is fruitful of evil consequences, not only depraving the minds of those engaged in it, but producing the most cruel separation of near connexions, and depriving its victims of almost every incentive to conjugal fidelity or correctness of conduct. Perhaps next in importance in meliorating the condition of slaves, is the adoption of regulations for their religious instruction, and the education of their children."

"And while the members of the several Societies are laboring in the good work of universal emancipation, the Convention would particularly urge them to use all suitable endeavours, mildly yet earnestly, to prevail upon slave holders to consider the injustice and impolicy of tolerating Slavery; and prevail, if possible, upon such individuals, to fall into some plan for its gradual and entire abolition in our otherwise free and favoured country."

We conclude with exhorting all those who are engaged with us in this important cause, to persevere, with the hope and confidence, that although our progress may be apparently slow, and our prospects sometimes appear discouraging, conformably to the dispensations of a Gracious Providence, truth and justice must, and will ultimately prevail.

All of which is respectfully submitted.

EDMUND HAVILAND, *Chairman*.[16]

274

F<small>ELLOW</small> C<small>ITIZENS</small>,—The American Convention for promoting the Abolition of Slavery, &c. now sitting at Washington, in the District of Columbia, having seriously taken into consideration the state of slavery in the said district, and in the United States generally, and viewed what furtherance the cause of freedom has received for some time past, are decidedly of opinion, that increasing efforts are at this time, emphatically called for, on the part of those who really think that "all men are created free and equal."

Memorial after memorial has been presented to Congress, but as yet they have produced but little visible effect. Small progress has been made towards abolishing slavery at the seat of our National Government. It has been a subject of much reflection what measures would be most likely to accomplish the grand object of our labours; and we would suggest whether greater success would not be likely to crown our efforts, by more widely disseminating a knowledge of the objects and principles of the different Anti-Slavery Societies throughout the Union. The subject has been referred at this session of our Acting Committee, but our funds are too limited to act as extensively as the great importance of the object requires. It is believed that a very large portion of the citizens of the United States are favorable to the emancipation of the people of colour, if it could be done upon legitimate principles, without infringing upon the rights of individuals or endangering the safety of the community; and if the dissemination of our principles was more generally attended to, co-adjuting societies would doubtless increase, and this Convention eventually become a body so numerous and respectable, that the National Government would not withhold its attention.

The proper education of the African race should form a prominent feature in all our efforts. It is with much gratification we are enabled to state that the address from New York, mentions a continued advancement in the literary improvement of the coloured children, and that from Philadelphia holds out the prospect of the establishment of a school for teaching them the higher branches of an English education and thus enabling them to act as teachers of their own isolated race. To break up the fallow ground, to sow the seed, and rear the tender plants of virtue in this degraded people, should be the wish of every heart and the effort of every hand. Let us establish schools, instruct the children, and show to the world that the mind of the African is not a soil where genius sickens and every virtue dies.

When we reflect that man is a being whose own interest generally forms the alpha and omega, beginning and end of life, a centre around which every passion and affection of his heart revolves, a boundary beyond which he seldom ventures, we are rather encouraged at the progress of our cause, than deterred by the magnitude of the work to be yet accomplished. Have not thousands been liberated, and the condition of tens of thousands improved? We believe there is a secret fire enkindled in the public bosom which will never be extinguished, until liberty be given to the captive and freedom to the oppressed. But this glorious principle needs to be encouraged and kept alive by the increasing efforts of its friends, to show to the world that they themselves are not weary of well-doing. Prejudices imbibed in youth and strengthened by age are to be broken down, and many an objection to be overcome.

In conclusion we would remark that although much censure has been cast upon us, we are renewedly convinced of the goodness and the justice of our cause. Let us exhort you to a patient continuance in your labours; and "the bread cast upon the waters, shall be found after many days."[17]

FOOTNOTES:

[1] Minutes of the Proceedings of a Convention of Delegates from the Abolition Societies, 1794, pp. 18-21.

[2] Minutes of the Proceedings of a Convention of Delegates from the Abolition Societies, 1795, pp. 26-31.

[3] Minutes of the Proceedings of a Convention of Delegates from the Abolition Societies, 1796, pp. 23-25.

[4] Minutes of the Proceedings of a Convention of Delegates from the Abolition Societies, 1796, p. 28.

[5] Minutes of the Proceedings of a Convention of Delegates from the Abolition Societies, 1797, pp. 22-25.

[6] Minutes of the Proceedings of a Convention of Delegates from the Abolition Societies, 1798, pp. 15-20.

[7] Minutes of the Proceedings of a Convention of Delegates from the Abolition Societies, 1800, pp. 20-23.

[8] Minutes of the Proceedings of a Convention of

Delegates from the Abolition Societies, 1801, pp. 42-46.

[9] Minutes of the Proceedings of a Convention of Delegates from the Abolition Societies, 1803, pp. 29-34.

[10] Minutes of the Proceedings of a Convention of Delegates from the Abolition Societies, 1804, pp. 35-39.

[11] Minutes of Proceedings of Tenth American Convention for the Abolition of Slavery, 1805, pp. 26-35.

[12] Minutes of the Proceedings of the Twelfth American Convention for promoting the Abolition of Slavery and improving the condition of the African Race Assembled at Philadelphia, 1809, pp. 26-31.

[13] Minutes of the Proceedings of a Convention of Delegates from the Abolition Societies, 1812, pp. 25-28.

[14] Minutes of the Proceedings of a Convention of Delegates from the Abolition Societies, 1827, pp. 20-22.

[15] Minutes of the Proceedings of a Convention of Delegates from the Abolition Societies, 1827, pp. 22-25.

[16] Minutes of the Proceedings of a Convention of Delegates from the Abolition Societies, 1828, pp. 28-30.

[17] Minutes of the Proceedings of a Convention of Delegates from the Abolition Societies, 1829, pp. 19-21.

CORRESPONDENCE

245 West 139th St.,
New York City,
January 11, 1920.

Carter G. Woodson, Ph.D.,
Editor, The Journal of Negro History,
Washington, D. C.

Dear Sir:

In the January, 1920, number of *The Journal of Negro History* there is an affidavit of Kelly Miller and Whitefield McKinlay to the effect that Mr. Cardoza, at one time secretary of State for South Carolina, stated to them that a number of colored men met and appointed a committee which was sent to Washington to get the advice of Charles Sumner and Thaddeus Stevens concerning the formation of the political organization for the newly enfranchised Negro shortly after the adoption of the 14th Amendment, pains being taken to keep the plans from both the native whites and the so-called carpet-baggers from the North, and that both Mr. Sumner and Mr. Stevens advised the committee to tender the leadership to native whites of the master class of conservative views, but that the plan was frustrated because they were unable to secure the consent of desired representatives of the former class to assume the proffered leadership.

I accept the fact that Mr. Cardoza made the statement as sworn to by Prof. Miller and Mr. McKinlay, but I must state with all of the emphasis that is possible that it is inconceivable to me how Mr. Sumner or Mr. Stevens could give such advice that would give the

278

leadership of the newly enfranchised Negroes to native whites of the master class, however conservative. All rebels were alike to Mr. Sumner and Mr. Stevens. No reference to conservative men of the master class will be found in the speeches or writings of either one.

I have read the speeches of both men on the Reconstruction measures as published in the *Congressional Globe* and I have failed to find one word uttered by either one that would lead me to believe that they would give the advice as stated in the affidavit. Both men held radical views as to reconstruction plans for the rebel States and were chiefly instrumental in having the Reconstruction Acts and the 14th Amendment passed. If it had not been for their untiring and persistent efforts, especially of Mr. Stevens, who practically dominated the House of Representatives from 1861 to the date of his death, I venture the assertion that the Reconstruction Acts and the 14th Amendment as passed could not have been passed.

It is possible that there were Negroes in South Carolina who had never felt the lash of the master class who were willing to curry favor with that class, regardless of the gratitude due the Northern men, white and colored, but I do not believe that the Northern Negroes (R. B. Elliott, Judge Wright, Judge Whipper, Henry W. Purvis, S. A. Swails, Dr. B. A. Bosemon, R. H. Gleaves, B. F. Randolph and others) would have deserted their Northern brethren, nor do I believe that the great men of the Republican Party (Conkling, Fessenden, Wade, Morton, Weed, Seward, Stanton, Chase, Boutwell, Washburne, Blaine, Sherman, Schurz, Phelps, Morrill, Bingham, Henry Wilson, Hoar and others) would have stood for the consummation of such a plan. I am sure, from what I knew of the Negroes of South Carolina, that they would have rebelled against the plan. If any committee went on to Washington it is possible that the members suggested the plan to Mr. Sumner and Mr. Stevens, but for them to advise along that line, a thousand times, no.

Everything done by Mr. Sumner and Mr. Stevens was done openly and above board and if they had given the advice as stated in the affidavit they would have had the courage of their convictions to have stated so publicly. It was not in their nature to play the cards from under the table.

Mr. Stevens, who was the author of the Reconstruction Act and most of the Reconstruction measures, ranking next to Alexander Hamilton as a constructive statesman, had embodied in the Act an oath that would have precluded men of the former master class, radical or conservative, from having anything to do with the Reconstruction legislation for the former rebel States. They could not register; therefore, they could not vote nor hold office until all of the provisions of the Reconstruction Acts, including the ratification of the 14th Amendment, were complied with, and their political disabilities removed. Practically all of the "cracker" element or "poor buckra" as designated by the Negroes could vote but the statement does not include that element.

The Republican Party was organized in South Carolina in July, 1867, and Northern men, white and colored, took an active part in the deliberations, R. H. Gleaves, a Northern Negro, being the President of the convention.

The Constitutional Convention met in Charleston, January 14, 1868, the Northern men practically dominating the proceedings, and before adjournment a State ticket was nominated. R. K. Scott, a Northern white man, was nominated for Governor. There were other white men (Northern) on the ticket. The Governor and Lieutenant-Governor were elected for two years and the other State officers for four years. This would indicate that the Northern men held the situation well in hand.

The South Carolina legislature under the Constitution of 1865, refused to ratify the proposed 14th Amendment on December 20, 1866. This legislature was composed of Democrats, all of the master class, conservative and radical, and in view of this it is incomprehensible to me how intelligent Negroes could have thought of tendering the leadership to any men of the master class. The conditions were such that men of the master class could not have accepted the leadership had they so desired after repudiating the 14th Amendment.

I have read Rhodes, Dunning, Burgess, Hart, Hollis, Pike, and Schouler, on Reconstruction, also S. W. McCall's *Biography of Thaddeus Stevens*, E. B. Callender's *Thaddeus Stevens, the Commoner*, and E. L. Pierce's *Memoirs and Letters of Charles Sumner*, and cannot find anything that would indicate that either Mr. Sumner or Mr. Stevens would give the advice as stated in the affidavit.

When Mr. Stevens introduced the proposed 14th Amendment it contained the following section:

Section 3.—Until July 4, 1870, all persons who voluntarily adhered to the late insurrection, giving it aid and comfort, shall be excluded from the right to vote for Representatives in Congress and for Electors for President and Vice-President.

This section was defeated but relative to it Mr. Stevens in a speech said:

"The 3rd section may encounter more difference here. Among the people I believe it will be the most popular of all the provisions; it prohibits rebels from voting for members of Congress and electors of President until 1870. My only objection to it is that it is too lenient.

281

I would be glad to see it extended to 1878, and to include all State and municipal as well as national elections."

There are two things about the advice that seem incongruous. First that intelligent Negroes would think that any men of the master class would join hands with them, some of whom had probably been their slaves, to govern the State. In the second place it is hard to believe that Sumner and Stevens, men of brilliant legal minds, would give advice that could not be carried out, even if practicable.

No man of the master class in South Carolina, however conservative, would stand for being called a scalawag.

There were practically no Union men in South Carolina. There were a few men who opposed secession at the time but when the ordinance of secession was passed a man who did not go with the State was considered a traitor. South Carolina was not considered a safe place for a white man who was opposed to secession after the ordinance was passed. This probably accounts for the statement in the last part of the affidavit relative to the frustration of the plans.

I regard the statement in reference to Messrs. Sumner and Stevens as a reflection on the memory of two of the greatest friends of the Negro.

History, unless it is based on facts, incontrovertible facts, is worthless.

If there are any readers of *The Journal of Negro History* who can produce "irrefragable evidence" relative to this matter I would be glad if they would do so. Truth is supreme and everlasting.

Prof. R. T. Greener, now of Chicago, Harvard's first Negro graduate, and the first and only Negro who occupied a chair in one of the old Southern universities, delivered on Public Day, June 29, 1874, in the historic South Carolina University, a most eloquent and scholarly address on "Charles Sumner, the Idealist, Statesman and Scholar." It made such an impression on the members of the faculty that they requested Prof. Greener to allow them to have it published and distributed. Professor Greener was the only Negro on the faculty. He occupied the chair of Mental and Moral Philosophy. Professor Greener was closer to Mr. Sumner than any other colored man, although very much younger, and enjoyed a friendship with the Senator vouchsafed to very few white men. It is possible that he may be able to throw some light on the subject in so far as Mr. Sumner is concerned.

Letters from scholars in this field will help us to learn the truth. A copy of a letter from J. F. Rhodes follows:

RAVENSCLEFT, SEAL HARBOR, MAINE,
Sept. 27, 1920.

HENRY A. WALLACE,

Dear Sir:

I have your valued favor of 23 with enclosure. It is now about fourteen years since I made my study of Reconstruction, and on some details my memory is not fresh, but I have no hesitation in saying that I never found anything that would lead me to believe that either Sumner or Stevens was in favor of the scheme outlined. The story told by the affidavit "does not fit into the situation" as Samuel R. Gardiner used to say. Nothing but irrefragible evidence could lead one to such a view. Your examination of the subject seems to have been thorough and I thank you for giving me the results of it.

	Very truly yours,	
enc. returned	Signed.	JAMES F. RHODES.

A Copy of a Letter from Samuel W. McCall

24 MT. VERNON ST., September 13, 1920.

MR. HENRY A. WALLACE,

245 West 139th St.,
New York, N. Y.

Dear Sir:

In reply to your favor of the 3rd inst., with enclosed copy of the affidavit concerning the position of Thaddeus Stevens and Charles Sumner upon the proposed policy of organization for the negroes, I would say that I do not remember ever having come across anything of the kind in my researches concerning Mr. Stevens, nor have I ever heard of it about Mr. Sumner.

Very truly yours,
Signed.   SAML. W. McCALL.

A Copy of a Letter from Hon. H. C. Lodge.

NAHANT, MASS.,
September 8, 1920.

My dear Sir:

I have received your letter of the 6th. I have never heard before of the point which you raise in regard to Mr. Sumner and really know nothing about it. As I am separated from my library, which is in Washington, I am sorry that I can give you no information about it, but if you would examine the Life of Charles Sumner by Edward L. Pierce, which is very elaborate and thorough, you would find something about it there, if anywhere.

Very truly yours,
Signed.   H. C. LODGE.

HENRY A. WALLACE, ESQ.,
245 West 139th St.,
New York, N. Y.

As the native white men of the master class were ineligible to hold office until the new Constitution and the 14th Amendment were ratified and their political disabilities were removed, even had they acted in an advisory capacity to the newly enfranchised Negroes, the Northern men being eliminated, only Negroes and white men of the "cracker" element could have held office and have been elected delegates to the Constitutional Convention.

There were some native white men of the "cracker" element in the Constitutional Convention and also in the first legislature elected.

Very respectfully,
HENRY A. WALLACE.

284

Carter G. Woodson, Ph.D.,
  Editor, The Journal of Negro History,
    1216 You St., N. W., Washington, D. C.

Dear Sir:

In connection with my letter to you of the 11th instant, pertaining to the affidavit of Messrs. Miller and McKinlay relative to the statement made by Mr. Francis Cardoza to them concerning Mr. Sumner and Mr. Stevens, as published in *The Journal of Negro History* for January, 1920, I respectfully invite your attention to a copy of a letter from Dr. J. W. Burgess, formerly of Columbia University. You will find him listed in "Who's Who in America."

Dr. Burgess is the author of two books covering the Civil War and the Reconstruction period, *The Civil War and the Constitution* and *Reconstruction and the Constitution*, and evidently made a thorough research in collecting the data for publication.

I regard this as a very important matter and the truth or falsity of the statement should be established. It is only by publicity that the facts can be established.

The names of Stevens and Sumner should be imperishable to the Negro race and any reflection on their attitude during the Reconstruction period should not go unchallenged.

A copy of letter from John W. Burgess follows:

Brookline, Mass.,
January 14, 1921.

Mr. Henry A. Wallace:

Your favor of January 12, forwarded to me here, interests me highly, and I thank you most sincerely for it. I am obliged to reply, however, that the affidavit of Messrs Miller and McKinlay astonished me very much. I cannot remember to have ever read anything of the kind anywhere and like you, I am very skeptical about it. I was in the world and a student at Amherst College in the year 1867, and was even then collecting the material for my history. I am pretty sure that I should have known of anything of this kind had it existed. I am going to try to run this assertion down, as I am here among the acquaintances and relatives of Sumner.

Very sincerely yours,
Signed.   JOHN W. BURGESS.

I have written to Dr. Burgess to inform me as to the result of his investigation and will let you know what he reports.

Yours very truly,
HENRY A. WALLACE.

BOOK REVIEWS

Rachel. By Angelina W. Grimké. Boston, Mass., The
Cornhill Company, 1920. Pp. 96. Price, $1.25.

Miss Grimké's drama of Rachel is a beautiful and
poetic creation. She has produced this effect by a
literary instinct which is fine and mainly cultivated. Its
native vigor carries the reader past an occasional
crudity, which it would seem to be hypocritical to
notice. The sweep of passion in the drama is
elemental. She has connected the story of a girl-
woman with the most woeful of earthly tragedies,
namely the crime of a great nation against one of its
component parts.

The feelings expressed in the drama, though
elemental, are uttered in the terms of modernity. The
structure of the drama is modern, and yet there is
something in the figure and movement of Rachel
herself which reminds the present writer of Antigone.
We do not see Antigone before the hour when she
has chosen to meet the doom that man's law has
decreed should she perform the task that human love
and religious faith have enjoined upon her. Antigone
goes to the death of her body declaring that in the
Infinite there is a longer time for love than there is on
earth.

But we do see Rachel before the ultimate choice has
come to her. She is a gay and happy girl. The drama
proceeds to the hour when she too must choose
between the issues of earthly love and those which
reach into eternity. She learns from her mother, Mrs.
Loving, that ten years before, they all lived in the
South and her father and her half brother were
lynched. Briefly summarized, this is Mrs. Loving's

story. As a young widow with a boy seven years old, she had married an educated man of color. She was a person of color herself. Mr. Loving owned and edited a paper in which he wrote on behalf of the people of color. A Negro innocent of all crime was murdered by a mob in that region. Mr. Loving denounced the murder and the murderers in his paper. He received an anonymous letter apparently written by an educated person, threatening him with death, if he did not retract what he had said. In the next issue of his paper he published an equally stern arraignment of the lynchers and their crime.

That night a dozen masked men broke into his house. Mr. Loving had a revolver. He defended his life and his home. Mrs. Loving tried to close her eyes. She could not. She saw all that happened in her bedroom. Four of the masked assailants fell. "They did not move any more ... after a little while." Then she saw her husband dragged out of the room. Her older boy, George, tried to help his stepfather. He was dragged out also. She went to the bedside of her two younger children. They were asleep. Rachel was smiling. The mother knelt down and covered her ears. When at last she let herself listen, she heard only the tapping of the branch of a pine tree against the side of the house. She did not know at first that it was *the tree*.

She fled with her two little children to the North. Those children had never before this day of revelation known how their father had died. The shadow of white cruelty to the body and souls of black folks had darkened somewhat over their lives in the North, but still they had been frolicsome and loving young creatures. Now they begin to realize the full significance of "race prejudice."

Rachel speaks to her mother: "Then, everywhere, everywhere throughout the South, there are hundreds of dark mothers who live in fear, terrible, suffocating fear, ... whose joy in their babies ... is three parts pain.... The South is full of ... thousands of little boys who one day may be, and some of whom will be lynched." "And the babies, the dear, little, helpless babies ... have *that* sooner or later to look to. They will laugh and play and sing and grow up, and perhaps be ambitious,—just for that."

"Yes, Rachel," answers her mother. The girl is one of those rare, feminine creatures whose soul and body are framed for maternity. In one swift rush of realization and of premonition, she comprehends all that the doom upon her race must eventually mean to her; she utters the cry of Africa's heart in America. "It would be more merciful to strangle the little things at birth.... This white Christian nation has set its curse upon the most beautiful, ... the most holy thing on earth ... motherhood."

Let us consider the historic background forth from which Miss Grimké has drawn her story. How do its incidents compare with known facts? In 1844, Massachusetts sent Judge Hoar to South Carolina to look after the interests of Massachusetts citizens of color there. The mob spirit showed itself so violently that this father of the future Senator was obliged to leave the South. More careful investigation into hidden causes for lynching would doubtless disclose more cases when educated men have been threatened or actually murdered. The rope with which to hang Wendell Phillips was actually carried into the hall where he was to speak. And the concerted plan had been to hang him on Boston Common.

The National Association for the Advancement of Colored People has investigated and published statistics showing that from 1889 to 1918 in the United States, 702 whites and 2522 blacks have been lynched, and that 11 of these victims were white women and 50 were women and girls of color. 6

whites and 142 Negroes were lynched for "no crime."

A few instances may well be cited. After some race riots in 1894 in which crimes had been committed on both sides, MacBride, "a respectable Negro of Portal, Georgia, was beaten, kicked, and shot to death for trying to defend from a whipping at the hands of a crowd of white men, his wife who was confined with a baby three days old." No offence on the part of the wife or the three days old baby is recorded, but the one of that helpless couple who could speak may have made about the riots remarks which disturbed the delicate sensibilities of these southerners who are so discriminating in their "chivalrous treatment" of women.

In 1895 a Negro in Texas was killed by a mob because he was accused of riding over a little white girl and seriously injuring her. "Later developments proved that the mob murdered the wrong negro." In 1899 in Louisiana "an attempt had been made to assault a white woman." Afterwards one Michael Curry saw a large Negro wandering in a field. For no reason whatever he decided that that man had been the assailant. Some white would-be murderers were quickly got together and shot the black man to death. Then it was discovered that he was an escaped lunatic, whose recent history did not square with the theory that he was the assailant.

In Georgia there was in 1911 a Negro woman described as "a good reliable servant" in her normal condition, but who was subject to attacks of violent mania. She killed a white woman in such an attack, as many years ago poor English Mary Lamb killed her own mother. The world knows with what chivalry her brother Charles shielded her through life. This Negro native of Georgia had once been adjudged to be a fit subject for an insane asylum; but the State institution was crowded and she was not then or now taken into it. Georgia took care of her in an easier way. Its lynchers put her into an automobile and placed a rope around her neck, fastened it to a tree, and started the car from under her, and left her to die. No arrests followed. But why mention that fact in this case? There are very few instances of mob murder when white murderers have ever been arrested.

In Oklahoma in 1914, two white men assaulted a seventeen-year-old girl of color. Her screams brought her brother to the rescue. There was a fight. He killed one of the men. The next day a mob came to the house in search of the brother. They could not find him so they killed the girl. In 1915 a sheriff in Georgia was murdered, and straightway five Negroes were killed. About a year later it was learned that all five were innocent. Sometimes "race prejudice" is given as the reason why certain Negroes were lynched. That probably means that in no such instance had the lynched Negro committed any offence, or at most none deserving the death penalty by any legal process.

The next historical question, which Miss Grimké's drama raises, was pertinently put to the present writer: "Was an educated, high-toned man like Loving ever lynched?" The answer as to probabilities is easily made. The American impulse towards mob-murder has always been strong whenever and wherever the rise of the Negro, either free or enslaved, has been considered vitally obnoxious to the community. In the slavery days, Northern mobs prepared often to kill William Lloyd Garrison, Wendell Phillips, and other Abolitionists, but they were foiled every time except when, in 1836, the Rev. Elijah P. Lovejoy, a white Northerner, was killed in Alton, Illinois, for denouncing, in his own paper, the burning to death of a Negro in Missouri. It was supposed, however, that the men who shot Lovejoy were Missourians and not Illinoisans.

The southern temper as to the educated Negroes was certainly voiced to a large extent, when in the eighties, the librarian of a large library in a southern town made answer to a question asked by a northern visitor: "Oh, no, the colored people don't come here to take out books. We don't believe in social equality, you know." And the Negro teacher in that town answered thus another Northerner's question: "Why don't you go there and ask for a book?" "I shouldn't like to do that, if I am going on living here."

In 1898 there were some terrible race riots in North Carolina. Two well educated Negroes owned and edited a small paper. Like the black Loving in Miss Grimké's drama, like the white historical Lovejoy, sixty-two years before, they printed editorials on the side of the Negroes. They were threatened. They fled and escaped pursuit. It is safe to assume that, had they been caught, they would have been lynched.

About a year ago, John R. Shillady, a white man, was engaged on a peaceful mission in Texas on behalf of the National Association for the Advancement of Colored People, whose agent he was. Prominent white citizens assaulted and beat him severely. It has always been the same story; white or black, educated or ignorant, in every part of this country the defenders of the Negroes have been liable to the decree or the abuse of the mob.

Still fresh is the memory of that shameful day when a white mob fired the Omaha jail where a Negro, still unconvicted of crime, was confined. He helped several of the other prisoners to get in line to leave the prison in safety, and then went down the steps himself to the mob which grabbed him and killed him. Meanwhile the ruffians had seized the Mayor of the town as he was on his way to try to enforce law and order. They hanged him, but somebody cut the rope before he was quite dead. There was strong evidence to show that the murdered Negro was innocent.

We come next to the question: What sort of men are they who make up these murderous mobs? Wendell Phillips once said, as to the North, that he had faced many mobs between the seaboard and the Mississippi, and that he never saw one that did not show that it was inspired if not actually led by "respectability and what called itself education." It is harder to know exactly what is the personnel of southern lynching parties. But a close study of known facts shows that "respectability and what calls itself education" has countenanced, approved, and participated in a large proportion of these orgies of horror. And the southern approval has developed in the South a most abhorrent type of white woman who holds up her babies to see a black man cut and burned to death. Miss Grimké's historical accuracy is unimpeachable when she allows "church members" to lynch Loving and his stepson.

George W. Cable said to the present writer in the winter of 1888-89, "You are right, the southerners do not want the Negroes to be educated." Miss Grimké, inferentially, dates her lynching somewhere in the decade of the nineties. The mass of black, brown, and olive-tinted ignorance at that time in the South, was appalling. It is appalling now—largely through the governing white man's fault. But still there were in the South at that time and before then many colored people who had obtained the rudiments of education and some who might be truthfully called well educated. Some of these became known to the whole country; but there might easily have been obscure ones like Loving scattered in many communities.

Now ordinary critics are sure to cry out against my

analysis of the historical situation and remind me of Booker Washington. They will say, "He was not lynched. He was accepted. Any Negro like him is safe, if he behaves himself." I answer that I have no fancy for mob murder or torture of any human being, ignorant or wise, good or bad. There are, moreover, other answers to the riddle of that great constructive educator's career. One is creditable to the white southerners. They are not all eager for Negro blood. There is yet another solution. Booker Washington surrendered many of the Negro's rights to southern prejudices. The South liked that surrender. Northern philanthropists occasionally liked it well enough to give money for purposes which would tend to make the Negro useful in the ways the whites wanted him to be, and yet to insure him a little intellectual comfort in his life.

To return to the direct consideration of Miss Grimké's Rachel; we see the girl, from the hour that she learns what things are done, and may be done, in the South to the dusky sons and daughters of America, she lives under a cloud—a sense of doom. Yet the cloud breaks now and then. She loves so much, and especially she loves so many little children, that she cannot fail to be happy sometimes. She also comes to love a man, and all the possibilities of marriage and motherhood open radiantly before her. But the shadow falls denser than ever upon her. She sees, even in the North, the grown men of her race, no matter how well educated, seldom able to get work befitting their ability. All this sort of thing would not happen in every northern town but every careful observer knows that such things do happen in many northern villages and cities.

Little children flock around her, drawn by the magic of her incarnated motherliness. She sees them ill-treated by their white school mates. She has adopted a little boy, Jimmy, and she sees him suffer. She sees a little girl, very black and ugly, but still a child, who has been frightened almost into idiocy by white children. Finally Rachel's ears are so filled with the sound of real wailing that her brain reels with the thought of the crying children all over the land, and at last voices come to her from the infinite spaces. Voices of unborn babies, the little babies who were meant to be born unto her.... They were begging her never to bring them into earthly existence. Now, like Antigone, she makes her choice; to soothe a ghostly pain no matter what may be her earthly doom.

Her lover leaves her. She cries after him once, as if to call him back. Then she ceases that cry, knowing that her fate is fixed, and her vow never to be a mother on earth is irrevocable. She begins to talk as to the pre-existent ghosts of her unborn children, and all the while the crying of her adopted child mingles fitfully with the wailing that seems to come to her from the caverns of the unknown regions.

The drama would probably have to be remoulded for use in the regular theatre, yet it is the present writer's opinion that to create the part of Rachel on the stage might well allure any actress who possesses the most delicate and passionate genius.

LILLIE BUFFUM CHACE WYMAN.

Songs and Tales from the Dark Continent, recorded from the Singing and Sayings of C. Kamba Simango, Ndau Tribe, Portuguese East Africa and Madikane Cele, Zulu Tribe, Natal, Zululand, South Africa. By NATALIE CURTIS BURLIN. New York, G. Schirmer, 1921. Pp. 170.

This work as its title imports does not cover a wide field of investigation and it was not done in Africa. The object of the author is to introduce Europeans and Americans to the soul of the African, who has too long been regarded merely as an object for exploitation. Believing that in the folk-music of a people is imaged the real soul, the author has made in this field researches, the results of which have been herein set forth. The aim finally is to show that the human family is near of kin and that basic emotions of love, of sorrow, of rejoicing and of prayer, whether men be primitive or advanced, white, yellow, red or black, are the same root-feelings planted in us all.

The book begins with a rather long introduction, discussing the geography, history, and institutions of Africa. Much space is here given to spiritual beliefs as a stimulus to the development of music. Then follows a discussion of song-poems and of the early music to which they were set. The actual contents begin with a treatment of songs, tales, and proverbs of the Ndau tribe by C. Kamba Simango. The reader, if he has found the details of the contents mentioned above a little tiresome, will have his interest quickened again by the explanation of the *Song of the Rain Ceremony*, the *Spirit-Song*, the *Love-Song*, the *Dance of Girls, Children's Songs, Laboring-Songs, Mocking-Songs*, and the like. There are also such folk-tales as the *Hare and the Tortoise*, the *Baboon, How the Animals dug their Well*, the *Jackal and the Rooster, Death of the Hare*, the *Legend and Song of the Daughter and the Slave*, and the *Sky-Maiden*.

After this portion of the book comes the Songs and Tales of the Zulu Tribe, recorded from the singing and sayings of Madikane Cele, a Zulu of royal blood. This includes such as the *Song of War, Song of Children, Dance Songs, Love Songs* very much like those mentioned above. It treats also of such folk-tales as

296

the *Creation Story*. The music to which these song poems have been set, doubtless will interest most the student of music. Along with this appear keys to the pronunciation of the dialects and translations of some of the songs.

The book is well printed and well illustrated with the art work of the Africans portraying in different ways another phase of African life.

Educational Adaptations. By Thomas Jesse Jones. Phelps-Stokes Fund, New York, 1919. Pp. 92.

This work presents valuable history in its introduction, which consists largely of a sketch of the life of the founder of the Phelps-Stokes Fund, Caroline Phelps Stokes. It is interesting to note that she was a descendant of English Puritan ancestors, eminent for their ability and Christian character. They early manifested interest in the relief of the poor and in the enlightenment of the heathen in foreign parts. From them, therefore, came much of the assistance given to promote the Sunday School movement, Bible and tract societies, missionary organization, the colonization enterprise, and the abolition of slavery. With this record before her it is not surprising, therefore, that Miss Caroline Phelps Stokes early united with the church with a desire "to live the years that still remained with a fixed and determined purpose to do her duty to God, regardless of how disagreeable that duty might be."

Measuring up to this ideal Miss Stokes became interested in the Negro race. She visited the South to inspect the schools for the education of the Negro and impressed with their needs she thereafter lavished upon them gifts which had a direct bearing upon the development of education among these people. Among these were donations to the Haines Industrial School, Hampton, and Tuskegee. Manifesting interest also in the local problems of the race, she undertook to secure better housing for the poor whites and blacks in New York City and established the Phelps-Stokes Fund for the improvement of tenement house dwelling in New York City for the poor families of New York City and for educational purposes in the enlightenment of Negroes, both in Africa and the United States North American Indians and deserving white students.

There follows then a brief account of how the provisions of this will have been carried out. Next one finds set forth a plan for educational-co-operation and the scope of the work of the committee on education which finally brought out the two-volume report of Dr. Thomas Jesse Jones, the Educational Director of the fund. This is followed by a brief statement on Negro education in the United States, which is a resumé of Dr. Jones's report. The more interesting part of this volume is that which sets forth in detail the manner in which this fund is being used by co-operation with the educational and religious agencies in the South, by giving fellowships to students in Southern universities to stimulate research into Negro life and history, by assisting the work of the University Race Commission on Race Questions, and that of the Southern Publicity Committee.

———————

The Negro Faces America. By HERBERT J. SELIGMANN, formerly Member of the Editorial Staffs of the New York Evening Post and the New Republic. New York and London, Harper and Brothers, 1920. Pp. iv., 319. Price, $1.75 net.

"There is, in fact, no race problem in the United States." A sociological study which within its first four pages makes this assertion must gain the reader's attention and interest at the start. That there is no solution to the race problem is a statement heard so often in America that it has become almost proverbial; that the solution is simple if our citizens would approach the problem fairly is an observation made less often; but that *there is no problem* would seem to be either the flippant remark of one who dabbles in sociology or the profound utterance of a new seer.

Mr. Seligmann, nevertheless, does not hesitate either to make this assertion or to attempt to demonstrate its truth. In "the conversational tone of the scientist," he cites the testimony of anthropologists, the opinions of students of racial and sociological questions, the conclusions reached by scientific surveys of rural and urban conditions, the observations of sworn eye-witnesses and the findings of grand juries in cases of inter-racial disturbance. The conclusion to be reached, to his mind, is that the so-called race problem is not a problem in itself, but a "blind spot" in the eye of the American public, a "color psychosis," a "habit of thought" by which questions of race and racial differences are connected, "frequently deliberately," with phases of American life with which they should have nothing to do,—in fact, with every phase of American life. This habit of thought, Mr. Seligmann says, is prevalent throughout the southern part of this country and is spreading through the North and West. In the cities, it makes the smallest and most natural examples of race tension "definitely subject to manipulation by political leaders and their allies in newspaper offices," raises the rent to Negro applicants for houses, protests against their living in certain localities, opposes the Negro in industry as he awakens to the strategic position which he occupies and uses such opposition in the fostering of race riots. In the rural communities of some parts of the South, it has created an "American Congo" in which peonage is practiced openly. In the World War, it made the United States'

300

"essential struggle" internal rather than external, brought about the rebirth of the Ku-Klux Klan on this side of the waters, and worked against the success of the Nation's arms abroad. In social questions it makes sex "the distorted glass by which the Negro is presented to view." It "lays its fetters upon science" and stifles the truths of anthropology with a blanket of myth. The spread of the habit of thought is in many cases part of a deliberate propaganda, the chief agent of which is the American newspaper, and "the only course for white Americans to pursue is to cultivate thorough-going skepticism as to everything which American newspapers publish about the Negro."

Such are the conditions. Meanwhile, Mr. Seligmann continues, a "new Negro" has been rising. His growth was not started by the War, as some think, but accelerated by it, for it was inevitable that he should come into being. He ranges, in type, from the radical editors of *The Messenger* to the "new bourgeoisie" which has learned to fight back and die, if need be, for the sake of principle and justice. This is the type of Negro who, in spite of differences of opinion within the race itself, is gradually working his way toward leadership; and this is the Negro who now "faces America." "Newly emancipated from reliance upon any white savior, [he] stands ready to make his unique contribution to what may some time become American civilization."

What is to be his future? It is Mr. Seligmann's opinion and conclusion that his future lies largely with the forces of labor, among whom "color and the habits of thought which come from emphasizing color distinctions must be subordinated to the need for joint consideration of common difficulties." "It depends largely," too, "upon the emancipation of the American people from their newspapers" and upon whether or not they will demand and obtain

301

"systematic information on matters concerning colored people and their relation to white people"; for a knowledge of the truth will set the nation free from the "color psychosis" under which it now labors.

That such a book as this should have been written is in itself an indication, let us hope, of the coming of the new day in racial relations toward which Mr. Seligmann points the way.

D. A. LANE, JR.

NOTES

Houghton Mifflin & Company has published John Drinkwater's *Lincoln, the World Emancipator*. This is not a biography of Lincoln but rather a type representing the ideals of the American nation and at the same time the bonds which have attached the people of the United States to those of England.

———

In the *Magazine of History* for November-December 1917, there appeared an important letter of Abraham Lincoln to the Mayor of New York bearing upon a proposed celebration of the Union victories in the West during the Civil War.

———

The article entitled "Fifty Years of Negro Citizenship," by Dr. C. G. Woodson which appeared in the last number of *The Journal of Negro History*, is now being used as supplementary reading by the Senior Class of the Law School of Howard University. This article has been reprinted.

———

In the January number of *The American Historical Review* appeared a number of documents entitled: "General M. C. Meigs on the conduct of the Civil War." In that same number is an interesting article entitled: "A Confederate Diplomat at the Court of Napoleon III," by L. M. Sears.

The Associated Publishers, a firm recently organized to publish books bearing on the Negro will soon bring out Dr. C. G. Woodson's work on *The Negro Church*. This is an intensive treatise of the development of religion among the American Negroes. The leading topics discussed are: The Attitude of the Early Missionaries toward the Negro, the Dawn of the New Day, Pioneer Negro Preachers, The Independent Church Movement, The Growth of the Negro Church, The Situation in the South before the Civil War, Preachers of Versatile Genius in the North, The Civil War and the Church, Religious Education, The Call of Politics, The Statistics of the Negro Church and The Negro Church Socialized.

This same firm in the near future will publish also Dr. Woodson's long delayed text book to be entitled *The Negro in Our History*. Because of the many upheavals in the publishing world, it has been impossible to bring out this work at an earlier date but this firm promises the publication of it by next fall.

THE JOURNAL
OF
NEGRO HISTORY

Vol. VI—July, 1921—No. 3

THE MATERIAL CULTURE OF ANCIENT NIGERIA.

The opinion of the Western World toward Africa and Africans is in the process of a very slow, yet very tremendous, change. The distant yet ultimate development of this process will bring about a most important revolution in the world of modern thought. It will be marked by a complete reversal of the prevailing present-day evaluation of the history of a continent and of the accomplishments and possibilities of a great people.

To the lay mind of the modern world, Africa is a gigantic jungle of barbarians, bamboo and baboons, where Livingstone traveled, Rhodes prospected, and Roosevelt hunted. Furthermore, it is only within the last twenty-five years or more that even that learned group whose profession is the exposition and interpretation of human history has begun to modify its opinions in this connection.

An insight into the spirit of learned opinion regarding Africa and the Africans only a comparatively short time ago may be gained from the following article, which appeared in a Berlin journal in 1891.[1] The article, in part, runs:

"With regard to its Negro population, Africa in contemporary opinion offers no historical enigma which calls for a solution, because from all the information supplied by our explorers and ethnologists, the history of civilization proper in the continent begins, as far as concerns its inhabitants, only with the Mohammedan invasion.

"Before the introduction of a genuine faith and a higher standard of culture by the Arabs, the nations had neither political organization nor, strictly speaking, any religion, nor any industrial development. None but the most primitive instincts determine the lives and conduct of the Negroes who

306

lack every kind of ethical inspiration. Every judicial observer and critic of alleged African culture must once for all make up his mind to renounce the charm of poetry and wizardry of fairy lore, all those things which in other parts of the world remind us of a past fertile in legend and song; that is to say, must bid farewell to the attractions offered by the Beyond of History, by the hope of eventually realizing the tangible impalpable realm conjured up in the distance which time has veiled within its mists, and by the expectation of ultimately wresting some relics of antiquity every now and again from the lap of the earth.

"If the soil of Africa is turned up today by the colonist's plough share, no ancient weapon will lie in the furrow; if the virgin soil be cut by a canal, its excavation will reveal no ancient tomb; and if the ax effects a clearing in the primeval forest, it will nowhere ring upon the foundations of an old world palace. Africa is poorer in record history than can be imagined. 'Black Africa' is a continent which has no mystery, nor history!"

But now this view of Black Africa and its peoples so widespread and well established a generation ago is being slowly dissipated and a new and revolutionary view of the mysterious contents is building itself in its stead. The facts and forces bringing about this great change fall into three main classes; they are of an historical, archaeological and ethnological character.

The real beginning of this change of opinion may be said to date from the capture of the old African city of Benin by the British military forces in the year 1897. The economic and political aspects of the incident do not concern us here, but from an anthropological point of view it proved to be one of the most important incidents of the nineteenth century. For as Ling Roth,[2] the noted traveler and ethnologist, has said, "the taking of Benin City opened up to us the knowledge of the existence of hitherto unknown African craft, the productions of which will hold their own among some of the best specimens of antiquity of modern times."

Many of these objects of art were carried away from Benin by the members of the invading expedition to

Europe, where they created a profound impression and astounding surprise in scientific circles throughout the continent. C. H. Read, in a paper before the Anthropological Institute of Great Britain and Ireland, on the "Art of Benin City," the year following their discovery, says: "It need scarcely be said that at the first sight of these remarkable works of art we were at once astounded at such an unexpected find."[3]

Just about this time, and continuing down to the present day, a number of Oriental scholars began to bring out modern language translations of the works of numerous Arab writers bearing upon African history—chief among them being the works of El Bekri, Ibn Batuta and Ibn Khaldoun. The most important, however, at least from one angle, was a translation of the *Tarikh es Sudan*, or *The History of the Sudan*, which is not the work of an Arab at all, but the joint work of several Sudanese blacks. In its original form it was written both in Arabic and in the Songhay languages. The book was translated into French by M. Houdas, the eminent French professor of the Oriental School of Languages of Paris.

"The book," says Lugard,[4] "is a wonderful document, the narrative of which deals mainly with the modern history of the Songhay Empire, relating the rise of this black civilization there in the fifteenth and sixteenth centuries and its decadence up to the middle of the seventeenth century.... But it is not merely an authentic narrative. It is for the unconscious light which it sheds upon the life, manners, politics and literature of the country that it is valuable. Above all, it possesses the crowning quality displayed usually in creative poetry alone, of presenting a vivid mind picture of the character of the men with whom it deals. It has been called the 'Epic of the Sudan.' It lacks the charm of form, but in all else the description is well merited. Its pages are a treasure house of information for the careful student, and the volume may be read many times without extracting from it more than a small part of all that it contains."

Barth, who obtained some fragments of an Arabic copy when he was on his way to Timbuctoo, goes so far as to say that the book forms "one of the most important additions that the present age has made to the history of mankind."[5] Like the unknown culture which the Benin bronzes revealed, the translation of these documents brought to the attention of the learned and academic circles of the Western World, in a more available form, surprising accounts of the sometime existence of powerful and age-old kingdoms and empires in the heart of Black Africa, which hitherto had scarcely been suspected.

Following close upon this was the cursory but illuminating report of *Une mission archeologique au Sudan francais*, headed by the soldier-ethnologist, Lieutenant Louis Desplaynes. The report, *Le Plateau Central Nigirien, Paris, 1907*, brought to Europe much valuable information bearing upon the past cultures of the practically unknown Nigerian plateau regions.

Passing over a few very important ethnological studies bearing for the most part upon present-day cultures, we come last of all to what is in the truest sense of the word the wonderful and astounding revelations regarding the pre-historic culture of an ancient Negro race on the West Coast of Africa. These revelations were brought to light as the result of the publications by Leo Frobenius of his *Der Afrika Sprach* in Berlin in 1913.[6] This was a popular account of the experiences and findings of the German Inner African Exploration Expedition during its travels in the Nigerian area for the years 1910-1912. As important as are the ethnological and archaeological finds of this expedition, which will be considered further on, one of its most significant features was its bold advocacy and support of an idea which has been hesitantly advanced in a few circles ever since the study of the Benin bronzes and the Nubian monuments, namely, the existence of a genuinely superior type of culture in Central Africa in pre-classical and pre-Christian times.

Such, then, by way of introduction is the nature of the sources from which comes the influence which is slowly and haltingly, yet surely, bringing about the change in current opinion regarding "Black Africa" as is evidenced by the timely but hitherto unsuccessful effort of Harvard University to treat the records of the African peoples scientifically in keeping with the standard set in the first volume of the *Varia Africana*. This paper, however, as may be inferred from its title, does not undertake to survey the facts covering the whole field, but restricts itself to materials of a more or less archaeological character, that is, to the architecture, tombs and the arts and crafts of a small section of this ancient land.

There are two reasons for approaching this whole subject in this way. First, the materials and facts herewith considered are in the main of a tangible and undisputed character; and, secondly, it is the study of architecture and the arts and crafts of this particular locality that has been the premier force in changing the old opinion of the world towards Africa. Let us then turn now for a somewhat detailed study of these materials.

As has been said in the introduction, it was the revelation incident to the taking of Benin by the British that marks the real beginning of a serious and scientific interest in the past cultures of Central Africa. The incident started a movement of both a forward and a backward reach. On the one hand, it led to subsequent searchings which ultimately resulted in the finding of additional evidences of culture in that territory, as well as to a reconsideration of the value of the reports of the travelers and adventurers on the West Coast from the fifteenth century on.[7] The combined result has been the bringing to light of objects and evidences of achievement which place the ancient and medieval African on a plane with, and in many cases above, his contemporaries in Europe and America.

The reports of earlier adventurers and travelers in the Benin territory previous to the British conquest gave us pictures of towns and buildings which, all things considered, are of no mean order, and which reflect the existence of a social and cultural development of a very long standing. The earliest recorded description of Benin City, according to Ling Roth,[8] is that of an old Dutch chronicler who wrote as "D. R." and whose works first appeared in Germany in 1604. His description is as follows:

"At first the town seems very large; when one enters it one comes at once into a broad street which appears to be seven or eight times broader than the Warme street in Amsterdam; this extends straight out, and when one has walked a quarter of an hour along it, he still does not see the end of the street.... At the gate at which one enters there is a very high bulwark, very thick and strongly made, with a very deep, broad ditch, but it was dry and full of high trees. This ditch extends a good way, but we do not know whether it extends around the town or not. That gate is a well-made gate, made of wood, to be shut according to their methods, and watch is always kept there. Outside this gate there is a large suburb.... One sees a great many lanes and streets on both sides, which also extend far and straight, but one can not see the end of them on account of their great extent.

"The houses in this town stand in good order, one close to the other, like houses in Holland. Houses in which well-to-do people, such as gentlemen, dwell, have two or three steps to go up, and in front have an ante-court where one may sit, which court or gallery is cleaned every morning by their servants, and straw mats spread for sitting on. Their rooms or apartments with (the court) are four square, having a roof all round, which, however, does not join in the middle, but is left open, so that the wind, rain and daylight may enter. In these houses they live and eat, but they have specially built little houses for cooking, as well as other huts and rooms.... The king's court is very large, being many square places within, surrounded by courts wherein watch is always kept. This king's court is so large that the end is not to be seen, and when one thinks he has come to the end, one sees through a gateway other places or courts, and one sees many, many stables."

311

Another description of Benin which seems to corroborate this former description, and which was itself substantiated by later and more recent reports, appeared in a book[9] published by one Dapper, a Dutchman, in Amsterdam in 1668. It seems that Dapper himself was never at Benin, but received most of his information about the country from the writings of a Sam Blomert, who, Dapper says, lived for many years in Africa.[10] As Ling Roth points out, subsequent reports and the recent finds seem to bear out the truth of his account.

According to Dapper,

"the town comprising the queen's court is about five or six [Dutch] miles in circumference, or, leaving out the court, three miles inside the gates. It is protected at one side by a wall ten feet high, made of double stockades of big trees tied to each other by cross beams, fastened crosswise and stuffed up with red clay solidly put together.... The town possesses several gates, eight or nine feet in height, and five feet in width, with doors made of a single piece of timber hanging, or turning on a peg like the peasants' fences here in this country. [Holland.]

"The king's court is square and stands at the right-hand side as one enters the town by the gate of Gotton, and is certainly as large as the town of Harlem, and entirely surrounded by a special wall like that which encircles the town. It is divided into many magnificent palaces, houses and apartments for courtiers and comprises beautiful long and square galleries about as large as the Exchange at Amsterdam, but one larger than another, resting on wooden pillars from top to bottom, covered with cast copper on which are engraved the pictures of their war exploits and battles, and are kept very clean. Most palaces and houses are covered with palm leaves instead of square pieces of wood [shingles], and every roof is decorated with a small turret, ending in a small point on which birds are standing, these birds being cast in copper, and having outspread wings cleverly made after living models.

"The town has thirty very straight and broad streets, each of them about one hundred and twenty feet wide or about as wide as the Heeren or Keezersgracht [canals] at Amsterdam from one row of houses to the other, from which branch out many side streets, also broad, but less so than the main streets.

"The houses are built alongside the street in good order, the one close to the other as here in this country [Holland], adorned with gables and steps and roofs made of palm or banana leaves, or leaves from other trees; they are not higher than a 'stadie,' but usually broad with long galleries inside, especially so in the case of the houses of the nobility, and divided into many rooms, which are separated by walls made of red clay, very well erected, and they can make and keep them as shiny and smooth by washing and rubbing as any wall in Holland can be made with chalk, and they are like mirrors. The upper storys are made of the same sort of clay; moreover, every house is provided with a well for a supply of fresh water."

Before going any further with this description, it may be well to state that the description of the nature and character of the finish of the walls given here is substantiated by accounts of travelers in these parts as late as the end of the nineteenth century. Captain Boisragon, one of the two survivors of the ill-fated white expedition to Benin in 1897, in comparing the houses of Benin with those of another nearby city, says that "the chief of Gwatto's house was very much superior; the walls, which were very thick, being polished till they were nearly as smooth and shiny as glass."[11] Mr. Cyrl Punch, who traveled in Yorubaland in the eighties of the nineteenth century, gives us a hint of the widespread practice of this sort of wall polishing even so late as forty-five years ago, and furnishes us with a very interesting account of how the polished effect was produced. "For giving a high polish to the clay walls in Yorubaland," says Punch, "the leaves of the *Moringa pterygosperinia* are mashed up and rubbed over the clay." Of a certain house in the town Brohemi he continues to say that "the walls were better polished than any in Benin. They were like marble."[12]

In comparing the earlier descriptions of Benin and other African cities in this general area with the descriptions of later writers, an important fact stands out, namely, that these cities had already reached their highest point of development before the coming of the white man; for in a description of Benin by another Dutchman, Nyendall, which appeared in 1704, we read the following: "Formerly the buildings in this village were very thick and very close together, and in a manner it was over-populated, which is yet visible from the ruins of the half remaining houses; but at present the houses stand like poor men's corn, widely apart from each other." His description otherwise is very similar to those previously given, yet his account does bring out an additional point which is worthy of note, namely, the reason for the use of clay in building. "The houses are large and handsome," he writes, "with clay walls; for there is not a stone in the whole country as large as a man's fist."[13] In the same connection, Legraing, who visited Benin in 1787, also hints at the reason for the extensive use of clay and wood as the principal structural materials. Around Benin, according to this observer, "the vestiges of an old earthen wall are still to be seen; the wall could hardly have been built of any other material, as we did not see a single stone in the whole journey up."[14]

The recent reports by Leo Frobenius on his findings further up into the interior, aside from giving us a picture of present-day conditions of cities which he believes to date back to pre-classical and pre-Christian times, also show the absence or scarcity of durable producing materials. But, most important of all, the report indicates the grandeur of African cities in ancient times. In discussing the buildings in the present-day city of Ilife, which he believes was the capital or center of an ancient African theocracy, he says: "There can be no doubt that the entire plan and style of architecture gives the city of Ilife a pleasantly dignified character. If, however, I am to summarize all the life and activities of this city of palms and divinities, I cannot, indeed, speak of anything great and sublime, because that lies buried too deep beneath the soil and debris of centuries, yet I can say that it has a dreamy respectability."

But speaking specifically upon the building which now serves as the palace of the great religious headman of Yorubaland, he says: "The edifice rests upon foundations not of sun dried, but of fine burnt brick." Taken as a whole, the present-day structure conveys "the impression of grandeur in decay." "Such," he says, "is a sketch of the city whose effect is heightened by the noble ruins of the palace of this Holiness and the consciousness of its traditional past."[15]

We may now turn for a brief consideration of those strange and most interesting structures of the Sudan, the tombs of their ancient dead. All through the Sudan, and especially in Nigeria, are to be found great conical dome-shaped structures of baked clay ranging in size from sixteen feet in height and sixty-six feet in basal diameter to seventy feet in height and two hundred and twenty feet in basal diameter. [15a] These structures were first mentioned by Lieutenant Louis Desplaynes in his report of *Une Mission archeologique au Sudan francais*,[16] but the first close study of these tombs was made by Frobenius in 1911. Frobenius tells us that these tombs are of three main types: first, a small size; second, an intermediate size; and third, a large size. This last type, he tells us, was an extraordinary large construction, averaging about seventy feet in height and six hundred and fifty to seven hundred feet in basal circumference. The external structure is connected with an underground structure composed of a number of subterranean chambers and compartments, extending in every direction of the compass, sufficient to accommodate the remains of a great number of notables and royal personages.

Frobenius states, regarding one of these subterranean chambers which he explored, that it contained a dome which was paneled and strengthened with wood from the borassus palm and the whole plastered with a sort of prepared clay.[17] Frobenius also believes that the external parts of the tombs, that is, the mound proper—was made layer by layer. Each layer of clay was first thoroughly worked, moulded, and baked. This process was repeated time and time again, until the mound was completed.

The veteran Egyptologist, Flinders Petrie, in the great mass of evidence adduced by him to show the African origin of the spirit and substratum of early dynastic Egyptian culture, points out that there is a very close connection between the subterranean structures of these tombs and many of those of the Egyptian pyramids, the inference being that the idea of the pyramids very probably had its origin in Central Africa.

As interesting and important as are these structures in this connection, they, like those previously mentioned and those yet to be described, are of interest in another direction; they bespeak the sometime existence here of a mighty people with a glorious past, now lying sleeping within the bosom of the earth, the silent witnesses of a world that has perished.

Beginning about three hundred years ago, and going back to an unknown period, it is evident from the above comments and extracts that the cultural life of the Negro on the West Coast of Africa, especially from the point of view of his architectural and tomb-building proclivities, was of a much higher type than anything he has produced since his contact with the European during the last four hundred years. The quality and quantity of work accomplished by these ancient black builders is especially notable when it is remembered that the type of material which they were forced to use, and the climatic conditions surrounding them, were of a most discouraging sort. The manner in which these very serious difficulties were overcome is itself a durable testimony of the ingenuity and resourcefulness of the African builder and craftsman of earlier days. One can hardly avoid the speculation of what might have been the nature of their accomplishments, had they been provided with a more suitable and durable building material.

The more we study the cultural products of these people, the more pregnant such a speculation becomes; for in those fields of endeavor where they were less handicapped, or better, perhaps, where they were in a better position to overcome the destroying influence of the climate and the lack of suitable structural materials, we find the African artisan and the craftsman producing a wealth of objects of art of a very superior type. Some of these objects are notable not only in that they are of a superior type judged according to the standards of a so-called primitive art, but they compare, so far as technique and artistic qualities are concerned, very favorably with much of the best of ancient civilized art. The last generation has brought to light evidence which shows that the Negroes of the West Coast of Africa were producing hundreds and even perhaps thousands of years ago objects of art which, from the point of view of technique and artistic perfection, equal some of the best works of the ancient Greeks and Romans, and compares favorably with the best masterpieces of the Solons of the Italian Rennaissance.

As was above stated, it has been the study of the technique, originality and artistic qualities as expressed in these recently found and comparatively little known African objects that has been the premier force in producing the change of opinion regarding the capabilities of African folk and the cultural history of the great continent. In this connection, however, it is perhaps well again to remind one of the fact that this change of opinion is not yet public in its scope, but is rather restricted to academic and especially to anthropological circles.

For the sake of clearness, the whole collection of African arts and crafts may be classified under three main heads, namely, carved works, glass and porcelain objects, including terra cottas, and metal castings. It will, of course, be impossible to treat exhaustively of the objects in any one of these fields. A considerable amount of selection will, therefore, be necessary; and in the interest of fairness it may be stated at the outset that the treatment and descriptions for the most part will be of the finest and best specimens so far obtained. In doing this, of course, we follow the general and most usual method of those engaged in making cultural studies. There is, however, an additional and very special reason for such a procedure in this case. It is the opinion of Dalton, Read, Ling Roth and Frobenius—perhaps the leading authorities on the whole subject—that the best objects are likewise the oldest objects; and since this purports to be a study of the ancient and medieval cultures, our purpose in following the above method of selection is doubly clear.

Among the large number of carved works discovered at Benin by the British Punitive Expedition are a large number of huge and splendidly carved elephant tusks. These objects have been carefully studied by Ling Roth, and the following is an abbreviation of his description of them:[18]

> "The tusks vary in length up to six feet and over, and are in themselves magnificent specimens of ivory, speaking eloquently of the peaceful life which the elephants must once have lived, in order to produce such tusks. The ornamentation to which the large tusks have been subjected while preserving their form is in two grades: the one is severely plain, and the other extremely ornate and decorative in effect. The former consists of a series of three to five incised bands of a plait pattern, a design very common in West Africa, placed at intervals, the bands diminishing in width as they approach the

tip of the tusk. The embellishment is consequently plain, but elegant, and does not call for further remark.

"The other grade consists in covering the whole tusk with a succession of boldly carved grotesque figures—human, animal, and symbolic—giving the tusk a rich embroidered-like look, the thick ends being finished off with a suitable diamond pattern belt and the tip finished with an equally appropriate series of carvings in the shape of a mascle studded foolscap, or a capsule supported by elongated cowries. The back appears to be cut to a uniform depth, and in spite of the multiplicity of figures there is neither overcrowding nor overloading."

There is another piece of carved ivory which appears to Ling Roth to be a piece of symbolic sculpture and which was probably used as a scepter. Roth says of this:

"The execution of the detail is rough—more rugged perhaps than the carved tusks—nevertheless there is considerable originality of design, and it is especially remarkable as showing an earlier stage of the application of hammered metal to carved work."[19]

Among the carved works in ivory are many splendidly carved armlets. Ling Roth gives a description of one which is particularly interesting as showing the ingenuity of the Negro artisan.

"While at first sight it appears to depict only one carved armlet, it is really two armlets, one being carved inside the other out of the same piece of ivory with only the space of a knife-blade thickness between them. When moved, the two armlets rattle against each other. The ornamentation consists of four figures: a king or chief belonging to the outer armlet, and four sets of two hands placed between the human figures belonging to the inner armlet. The whole shows skill and ingenuity on the part of the artist who planned this difficult piece of work, so remarkable from a technical point of view. But although the beauty of design is not its chief attraction, it is nevertheless a piece of work which can not fail to be admired from the artistic standpoint also."

Another object of interest described by Ling Roth is a highly ornate fragment on an article which originally had the shape of a brass sistrum, consisting of two bell forms, a large and a small one, grafted onto one

319

handle. Its delicate treatment is described as differing somewhat from the rugged workmanship of the objects above described, but it is said to err in its excessive elaboration.

"Yet there are good points," says Roth, "such as the blending of the two bell forms into the common handle, the happy tapering of the ornamentation into the Normian bird's beak; the increasing size of the side cups as they rise to correspond to the enlarged opening of the bell form; the truthfulness to nature in an essential like the bust of the Negro, all of which betoken a fair amount of artistic feeling. The craftsman who probably designed execution of the smallest detail."[20]

It is the opinion of collectors that there existed in Benin at one time a very large amount of carved objects in wood, but, unfortunately, most of these must have been destroyed when the British burned the city in 1897. Very little of such work, therefore, has survived. What it may have been like cannot be definitely said, yet some hint might be gained from a few specimens that escaped the fire, though these specimens are probably modern in their execution.

One such object is a wooden casket in the form of a bullock's head, with two hands jutting out of the forehead and grasping the horns of the animal. The casket is supported by a pedestal of appropriate size and is decorated to represent cowries. "The ears of the bullock's head are covered with embossed brass work, and there are strips of brass of scroll pattern running down the bullock's face and fastened on with small brass staples."[21]

In this connection it might be mentioned that there are some carved coconut shell in which the Negro carver often expressed his ingenuity. These represent in their carving a varied number of forms, including human beings, animals and plants. The interest in these carvings, as Roth tells us, "lies in their demonstration of the adaptability of the native to perform creditably on a material very different from ivory. Fair ingenuity is displayed in the manner in which the figures are grouped on a confined surface without overcrowding. In fact, the feature of the work is the careful distribution and general freedom of treatment. The details of the carvings are throughout in low relief, remarkably clean and neat and of a uniform depth."[22]

So far no carved objects in stone, granite, marble, or the like, have come to view in the immediate Benin territory. This, of course, is natural enough when it is remembered, as has been pointed out, that there are no such materials to be found in the country. In 1911, however, Leo Frobenius discovered in his excavations of Ilife, a few hundred miles farther back in the interior, a number of carved stone objects which are interesting from several points of view. In the first place, might be considered the circumstance and position in which these objects were found. Many of these objects were dug up out of the earth at a depth of from eighteen to twenty feet, but several were found set up in tombs and isolated spots in the African forest. These forests are described by Frobenius as being sacred groves where the present-day natives worship their gods. Frobenius testifies that there were an extraordinary number and variety of these stone figures, and that they represent very different periods. Some show a coarse type of workmanship, but others represent a very superior grade of work. The following is, in the main, Frobenius's description of these objects:

"When, on leaving the main road, we arrived at the first small palm plantation, a group of quite coarse little stone pillars about waist high came into view. They are angular, roundish, and at all events roughly hewn or chipped off, absolutely bare of any detail. Going forward we came to another, rather more to the left. Here there is a wilderness of weeds, a mass of roof battens and the straw of a collapsed thatch, surmounted by a few stakes and climbers amidst which rises a stone image. This is about thirty-two inches high, roughly executed and defaced. It has one chain around its neck and another hangs over an apron skirt down to the hands folded over the stomach. On its left side it has a peculiar hanger, something like the tassels of a Houssa sword."[23]

In another nearby spot he describes the find of a smaller statue:

"When I first made its acquaintance," he writes, "it was housed in a badly damaged little hut whose thatch almost hid it. It is a granite figure about thirty-six inches high above ground level. I could not find out whether its feet were covered by the earth. It is exactly like the other figure, with the hands over the belly, aproned and ornately tasseled on its left. It has armlets and a ruff-like ornament round its neck. The interesting part of the statuette is most decidedly its head, which had been knocked off and only insecurely replaced, when I first set eyes on it. The thick-lipped, broad-nosed face is negroid in type.... The treatment of the hair in this granite head is especially of the very greatest interest. The hair is represented by little iron pegs inserted in small holes; here, for the first time, we come upon this singular use of iron, which metal, as we shall see, played a quite extraordinary part in the realm of Ilifian antiquities."[24]

Under these same circumstances, he continues,

"a group of all kinds of well-preserved relics is met with in a carelessly constructed hut in the fourth and last enclosure. Symmetrically placed there is a stone crocodile to the right and left in front of a stone block artificially rounded and set on end. These vary but little in shape between a drop and an egg or onion, always inclining toward the first, so that I would like to call them 'drop stones,' ... before such of these drop stones, the more oval of which is twenty-four, and the more conical one nineteen and a quarter inches high, there is a crocodile. The larger and better finished of the two is twenty-four and three eighths and the other twenty-one and a quarter inches long."[25]

Frobenius further states that he had seen several other similar objects, made both of quartz granite and of other kinds of stone. In another sacred grove he reports finding several other very interesting stone objects:

"Here within a small space surrounded by a low wall there is a ring of holy stones," he writes, "some of them very valuable. Firstly, there is a twenty-nine and a half inch long sandstone block of no very remarkable general aspect, weather-worn and abraded, but ending in a jagged crowned head of some such animal as a fish. The second is a block of quartz, like the drum of a column, damaged in places by exposure, but still recognizable as a fine piece of antique work."

Finally, we come to what Frobenius calls the stone "stools," of which "there are quite a number." According to Frobenius, these stools very much resemble the stools made and used by the present-day Negroes and remind one of "negro stools with carriers." He says further:

"These are stumpy columns from fourteen to twenty-four inches high. Sometimes the flat surfaces have a ring between them and sometimes not. Both quartz and granite examples are characterized by extraordinary uniformity of shape and surface polish. Their single handles at the side, mostly broken off, is the strangest part."

Frobenius comments especially upon the tendency of these objects to "monumental form." In this connection he says:

"Following the lines of everything taught us in the development of historical art, I can not well help drawing the inference that this idea of working in stone was introduced by a people who felt themselves impelled to monumental expression."[26]

The origin and variety of these carved objects in stone offer us a very interesting point, yet one may reasonably infer from his other statements that here in the Ilife, as in the Benin region, granite, quartz and hard stone materials are in their natural state very, very limited, if not altogether absent. Like Benin, Ilife is in the Niger delta region, and, as Frobenius points, is of rather a swampy character. It is a geological fact that hard stone in any quantity is seldom to be found in such regions. In addition to this, Frobenius, as was pointed out above, states that the foundations of the ancient buildings are of burnt brick rather than sun-dried brick or stone. It is very reasonable to suppose that hard stone, had it been in any way common to this area, would certainly have been used for building

323

operations. One seems more or less justified in concluding, then, that the materials out of which the above-described objects were made were not of local origin. This circumstance is very important, for it seems to indicate that either these materials were imported from a distance and fashioned on the spot or else they were imported already in their finished form. If the first view be accepted, it would seem in a measure to account, on the one hand, for the obvious lack of skill on the part of the African artist as expressed in the archaic human and animal forms; but, on the other hand, it would, as is seen in the case of the "stools" mentioned above, seem to indicate a rather remarkable liberty and grace on the part of the Negro artist, implying his ability to become a master even when working with a comparatively unfamiliar material. For as Frobenius says, "the dexterity acquired in treating quartz and granite is very considerable. There is a quantity of eminently beautiful examples of such skill in this country."[27]

If we accept the latter view, namely, that the objects were imported ready made, it would seem to indicate that there must have been a rather extensive trade with some other Negro folk having a rather advanced form of culture, for it is obviously apparent from the distinctively Negro features of the statuettes and the undoubted Negro influence as expressed in the style of the "stools" that these objects must have been the products of a Negro people. A slight hint for such an origin may be gleaned from the finding by Frobenius of the handle of an antique cup, of which he testifies that the carved figure thereon resembles very much the effigy of the Ethiopian or Nubian god Bes,[28] and which, according to Budge,[29] is held to have been of Sudanese origin.

Such, then, is an abbreviated account of the carved works which during the last generation have been discovered to have been produced by black folk on the West Coast of Africa in ancient and medieval times.

We shall next turn for a brief consideration to the glass and porcelain objects, including terra cottas. So far as can be determined, very little or no work of importance which can be classed under this head had come from the Benin country. By stretching the category, however, one might include under this head the finely polished marble-like walls which have been described in connection with the houses of the Benin territory. One might also include under this head the benches which were seen in the Benin houses in former times. The typical character of these benches may be noted from the brief description given by Captain Jas. Fawckner,[30] who visited the country in 1825. After describing the houses, he says that "in the center is a bench formed of brown clay, which by frequent rubbing with a piece of coconut shell and wet cloths has received a polish, and, when dry, looks like marble."

A few hundred miles to the West, in the Gold Coast region, is the home of the famous "aggry" beads. These beads, the manufacture of which is now a lost art, were found in the possession of natives by the earliest European explorers.[31] The beads are of two kinds, a plain type and a variegated. "The plain aggry beads," say Bowdich, who made a careful study of them, "are blue, yellow, green or a dull red; the variegated consist of many colors and shades; the variegated strata of the aggry bead are so firmly united and so imperceptibly blended that the perfection seems superior to art. Some resemble mosaic work; the surface of others is covered with flowers and regular patterns so very minute and the shades so delicately softened one into the other and into the ground of the bead that nothing but the finest touch of the pen could equal them. The agate parts disclose flowers and patterns deep in the body of the bead and thin shafts of opaque colors running from the center to the surface. The coloring matter of the blue bead has been proved by experiment to be iron; that of the yellow, without doubt, is lead and antimony, with a trifling quantity of copper, though this latter is not essential to the production of the color. The generality of these beads appears to be produced from clays colored in thin layers, afterwards twisted together into a spiral form, and then cut across; also from different colored clays raked together without blending. How the flowers and delicate patterns on the body and on the surface of the rarer beads have been produced cannot be so well explained."[32]

In the earlier days, when much less was known of the technical and artistic ability of the African, the origin of these beads was quite a problem. The fact that similar beads were sometimes found in tombs in North Africa and in the graves and tombs of ancient Egypt and India led some to suppose them of probable Phoenician origin. Such a theory implies the existence of a rather extensive trade between the ancient Phoenicians and the ancient Africans of the West Coast. This may have been the case, for from Herodotus, and from the fragments of Hanno from the Temple of Milcarth in Carthage, we learn that frequent voyages were made beyond the Straits of Gibraltar and to the Gold Coast hundreds of years before Christ by Phoenicians as well as the Egyptians. This theory would, however, imply an act of conservation and preservation of minute objects over a period of thousands of years on the part of African "savages," which, to say the least, would be very remarkable. It is likely, in the light of recent research upon the subject, that the Phoenician theory will have to be made with caution; for, as will be pointed out,

326

there is now available much evidence which seems to indicate that these beads were of indigenous African origin.

Further up in the interior of the Ilifian region a number of important glass objects have been found. Frobenius, commenting on the find of this character made as a result of his excavation in the neighborhood of the ancient "Holy City," testifies that "these furnish proof that at some remote era glass was made and moulded in this very land, and that the nation which here of old held rule was brilliant exponents of apt dexterity in the production of terra cotta images."[33] The spot where the objects were excavated is "located about a mile or more to the north of Ilife and undoubtedly marks the impression of an ancient cemetery." It is located today in what is a vast forest, and "is about half a mile broad, did hide and still in fact hides quite unique treasure." Frobenius in describing the excavations here, planned by himself and executed under the direction of Martins, the engineer of the expedition, gives the following account:

"We went down some eighteen feet or so, near the ground water, and can report as follows, viz., the top layer consisted of about two and a half feet of extraordinary hard and compacted soil. Even in this we turned up several glazed potsherds.... At about six and a half feet we found pottery. But the actual adit averaged about eighteen feet below the surface. For we came upon charcoal and ash heaps at this depth. This thoroughly verified the native statements as to the finding of either pearl jars or ashes so far down.[34] The old excavations made by the inhabitants reached from twelve to twenty-four feet or thereabouts."

Frobenius, in describing the objects discovered by this expedition, says: "The substance of the pots is a sort of cement or stoneware. They are from fourteen to twenty four inches high and from three and three quarters to sixteen inches in diameter; they are generally uniform. The aperture is at the under and upper ends of the walls from about three quarters to one and a quarter inches thick. The upper of these portions is covered with an irregular glaze, varying from one thirty sixth to one eighteenth of an inch thick inside. They were similarly glazed outside as the edges proved, but this has perished. A convexly carved plate or cupola in which there are three or four holes for finger holds seem to have been lids. Inside the pots are glass beads, rings, irregular bits of glass tubing, and always at the bottom a mass of fused bits of glass from one eighth to one quarter of an inch in depth. The colors of the beads and the glaze on the jars vary from light green, greenish white, dark red, brown and blue." Frobenius, commenting upon these finds, concludes that "the great mass of potsherds, lumps of glass, heaps of slag, etc., which we found proves at all events that the glass industry flourished in this locality in ages past. It is plain that the glass beads found to have been so common in Africa were not imported, but were actually manufactured in great quantities at home."[35]

In addition to these objects of stoneware and glass, there were a large variety of terra cotta objects which range from the "simplest little pots and saucers to the most artistic shapes and portraits." To appreciate the real significance of these objects in view of the inability to see the originals themselves, one should make a special effort to see the drawings and photographs of these objects as contained in Frobenius's *Der Afrika Sprach*, or its English translation, *The Voice of Africa*. Accompanying these illustrations there are a few brief descriptions of the more important objects. There is, for instance, "a specimen which seems to be the mouth or collar of an urn. On its inner edge there is a mouth below, an ear on either side, and a pair of eyes…. It looks as if this might have been a portion of a tube which might have been put over a grave, through which offerings might have been made to the dead beneath."[36] This explanation for the original purpose of this object is very plausible, as a study of the burial customs of various parts of Africa will show.

Frobenius is of the opinion that the dress of these ancient peoples "must have been very rich and handsome." A terra cotta truss brought to light by these excavations is described as showing a "noteworthy completeness. In the holes scattered on the breast plate and shoulder piece there were formerly inserted metal or iron pegs as ornaments. The end of the garment which is thrown over the shoulder is patterned like the old textures,"[37] which Frobenius believed had reached a very high degree of development. "Among our terra cottas," continues Frobenius, "some may have served as pedestals for the heads or busts." He describes a peculiar "fragment belonging possibly to some sort of vessel; on one side is seen an owl, whose hooked beak is badly damaged; on the other a complete figure holding a weapon." Like the beautifully carved stone handle mentioned above, Frobenius testifies that this object also resembles the ancient Sudanese and Ethiopian god Bes,[37a] and hints of an ancient connection between these two countries.

Another object, not dug up in the cemetery, but in the town of Ilife proper, is a "fired," square thin plaque showing a crocodile in the shape of the letter S, so shaped that it seems to finish in a tightly bound head. The details are not easily seen, but the position of the legs seems to indicate that the beast is bound there with cords and is meant to seem fastened to the surface, with a sort of hood over the eyes ending in a string work and tassels as if in a cunningly made basket. Frobenius and his associates were of the opinion that this object is that of a tile which in ages past formed part of the decorative design of one of

329

the ancient buildings.[38]

Passing over a list of similar objects, we finally come to the world-famed terra cotta heads. Like the other terra cotta objects, these are fully illustrated in the above-named work. They are of "infinite variety" and "every observer may well see that they are patently portraits." They represent many varieties of Central Africans, from the restricted minority group of prognathous flat-nosed, thick-lipped type of the coast to the more delicate and sharper featured types to which the majority of Africans belong. In other words, these terra cottas represent almost every African type suggesting, therefore, a civil life very cosmopolitan in character and the probable existence of a *jus commercii* as well as a *jus connubii*, which in turn argues well for the existence of a demogenic form of association of a very great age. Frobenius testifies that these heads are of "great beauty and amazing to those who inspect them." Commenting upon these terra cottas in general, he says: "I do not think that there can be the least doubt but that we are faced with a local form of art whose perfection is absolutely astounding," and commenting upon one particular head which he calls *mia* after the native term for it, he concludes that it "must be regarded as the most important object hitherto found on African ground and as the finest work of art so far discovered outside the narrow Nile valley, on the further side of the old Roman jurisdiction."[39]

We may now turn for a brief study of what is beyond all doubt the most important division of the whole group of African arts and crafts—the metal castings. As was mentioned in the Introduction, the conquest of the city of Benin by the British in 1897 opened up to the knowledge of the white world a hitherto unknown field of Negro art, "the productions of which," according to Ling Roth, "will hold their own among some of the finest specimens of antiquity or modern times."[40] The excavations of Frobenius's expedition discovered in the heart of this part of Negro-land, aside from the terra cottas already described, metal works which are characterized as being "indeed like the finest Roman examples."[41]

The amount and variety of these works are tremendous and they have been carefully studied and reported upon by various writers. The following extracts, taken from the most noted among them, will give some idea of the nature and character of these objects. The chief feature of the personal ornaments, according to Ling Roth, is their variety. Another feature is their play upon patterns. For example, the same pattern which is seen in one bracelet is so adapted and reduced in another as to produce a very different effect. Spirals as a basis of design are not uncommon. "And they are often so twisted and interwoven that they produce quite a novel effect." Some of the bracelets are furnished with studs set with agate or coral. Some gold-plated ornaments have been found, among them a "bracelet formed by a double-headed snake grasping between its jaws a decapitated human head and a snake about four inches long." Ling Roth, commenting upon the workmanship of these smaller objects, says that generally speaking it is good, but "it is not as a rule equal to that of the large Benin metal workings; this is no doubt due to the greater difficulty presented by the smaller surfaces on which the artisans have had to work."[42]

Speaking of what he calls a curious class of objects, namely, the long armlets and leglets "so fashionable in West Africa," Ling Roth declares them to be "elegantly finished productions and good examples of Benin art.... They are provided with loops for hawk bills, which turn up everywhere in unexpected places

331

through Benin metal work." In describing one such bracelet, which, however, is of modern make, he says that it is "interesting as exhibiting a conventionalized leopard's face on the top, as well as a European's face on the bottom, likewise developing into a form of ornament ... the fertility in design is in all of these forms manifest indeed; it is a feature in the art of Benin natives which any of our jewelers might do well to copy."[43]

Passing to a consideration of some of the larger forms of metal casting, we have the following description by Ling Roth of a bronze vase "whose ornamentation consists of four mask-like faces in high relief, two plain and two ribbed, set alternately; above each of the ribbed masks there is a flat spiral on which rests an ornamental triangle on its apex. Between the heads are placed bands of very plain guilloche, each band consisting of alternate three or four rows each, above and below concentric circles of imitation (coral?) bead work, all in low relief, and helping to fill in the ground. The whole arrangement forms a combination of decidedly artistic effect. There is no enchasing or punching of any sort, nor is there much ornamentation, but what ornamentation there is, is designed in such a spirited manner as to produce a result which hardly can be surpassed by Europeans at the present day."[44]

As another example of this same sort of thing, we may take the description of another object, a curious metal casket brought to Europe by a member of the Punitive Expedition. In design, according to Ling Roth, this casket "is bold and artistic; the high relief of the bizarre face and the zigzag conventionalized serpents and tadpoles being well thrown up by enchasing of the ground work. The proportions are all good, and this is especially the case with an enchasing of the enclosed lines." Ling Roth says that the relief portions

332

are somewhat roughly cast, and the enchasing sometimes irregular, but, "on the other hand," he continues, "the great variety of objects exhibited without any over-crowding, the general grouping, the tones background, the real beauty" of the major portion of the design show that the artist was "a man of considerable taste, judged not only as a Negro, but as a man of culture."[45]

Another object which Ling Roth mentions as being especially remarkable for its technique is that which he has ventured to call a *sistrum*. It consists of what appears to be two brass bell bodies, a larger and a smaller welded together at the tapering ends. On the face of the larger bell is represented the now well-known group of a king or chief with a sort of Persian head-dress, with a harpoon-like projection at the top. He is supported on both sides by similarly dressed individuals; somewhat above the level of his head the chief is flanked by two tablets, each upheld by a hand emerging from the background. The background is enchased with an elegant foliated design somewhat Bornean in character. The back of the bell, with a few exceptions, has a similar relief. After describing the smaller bell, which is of a somewhat different character, Ling Roth concluded with these rather significant remarks:

"Taken as a whole the *Sistrum* is an elegant piece of workmanship. The thoroughness of the details of execution is worthy of the Japanese, even the inaccessible and almost hidden portion of the smaller bell being enchased with a pattern."[46]

As excellent as are these types of castings, the finest works of these Negro sculptors were achieved, not in works of this character, but, according to critics like Dalton, Read, and Ling Roth, rather in works that are done in the round.[47] Dalton, speaking of a bronze head of a Negro girl now in the British Museum, declares it to be "the most artistic and perfect of all the castings in the round." Ling Roth, speaking of the same head, declares it to be the "finest piece of cast bronze art obtained from Benin."

A find by Frobenius during his excavations at Ilife seems to support these conclusions. For of all the objects found by him at that site, his most important discovery he declares to be a bronze head, which he thinks is that of an ancient African god. The head wears a diadem with a staff. From the very tip of the diadem staff to the chin the object measures thirty-one and a quarter inches. "It is cast in what we call *cere perdue*, or hollow cast, and is indeed finely chased, suggesting the finest Roman examples. The setting of the lips, the shape of the ears, the contour of the face, all prove, if separately examined, the perfection of a work of true art, which the whole of it obviously is."[48]

Some attention may now be given to the method by which these objects were made and to the question of their age and origin. In a report before the Anthropological Institute of Great Britain and Ireland in February, 1898,[49] Mr. C. H. Read and Mr. O. M. Dalton described these objects as having been cast in moulds. They testified as to the difficulties attendant upon such methods in sculpture, announcing that they had "been overcome with the certainty and skill which only long practice of a familiar art could produce. This alone goes to prove that at whatever period the objects were made they were produced by a people long acquainted with the art of casting metals."[50]

Their report continues: "The method by which the objects were produced can only be that known as *cere perdue* process. By no other is it conceivable that so much extravagant relief and elaborately undercut detail could be represented with success. The process may be described in a very few words. The model is first made in wax, and every part of its surface is then covered with fine clay; the whole work is then hidden in a mass of clay. An outlet is then made for the wax to escape, and the mass is then heated until the wax has melted out, leaving, of course, a mould of exactly the design of the wax in the original state. The metal is then poured in and fills every hollow space left by the wax." Read and Dalton, as well as Ling Roth, testify that when casting objects in the round, or any object for that matter, where there was considerable internal bulk or projections, a core of sand was used as a base and the wax and clay respectively placed over this. This method, aside from insuring lightness, also saved considerable metal. Ling Roth, in this connection, points out that "the ancient Etruscans and Greeks made their castings solid without any sand core, while the Beni were evidently adept in the superior method practiced by the ancient Egyptians."[51] Read and Dalton likewise conclude that "this *cere perdue* process is that by which many of the finest Italian bronzes of the best period were produced."[52] Thus it is that we find the Negroes of West Africa, as Dalton concludes, "using with familiarity and success a complicated method which satisfied the fastidious eye of the best artists of the Italian Rennaissance."[53]

Such, then, is an abbreviated account of the arts and crafts which have been discovered in a restricted part of West Africa during the last generation. Whether the results be considered large or small, it should be remembered that they represent the outcome of but a small amount of scientific investigation, only one expedition of scientific qualifications having so far operated in these parts. What the future holds or may bring forth yet remains to be seen.

There has been, and still is, considerable difference of opinion regarding the origin and antiquity of the culture which these objects represent. Some hold it to be of great age and of a more or less indigenous origin, while others are of the opinion that it is comparatively modern and that it was introduced, some say, by the Arabs and Mohammedans, while others believe it was brought by the Portuguese, at varying dates down to and including the fourteenth and fifteenth centuries.

Dealing with the latter view first, one hardly considers it unfair to say that there has never been any serious evidence for such opinion. The main reason for ascribing this culture to the Arab or Portuguese origin was due, on the one hand, to a failure to study seriously the culture itself, and, on the other hand, a kind of *a priori* conception of the very limited potentialities of Negro peoples. Basing their opinion upon the popular conception that the Negro represented the lowest form of human development, it was thought by early critics of the culture that the Negro could not have produced objects of art capable of holding their own among the highest forms of human creations; and so in the exigencies of the situation the theories of Arab or Portuguese origin were brought to the fore. The advance of ethnological science during the last generation, the serious study of the Benin objects in an objective sense, and finally the results of Frobenius's Expedition, all combined, have not only weakened the theories of a modern Arab and Portuguese origin, but have practically destroyed them altogether.

Let us take a summary view of some of this evidence against these theories. In the first place, there might be mentioned the changing opinion regarding the supposed mental difference between so-called cultured and primitive peoples. As a result of many scientific studies, and some scientific expeditions both in Africa and Oceania, it is now practically the belief in scientific circles that there is no potential difference in quality of mind of the various races or of widely differentiated cultural groups. This removes at the outset the belief heretofore held as to the inherent limited capacity of the Negro peoples. According to this modern point of view, then, the objects above described *could* have been created by native blacks of

337

Central Africa.

As a next step, Ling Roth has pointed out that as there is hardly a traveler from Africa who has not recorded the art of iron smelting among the Negro or Bantu tribes, "we may accept as a fact that the art of smelting iron is a very old one in Africa." Not only does the recent evidence point out that iron smelting *per se* was an old and widespread practice in Africa, but, in addition, reports a similar method of metal working as discovered in the Benin country to have been in vogue in other and widely separated parts of Africa. For example, Bowditch[54] describes a method of casting on the Volta River, where a wood core was used instead of sand, while Robinson[55] states that at Kano "there are on sale swords, spears and many other objects made of native wrought iron. The article desired is first formed in wax and from this clay model is made into which the molten iron can be poured."[56]

This, it would seem, reduces considerably the need for postulating modern influence so far as the *method* is concerned. And even if modern influence were responsible, it could hardly have been Arab or Portuguese, for up to date no such objects as above described have been found among the ruins of the Islamic civilization. And on the other hand, as Ling Roth has said, "we are still quite in the dark as to the existence of any such high-class art in the Iberian peninsula at the end of the fifteenth century; and we know that there was not much of this art in the rest of Europe."[57] The only serious evidence, if even it might be so called, which was ever advanced as indicating Portuguese origin for this art was the fact that on some of the plaques from Benin there were found Portuguese heads or figures. But this, instead of indicating a Portuguese origin, gives, when carefully studied, reasonable evidence to the contrary.

Let us make a brief study of one of these objects. An

object described by Ling Roth[58] as the "head of the staff or wand of offices" may be used as an illustration. The design is "that of a leopard supporting a column on its back. The uppermost portion of this staff head consists of a band of engraved basket work patterns with grained open ground. This is followed by a band of fish-scale patterns ornamented at the lower corners of contact pinched indents. On this band there is an upper series of ornaments in relief. The upper series consists of four faces; that on the front being probably that of a Negro and that on the back that of a European. Both faces are boldly and clearly executed, while the two faces on either side are of Europeans, both of them flat and poorly executed, and in profile with the mouth curiously twisted into the full face. The European figures on either side of the leopard in their flatness and general crudeness are quite out of keeping with the rest of the work. "Yet," he says, "one cannot help admiring the boldness with which the leopard has been modelled, or the firmness with which its claws grasp the ground; while the vigorous way in which the tail is made to support the back of the column should be remarked. Equally admirable are the suitable proportions of the bands of ornament. The upper band is thoroughly subdued so that the faces next to it are brought more prominently into relief."

It is evident that in every feature, excepting the European faces, this object is obviously the product of a master. How, then, are we to account for the crude and archaic appearance of the European figures? It would seem either that it was done purposely out of disrespect for the European or else it was the result of an unfamiliarity with the subject on the part of the artist. If the African artist had been indebted to the European for his apprenticeship, it is highly improbable that either of the conditions

339

present here would have been likely to occur.

In this same connection a statement by Ling Roth testifies that "the Beni almost invariably give their fellow Africans sturdy lower limbs while they do not do so invariably to Europeans. The latter of a certain type are made to stand on well planted feet, while such Europeans as are in any way about to use their guns have their legs bent and puny."

That the work of the African artist, when dealing with Europeans, was necessarily of an inferior grade must not be assumed to be the rule, however, though it does seem from the evidence that there is more unaccountable archaicness in objects of this character than in any others. Ling Roth, speaking in this same connection, calls attention to the fact that Benin was not discovered by the Portuguese until about 1472, and that by the middle of the sixteenth century (*e.g.,* 1550) we have an almost perfect figure of a European, presumably made by a native. "It is inconceivable," he concludes, "that an introduced art could have developed at so rapid a rate that in seventy years, probably less, for this art would hardly have been introduced the first day, such a high pitch of excellence could have been attained by the natives."

If the Portuguese theory is untenable, the Arabic or Islamic theory is equally, if not more, unacceptable. In the first place, as has already been pointed out, Arabic or Islamic art shows absolutely nothing in art approaching objects of the Benin type. Furthermore, Islam itself did not appear in Central Africa until the eleventh century, and then only in the northern and western parts of the Sudan. And it was, moreover, not until the fourteenth century that it made itself a real part of the life of the northern country, and not until the eighteenth that its influence spread into Yorubaland. And then its influence was only felt in the

340

back country.[59]

Furthermore, according to Frobenius and Ling Roth, respectively, both the Ilifian region and the Benin territory remain until the present-day non-Mohammedan in character. This would seem to indicate Islamic influence in those countries where most of these objects above described were found has been necessarily very slight; yet such a culture as the above objects represent was unquestionably a very integral part of the life of the country and could not possibly have been due to such an influence. Furthermore, if additional evidence were needed to disprove the theory, it might be cited that it is a well-known fact that one of the fundamental tenets of the Islamic faith is the proscription of the representation of the human form in its art in any whatsoever. And since the height of the material side of this culture was reached in this kind of art, it appears doubtful that this culture could have arisen from such a source.

It would seem, therefore, that this culture at least antedates the coming of the Portuguese and the Arab influence in this part of West Africa. To state definitely its place of origin, or the exact date of its origin, is at present, however, impossible, because of the relatively small amount of scientific work and study carried out in this part of the Continent. But in spite of this sufficient evidence is already available to warrant the opinion on the part of all the critics previously referred to that this culture is essentially African in origin and very, very old. Frobenius is convinced that it is at least pre-classical and pre-Christian in its beginning.

Such, then, and until now, is the character of the material culture of this restricted spot of Black Africa. What the future will bring let the future tell, but of this let the present be convinced: that at least this part of Black Africa is *not* "beyond the reach of

341

interest in the history of the world; always in a state of apathy asleep to progress and dreaming its day away." And of this may the present be ever sure that Black Africa is *not* "a continent which has no mystery, nor history!"

WILLIAM LEO HANSBERRY.

FOOTNOTES:

[1] Quoted by Leo Frobenius, *Voice of Africa*, Vol. 1, p. 1.

[2] H. Ling Roth, *Great Benin*, p. 217.

[3] *Jour. Anthrop. Inst.*, February, 1898, p. 371.

[4] F. L. Lugard, *A Tropical Dependency*, p. 154.

[5] Lugard, *A Tropical Dependency*, p. 154.

[6] Translated into English by Rudolf Blind. Published by Hutchinson and Company, London, 1913.

[7] Old Dutch and Portuguese manuscripts have been collected and studied by Ling Roth and the findings appear in his *Great Benin* quoted in this paper.

[8] Ling Roth, *Great Benin*, p. 157.

[9] Dr. Olfert Dapper, "Nauwkeurige. Beschrijvenge der Afrikansche Geweslen." (As listed and quoted by Ling Roth, in *Great Benin*.)

[10] Ling Roth, *Great Benin*, p. 2.

[11] *The Benin Massacre*, p. 81.

[12] Quoted by Roth in *Great Benin*, p. 161.

[13] *Ibid.*, p. 162.

[14] *Ibid.*, p. 163.

[15] Leo Frobenius, *Voice of Africa*, Vol. 1, pp. 21-25.

[15a] Leo Frobenius, *Voice of Africa*, Vol. 1, pp. 21-25.

[16] *Le Plateau Central Nigerien*, Paris, 1907.

[17] Frobenius, *Voice of Africa*, Vol. 1, p. 25.

[18] Ling Roth, *Great Benin*, p. 193.

[19] Ling Roth, *Great Benin*, p. 196.

[20] Ling Roth, *Great Benin*, p. 205.

[21] *Ibid.*, p. 209.

[22] Ling Roth, *Great Benin*, p. 209.

[23] Frobenius, *Voice of Africa*, Vol. 1, p. 297.

[24] *Ibid.*

[25] *Ibid.*, p. 302.

[26] Frobenius, *The Voice of Africa*, Vol. 1, p. 305.

[27] Frobenius, *The Voice of Africa*, p. 305.

[28] *Ibid.*, p. 105.

[29] E. A. W. Budge, *The Egyptian Sudan*, Vol. 1, p. 526.

[30] Fawckner, *Travels on the Coast of Benin*, London, 1837, p. 32.

[31] A. B. Ellis, *A History of the Gold Coast*, p. 9.

[32] Bowdich, *Mission to Coomassee*, p. 218. Quoted by Ellis.

[33] Frobenius, *The Voice of Africa*.

[34] It was such reports by the natives and the nature of the objects which they claimed to have found at this place that led Frobenius to excavate here. See pages 306-307 of his *Voice of Africa*, Vol. 1.

[35] Frobenius, *The Voice of Africa*, p. 309.

[36] *Ibid.*, p. 313.

[37] Frobenius, *The Voice of Africa*, p. 313.

[37a] Frobenius, *The Voice of Africa*, p. 313.

[38] *Ibid.*, p. 313.

[39] Frobenius, *The Voice of Africa*, p. 313.

[40] Ling Roth, *Great Benin*, p. 217.

[41] Frobenius, *Voice of Africa*, p. 310.

[42] Ling Roth, *Great Benin*, p. 31.

[43] *Ibid.*, p. 33.

[44] Ling Roth, *Great Benin*, p. 225.

[45] *Ibid.*, p. 223.

[46] Ling Roth, *Great Benin*, p. 223.

[47] See an article by Dalton and Read in the *Journal Anthrop. Inst.*, February, 1898, p. 372; also Ling Roth, *Great Benin*, p. 216.

[48] Frobenius, *The Voice of Africa*, Vol. 1, p. 310.

[49] "Works of art from Benin City," *Jour. Anthrop. Inst.*, 1898, p. 321.

[50] *Ibid.*

[51] Ling Roth, *Great Benin*, p. 226.

[52] *Jour. Anthrop. Inst.*, 1898, p. 372.

[53] *Ibid.*, p. 272.

[54] *Mission to Ashanti*, pp. 311-312.

[55] *Haussaland*, p. 118.

[56] Quoted by Ling Roth, in *Great Benin*, p. 232.

[57] *Ibid.*, p. 232.

[58] *Ibid.*, p. 219.

[59] Lugard, *A Tropical Dependency*.

THE NEGRO IN BRITISH SOUTH AFRICA.[1]

It was in the United States Senate, during the summer of 1919, that there was in progress a debate concerning the ratification of the Treaty of Peace with Germany and the consequent ratification of the covenant of the League of Nations. Speaking to this question the words of Senator William Edgar Borah of Idaho were, in substance, these: "The President of the United States has said that if we fail to ratify the covenant of the League of Nations we will 'break the heart of the world.' ... But, sir, failure to ratify this covenant will not break the heart of China, which constitutes a third of the world; it will not break the heart of India; *it will not break the hearts of the natives of the South African Republics.*"

How could the Senator from Idaho state so confidently that the failure of the League of Nations, under which Great Britain retained her rôle as protector of British South Africa, would not be a source of grief to the natives of the republics thus protected? What is the status, political, economic and social, of these people? For what do they stand on the African continent? How have they withstood the characteristic onslaught of British colonization and imperialism? What does "the autonomous development of small nations" mean to them? Any reasonable attempt to answer questions of this nature necessitates a review, however brief it may be, of the history of South African colonization by the English and of its relation to the native.

British South Africa, which occupies the entire southern horn of the African continent, from the southern coast to the Zambesi River, and from the Indian Ocean on the east to the Atlantic on the west, has a population of about 6,500,000 people, fully five-sixths of whom are of Negro extraction, the other one-sixth being of European—British and Boer. It is a "southern black belt" in every sense of the term, and its Negro or Negroid inhabitants belong to the subdivision of the race to which ethnologists have given the name "Bantu," a native African word meaning "the people." Their origin is unknown, and no authentic history of their racial and tribal movements is available. All that is known of their past is what has been gleaned by surmise and deduction from the condition in which they were found by missionaries and traders making their way into South Africa. A nomadic, patriarchally governed people—polygamists, ancestor-worshipers, tillers of the soil, sheep-raisers, raiders upon neighboring tribes—such were the primitive Bantu. Let the reader substitute "Bantu" for "Germani" in Tacitus's classic description, or for "Britons" in any accurate portrayal of the manners and customs of the early inhabitants of the British Isles, and he will catch the true *spirit* of life as it was among the primitive Bantu before the advent of the European missionary and trader.

The missionary, first as civilizer and educator, later as protagonist of the political rights of the Bantu, has been a potent factor in their development. "To the Bantu, perhaps more than to any other people," says Mr. S. M. Molema, himself a member of that race, "the missionaries have stood for civilization, Christianization and education."[2] Niggardly and inadequate governmental appropriations for common schools have been supplemented by missionary funds, and in many cases missionary funds alone have supported and are still supporting native schools. "In short, every educated member of the Bantu race, no matter how great or small his

346

education may be, is directly or indirectly a product of the mission school."[3] This fact should be borne in mind whenever one considers the relations which exist between the native and the government. The Bantu feel that the missionary, and not the government, is responsible for their enlightenment, and it is to the missionary that their gratitude is poured out.

What has been the attitude of the other class of Dutch and British newcomers, of the trader and colonist group, toward the natives whom they found living under native law and custom? Some will call it a credit, others a discredit, to the European regime that more than a century and a half passed before any inroads were made upon native independence and sovereignty. Members of the Dutch East India Company, under Jan van Riebeek, landed on the Cape of Good Hope as early as 1652; the British occupied the Cape in 1806, but it was not until 1846 that any portion of the South African territory came under British control. Before this time the Boer and Briton had been bent almost solely upon the establishment of amicable and successful trade relations with the natives. The Boer had come to the Cape to find an ocean port for his vessels, and while it is true that wars were waged between Boer and Bantu for the duration of a century, the natives were only driven inland and no attempt was made to establish European sovereignty over them.

In 1806, however, the British obtained final control of the Cape, and in 1846 put an end to their former policy of "hands off" by making a British province, called Kaffraria, of all the country lying between the Kei and the Keiskama Rivers. In 1865 this province was formally annexed to and incorporated in the English state, called Cape Colony, which had been set up on the Cape. From this time colony after colony was formed, annexed and incorporated by both British and Boers, the latter of whom had marched northward in "the Great Trek" of 1836. The Boers formed the Republic of Natal in 1838, but moved out in 1842, and Natal was annexed to the British Cape Colony in 1844. The Boers, continuing northward, next set up Transvaal and the Orange Free State. The constitution of the latter bears the date 1854, and of the former 1858.

Cape Colony, Natal, Transvaal and the Orange Free State, then, are the South African States which were set up by British and Boer—now five-sixths Negro and one-sixth European in population. An examination of the constitutions and laws of these republics, as they appear on the statute books and in practice, reveals that the relationship between European and native has not been the same in all of the states.

CAPE COLONY

Cape Colony, farthest south and the oldest of the four states, was founded upon the principle of political equality of all inhabitants, black and white. A proclamation of the Duke of Newcastle (1853) contained the following statement:

> "It is the earnest desire of Her Majesty's Government that all her subjects at the Cape, without distinction of class or colour, should be united by one bond of loyalty, and we believe that the exercise of political rights by all alike will prove one of the best methods of attaining this object."[4]

At the first, every activity of the British colonizers seemed to be pointing toward the day when they would relinquish all direct governmental authority and turn it over into the hands of the natives. Districts were under the control of native boards elected by popular vote and sending representatives to the Grand Council. Black and white alike shared the privilege of franchise. Such social distinctions as were made were personal, not sanctioned by law.

NATAL

Natal is likewise a British colony, but from the first has adopted a policy toward the native entirely different from that of Cape Colony. Politically shrewd, she does not flatly deny the right of the native to vote, but by carefully worded legal phraseology so limits the voting class that, in effect, her policy is "No votes for natives." Under date of August 24, 1865, appears a law "disqualifying *certain* natives from exercising electoral franchise" (the italics are in all cases ours). The following extract is taken from this law:

> "Be it therefore enacted by the Lieutenant-Governor of the Colony of Natal, etc., as follows:
>
> "1. Every male native, resident in this Colony, or having the necessary property qualifications therein, whether subject to the operation of the native laws, customs and usages in force in this Colony or exempted therefrom save as in this law provided, shall be disqualified from becoming a duly registered elector, and shall not be entitled to vote at the election of a member of the Legislative Council for any electoral district of the Colony of Natal."[5]

Certain natives, however, may vote. The conditions of their voting are these:

> "2. Any male native inhabitant of this Colony who shall show to the satisfaction of the Lieutenant-Governor that he has been resident in this Colony for a period of twelve years, ... and who shall possess the requisite property qualifications, and shall have been exempted from the operation of Native Law for a period of seven years, and who shall produce to the Lieutenant-Governor a certificate signed by three duly qualified electors *of European origin* ... a statement to the effect that the Justice or Magistrate endorsing said certificate has no reason to doubt the truth of said certificate, ... shall be entitled *to petition the Lieutenant-Governor* of Natal for a certificate to entitle him to be registered as a duly qualified elector....
>
> "5. The Lieutenant-Governor may, *at his discretion, grant or refuse* to any native applying in manner aforesaid for such certificate entitling him to be registered as a duly qualified

elector...."[6]

This franchise law was amended in 1863, as follows:

"6. No person belonging to a class which is placed by special legislation under the jurisdiction of Special Courts, or is subject to special laws and tribunals, shall be entitled to be placed on the Voters' List...."[7]

When it is understood that special laws for natives, and for natives only, are actually a part of the Natal Code, the effect of this amendment may be seen.

TRANSVAAL AND THE ORANGE FREE STATE

The two republics founded by the Boers have at least the virtue of frankness in their make-up; for, without the circumlocution of their neighbors in Natal, they flatly and expressly withhold from the native all rights of citizenship. The following extracts from Transvaal law are sufficient evidence of this fact:

From the Grondwet (or Constitution) of Transvaal (February, 1858):

"9. The people desire to permit no equality between coloured and white inhabitants, *either in church or state*.

. . . .

"31. ... No coloured person or half-castes shall be admitted to our meetings."

From a law of June 12, 1876:

"No person not regarded as belonging to the white population of the South African Republic shall be enrolled as a burgher possessing the franchise according to Article 9 of the Grondwet."[8]

A resolution of the Volksraad, June 18, 1885, runs thus:

"159. When a male person has been recognized as a burgher of this Republic, his wife shall thereby also be recognized and remain a burgheress of this Republic.

350

> "*All coloured people are excluded from this provision*, and (in accordance with the Grondwet) they may never be given or granted rights of burghership...."

So much for Transvaal. The Constitution of the Orange Free State, adopted April 10, 1854, contains a provision restricting the right of suffrage by incorporating throughout the law the term all white persons. In short, the Boer plainly and bluntly disdains to use the diplomatic phraseology of the British statesman. He shuts the door of hope in the native's face, without apology or equivocation.

THE UNION OF SOUTH AFRICA

Such was the state of affairs in 1910, Cape Colony granting absolute citizenship to all inhabitants, Natal cleverly refusing it to natives, Transvaal and the Orange Free State flatly withholding it. In 1910, however, long-continued propaganda in favor of bringing the Boer and British states together, to be thenceforth under a common government, bore fruit, and the four republics united to form the Union of South Africa.

The day of the passage of the act of union (called the South Africa Act) was an ill one for the South African native. Cape Colony, the one benevolent and fair-minded state, could not help but be over-ruled by the three states whose policy toward the native was one of oppression and political non-representation. Hence the South Africa Act (1909) contains the following provisions:

> "IV.—(26) The qualifications of a senator shall be as follows—
> He   must
>
> .   .   .   .
> be a British subject *of European descent.*
>
> .   .   .   .
>
> 36. ... the qualifications of parliamentary voters, as existing in the several colonies, at the establishment of the Union, shall be

351

the qualifications necessary to entitle persons in the corresponding provinces to vote for the election of members of the House of Assembly.

. . . .

44. The qualifications of a member of the House of Assembly shall be as follows—He must ... be a British subject *of European descent.*"[9]

In other words, no native can be a member of the South African Parliament. Even if the natives of Cape Colony, who have the right of franchise under section 36 above; for they had it "at the establishment of the Union"—even if they should elect one of their number to represent them, such duly elected person could not be seated. Under the laws of the Union, then, the Cape Colony right of franchise has been nullified and "the Bantu and coloured people in the Provinces of Natal, Transvaal and Orange Free State are unrepresented in the Union Parliament, and those of the Cape Province are but indirectly represented. The five million coloured peoples in the Union have no direct representation, and the one million, five hundred thousand white people have all the representation and say."[10]

Now, although the natives are not eligible for election to the South African Parliament, they have a deliberative body, known as the South African Native National Congress, to which native representatives are sent from all districts. With no legislative authority, however, this body can only *discuss* legislative measures which have been proposed before the South African Parliament when such measures affect the natives, and it may use "all available constitutional methods" for or against the proposed measures. But of what avail to protest against a law when the persons to whom the protest must be made are those who have enacted the law? An appeal to the British government would be useless, for the British government has declared that the Union of

South Africa is "self-governing."

Such, in brief, is the political status of the Negro in British South Africa, and the government of Great Britain, having set up "self-governing South Africa," has thus far refused to come to the rescue of the natives. As a member of the British Parliament said during the debate on the Union Bill, "it [the proposal for unification] is the unification of the white races to disfranchise the coloured races, and not to promote union between all races in South Africa." The passage of the Union Bill sounded the political death knell of the South African native.

His economic condition is equally as disheartening. When the Union was set up, native employees of the government in the railway, post office, telegraph and civil service systems were discharged in large numbers and their places were given to Europeans. Enforced labor of natives is statutory in Natal, and a tax upon natives, from which they are exempted upon certification that they have worked for a certain number of months during the year, is levied throughout Cape Colony. The most iniquitous feature of the economic status of the native South African, however, is that which resulted from the passage, in 1913, of the Natives' Land Act "to take effective measures to restrict the purchase and lease of land by natives" by setting apart certain areas in which natives were not permitted to acquire land. It assigned approximately 21,500,000 acres of land to the 5,000,000 natives, reserving 275,000,000 acres for the 1,500,000 white inhabitants. Natives who were living within the area set aside for white inhabitants had to sell their grain and stock and either move their families to an area assigned to natives or hire themselves out to white men. This condition has existed, moreover, since 1913. Recently, however, the Natives' Land Act has been declared to be without effect, because its provisions conflict with those of the original South Africa Act; but, as Mr. Molema remarks, the South Africa Act is easily amended. There is nothing in the past record of the Union to indicate that an amendment to cover the Natives' Land Act will not be incorporated in the Constitution, thus making the natives' serfdom permanent.

Since the native South African is a political and economic nonentity, it is not surprising to note that, socially, he is on one side of a great gulf fixed between him and his white neighbors. The South African native is indeed a social outcast. Portions of the following extract, describing social relations in South Africa, should ring familiarly in American ears:

"The peculiar colour-prejudice of South Africa ... finds expression everywhere—in the streets, in the public buildings, in the public conveyances, in the press, nay, in the church itself. Thus, if a black man were to try to get into an hotel, let his education be what it will, he would be refused admission; but supposing he did manage to enter somehow, if he appeared at table, all the whites would leave it.... All over South Africa whites will not mix with blacks in railway compartments, tramcars or post-carts....

"Bantu children and European children are provided with separate schools.

" ... On that lavatory you see written 'Gentlemen,' and there only white men may go. On that other lavatory you see written 'Amadoda' (men), and this is meant for black men.

"One would expect that the distinction would not go the length of the church, but it does so with sober earnestness....

"The *average* white man in South Africa would never think of shaking hands with a black man. The ordinary terms of courtesy are purposely avoided by him, and such a prefix as 'Mr.' or 'Mrs.' in association with a black man's or woman's name never escapes his lips....

"'A single case of marriage between white and black by Christian rites will fill the newspapers with columns of indignant protest, but illicit intercourse, even permanent concubinage, will pass unnoticed.'"[11]

The American Negro, it may be said, habitually thinks of himself as the most unfortunate of God's creatures, but his South African brother is still more unfortunate. Separate schools, separate churches, separate waiting-rooms, "jim crow cars"—with these the American Negro is familiar. With few exceptions, however, he may work independently, unlike the South African native, and at his own calling. He may acquire as much property as he can pay for. If he will "go North" for his education, he may sit at the feet of the best scholars his country produces. Direct representation in state legislative bodies is not unknown to him, and direct representation from some districts to the National Congress seems to be at hand. The trend of the American Negro is upward, but the South African native remains on an unchanging plane of misery and oppression. For the American Negro, in spite of discrimination, lynching and riot, the star of hope shines with ever-increasing luster, but its beams, at the present time, seem scarcely to reach his South African brother. The British protectorate of self-governing South Africa has not been a boon to the South African native, for the home government has abandoned him to the hands of his oppressors.

D. A. LANE, JR.

FOOTNOTES:

[1] The facts concerning South Africa herein given are obtained from select constitutional documents in the appendix of *The Bantu*, by S. M. Molema. This book was published by W. Green and Son, Ltd., Edinburgh, 1920.

[2] Molema, *The Bantu*, p. 220.

[3] *Ibid.*, p. 237.

[4] Molema, *The Bantu*, p. 241.

[5] Molema, *The Bantu* (appendix), p. 378.

[6] *Ibid.*

[7] *Ibid.*, p. 378.

[8] Molema, *The Bantu*, p. 368.

[9] Molema, *The Bantu* (appendix), p. 384.

[10] Molema, *The Bantu*, pp. 245-246.

[11] Molema, *The Bantu*, pp. 264-266.

THE BAPTISM OF SLAVES IN PRINCE EDWARD ISLAND

Somewhat early in the history of Christianity the thought became manifest that it was at least questionable for one to hold a fellow-Christian in slavery. This went so far that at length it became "fireside law" that the baptism of a pagan slave *ipso facto* effected his emancipation. There was no foundation for this view in positive law, but it appears from time to time in non-legal and quasi-legal writings.

For example, *The Mirror of Justice*, written in Norman French in Plantagenet times, about the end of the thirteenth century, has it: "Serfs devenent francs en plousours maneres, ascuns par baptesme sicom est de ceux Sarrazins qe sont pris de Christiens ou achatez e amenes par de sa la meer de Grece e tenent cum lur serfs ..."; *i.e.,* "Slaves become free in various ways— some by baptism, as is the case with those Saracens who are captured by Christians or purchased and brought from beyond the Sea of Greece and held as their slaves." *The Mirror*, while received as high authority even by so learned and capable a lawyer as Sir Edward Coke, Lord Chief Justice of England, is now quite discredited, the latest editor, Sir Frederick Maitland, going so far as to say of the author, "The right to lie he exercises unblushingly."

Nevertheless the book, while nearly, if not quite, worthless as an authority as to what the law actually was, is very valuable as showing what an intelligent layman at the time thought it was. The fear that baptism set a slave free was undoubtedly present among both the French and the English planters in

America, including the West Indies; and this fear had much to do with their determined objection to missionary effort among the slave population. The Code Noir relieved the fears of the French in this regard; but I find no legislation on the matter in the English Settlements until 1781.

Prince Edward Island (formerly the Island of St. John) had a number of slaves, as had the other British North American Colonies; and in 1781 the Legislature of the Province passed an act respecting them (21 George III, c. 15 (P. E. I.)). This act, with the others passed in the same session, was transmitted by Governor Walter Patterson to the Home Government in a dispatch, March 1, 1781, to Lord Stormont (Earl of Mansfield), in which he says: "There will be no need to trouble your Lordship with more than the titles of the above-recited acts to show the reasons which induced me to consent to their becoming laws." From a perusal of the act it will at once be seen that the statute went far beyond the title and fixed the status of slavery upon "all Negro and Mulatto servants" then on the island, or thereafter to be imported (being slaves), and provided that they should continue to be slaves until freed by the owner. The act reads:

"AN ACT declaring that baptism of slaves shall not exempt them from bondage.

"WHEREAS some Doubts have arisen whether Slaves by becoming Christians, or being admitted to Baptism, should, by Virtue thereof, be made free:

"1. Be it therefore enacted by the Governor, Council and Assembly, That all Slaves, whether Negroes or Mulattos, residing at present on this Island, or that may hereafter be imported or brought therein, shall be deemed Slaves, notwithstanding his, her or their Conversion to Christianity; nor shall the Act of Baptism performed on any such Negro or Mulatto alter his, her or their Condition.

"2. And be it further enacted, That all Negro and Mulatto Servants who are now on this Island, or may hereafter be imported or brought therein (being Slaves), shall continue such, unless freed by his, her or their respective Owners.

358

"3. And be it further enacted by the Authority aforesaid, That all Children born of Women Slaves shall belong to and be the property of the Masters or Mistresses of such Slaves."

This statute had absolutely no effect to stay the evolution of a strong public opinion against the institution of slavery. The latest recorded sale of a slave was in 1802, and slavery gradually died out as a fact, although it was possible in law until the Imperial Act of 1833, freeing all slaves under the British flag.

Before the culminating emancipation act, however, the Provincial Legislature had repealed the obnoxious statute of 1781. The act of 1825, 5 George IV, c. 7 (P. E. I.), reads:

"AN ACT, to repeal an Act, made and passed in the twenty-first year of His late Majesty's Reign, intituled 'An Act declaring that BAPTISM OF SLAVES shall not exempt them from BONDAGE.'

"WHEREAS by the aforesaid Act Slavery is sanctioned and permitted within this Island, and it is highly necessary that an Act so entirely in variance with the laws of England and the Freedom of the Country should be forthwith repealed, and Slavery forever hereafter abolished in this Colony.

"Be it therefore enacted by the Lieutenant Governor, Council and Assembly, That from and after the passing hereof the said Act, intituled 'An Act declaring that Baptism of Slaves shall not exempt them from Bondage,' and every Clause, Matter and thing therein contained, be, and the same is hereby, repealed.

"Provided always, That nothing herein contained shall have any effect until His Majesty's Pleasure shall be known."

The act was transmitted by the Lieutenant-Governor, Colonel John Ready, in a dispatch to Secretary of State George Canning, of date November 8, 1825, in which he says: "The preamble explains the reasons for passing this act." The bill received the Royal approval and became law. But it will be seen that, while the act of 1781 went further than its preamble, that of 1825 fell far short. It did not abolish slavery, but simply repealed the previous act.

359

WILLIAM RENWICK RIDDELL.

OSGOODE HALL,
    TORONTO, MARCH 24, 1921.

DOCUMENTS

From the Proceedings of the American Convention of Abolition Societies may be obtained valuable information in the form of the reports as to slavery, the appeal of the anti-slavery groups to Congress, and their addresses to the citizens of the United States. There is unconsciously given in these documents most interesting facts as to what the Negro was doing and what was being done for him. The important documents falling within these three groups follow.

The Report of the Committee on the State of Slavery in the United States, being again considered, was amended and adopted as follows.

To the American Convention for the Abolition of Slavery, Ec.

The committee appointed (at the last session of the Convention) on the state of slavery in the United States, beg leave to report as follows:

Your committee were rather at a loss to perceive the precise design of the Convention, in the appointment of a committee on the state of slavery in the United States. But have thought proper to review the subject; first with reference to its progress; secondly in reference to the situation or treatment of slaves; and thirdly in reference to the prospect of its diminution or final removal.

First. In reference to the progress of slavery in the United States, your committee find that at the time of the first census under the Constitution in 1790, there were 694,280 slaves in the Union. These were with

361

the exception of about 40,000, confined to a surface of about 212,000 square miles. In 1800, the number was 889,118 on a surface of 289,000 square miles or nearly so! In 1810, the number was increased to 1,191,364 and covered an extent of territory of about 431,000 square miles! At the time of the last census in 1820, the slaves in the United States and territories amounted to 1,538,178, and your committee have good reason to believe that the number at the present time or at the census of 1830, will be found to be about two millions, occupying a territory including Arkansas, of nearly 600,000 square miles!!

Your committee have been surprised at the result of their own enquiries, for they had fondly hoped that the dreadful evil was if not diminishing, at least advancing with less rapidity. From various estimates, on which your committee place much reliance, they are confirmed in the opinion, that the increase (independent of clandestine importations) must amount at the present time to at least near 50,000 per annum.

As this increase like that of population generally, is in its nature, a geometrical progression, it must continue to augment, as long as subsistence can be obtained. This view of the subject is truly alarming; but when we consider the extent of territory which is overspread by this foul blot on the map of our beloved country, the heart sickens at the prospect.

To behold 600,000 square miles of the best land in North America, teeming with slaves,—a surface greater, than that of many European kingdoms, held too by men who are constantly boasting of their love of liberty; sending up daily to Heaven, the sighs and groans of millions of broken hearts, while the sweat and tears and even the blood of thousands moisten its soil, must excite deep emotion in every breast, not dead to those feelings which become the patriot, or animate the Christian. But furthermore your committee are of opinion that if the scheme, of adding a large portion of Mexican territory, to our south-western border, should be consummated, the price of slaves will be so enhanced and the facilities of smuggling so much increased, that the African slave trade will be greatly augmented, as well as the practice of kidnapping in the more eastern parts of our own country. So that upon the whole, your committee are of opinion, that slavery is fearfully on the increase, and that every effort is making, by many of those interested in its continuance, to multiply its victims and extend its influence. This state of things calls loudly on every friend of his country, on every friend of man, to use every effort in his power, to arrest the torrent of misery and crime.

Secondly. On the treatment of slaves,—your committee have long indulged an opinion which they believe is common with their fellow-citizens, that slaves in this country are somewhat better treated than formerly. This opinion seems to prevail to an extent which your committee fear, is not sustained by facts. A writer in Niles's Register for 1818, says, speaking on this subject, "The favourable change which has occurred in the treatment of negro slaves in this state (Maryland) since the revolution, must be to every benevolent mind a source of very agreeable reflections, our oldest citizens well remember when it was very customary to inflict on the manacled and naked person of the slave, the most intolerable punishments for very trivial offences. *Within the last twenty years* it has been the practice to muster all the slaves on a farm once a week, and distribute to each his peck of corn, leaving him to walk several miles, to some neighbours hand mill, to grind it himself, under cover of night, when exhausted nature called for rest from the labours of the day; in many cases they

363

received not an atom of animal food, and their usual bedding was a plank, or by particular kindness a single blanket."

The above writer does not specify any particulars in which the improvement spoken of is apparent, but we think all will admit that a very considerable improvement might be accomplished, and yet the treatment might be such as could not be called *good*. He adds however that "much remains to be done, which the obligation of *humanity* require."

Your committee are of opinion, that in consequence of what has been written, spoken, and done by the friends of abolition, much light has been diffused through the community even in the slave holding states, and many masters restrained by the force of public opinion, thus enlightened, have abstained from cruelties which they would otherwise have inflicted; yet we cannot but believe, that very much anguish of heart, and exquisite sufferings of body are endured by this unhappy race, even in Maryland: (and we believe they are used as well here, as in any other part of our country.)

The multitudes that are annually sold to the southern markets, by which parents and children are violently separated, and all the ties of consanguinity rent asunder, if no other indication of bad treatment were discovered; would itself speak volumes.

The treatment of slaves may be estimated with some degree of accuracy by the laws which are in force respecting them. The laws of the land are always understood to be intended for the protection of the subject, but with respect to negro slaves (in the slave states) they have an effect directly the reverse. So far from securing him in the enjoyment of happiness, his very life is placed at the mercy of any white man, (especially of his master or overseer) who may take the opportunity to kill him in the absence of any other free white person. Resistance to the will of the master, may be punished with stripes, and if the resistance amount to striking, may be punished by imprisonment and whipping; and for a third offence the slave may suffer death! It will be perceived that by the operation of those laws, a virtuous female slave, may suffer death for defending her chastity against the ruffian assaults of a debauchee. The manner in which those laws are administered in some of the states, frequently occasions great outrages upon the common charities of our nature. The discretion rested in a court of two or three freeholders, or a single magistrate, over the persons of the accused is often exercised with great severity. In Stroud's Slave Laws, we have an account of the burning to death of a negro woman, under a law of South Carolina, so late as 1820. (See page 124, in the note.)

It appears also that the mental improvement of the slave is a thing generally deprecated by the master, and in some cases provided against by law. (See Niles's Register, April 21, 1821.)

How deplorable must be the state of that community, which supposed its safety to depend on keeping one half of its members totally ignorant, and not even able to read the Holy Scripture.

How contrary to the nature of man? how offensive in the sight of that God who "*has made of one blood all nations of men to dwell on all the face of the earth*!"

It furthermore appears that in transporting slaves from one part of the nation to another, either in the domestic slave trade or in large bodies by removals of planters, &c. they are usually chained and handcuffed, or otherwise manacled, like the vilest criminals, &c. &c.

In considering the treatment of slaves, your

committee deem it necessary to notice the amount and quality of labour required of them. In some cases this is known to be extremely severe, and attended with many aggravating circumstances. Such as scarcity of supplies which are sometimes insufficient, and frequently of very inferior quality: exposure to disease, and want of proper attention in the incipient states of sickness. The cultivation of rice one of the great staples of the Carolinas, is an instance to illustrate this point. Mr. Adams in his Geography says, "the cultivation is wholly by negroes. No work can be imagined more laborious or more prejudicial to health. They are obliged to stand in water often times mid-leg high, exposed to the scorching heat of the sun, and breathing an atmosphere poisoned by the unwholesome effluvia of an oozy bottom and stagnant water."

It appears therefore, that in the treatment of slaves in general, as well as in the legal provisions respecting them, the interest, convenience, security and inclinations of the master, constitute the only object in view; the comfort or even safety or health of the slave makes no part of the consideration, any further than it is supposed, to promote one or the other of the former. Finally after taking a rapid view of this part of the subject, your committee are led to doubt whether the evils of slavery are materially lessened in certain portions of our beloved country, notwithstanding all that has been done in favour of manumission, colonization and abolition of the slave trade, &c. &c. and what it might have been at this time, if no efforts had been made to arrest its progress, is beyond human wisdom to determine.

Thirdly, In reference to the diminution or the final extinction of slavery in the Union, your committee remark, that it seems to be the expectation of all, that it must at some period cease to exist, an evil so tremendous—a practice so completely at war with all the principles of justice, mercy and truth, so repugnant to all the best feelings of human nature, and fraught with such fearful consequences to society; cannot but excite in every reflecting mind a strong desire that it should be removed. In view of the divine government, which rules all with justice and righteousness, the human mind is naturally led to expect that such oppression and cruelty must have an end.

But how this revolution in society is to be brought about, perhaps no human foresight can yet divine. If our slave holding fellow citizens could be induced to establish schools for the instruction of the rising generation among the blacks, and thus qualify them for self government, which every principle of equity requires they should do, and to teach them by precept and example the importance of moral obligation; one of the greatest obstacles would be removed. If they would introduce among them a sacred regard for the social duties, arising from marriage, and from the relations subsisting between parents and children; they might with perfect safety and great advantage to the state, be emancipated. A few years of effort of this kind, would form a class of men from whom the nation would not only have nothing to fear; but on whom she could safely rely for aid in her greatest emergency. In their present condition of abject slavery what can be expected of them, but that they should lay hold on every apparent opportunity, of regaining their freedom, and ever retorting on the masters the evils they have suffered?

Facts uniformly sustain this position; what multitudes of slaves joined the enemy during his temporary invasions of our southern coasts in the late war, notwithstanding all the efforts of the whites to

367

prevent it? While on the contrary none were found more efficient in repelling his attacks than the free blacks of the south. Such was their zeal and valour in defence of Louisiana, that General Jackson, the present Chief Magistrate of the Union; bestowed on them the following eulogium.

"To the Men of Colour."

"Soldiers! From the shores of Mobile I collected you to arms; I invited you to share in the perils, and to divide the glory of your white countrymen. I expected much from you, for I was not uninformed of those qualities which must render you formidable to an invading enemy. I knew that you could endure hunger and thirst, and all the hardships of war.—I knew that you loved the land of your nativity! and that like ourselves you had to defend all that is dear to man. But you *surpass my hopes*. I found in you united to those qualities, that noble enthusiasm which impels to great deeds." In a subsequent communication, the General in numerating the officers whose commands had distinguished themselves, makes honourable mention of the one who led these troops in the different actions of that memorable campaign. There are many circumstances which encourage the hope, that the time is drawing nigh when the African race shall enjoy the sweets of liberty. Their successful attempt at self government in St. Domingo, under so many disadvantages, the abolition of slavery in several of the South American provinces, and recently in Mexico, and the efforts of the British nation in their behalf, together with many other co-operating causes seem to indicate the interposition of Divine Providence in favour of the oppressed. In HIS Almighty hand, the most inefficient causes sometimes produce the most astonishing effects, and often the very means made use of to rivet the chains of oppression are so overruled by Him as to burst the bonds they were designed to perpetuate. We may therefore rest assured that He will in his own good time crown our labours with complete success, by bringing deliverance to the captive "and the opening of the prison doors to them that are bound." In the mean time let every friend of the cause remember that he has a duty to perform. Let the result be what it may, he is equally bound to oppose as far as possible, the growing evil.

It becomes us therefore to enquire how this may most effectually be done. Our opposition should be peaceable but firm. It should be the opposition of brothers not of enemies, it may be shewn by acts of kindness and forbearance, but it *must be opposition* and it *must be shown*. It may exhibit itself in peaceable efforts to protect the rights of free blacks, and instructing their offspring, or it may be shown by rational attempts to enlighten the public mind on the subject, or in encouragement of those publications that are so employed; or by memorials to congress and the state legislature, &c. &c.

Our means of considerable efficiency for exciting the public mind to the consideration of the injustice and impolicy of slavery, may probably be found in the persevering efforts now making on the part of many friends of abolition to encourage the creation and consumption of the products of free labour.

We cannot withhold the tribute of our respect and admiration from those patriotic females, who have associated for this purpose both in England and America, and heartily, recommend their example, as one worthy of universal imitation.[1]

WM. KESLEY, Chairman.

A Table shewing the recommendations and requisitions of the Convention of 1796, and of former Conventions, and how far they have hitherto been complied with by each Society.

I. *To send delegates to a Convention to meet at Philadelphia in May, 1797.*

Society,		New-York complied.
society,		New-Jersey ditto.
society,		Pennsylvania ditto.
	Maryland society,	(*at Baltimore*) ditto.
(*Maryland*)	Choptank society,	ditto.
(*Virginia*)	Alexandria society,	ditto.
	Virginia society,	(*at Richmond*) ditto.

Rhode-Island, Connecticut, Washington (*Pennsylvania*,) Wilmington, (*Delaware*,) Delaware, Chester-town (*Maryland*,) Winchester, (*Virginia*) and Kentucky societies sent none.

II. *To transmit certified copies of all the laws in the respective states relating to slavery; as well of those repealed as of those in force.*

Connecticut transmitted. . . . . in 1795.

New-York, ... in 1797.

New-Jersey, ... in 1796.

Pennsylvania, ... in 1797.

Maryland, ... in 1797.

Virginia and Alexandria . . . . in 1797.

a copy of professor Tucker's dissertation on slavery, which contains the substance of all the laws of Virginia respecting slavery from its settlement till 1794. Copies of the laws since that period also sent.

Rhode Island, Delaware, and Kentucky societies have not yet

370

transmitted.

III. *To forward correct lists of the officers and other members of each respective society.*

New-York complied in 1796 and 1797, number of members two hundred and fifty.

New-Jersey complied partially.

Pennsylvania complied in 1797. Members five hundred and ninety-one.

Wilmington complied in 1796. Members about sixty.

Maryland complied in 1797. Members two hundred and thirty-one.

Choptank complied in 1797. Members twenty-five.

Alexandria complied in 1797. Members sixty-two.

Virginia complied in 1796 and 1797. Members one hundred and forty-seven.

Rhode-Island, Connecticut, Washington, Delaware, Chester-town, Winchester and Kentucky societies have not yet sent lists of their members.

IV. *An account of the proceedings of each society in relieving persons unlawfully held in bondage.*

New-York. Since January 1796, have had complaints from ninety persons, Africans or of African descent—twenty-nine freed on the law prohibiting importation—seven as free born—two unsuccessful—heavy damages recovered in some instances—twenty-one cases now in suit—nineteen under consideration.

New-Jersey, Society. Many manumissions have been effected since January 1796, but no precise information is yet received to what number and under what circumstances.

Pennsylvania Society. It appears from the minutes of the acting committee of the society, that many hundreds of Africans have been liberated through their aid since the institution of the society.

Wilmington Society. Has sent a list of persons liberated by their agency up to 1796, amounting to eighty since 1788.

Maryland Society at Baltimore. A variety of suits were instituted against the unlawful holders of slaves last year, and in consequence many have been liberated—there are several

371

suits now pending in law, which are expected to have the like favorable issue.

Choptank Society. This society has exerted itself in favor of the Africans, for seven years; and been the instrument of liberating more than sixty individuals, and has failed but in a single application to a court of justice in their behalf.

Alexandria Society. Twenty-six complaints made to the society —six persons relieved on the law against importation; five will probably be relieved, the other fourteen cases on which as well as on the above suits are pending are doubtful. A suit in Norfolk court and one in North Carolina now carrying on at the expense of this society.

Virginia Society. Nothing of material importance since the convention of 1796. Suits commenced before now pending in behalf of between twenty and thirty persons.

Rhode-Island, Connecticut, Washington, Delaware, Chestertown, Winchester, and Kentucky societies sent no account.

V. *A Statement of the condition of the blacks in each State both bond and free, with respect to the property of the free, and the employment and moral conduct of all.*

New-York. The number of people of color in the state of New-York not known—exceeds two thousand—in the city names of one thousand collected—of these more than half are free, employed as servants, labourers, sailors, mechanics, &c.—a few are small traders—condition tolerable—many in town and country freeholders—several worth from three hundred to thirteen hundred dollars—various associations among the free blacks for mutual support, benefit and improvement—one has a lot for a burying ground and the site of a church worth fifteen hundred dollars. In a state of progressive improvement.

New-Jersey. Condition, as to enjoyments of life and respectability, much the same as in New-York.

Pennsylvania. Complied with in 1796. See the minutes of the convention of that year—page 20 and 21.

Maryland at Baltimore & Choptank. The condition of the blacks from the information this society has received is greatly ameliorated, and some few of the free are enabled to provide for themselves without manual labor—moral conduct equal to that of the whites in like circumstances—minute information not yet obtained.

Alexandria. Generally slaves—their treatment less rigourous than formerly—moral conduct of the free generally good—as labourers preferred to the whites.

372

From Rhode-Island, Connecticut, Washington, Wilmington, Delaware, Chester-town, Virginia, Winchester and Kentucky Societies,—none sent.

VI. *Reports of trials and adjudications relative to Africans.*

New-York. A bill for the gradual abolition of slavery brought into the Legislature at their last session, but postponed till the next session.

New-Jersey. A bill brought into the last session of the Legislature for a gradual abolition of slavery which is postponed to the next session as in New-York.

Pennsylvania. A bill for the total abolition of slavery was brought into and read in the House of Representatives near the close of the last session of the Legislature, but lies over to the next session.

Maryland at Baltimore. No attempt has been made since the Convention of 1796.

Alexandria. Have drawn up and mean to present to the next Legislature, a remonstrance against a late law of the State which is peculiarly severe against Africans.

Rhode-Island, Connecticut, Washington, Wilmington, Delaware, Chester-town, Choptank, Virginia, Winchester, and Kentucky societies transmitted no information.

VIII. *The progress made in extending to Africans the benefits of instruction.*

New-York. House and lot for a school purchased by the society since January 1796—school has existed many years—more flourishing now than ever—property of the society for its accommodation worth upwards of three thousand five hundred dollars—annual expense of the school one thousand dollars—has a master, usher and mistress—scholars taught reading, penmanship, arithmetic, English grammar and geography—girls (additionally) needle work—number one hundred and twenty-two—boys sixty three girls fifty-nine—improve fast and behave as well as any other children—evening school in the winter for free blacks, adults—taught by the master and usher of the society's school—number, forty-four—usher a black man.

New-Jersey. Nothing done by the society—a bill is now pending before the Legislature providing for the instruction of all children in the state, which, if carried, will include the Africans as well as the whites.

Pennsylvania. Within the city and liberties of Philadelphia there are at present seven schools for the education of people of colour; at which perhaps near three hundred scholars of both sexes usually attend—two other schools are about to be opened for the same purpose.

Maryland at Baltimore. Several children of Africans and other people of color now under a course of instruction—an academy (of which no notice was given to the last convention) will be opened the ensuing season, and suitable teachers provided.

Alexandria. A Sunday school opened by this society in December, 1795, for the reception of Africans and their descendants—the number of scholars who usually attend is one hundred and eight—they are instructed in reading, penmanship and arithmetic.

From Rhode-Island, Connecticut, Washington, Wilmington, Delaware, Chester-town, Choptank, Virginia, Winchester, and Kentucky societies—no information received.

IX. *To establish periodical discourses on the subject of slavery and the means of its abolition.*

Connecticut. No information this year—there have been seven or eight discourses delivered before the society, the greater part of which have been printed and circulated extensively.

New-York. The first annual discourse delivered before this society the twelfth of April, 1797.

Pennsylvania. Not deemed necessary in this state, where the general sentiments of the people are, in a great degree, congenial with those of the society.

Maryland. Complied with.

Rhode-Island, New-Jersey, Washington, Wilmington, Delaware, Chestertown, Choptank, Alexandria, Virginia, Winchester, and Kentucky Societies transmitted no information on the subject.

X. *To keep accurate registers of all deeds of manumission executed within the precincts of each society.*

New-York. Attended to by this society from the first, so far as depended on itself.

Pennsylvania. A register of manumissions kept by the acting committee.

Maryland at Baltimore, and Choptank. The society preserve a register—and all manumissions are matter of record in the county courts.

Alexandria. A register is kept by the society, manumissions are recorded in the court of Common Pleas.

374

Virginia. Deeds of emancipation are recorded in the county courts.

From Rhode-Island, Connecticut, New-Jersey, Washington, Wilmington, Delaware, Chester-town, Winchester and Kentucky societies—no information.

XI. *To distribute suitable publications tending to promote the design of the institutions.*

New-York. Attended to partially.

New-Jersey. Attended to generally.

Pennsylvania. Faithfully attended to.

Alexandria. Attended to, and a new publication is soon to be made on the subject of slavery.

From Rhode-Island, Connecticut, Washington, Wilmington, Delaware, Maryland, Chester-town, Choptank, Virginia, Winchester, and Kentucky societies—no information.

XII. *To endeavour to free negroes from St. Domingo retained here as slaves, contrary to the decree of the National Convention of France.*

Pennsylvania. Acted on as cases have occurred—from the other societies—no information.

XIII. *To discourage the use of articles manufactured by slaves.*

No particular measures on this subject are represented as being adopted by any of the societies.

XIV. *To distribute the address to the free people of color from the convention of 1796.*

New-York, New-Jersey, Pennsylvania, Maryland, and Alexandria societies,—done.

Choptank society. Not received till late by this society.

Virginia society. Done in part.

From Rhode-Island, Connecticut, Washington, Wilmington, Delaware, Chester-town, Winchester, and Kentucky societies—no information.

XV. *To send copies of the constitutions of the respective societies.*

Connecticut. Sent.

New-York. Sent the original in 1796, and the revised one in

375

1797.

New-Jersey. Sent in 1796.

Pennsylvania. ditto.

Wilmington. ditto.

Maryland. ditto.

Alexandria. Sent in 1797.

Virginia. Sent in 1796.

Rhode-Island, Washington, Delaware, Chester-town, Choptank, Winchester, and Kentucky societies sent none.[2]

A PLAN FOR THE GENERAL EMANCIPATION OF SLAVES.

"We hold these truths to be self-evident, that all men are created equal; that they are endowed by their Creator with certain unalienable rights; among these are life, liberty, and the pursuit of happiness that to ⸌ secure these rights, governments were instituted, deriving their just powers from the consent of the governed." (Declaration of Independence.)

These self-evident truths, thus solemnly promulgated, and always admitted in theory; at least in relation to ourselves; are well-known to be partially denied or disregarded, in most sections of the union, in relation to the descendents of the African race. That a nation professing the justice of its laws, should contain a population, amounting to nearly one-seventh of the whole, who know little of the operation of those laws, except as instruments of oppression, is one of those political phenomena, which prove how little the patriot's boast, or the creator's declamation is guided by the light of truth.

It must be admitted that it would neither be politic nor safe, for the present system of slavery in the United Sates to be long continued, without providing some wise and certain means of eventual

376

emancipation.

Slavery with its present degrading characteristics, is a state of actual hostility between master and slave, in which "a revolution of the wheel of fortune, in exchange of situation, is among possible events; and this may become probably by supernatural interference! The Almighty has no attribute which can take part with us in such a contest."—*Jefferson.*

It is a truth generally acknowledged, that Slavery is an evil, not only by those whom principle, or education have taught to proscribe the practice, but by men of reflection, even in the very vortex of slavery. To condemn then, what few, if any, will presume to defend is rendered unnecessary; and the ingenuity of the philanthropist would be more judiciously exercised in devising a practicable remedy for this deep-rooted disease, than in heaping reproaches upon these, who, by the conduct of their ancestors, are placed in the condition of masters of slaves. Few of those who from their childhood, have been placed in situations far removed from the scenes which slavery exhibits, can fully appreciate the difficulties, the vexations, and the anxieties, incident to the life of a slaveholder. To devise a plan, then, by which the condition, both of the master and slave may be meliorated, is a desideratum in the policy of this country:—A plan which will promote the immediate interest of the master, in the same ratio, that the slave is made to rise in the scale of moral and intellectual improvement; and which will eventuate in the ultimate enfranchisement of the long injured and degraded descendants of Africa. The evils of slavery being generally acknowledged, and its impolicy fully evinced, the important question which remains to be solved, will naturally present itself: What are the means by which this evil is to be removed, consistently with the safety of the master, and the happiness of the slave?

Perhaps to some, this question, considered on the ground of absolute justice, may appear of easy solution: *Immediate, universal emancipation*.

But however pleasing the prospect may be to the philanthropist, of getting clear of one of the evils of slavery, yet a full examination of local circumstances, must convince us that this would be, to cut, rather than untie the Gordian knot.

Reformation on a large scale, is commonly slow. Habits long established, are not easily and suddenly changed. But were it possible to induce the inhabitants of the slaveholding states, to proclaim liberty to the captives, and to let loose at once the whole tide of black population, it may reasonably be questioned whether such a measure would not produce as much evil as it would cure. Besides, such a measure, if it were practicable, would fall short of simple justice. We owe to that injured race, an immense debt, which the liberation of their bodies alone would not liquidate. It has been the policy of the slaveholder to keep the man whom he has doomed to interminable servitude, in the lowest state of mental degradation: to withhold from him as much as possible the means of improving the talents which nature has given him. In short, to reduce him as near to the condition of a machine as a rational being could be. Every inducement—every excitement, to the exertion and development of native talent and genius, is wanting in the slave.—Hence, to throw such a being, thus degraded, thus brutalized, upon society, and then expect him to exercise those rights which are the birthright of every son and daughter of Adam, with advantage to himself, or to the community upon which he is thrown, is to suppose that the laws established for the government of universal nature, should in this case be changed. As well might we expect a man to be born in the full maturity of his

378

mental faculties, or an infant to run before it had learned the use of its limbs.

A plan, then, for universal emancipation, to be practicable, must be gradual. The slave must be made to pass through a state of pupilage and monority, to fit him for the enjoyment and exercise of rational liberty.

"If then the extremes of emancipation, and perpetual, unlimited slavery be dangerous," and impolitic, "the safe and advisable measure must be between them." And this brings us again the question, How can we get clear of the evils of slavery, with safety to the master, and advantage to the slave? For the solution of this difficult problem, the following outlines of a plan for a gradual, but *general* and *universal* emancipation is proposed. Let the slaves be attached to the soil,—give them an interest in the land they cultivate. Place them in the same situation as their masters, as the peasantry of Russia, in relation to their landlords. Let wise and salutary laws be enacted, in the several slave holding states, for their general government. These laws should provide for the means of extending to the children of every slave, the benefits of school learning. The practice of arbitrary punishment for the most trivial offences, should be abolished.

An important step towards the accomplishment of this plan, would be, to prohibit by law the migration, or transportation of slaves from one state to another:—and also to provide, that no slave should be sold, out of the county, or town in which his master resides, without his own consent. Provision should then be made for the introduction of a system of general instruction on each farm or plantation; each slave who has a family should be furnished with a hut, and a portion of land to cultivate for his own use; for which he would pay to the landlord an annual rent. For each day he was employed by the master or landlord, he should be allowed a stipulated price: out of the proceeds of his stipulated wages, those things necessary for his comfortable maintenance, should be deducted; if furnished by the master.

The time given him to cultivate his allotment of ground should be deducted from his annual hire. A wise and equitable system of laws, adapted to the condition of blacks, should be established for their government. Then a character would be formed among them; acts of diligence and fidelity would meet their appropriate reward, and negligence and crime would be followed by their merited chastisement. The execution of this plan, in its fullest extent, would be followed by increased profits to the landholder.

It would be productive of incalculable advantage to the slave, both in his civil, and moral condition:—And thus the interest of the master, and the melioration of the condition of the slave, would be gradually and reciprocally advanced in the progress of this experiment. Although legislative provisions would greatly facilitate the adoption of this plan, it is not necessary for individuals to wait the movement of government. Any one may introduce it on his own plantation, and reap many of its most important advantages.

The plan now proposed is not new. It is not a Utopian and visionary theory, unsupported by experience. It has been successfully tried in the Island of Barbadoes, by the late Joshua Steele; and the result exceeded his most sanguine expectations. "The first principles, of his plan," says Mr. Dickson, "are the plain ones, of treating the slaves as human creatures: moving them to action by the hope of reward, as well as the fear of punishment: giving them out of their own labours, wages and land, sufficient to afford them the plainest necessaries:—And protecting them against the capricious violence, too often of ignorant, unthinking, or unprincipled, and perhaps drunken men and boys, invested with arbitrary powers, as their managers, and 'drivers.' His plan is founded in nature, and has nothing in it of rash innovation. It does not hurry forward a new order of things;—it recommends no fine projects of ticklish experiments; but, by a few safe and easy steps, and a few simple applications of English law, opens the way for the gradual introduction of a better system." "To advance above three hundred debased field Negroes, who had never before moved without the whip, to a state nearly resembling that of contented, honest and industrious servants; and after paying them for their labour, to triple, in a few years, the annual net clearance of his estates—these were great achievements, for an aged man, in an untried field of improvement, preoccupied by inveterate vulgar prejudices. He has indeed accomplished all that was really doubtful or difficult in the undertaking; and perhaps all that is at present desirable, either to owner or slave. For he has ascertained as a fact, what was before only known to the learned as a theory, and to practical men as a paradox:—that the paying of slaves for their labour, does actually produce a very great profit to their owners."[3]

To the American Convention for promoting the Abolition of Slavery, and improving the condition of the African Race.

The Committee appointed to take into consideration the subject of the Internal Slave Trade, and report such facts as they may deem suitable for publication, in relation to it,

Respectfully Report—That they consider the subject as one of the greatest magnitude and importance that can gain the attention of this Convention. That such a trade should be permitted to be practised by the Laws of the United States of America, is a matter of the deepest regret, and can only be reconciled by a consideration of the frailty of all human institutions. From the short time afforded the Committee they have been unable as fully to consider the subject as they desired, but from the enquiry they have been able to make, the following appears to be at present the principal markets for the sale of human beings in the United States, viz. the Territories of Florida and Arkansas, the states of Georgia, Alabama, Mississippi, and Louisiana; these states and territories are supplied with their victims of oppression and cruelty, from the states of Delaware, Maryland, the District of Columbia, Eastern and Northern parts of Virginia, Kentucky and Tennessee. The principal depots where men, women, and children are collected, frequently kept in irons and exhibited for sale are—Patty Cannon's house, situated on the confines of Delaware and Maryland; a large establishment in the city of Baltimore; the Jail of Baltimore County; one at Saddler's Cross Roads, and the Jail in the city of Washington a public tavern in the same place, and several places in the town of Alexandria; and in most of the towns of Virginia, and in the city of Charleston, S. C. In addition to the evils of legalized Slavery, we may add, as growing out of the trade, acts of kidnapping not less cruel than those committed on the Coast of Africa. Individuals are well known, who have made a business of decoying free people of Color on board their vessels, and of selling them for Slaves; two instances came particularly under observation in one of our principal sea ports, (and we believe they are numerous in other places,) one a boy of about 12 years of age, was decoyed on board a vessel and taken to one of the above places of deposite, from thence sent in their chain of communication to the home of the purchaser. Another instance occurred by the next trip of the vessel, of a woman being taken in the same manner, who on attempting to leave the cabin was knocked down, gagged, and severely whipped, to intimidate, and make her acknowledge herself a slave. She was taken to the same place of deposite, but apprehending it was to be searched, they removed her with two others, free persons, (one of them stolen within twelve miles of the place,) to the woods, where they were chained, with but little clothing, and exposed day and night in the open air; one of the persons so confined released himself from the tree to which he was attached and with an axe extricated the others. The woman above alluded to has since arrived and gave the information, and in addition says, they have pits to conceal their captives when close pursuit is apprehended, which they cover with earth and leaves. It may be asked, as the persons are known, why not bring them to justice? We may reply, that notwithstanding we could bring some of the persons last alluded to, to identify their kidnappers, yet their evidence, on account of their color, is not allowed to be received in the Courts of Slaveholding States. Many other instances have occured: and many instances of persons who were entitled to their freedom after serving a limited time, being sold into irredeemable Slavery in other states are deplorably numerous; the covert manner of doing which is generally such as to elude detection. It is suggested whether Legislative enactments requiring that persons so situated, should be required to be registered every time they change masters would not obviate in some measure this evil—humane persons could then trace individuals so circumstanced, and bring offenders to justice:—all which is respectfully submitted.

Some of your Committee have been the unwilling witnesses of gangs of men, women and children, being driven off in chains from some of the above places to be sold like cattle. The shrieks and groans of the wretched victims, would have melted any heart but that of a Slave Trader, steeled by avarice or petrified by cruelty: and as if in utter defiance of the laws of God and man:—the Sabbath is the day generally chosen for receiving and sending off the unfortunate objects of their cupidity and so blunted has public opinion become from the long existence of this unhallowed traffic, that individuals in the city of Alexandria, publicly advertise their having prepared their prisons and furnished themselves with every accommodation for selling men, women, and innocent children, to any purchaser.

The number transported by sea from the single port of Baltimore by a noted trader of that place is believed to exceed several hundreds per annum. How long, may we ask, is our land to be polluted with such abominations? Is there no fear of the awful vengeance of him who has declared, "Is not this the fast that I have chosen, to loose the bonds of wickedness, and that ye let the oppressed go free, and that ye break every yoke?" If cruelty to the Israelites, (and their acts of oppression was mildness, in comparison with ours,) what may we not expect, we who have received the blessings of divine revelation, who proclaim the goodness of God, in having freed us from the political bondage of Great Britain.

Respectfully submitted, on behalf of the Committee,

—THOMAS SHIPLEY, *Chairman*.[4]

TO THE AMERICAN CONVENTION, &c.

The Committee appointed at the last Convention to procure information of the cultivation of Sugar, Cotton, &c. by free labor, &c.

Respectfully Report—That they have given some attention to the subject of their appointment, but have not been as successful as could have been desired. They have been enabled to procure some general information, relative to the production of sugar and cotton by the labor of emancipated slaves, and other free persons of color, in the West Indian Islands and on the American Continent; but have not had it in their power to obtain such particulars concerning it as will shew the extent of the pecuniary advantages which this mode of proceeding undoubtedly possesses over that of cultivating the land by slave labor.

We are credibly informed that the article of sugar is now produced by free labor, in two or more of the West Indian Islands, of a quality fully equal to that of any other, and is, also, brought into the market upon quite as favourable terms. Coffee is also produced in abundance in the island of Hayti, and some parts of South America, by free labor. These productions, unstained by slavery, may now be had in the cities of New York and Philadelphia, and likewise at Wilmington in Delaware.

In the Territory of Florida, we learn, that a company, composed principally of citizens of the United States, have purchased a large tract of land, with the view of cultivating the sugar cane and other tropical productions, by the labor of free men. Samples of the sugar made by this company have been shewn to some of the members of your committee, and have been pronounced to be of a good quality. In Louisiana, likewise, we are informed that sundry persons are engaged in producing sugar in the same way, but we have not ascertained to what extent they have carried their experiments.

Sundry cotton planters in the states of North Carolina and Alabama, have, for several years cultivated their lands by free hands. They have disposed of considerable quantities of cotton in New York and New England, and we are informed appear well satisfied to continue the practice of employing free laborers to the total exclusion of that of slaves.

A gentleman in Rhode Island has manufactured some of this cotton separately into coarse muslins, which may also be had as above stated. A few of the citizens of Pennsylvania and Delaware, have likewise purchased some of this cotton, and manufactured it into calicoes and other fabrics. We presume, however, that this has not been done to any considerable extent; neither have we ascertained the degree of encouragement held out to those engaged in the enterprise.

The article of tobacco, has, for some years, been successfully cultivated in the state of Ohio, where it is known that slavery does not exist; and we learn that it can be afforded in the Baltimore market at a lower price than that produced in the state of Maryland, by the labor of Slaves, after defraying the expenses of transportation some hundreds of miles further than the latter. But we are informed that even in the Province of Upper Canada, sundry colored persons from Kentucky, have made a settlement, and have raised large quantities of this article which has been disposed of to advantage in some of our Atlantic ports.

But the most particular account your committee have obtained respecting the experiment of free, contrasted with slave labor, has been obtained from Ward's Mexico, a work lately published in London. The author was an Envoy of the British Government, and the most entire reliance may be placed on his statement, which, as in every other fair experiment completely proves the advantages of cultivation by freemen. It appears, from his account, that the experiment was tried in consequence of the difficulty of procuring slaves during the war, and the great mortality which always took place on the first introduction of the slaves, from a change of climate. Being desirous to produce a race of free laborers, a large number of slaves were manumitted and encouraged to intermarry with the native Indians, which they soon did to a great extent, and so beneficial was the plan found to the master's interest, that in the year 1808 on most of the largest estates, there was not a slave to be found. From a personal inspection the author above alluded to declares that their tasks were performed with great precision and rapidity, (vol. 1, p. 67, 68.). A most important improvement appears also to have taken place; the whip being banished from the field and the females released from the field labor. From 360 to 450 tons of sugar are produced by 150 free laborers, while in Cuba, where the soil is superior in fertility the same number produce but 180 tons.

Should the Convention think proper the committee are willing to continue the further investigation of the subject.

Respectfully submitted,
B. LUNDY, Chairman.[5]

To THE AMERICAN CONVENTION,—The committee appointed to procure information in relation to the culture of sugar, cotton, &c. on this continent by free labor.,

Respectfully State—That owing to the inadequacy of the means to make the requisite investigations, your committee has not been able since the last session of the Convention to acquire much information of any farther general facts. The following notice of the cultivation of sugar in Mexico, to which your committee then briefly advertised has been obtained through the medium of the London Anti-Slavery Monthly Reporter for August, 1829. It is an extract of a letter from Mr. Ward, Mexican Envoy of the British Government to the Right Honourable George Canning, viz.

Mexico, March 13, 1826.

"Sɪʀ,—The possibility of introducing a system of free labour into the West India Islands having been so much discussed in England, I conceived that it might not be uninteresting to His Majesty's Government to receive some details respecting the result of the experiment in this country, where it certainly has had a fair trial.

"I accordingly took advantage of Mr. Morier's prolonged stay here to visit the Valley of Cuernavaca, and Cuantla Amilpas, which supplies a great part of the federation with sugar and coffee, although not a single slave is at present employed in their cultivation.

"I have the honour to inclose a sketch of the observations which I was enabled to make upon this journey, together with such details as I have thought best calculated to show both the scale upon which these estates are worked, and the complete success with which the abolition of the slavery has, in this instance been attended.

"The valley which extends almost uninterruptedly from Cuernavaca to Cuantla Amilpas and Juncar (covering a space of about forty miles,) is situated on the road to Acapulco, at the foot of the first range of mountains by which the descent from the Table Land towards the south-west commences, about fifty miles from the Capital.

"It is about 2,000 feet lower than the Table Land of Mexico. The difference of temperature is proportionably great, so that two days are sufficient to transport the traveller into the very midst of Tierra Caliente.

"It is believed that the sugar-cane was first planted there about one hundred years ago; from that time the number of sugar-estates has gone on increasing, until there is now hardly an acre of ground on the whole plain which is not turned to account.

"The cultivation was originally carried on entirely by slaves, who were purchased at Vera Cruz, at from 300 to 400 dollars each.

"It was found, however, that this system was attended with considerable inconvenience, it being impossible to secure a sufficient supply of slaves during a war. The losses likewise, at all times, were great, as many of the slaves were unable to support the fatigue and changes of temperature, to which they were exposed on the journey from Vera Cruz to Curnavaca, and perished, either on the road, or soon after their arrival.

"Several of the great proprieters were induced by these circumstances to give liberty to a certain number of their slaves annually, and by encouraging marriages between them and the Indians of the country, to propagate a race of free labourers, who might be employed when a supply of Slaves was no longer to be obtained.

"This plan proved so eminently successful that on some of the largest estates there was not a single slave in the year 1808.

"The policy of the measure became still more apparent

on the breaking out of the revolution in 1810.

"The planters who had not adopted the system of gradual emancipation before that period saw themselves abandoned, and were forced, in many instances, to give up working their estates, as their slaves took advantage of the approach of the insurgents to join them en masse; while those who had provided themselves with a mixed cast of free labourers, retained even during the worst times, a sufficient number of men to enable them to continue to cultivate their lands, although upon a smaller scale."

The same work for September 1829, speaking of free and slave labour, remarks.

"The controversy is fast tending to its termination. The march of events will scarcely leave room much longer, either for misrepresentation or misapprehension. The facilities already given in Bengal by Lord W. Bentinck, to the investment of British capital and the development of British skill in the cultivation of the soil; the almost certainty that those fiscal regulations which have hitherto depressed the growth of sugar in Bengal, and prevented the large increase of its imports into this country, will soon be repealed; the prospect of an early removal of the other restrictions which still fetter the commerce of our Eastern possessions: the rapidly increasing population and prosperity of Haiti; the official statements of Mr. Ward, as to the profitable culture of sugar by free labour in Mexico; and the rapid extension of the manufacture of beet root sugar in France; a prelude as we conceive, to its introduction into this country, and especially into Ireland; all these circumstances combined, afford a promise which can scarcely fail of seeing a death blow inflicted on the culture of sugar by slave-labour, which all the misrepresentations of all the slave holders in the world, with all their clamourous partisans in this country cannot avert, or even long retard."

Since their views have been directed to the subject, your committee are fully satisfied that its further investigation will be highly important; and that at no very distant period, *the results of very interesting experiments nearer home may be obtained*.

Respectfully Submitted,
B. LUNDY, Chairman.[6]

Baltimore, December 1, 1829.

AN ACT TO PROHIBIT THE CARRYING ON THE SLAVE-TRADE,
FROM THE
UNITED STATES TO ANY FOREIGN PLACE OR COUNTRY.

Section I. *Be it enacted by the Senate and House of Representatives of the United States of America, in Congress assembled.* That no citizen or citizens of the United States, or foreigner, or any other person coming into, or residing within the same, shall, for himself or any other person whatsoever, either as master, factor or owner, build, fit, equip, load or otherwise prepare any ship or vessel, within any port or place of the said United States; nor shall cause any ship or vessel to sail from any port or place within the same, for the purpose of carrying on any trade or traffic in slaves, to any foreign country; or for the purpose of procuring, from any foreign kingdom, place or country, the inhabitants of such kingdom, place or country, to be transported to any foreign country, port or place whatever, to be sold or disposed of, as slaves: And if any ship or vessel shall be so fitted out, as aforesaid, for the said purposes, or shall be caused to sail, so as aforesaid, every such ship or vessel, her tackle, furniture, apparel and other

391

appurtenances, shall be forfeited to the United States; and shall be liable to be seized, prosecuted and condemned, in any of the circuit courts or district court for the district, where the said ship or vessel may be found and seized.

Section II. *And be it further enacted*, That all and every person, so building, fitting out, equipping, loading, or otherwise preparing, or sending away, any ship or vessel, knowing, or intending, that the same shall be employed in such trade or business, contrary to the true intent and meaning of this act, or any ways aiding or abetting therein, shall severally forfeit and pay the sum of two thousand dollars, one moiety thereof, to the use of the United States, and the other moiety thereof, to the use of him or her, who shall sue for the prosecute the same.

Section III. *And be it further enacted*, That the owner, master or factor of each and every foreign ship or vessel, clearing out for any of the coasts or kingdoms of Africa, or suspected to be intended for the Slave-trade, and the suspicion being declared to the officer of the customs, by any citizen, on oath or affirmation, and such information being to the satisfaction of the said officer, shall first give bond with sufficient sureties, to the Treasurer of the United States, that none of the natives of Africa, or any other foreign country or place, shall be taken on board the said ship or vessel, to be transported, or sold as slaves, in any other foreign port or place whatever, within nine months thereafter.

Section IV. *And be it further enacted*, That if any citizen or citizens of the United States shall, contrary to the true intent and meaning of this act, take on board, receive or transport any such persons, as above described, in this act, for the purpose of selling them as slaves, as aforesaid, he or they shall forfeit and pay, for each and every person, so received on board, transported, or sold as aforesaid, the sum of two hundred dollars, to be recovered in any court of the United States, proper to try the same, the one moiety thereof, to the use of the United States, and the other moiety to the use of such person or persons, who shall sue for and prosecute the same.

FREDERICK AUGUSTUS MUHLENBERG,
Speaker of the House of Representatives.

JOHN ADAMS, *Vice President of the United States, and President of the Senate.*

Approved—March the twenty second, 1794,

Go. Washington,
President of the United States.

AN ACT IN ADDITION TO THE ACT, ENTITLED, "AN ACT TO PROHIBIT
THE CARRYING ON THE SLAVE-TRADE FROM THE UNITED
STATES TO ANY FOREIGN PLACE OR COUNTRY."

Section I. *Be it enacted by the Senate and House of Representatives of the United States of America, in Congress assembled,* That it shall be unlawful for any citizen of the United States, or other person residing within the United States, directly or indirectly to hold or have any right or property in any vessel employed or made use of in the transportation or carrying of slaves from one foreign country or place to another, and any right or property belonging as aforesaid, shall be forfeited, and may be libelled and condemned for the use of the person who shall sue for the same— and such person transgressing the prohibition aforesaid, shall also forfeit and pay a sum of money equal to double the value of the right or property in such vessel which he held as aforesaid, and shall also forfeit a sum of money equal to double the value of the interest which he may have had in the slaves which at any time may have been transported or carried in such vessel after the passing of this act, and against the form thereof.

Section II. *And be it further enacted*, That it shall be unlawful for any citizen of the United States or other person residing therein, to serve on board any vessel of the United States employed or made use of in the transportation or carrying the slaves from one foreign country or place to another, and any such citizens or other person voluntarily serving as aforesaid shall be liable to be indicted therefor, and on conviction thereof, shall be liable to a fine not exceeding two thousand dollars, and be imprisoned not exceeding two years.

Section III. *And be it further enacted*, That if any citizen of the United States shall voluntarily serve on board of any foreign ship or vessel which shall hereafter be employed in the Slave-trade, he shall on conviction thereof, be liable to, and suffer the like forfeitures, pains, disabilities and penalties as he would have incurred had such ship or vessel been owned or employed in whole or in part by any person residing within the United States.

Section IV. *And be it further enacted*, That it shall be lawful for any of the commissioned vessels of the United States, to seize and take any vessel employed in carrying on the trade, business or traffic contrary to the true intent and meaning of this or the said act to which this is in addition, and such vessel, together with her tackle, apparel and guns, and the goods or effects other than slaves which shall be found on board, shall be forfeited and may be proceeded against in any of the District or Circuit Courts, and shall be condemned for the use of the officers and crew of the vessel making the seizure, and be divided in the proportion directed in the case of prize; and all persons interested in such vessel, or in the enterprise or voyage in which such vessel shall be employed at the time of such capture, shall be precluded from all right or claim to the slaves found on board such vessels as afore said, and from all damages or retribution on account thereof, and it shall moreover be the duty of the commanders of such commissioned vessels to apprehend and take into custody every person found on board of such vessel so seized and taken, being of the officers or crew thereof, and him or them convey as soon as conveniently may be, to the civil, authority of the United States in some one of the Districts thereof, to be proceeded against in due course of law.

Section V. *And be it further enacted*, That the District

and Circuit Courts of the United States shall have cognizance of all acts and offences against the prohibitions herein contained.

Section VI. *Provided nevertheless, and be it further enacted*, That nothing in this act contained, shall be construed to authorize the bringing into either of the United States any person or persons, the importation of whom is by the existing laws of such state prohibited.

Section VII. *And be it further enacted*, That the forfeitures which shall hereafter be incurred under this or the said act to which this is in addition not otherwise disposed of, shall accrue and be one moiety thereof to the use of the informer, and the other moiety to the use of the United States, except where the prosecution shall be first instituted on behalf of the United States, in which case, the whole shall be to their use.

THEODORE SEDGWICK, *Speaker of the House of Representatives.*

THOMAS JEFFERSON, *Vice President of the United States, and President of the Senate.*

Approved—May 10th A. D. 1800,

John Adams, *President of the United States.*[7]

AN ACT TO PROHIBIT THE CARRYING ON THE SLAVE TRADE, FROM
THE UNITED STATES TO ANY FOREIGN PLACE OR COUNTRY.

Section I. *Be it enacted by the Senate and House of Representatives of the United States of America, in*

396

Congress assembled, That no citizen or citizens of the United States, or foreigner, or any other person coming into, or residing within the same, shall, for himself, or any other person whatsoever, either as master, factor or owner, build, fit, equip, load or otherwise prepare any ship or vessel, within any port or place of the said United States, nor shall cause any ship or vessel to sail from any port or place within the same, for the purpose of carrying on any trade or traffic in slaves to any foreign country; or for the purpose of procuring, from any foreign kingdom, place or country, the inhabitants of such kingdom, place or country, to be transported to any foreign country, port or place whatever, to be sold or disposed of, as slaves; And if any ship or vessel shall be so fitted out, as aforesaid, for the said purposes, or shall be caused to sail, so as aforesaid, every such ship or vessel, her tackle, furniture, apparel and other appurtenances, shall be forfeited to the United States; and shall be liable to be seized, prosecuted and condemned, in any of the circuit courts or district court for the district, where the said ship or vessel may be found and seized.

Section II. *And be it further enacted*, That all and every person, so building, fitting out, equipping, loading, or otherwise preparing, or sending away, any ship or vessel, knowing, or intending that the same shall be employed in such trade or business, contrary to the true intent and meaning of this act, or any ways aiding or abetting therein, shall severally forfeit and pay the sum of two thousand dollars, one moiety thereof, to the use of the United States, and the other moiety thereof, to the use of him or her, who shall sue for and prosecute the same.

Section III. *And be it further enacted*, That the owner, master or factor of each and every foreign ship or vessel, clearing out for any of the coasts or kingdoms of Africa, or suspected to be intended for the Slave-trade, and the suspicion being declared to the officer of the customs, by any citizen, on oath or affirmation, and such information being to the satisfaction of the said officer, shall first give bond with sufficient sureties, to the Treasurer of the United States, that none of the natives of Africa, or any other foreign country or place, shall be taken on board the said ship or vessel, to be transported, or sold as slaves, in any other foreign port or place whatever, within nine months thereafter.

Section IV. *And be it further enacted*, That if any citizen or citizens of the United States shall, contrary to the true intent and meaning of this act, take on board, receive or transport any such persons, as above described in this act, for the purpose of selling them as slaves, as afore said, he or they shall forfeit and pay, for each and every person, so received on board, transported, or sold as afore said, the sum of two hundred dollars, to be recovered in any court of the United States, proper to try the same, the one moiety thereof, to the use of the United States, and the other moiety to the use of such person or persons, who shall sue for and prosecute the same.

FREDERICK AUGUSTUS MUHLENBERG,
Speaker of the House of Representatives.

JOHN ADAMS,
Vice President of the United States,
and President of the Senate.

Approved—March the twenty second, 1794,

Go. Washington,
President of the United States.

The memorial and petition of the Delegates from the several Societies, formed in different parts of the United States, for promoting the abolition of slavery, in Convention assembled at Philadelphia, on the first day of January, 1794.

Respectfully shew,

That your memorialists, having been appointed, by various Societies, in different parts of the Union, for the benevolent purpose of endeavouring to alleviate or suppress some of the miseries of their fellow-creatures, deem it their duty to approach the Congress of the United States with a respectful representation of certain evils,—the unauthorised acts of a few, but injurious to the interest and reputation of all.

America, dignified by being the first in modern times, to assert and defend the equal rights of man, suffers her fame to be tarnished and her example to be weakened, by a cruel commerce, carried on from some of her ports, for the supply of foreign nations with African slaves.

To enumerate the horrors incident to this inhuman traffic, of which all the worst passions of mankind form the principal materials, would be unnecessary, when we offer to prove its existence.

Nor is it requisite to consume much of your valuable time in the endeavour to prove it a national injury.

While it exposes the lives and the morals of our seamen to peculiar danger, it renders all complaints of retaliation unjust; for those who deprive others of

399

their liberty, for the benefit of foreign countries, cannot reasonably murmur, if, by other foreign nations, they are deprived of their own.

True it is, that the captivity at Algiers is not without a hope, and that the slavery of the West-Indies terminates only with existence; but, in proportion as that to which we are accessary is more severe, the duty of desisting from it becomes more urgent.

Your memorialists observe, and mention with pleasure, that this venal cruelty is at present confined to a few ports, and a few persons. Hence it becomes more easy to destroy a degrading exception from the general dignity of our commerce, and to restore our citizens to their former fame, of preferring the spirit of freedom to the delusions of interest.

An additional reason for the legislative interference, now requested, arises from the natural consequence of the facts already suggested.

Foreigners, seduced by the example, and believing that they may commit without reproach, what American citizens commit with impunity, avail themselves of our ports to fit out their vessels for the same traffic. Thus we become the accomplices of their offences, and partake of the guilt without the miserable consolation of sharing its profits.

Your memorialists, therefore, trusting that a compliance with their request, will not exceed the constitutional powers of Congress, nor injure the interests or disturb the tranquility of any part of the Union, respectfully pray, that a law may be passed prohibiting the traffic carried on by citizens of the United States for the supply of slaves to foreign nations, and preventing foreigners from fitting out vessels for the slave-trade in the ports of the United States.

MEMORIAL

To the honourable the Senate and House of
Representatives
of the United States of America, in Congress assembled,

The Memorial of the American Convention for promoting the Abolition of Slavery, and improving the condition of the African Race,

Respectfully sheweth,

That, in the pursuit of the object of their association, your memorialists feel it their duty, to call your attention to the territory over which Congress holds exclusive legislation. The patriot, the philosopher, and the statesman, look to this spot, where the legislative authority of the Republic has an uncontrolled operation, for that perfect system of laws, which shall at once develope the wisdom of the government, and display the justice and benevolence of its policy.

Is it not an incongruous exhibition to ourselves, as well as to foreigners who may visit the seat of the government of the nation, whose distinguishing characteristic is its devotion to freedom, whose constitution proclaims that all men are born free, to behold, on the one hand, the representatives of the people, asserting, with impassioned eloquence, the unalienable rights of man; and, on the other, to see our fellow men, children of the same Almighty Father, heirs like ourselves of immortality, doomed, for a difference of complexion, themselves and their posterity, to hopeless bondage?

Deeply impressed with this sentiment, your memorialists do earnestly, but respectfully, request your honourable body, to take into your serious

401

consideration, the situation of Slavery in the District of Columbia; to devise a plan for its gradual, but certain abolition, within the limits of your exclusive legislation; and to provide that all children born of slaves, after a determinate period, shall be free.

Signed on behalf and by order of the American Convention, assembled at New-York, November 28th, 1821."[9]

The report of the committee was accepted: and the Memorial proposed,

To the Senate and House of Representatives of the United
States of America, in Congress assembled,

The American Convention for promoting the Abolition of Slavery, and improving the condition of the African race, being deeply impressed with the magnitude of the evil of involuntary servitude, beg leave to call the attention of Congress, to the devising of such means as may be practicable for preventing its extension.

When we reflect on the praiseworthy regard shown to the rights of man by the Republics of South America, in their public acts respecting Slavery, we cherish a hope that the United States will emulate their example, so far as the constitution will allow; and thus assist in hastening the period, when our country will no longer afford the advocates of despotism arguments in its defence, drawn from the inconsistency of Republicans;—when it will no longer furnish an exemplification of the truth, that those who are most zealous in asserting political and religious liberty for themselves, are too prone to trample on the claims of others to those blessings.

The evils of slavery, and its injustice, abstractedly considered, are so generally admitted by the citizens of all the states, that we deem it unnecessary to adduce arguments for their proof. A favourable occasion for circumscribing these evils, and discountenancing this injustice, is, we conceive, now offered to Congress, in the power and opportunity of legislating for the newly acquired territory of the Floridas.

The first Congress after the adoption of the American Constitution, composed partly of the framers of that instrument, having, with great unanimity, forbidden the introduction of slaves into the territory northwest of the Ohio; and more than three-fourths of the last Congress, having, after a full discussion of the constitutionality of the act, voted in favour of restricting the migration of slaves to another territory of the United States; the right of imposing such a restriction with regard to the Floridas, appears sufficiently established. Such being the case, we beseech you, by your duty to that Almighty Being who controls the destinies of nations, to strive to mitigate and limit an evil, so universally acknowledged and deplored. And may you, from so doing, reap a satisfaction, beyond any to be derived from possessing the fruits of the industry of thousands—the satisfaction of having been governed, in your conduct, by the principles of reason, humanity, and religion!

Though the motives already urged, appear sufficient to induce a prohibition of the further introduction of slaves into the Floridas, yet we will briefly mention some additional ones, supposed to possess considerable force.

The vacant lands within the new states and territories, have been looked upon as a field of promise,—a common patrimony for all the sons of the

Republic who may choose to partake of it. The introduction of many slaves into a territory, will totally prevent the settlement of free labourers within it. As the states, adapted to the cultivation of the valuable staples, cotton, sugar, and tobacco, having been hitherto open to the migration of slaves, it appears but equitable, now to reserve a district, for the free labourer to occupy in the culture of these articles. It is but just, that the citizens of those states where slavery is interdicted, should be enabled, without a sacrifice of their principles, to obtain a portion of the profits arising from the settlement of those new lands, which are suitable for rearing such products as are most in demand, and are, consequently, the most lucrative.

Signed on behalf, and by order of the American Convention, held at New York, the 28th of November, 1821.[10]

To the Senate and House of Representatives of the United
States, in Congress assembled.

The Memorial of the American Convention for promoting the Abolition of Slavery, and improving the condition of the African race, respectfully sheweth:

That your memorialists, acting in accordance with the designs of their Association, and prompted by their love of country and the paramount obligations of Christianity, earnestly solicit your attention to the condition of the population of the territory over which your honourable body holds exclusive jurisdiction. More than half a century has elapsed since the representatives of the American States, in Congress assembled, declared to the world, as "self-evident truths: that all men are created equal, and endowed by their Creator with certain inalienable rights, among which are life, liberty, and the pursuit of happiness." But that Congress, one of the greatest and most dignified bodies the world ever beheld having but limited jurisdiction, were unable to do more than to proclaim these truths, as the basis of the government they were about to establish. The Constitution since framed, has delegated no authority to the General Government to enforce their views in relation to slavery, existing in any of the States; but that instrument, so far as it respects the District of Columbia, has invested Congress with an unrestrained privilege.

To this spot the eyes of the friends of equal rights are directed: to this spot the patriot, the philosopher, and the statesman, look for that perfect system of laws which at once develope the wisdom of the Government, display the justice and benevolence of its policy, and exhibit a practical illustration of the principles proclaimed in our declaration of independence.

Within this District, however, slavery yet exists; many of the African race, purchased for a distant market, are concentrated here, where the sounds of the clanking fetters mingle with the voice of American statesmen, legislating for a free people!

We, therefore, most respectfully, but most earnestly, entreat your attention to the subject of slavery in the District of Columbia; and especially we solicit that your honorable body may designate a period by law, after which no child, born within the District, shall be held a slave. We respectfully submit that the honor of our common country, a decent respect for the opinions of mankind, and the strong injunctions of Christianity, alike call for your interference upon this momentous subject.

WM. RAWLE, *President*.[11]

Edwin P. Atlee, *Secretary*,
Philadelphia, Oct. 1827.

The American Convention for promoting the abolition of slavery and improving the condition of African race, most respectfully represent:

That an opportunity is now offered, in which, without violating any supposed private rights, or encroaching upon any state sovereignty, the exalted principles of liberty, on which our constitution was founded, may be fully displayed and enforced by your honourable body.

The eminent rank, which these United States have so rapidly attained among nations, is mainly attributable to the high dignity and undeviateing rectitude of their public proceedings—to the equal rights and universal freedom of their citizens. Our enemies can cast on us but one reproach, but, of that reproach they are not sparing. Why, they ask, if all men are born free and equal, is the slavery of so large a portion of your inhabitants still continued among you? To this enquiry no better answer can be given than, that at the period of our political emancipation, the situation of the Southern States was supposed to render the measure of domestic emancipation dangerous, if not impracticable. Yet those who had the misfortune to be subjected to this evil, would willingly have commuted a species of precarious and artificial property for any other more substantial in itself, and more consonant with their own moral feelings. It has since been the

406

frequent effort of Southern legislation to diminish the quantity of the evil, which, it is was supposed, could not wholly be removed. Hence their concurrence in the suppression of the slave trade, and hence, in some instances, their refusal to admit other slaves from other States into their own precincts. In all similar efforts, we doubt not that the legislature of the United States would accordingly coöperate, but the defect of power sometimes impedes the wishes of benevolence and the dispensation of justice.

Aware that however consonant the opinions of your honourable body on this subject may be with our own, your constitutional powers as thus limited, we abstain from preferring any request to which you cannot accede; but we respectfully submit that in the late acquisition of an extensive tract, in a great part yet unsettled, the absolute dominion and internal regulation of which belong to Congress alone, the trial might be made, whether a southern latitude necessarily requires the establishment of domestic slavery; or whether in the Territory of Florida, as well as in other places, the cultivation of land, and the general prosperity of the country, would not be eminently promoted by the use of free labor alone. If the few persons who are already settled there, desire to retain their fellow creatures in bondage, let the example of the superior productiveness of free labor be set before their eyes, and let Congress avail itself of the happy opportunity to elevate the Territory itself to a pinnacle of prosperity, while it supports our national character, in the preservation of human rights and consistent justice.

Another consideration may be added to the foregoing. The extensive unsettled coast of this Territory, and its vicinity to the West India Islands, render the evasion of the existing laws against the slave trade easy—whereas, if it were settled by a free yeomanry, it would form an effectual barrier to such illicit trade, and a strong protection to the slave holding states against the invasion of a foreign enemy.

Our most respectful request is, that Congress will be pleased to prohibit, by law, the further introduction of slaves into the Territory of Florida.

Wm. Rawle, *President*.[12]

Edwin P. Atlee, *Secretary*,
Philadelphia, Oct. 1827.

To the Senate and House of Representatives of the United
States in Congress assembled.

The memorial of the American Convention for promoting the Abolition of Slavery, and improving the condition of the African Race,

Respectfully Represents,

That your memorialists being citizens of this free republic, and feeling in a high degree thankful for the favours and protection of its benign government, are solicitous, in common with all the advocates of true liberty, that its benefits should be extended to the whole human family—that all mankind might be permitted to enjoy peaceably, the full fruition of national rights, and the great blessings of heaven, while here on earth, the right to "life, liberty, and the pursuit of happiness."

Your memorialists, without presuming to question the dignity, superior wisdom, and qualifications of your honourable body, would ask leave most respectfully to urge, as a sentiment, every day gaining a wider spread, and a deeper root, in the best feelings of freemen, that slavery is alike derogatory to the present enlightened condition of man, and a solecism in the institutions of our country: without, in any degree, wishing to appeal to the prejudices, either sectarian or geographical, of any portion of your honourable body, your memorialists cannot consent to withhold themselves from the influence of the irresistible current, manifest in the march of mind, towards perfection, and are therefore free to acknowledge, that they cannot, as consistent republicans, omit to raise their voices, in a respectful petition to their government on behalf of the sufferings, the privations, and the unmerited degradation of their fellow-men the colored people of America.

That the several states in this confederation, are, to a certain constitutional extent, sovereign and independent, is readily admitted; but that their independence is qualified by the federal constitution, is equally certain. No state, has a right to injure or destroy the fair fame of the republic: and no state has a right, unnecessarily to jeopardize the peace of prosperity of any other state. And that all the states, and all the people of each and every state in the union, are indissolubly bound to submit to the majority, is a fundamental principle of the union.

With these preliminary remarks, your memorialists will ask your paternal and special attention to the subject of *slavery in the District of Columbia*. This District, the seat of the national councils, and the common property of the whole republic, is by the constitution of the country, under your immediate care, and exclusive government—and to the combined wisdom, patriotism and prudence of your honourable body, is the common mind turned, with intense anxiety, knowing that nothing can exempt any portion of us

409

from the shame and mortification that may attach to the character of its public laws and institutions; while nothing can prevent their participation in the splendour and renown of its wisdom, prosperity, and happiness. The District of Columbia, then, being the common property of the nation, the nation has an indubitable right, and it is consistent with the fitness of things, to have the institutions and the laws of the District, conformably to the aggregate sentiment of the whole people. The clearly expressed public opinion is against the continuance of slavery—and, by every rule of right, slavery should cease, as soon as practicable, within the national domain.

Under a full conviction of the truth of this doctrine, and the justice of their cause, your memorialists ask of your honourable body, the immediate enactment of such laws as will ensure the abolition of slavery within the District of Columbia, at the earliest period that may be deemed safe and expedient, according to the wisdom of Congress. They ask this, conscientiously believing that this is the sentiment and expectation of the nation: and believing furthermore, that the example will be gradually followed by many of the southern States, as the evils, impolicy, and injustice of slavery are more and more developed.

Commending you and themselves, with the best interests of humanity, to the mercies of a just God, your memoralists very respectfully and earnestly entreat your prompt attention to the subject.

Signed by direction of the Convention.[13]

The following Memorial was reported by Mr. Kesley, and having been amended, was adopted as follows:

To the Hon. the Senate and House of Representatives, of the United States, in Congress Assembled.

The Memorial of the American Convention, &c.,

Respectfully sheweth—That your memorialists, citizens of the United States, feel grateful to that Divine Providence, who hath so gloriously protected this nation in the enjoyment of all the privileges of freemen; and whose parental care still preserves to us untrammelled, the right of conscience, and affords to our free citizens all needful facilities in the pursuit and enjoyment of as full a share of happiness as the present condition of man is susceptible of. But while thus enjoying all the blessings of Heaven's richest bounty, your memorialists have viewed with deep regret and heartfelt sorrow, the dark stain on our national character, which is inflicted by the existence of slavery in the District of Columbia. That district being the common property of the nation, and immediately under the control of congress; whatever enormity may be legally permitted therein, becomes the common concern of the whole confederacy. Furthermore if slavery be an evil both moral and political as is generally admitted at the present day, it would seem that the whole nation becomes implicated in its support, so long as it remains sanctioned by law in that district which is the seat of our government, and depository of our rights. Your memorialists therefore, feeling in common with many thousands of their fellow citizens, unwilling to sanction so great an evil, and desirous to do all that is in their power towards its removal, beg leave, earnestly, yet respectfully, to urge the consideration of this subject, on the attention of congress.

Your memorialists are aware that difficulties are found in the way of an immediate emancipation of those slaves now existing; arising out of a supposed right of property in those who hold them; as well as from a disqualification for self-government on the part of the slaves themselves, but which would be entirely

411

obviated by an enactment providing that from and after a given date all persons born within the district, shall be free at a given age. By the enactment of such a law the wishes of a very large proportion of the individuals represented by your honourable body, it is believed would be met; and that so much at least, ought to be done by the national legislature, seems to be demanded not only by the claims of humanity and justice, but also by those of patriotism and consistency. Amongst the first acts of the congress of this Union, was one to abolish the African slave trade; and our whole existence as a nation is based on the principle that "all men are created equal;" and shall the congress of these states at the present day, hesitate to declare, that henceforth and forever, the child that is born within the limits of its special legislation, shall breathe an atmosphere of liberty?

Under a full conviction that the true interest of the nation requires the interposition of congress in this important matter; and with a full and entire reliance on the wisdom of your honorable body; your memorialists decline any argument to prove the justice or reasonableness of the prayer, or to show the obligation that lies upon the legislature of this happy country, to interpose its authority in behalf of the offspring of these subjects of oppression, and thus remove the odium which attaches to the American name by the existence of slavery in the national domain.

Your memorialists would also intreat your attention to the necessity of passing laws for the prevention of kidnapping, and the scenes of cruelty connected with the slave trade in the District of Columbia, until its final abolition.

Many of the African race, purchased for a distant market, are concentrated here, where the sounds of the clanking fetters mingle with the voice of the

412

American statesmen, legislating for a free people.

This district, from its central situation, has become a depot of slaves, purchased and introduced by dealers from other states, and here incarcerated till the time of their transportation arrives. In near view from the capital, are private jails, from whose walls issue the agonizing cries of those separated from kindred and friends, revolting to every citizen and philanthropist. Here, through the defect of existing laws, facilities are afforded persons denominated slave traders, to consign to perpetual bondage those who are entitled to freedom after a term of years, and the people regard with abhorrence and pain, a traffic extensively carried on by those who prefer wealth to the love and esteem of mankind.

In this district whether its citizens be the friends or opponents of the abolition of slavery, they regard this traffic as alike dishonorable to our character as Americans and Christians, and demanding the interposition of the government. The honor of our common country, a respect for the opinions of mankind, the ardent desire of our patriots and statesmen to remove the curse of slavery entailed on us while colonies, when it can successfully be done, call for your interference on this momentous subject. [14]

———

To the American Convention, &c.—The committee appointed to draft a memorial to the legislatures of the several states praying that their representatives in Congress may be requested, and their senators instructed to use their exertions to produce the passage of an act for the gradual abolition of slavery in the District of Columbia,

413

Respectfully report, That they have prepared and herewith present the draft of such a memorial for the consideration of the Convention.

JAMES OSWALD GRIM,
Chairman.

December 11, 1829.

To the Honourable the legislature of the state of

The Memorial of "The American Convention for promoting the Abolition of Slavery and improving the condition of the African race" assembled at Washington, in the District of Columbia.

Respectfully Represents,—That feeling a strong solicitude to advance the object for which they are associated, your memorialists approach your honorable body for its concurrence and aid upon a matter which they conceive to be of great interest to the American people. That the existence of slavery within the United States is a great evil and one for which an adequate remedy is, of all national objects the most to be desired, is a truth in which the whole body of our fellow-citizens have for a long time acquiesced; but whether its ultimate and entire removal is ever to be affected, compatibly with that justice to the parties concerned upon which it should be based, is a problem that remains to be solved, but to which philanthropists are now daily directing their attention.

The success, however which has attended the efforts of many of the States of the Union, who at an early period of our national history were encumbered by the same evil in a lesser degree but who have since been successful in removing it, induce a hope in your memorialists that slavery may be abolished in the District of Columbia. That if possible it *ought* to be,

414

some interesting considerations of a local character, peculiarly dictate. The significant and peculiar silence discovered upon the face of the constitutional compact of the land, upon the great subject of human servitude with which the country then was burthened, the care which was observed by the sages, who framed the instrument, not to employ a term in its structure which might in after years and in times of universal freedom, be appealed to for the purpose of accusation or reproach, enjoin it, we think as a strong and imperative duty to their successors to remove this growing evil from the seat of the councils of the nation and the limits emphatically of the national domain. Without therefore attempting to interfere with the exclusive duties of state sovereignties, it is incumbent we think upon national legislators, to give effect to the noble and benign spirit of the great charter under which they are convened, by devising and enacting measures for the gradual emancipation of all who are in a state of servitude in the District of Columbia. Nor can we for a moment believe that it is a subject upon which local situation can give rise to any diversity of sentiment among Americans at large. The dictates of patriotic pride and of national consistency must have the same force with all of them.

The people of these states have cause to be distinguished for numerous occasions upon which, and that too in many instances by discarding all interested considerations they have sought the establishment of great national principles. Without advertising to the events connected with the origin of their independence, further than to say that they were founded in a regard for free principles in the abstract, more than in any practical evil under which they were suffering, we may mention the extension of the principles of free trade, the abolition of private warfare on the ocean, the denunciation of the African slave trade as piracy, &c. as propositions by which our country has endeavoured to discharge its duty in the great family of nations. From a people thus naturally disposed, what may not be expected? What circumstances of accident or temporary advantage will be able to stifle the strengthening voice of freedom and manly justice?

The friends of Abolition must indeed expect that the object can only be obtained by very gradual means, but a period no matter how distant, for the certain operation of any principle which may have the desired effect, must afford a great degree of satisfaction to every friend of equal rights and every well wisher of the reputation of his country.

This object however, cannot be obtained except perhaps at a distance of time now invisible, unless the wishes of the states with regard to it are audibly expressed. Congress have been heretofore memorialized on this subject, but as they were not guided by any expression of the wishes of their constituents, no satisfactory result was produced. But the great body of the American people never can be indifferent to a matter of this nature, and the friends of the cause of Abolition have taken measures to draw the attention of Congress once more to it.

Your memorialists therefore respectfully request your Honorable body to instruct your senators and request your representatives in Congress, to use all their effort for the passage of a law, which may have for its end the gradual abolition of slavery in the District of Columbia, upon principles of justice and a regard to the rights of individuals.

Thomas Earle presented the follow report, which was read and accepted Viz.

The committee to whom was referred the

consideration of the various proposed schemes for effecting the abolition of slavery and improving the condition of the African race, respectfully report:

That it has been proposed, as a preliminary to complete emancipation, to reduce slaves to the condition of the serfs of Poland and Russia, fixed to the soil, without the right on the part of the master to remove them. It appears extremely doubtful to your committee whether such a measure would in any degree accelerate entire emancipation. The proposition moreover, has not received that degree of public approbation which is necessary to justify any expectation of its speedy adoption.

Some individuals have believed it perfectly safe and judicious, to obtain, if practicable, legislative enactments for the immediate liberation of all slaves. Propositions of this nature are met by a reprobation so universal on the part of the citizens of those states where slavery exists, who have undoubtedly the best means of judging of the probable consequences, that it may be considered certain they will not be adopted. Gradual abolition is the only mode which at present appears likely to receive the public sanction.

Another proposition has been that those who are not owners of slaves should abstain from the products of slave labour, and thus by destroying the market compel emancipation. Your committee are of opinion that it would be far easier to persuade the majority of the people to pass laws for the abolition of slavery than to break off all commercial intercourse with slave holders. The more practicable measure would render the less practicable, unnecessary.

It seems probable, however, that the example of individuals who, from conscientious motives, abstain from the produce of slavery, will have its uses in exciting public attention to the nature and magnitude of the evil which leads to these instances of self-denial.

It has been strenuously urged that there is less pecuniary profit in the employment of slave labour, than in that of freemen, and that the extensive promulgation of this truth will be effective in inducing slave holders, from motives of interest, to consent to emancipation. Although this doctrine has been promulgated for several years, facts have not been adduced sufficient to carry general conviction to the minds of those interested. Unless some evidence of a more conclusive or effectual nature can be adduced, it appears that little good can be expected from the agitation of this matter.

But in whatever degree the question of immediate pecuniary profit may be unsettled, the evils of slavery in affecting the morals and happiness of society, in abridging public and private enterprize, in promoting idleness and extravagance, and in accelerating the impoverishment of land, are sufficiently capable of demonstration, and are indeed freely admitted by many slave holders. To continue to call the attention of the people to these effects, will undoubtedly be useful in the furtherance of the grand object of our aim.

The passage of laws by our state legislatures, fixing a certain period after which all shall be born free, or shall be free at a certain age, is a proposed measure which has formerly received the sanction of this Convention. It is analagous to those which have already been adopted in some of our states, and it is that by which the final extinction of slavery will probably be effected throughout our country. But it seems unlikely that those states where slaves are very numerous, will consent to the measure, until the proportion of slaves has been considerably reduced by other means. It can hardly be expected that the whites, where they are a minority, will, at any near period of time, consent to surrender political power into the hands of a race which they are accustomed to look upon as inferior and degraded, or that they will be free from apprehension of a contest for property as the probable result. History furnishes no instance of the passage of a law for abolishing slavery in a nation where the slaves at the time of its passage were nearly equal in number to the freemen. We have no evidence to justify the assumption, that mankind in future will act differently. The condition of some of our states, never-the-less, is such, that measures of this kind may with great propriety be urged, and kept constantly in view of the public.

Appeals to a sense of justice, and the dictates of religion, operating on individuals to produce voluntary emancipation, have been the chief means by which slavery has been abolished or greatly reduced, in most countries where it once extensively existed. Such were the means of the liberation of serfs in Great Britain and other European countries.[15] They are those which have produced the emancipation of most of the free coloured people now existing in the United States. They are those which must be looked to, for so far diminishing the evil, as to produce that state of society in which the passage of laws for complete abolition may be obtained. But unfortunately a sense of danger, mingled with other motives or interest, has produced the enactment of laws in most of the slave holding states, prohibiting or greatly limiting the exercise of benevolent feelings in this way. The repeal of these laws must be the first or an early measure towards the completion of the great work.

It has been supposed that adequate provision of the colonization of emancipated persons in Africa, Hayti, or other foreign or domestic territory, would tend to produce the repeal of those laws, as well as of those which restrict the education of slaves, and would thus pave the way for the adoption of laws for complete emancipation. If, in this way, the number of slaves could be kept stationary, while that of the free whites should continue to increase, the relative proportions would ere long be obtained which would justify the hopes of legislative interference. The interference of legislatures does not depend so much on the number of slaves, as upon their proportion to the free inhabitants. This position is illustrated by the fact that in New York where slavery is now extinct, the number of slaves in 1820 was ten thousand and eighty-eight, while in Delaware, where no laws for emancipation have been passed, the number was only four thousand five hundred and nine.

We are informed that a conviction of the injurious effects of the presence of free blacks, is general in the slave-holding states, even perhaps among those citizens who have no property invested in slaves. We are also assured and believe that there are great numbers of persons in those states who would emancipate their slaves, if a suitable asylum abroad were provided for them; and that the number of individuals of this description is likely greatly to increase if ample means of emigration are provided. [16]

The question therefore arises, whether colonization to any considerable extent is practicable. The solution of this question depends, in a degree, upon the expense, and the means which there is reason to hope may be commanded. The public mind in the greater portion of our country appears more favorable to colonization than to any other proposed means of emancipation, as may be gathered from the resolutions and laws adopted by Congress, and by various State Legislatures, as well as from inquiry into the sentiments of private individuals. Consequently, if adequate colonization could be effected by the national government without materially embarrassing its operations, or requiring the imposition of new taxes upon the people, there is reason to hope for its realization. The question of expense, and practicability is, we apprehend, too often decided hastily, and without those accurate calculations which can alone justify a positive conclusion.

We will therefore state the results of some of our inquiries. The number of slaves in the United States is rather under two millions:[17] and the annual increase is something less than two and a half *per centum* on the population of the preceding year.[18] The total increase per annum, is therefore short of fifty thousand. The expense of transportation to Africa in merchant vessels will not exceed thirty dollars per head, and to Hayti from ten to fifteen dollars per head. The expense of transporting the increase, half to each of the above named countries, would therefore be from one million to one million one hundred and twenty-five thousand dollars yearly. If we add two dollars per head for corn to maintain the emigrants until they can provide for themselves, the total expense will not exceed one and one fourth million of dollars per annum.

The average annual revenue of the national government may be estimated at twenty-three millions;[19] and the annual expenditure exclusive of the public debt, is about twelve millions. As the public debt will be extinct in four or five years, there will shortly be a surplus revenue of about eleven millions yearly. One eighth of this sum will be sufficient for transporting the whole increase of slave population.

Again: the annual expenditure of the Naval Department of the United States, was estimated in 1827 at $4,263,877, and in 1828 at $4,420,000. This expenditure is more than treble that of the same department, at some periods of our history. Without expressing any opinion of the propriety of this expenditure, a question not proper for this Convention to decide, we may remark that rational men will readily admit that it would be wiser to reduce the expenditure one half, and abolish slavery, than to continue both the expenditure and the servitude. A reduction of one half in the naval expenditures would produce a fund of $2,200,000 per annum; a sum sufficient to transport to Africa and Hayti, ninety thousand slaves per annum, or forty thousand more than the annual increase. We offer this observation merely in illustration of the ease with which the government *can* command the necessary funds without any sacrifice that is not greatly overbalanced by the importance of the subject. There would, however, be no occasion for retrenching any of the present expenditures of the government.

It has been suggested that the public vessels of the nation, most of which are useless during peace, should be employed in the transportation of emancipated persons. The number of these vessels is about fifty, and the average number of persons which they could transport at a voyage, may be estimated at one thousand, although the ships of the line, of which there are twelve built and building, can transport two thousand five hundred each, at a voyage. These vessels going one half to Africa, and one half to Hayti, and the former making two and the latter four voyages per year, would transport one hundred and fifty thousand persons per annum, or three times the increase of slaves; and would at this rate extinguish slavery in twenty years. The whole increase of slaves might therefore be transported in public vessels, without interfering with other national objects, or very materially increasing the national expenses.

We will now consider the effect of transporting the increase. The present population of the slave holding states is about 5,800,000, of which above 3,800,000, are freemen; perhaps from one third to one half the free people are interested in slave property. If the increase of slaves were colonized, in about twenty-five years there would be in the slave states, seven millions of free people to two millions of free people to the above number of slaves, or a proportion of ten to one. The consequent increased ease, safety, and probability of obtaining laws for total emancipation, is manifest.

Thus the practicability of great benefit, with little sacrifice, from the aid of government in the work of emigration, is very apparent. A great recommendation of the measure arises from the fact, that it is the only efficient one which is likely to be speedily sanctioned by the people; and is the only one by which voluntary emancipation, in most of the slave holding states, can be effected.

Even if colonization should not be adopted to the extent of carrying away the whole increase, it ought still to be encouraged. It is considered a great and good work to have obtained by law, the emancipation of about fourteen or fifteen thousand persons in New York and Pennsylvania. If so, the emancipation of no more than that number, by aid of emigration to suitable countries, would also be a work worthy the united efforts of the friends of abolition.

Your committee do not look to the transportation of the whole coloured population from this country, at any period. Emancipation will be effected without it. But partial emigration may greatly aid the cause; particularly in its early stages, by preparing the way for the repeal of the laws against education and against voluntary emancipation.

Under the influence of the foregoing considerations your committee would recommend, that the friends of emancipation persevere in their efforts to convince the whole community of the pernicious effects of slavery on the morals, the enterprize, and the happiness of a people.

That they continue in temperate and conciliatory language to illustrate the inconsistency of bondage, with sound political doctrines, as well as with the obligations of justice and religion.

That they constantly endeavour to procure the repeal of those laws which restrict the education and emancipation of slaves.

That they exert themselves, particularly in the states where slaves are the least numerous, to procure the speedy passage of laws for gradual abolition.

That they endeavour to procure from the National Government the appropriation of adequate funds to aid the voluntary emigration of all emancipated people of colour, to any country where a suitable asylum may be found: and that, as an auxiliary means, they petition the state legislature for the passage of resolutions approbatory of such measure.

That they cordially aid in any just mode of promoting abolitions which is favourably received by the people, without insisting on a preference of other modes, which might be abstractedly the best, but are not likely to be generally adopted.—All of which is respectfully submitted.

On behalf of the
Committee,[20]
T. EARLE, Chairman.

December 11th, 1829.

TO THE CITIZENS OF THE UNITED STATES.

The address of the Delegates from the several Societies, formed in different parts of the United States, for promoting the abolition of slavery, in Convention assembled at Philadelphia, on the first day of January, 1794.

Friends and Fellow-citizens,

United to you by the ties of citizenship, and partakers with you of the blessings of a free government, we take the liberty of addressing you upon a subject, highly interesting to the credit and prosperity of the United States.

It is the glory of our country to have originated a system of opposition to the commerce in that part of our fellow-creatures, who compose the nations of Africa.

Much has been done by the citizens of some of the states to abolish this disgraceful traffic, and to improve the condition of those unhappy people, whom the ignorance, or the avarice of our ancestors had bequeathed to us as slaves; but the evil still continues, and our country is yet disgraced by laws and practices, which level the creature man with a part of the brute creation.

Many reasons concur in persuading us to abolish domestic slavery in our country.

It is inconsistent with the safety of the liberties of the United States.

Freedom and slavery cannot long exist together. An unlimited power over the time, labour, and posterity of our fellow-creatures, necessarily unfits men for

425

discharging the public and private duties of citizens of a republic.

It is inconsistent with sound policy; in exposing the states which permit it, to all those evils which insurrections, and the most resentful war have introduced into one of the richest islands in the West-Indies.

It is unfriendly to the present exertions of the inhabitants of Europe, in favour of liberty. What people will advocate freedom, with a zeal proportioned to its blessings, while they view the purest republic in the world tolerating in its bosom a body of slaves?

In vain has the tyranny of kings been rejected, while we permit in our country a domestic despotism, which involves, in its nature, most of the vices and miseries that we have endeavoured to avoid.

It is degrading to our rank as men in the scale of being. Let us use our reason and social affections for the purposes for which they were given, or cease to boast a preeminence over animals, that are unpolluted with our crimes.

But higher motives to justice and humanity towards our fellow-creatures remain yet to be mentioned.

Domestic slavery is repugnant to the principles of Christianity. It prostrates every benevolent and just principle of action in the human heart. It is rebellion against the authority of a common FATHER. It is a practical denial of the extent and efficacy of the death of a common SAVIOUR. It is an usurpation of the prerogative of the GREAT SOVEREIGN of the universe, who has solemnly claimed an exclusive property in the souls of men.

But if this view of the enormity of the evil of domestic

slavery should not affect us, there is one consideration more which ought to alarm and impress us, especially at the present juncture.

It is a violation of a divine precept of universal justice, which has, in no instance, escaped with impunity.

The crimes of nations, as well as of individuals, are often designated in their punishment; and we conceive it to be no forced construction, of some of the calamities which now distress or impend our country, to believe that they are the measure of evils, which we have meted to others.

The ravages committed upon many of our fellow-citizens by the Indians, and the depredations upon the liberty and commerce of others of the citizens of the United States by the Algerines, both unite in proclaiming to us, in the most forcible language, "to loose the bands of wickedness, to break every yoke, to undo heavy burthens, and to let the oppressed go free."

We shall conclude this address by recommending to you,

First, To refrain immediately from that species of rapine and murder which has improperly been softened with the name of the African trade. It is Indian cruelty, and Algerine piracy, in another form.

Secondly, To form Societies, in every state, for the purpose of promoting the abolition of the slave-trade, of domestic slavery, the relief of persons unlawfully held in bondage, and for the improvement of the condition of Africans, and their descendants amongst us.

The Societies, which we represent, have beheld, with triumph, the success of their exertions, in many

427

instances, in favour of their African brethren; and, in a full reliance upon the continuance of divine support and direction, they humbly hope, their labours will never cease, while there exists a single slave in the United States.[21]

To the Citizens of the United States.

Friends and Fellow Citizens,

Various Societies having been formed, in different parts of the Union, for the purpose of promoting the Abolition of Slavery, they have several times met in convention to deliberate on the best means of furthering the humane work they have undertaken.— We, the seventh association of Delegates from these bodies, now convened in the city of Philadelphia, appealing to the Searcher of hearts for the rectitude of our intentions, believe it our duty to address you with a few remarks, to which we solicit your candid consideration and attention. Believing as we do, that the benevolent Author of nature has made no essential distinction in the human race, and that all the individuals of the great family of mankind have a common claim upon the general fund of natural bounties, we have never hesitated to avow the objects of our institutions, now the honest means by which we hope for their ultimate attainment. Yet we are sensible that many of our fellow citizens have laboured under mistaken impressions on both these points, and have ascribed to us views as inconsistent with the policy of our country, as with our real prospects. It is true we contemplate the deliverance from slavery of all the blacks and people of color in these states, sooner or later, by such means as your humanity, and the wisdom of our rulers may suggest; and though we think the existing laws of some of the states unnecessarily severe; yet we pointedly disavow

428

any wish to contravene them, while they remain in force, or to hazard the peace and safety of the community by the adoption of ill advised and precipitate measures.

In common with the rest of our fellow citizens, we sincerely deplore the late attempts at insurrection by some of the slaves of the southern states, and participate in the dreadful sensations the inhabitants in their vicinity must have felt on so awful an occasion. It is fervently to be hoped that they may induce a weighty consideration of the source of the evil, and of the best means of its future prevention. We are convinced, that so long as a relation subsists between cause and effect, and the present policy of those states is pursued, so long the deprecated calamity is to be dreaded; and while we all revolt with horror from the anticipation of an organization on the part of the slaves, we conceive there is a certain state of degradation and misery to which they may be reduced, a certain point of desperation to which the human mind may be brought, and beyond which it cannot be driven.—If then the premonitory signs of this crisis have appeared, if a recurrence of the desperate feelings which gave birth to the design is to be so awfully dreaded, ought not the attention of every humane mind to be exerted in devising adequate means for averting so enormous a danger? We advance with confidence our firm belief, a belief founded on mature reflection, that to be effectual they must be in many respects different from those which have heretofore been adopted. An amelioration of the present situation of the slaves, and the adoption of a system of gradual emancipation, while it would tend to remove the charge of inconsistency, between the constitutional declaration, and the legal provisions of some of the states; would also be an effectual security against revolt. If the severity of their treatment were lessened, and the hope of freedom

429

for them or their posterity were held forth as the reward of good behaviour, the slaves would be bound by personal interest to be civil, orderly, and industrious. It has been argued, that they are not qualified to enjoy the blessings of freedom, even under a gradual emancipation: but are they not rational creatures, and why will not the same method which have civilized others, in the course of time also civilize them? A principal mean of effecting this purpose, would be to instruct them in the duties and obligations of religion, morality, and social justice. We find that the cultivated inhabitants of different countries and even the individuals of the same country, have very different ideas on these subjects. Is it therefore to be wondered at that the poor illiterate blacks, who are so little instructed in the principles of Christianity, and strangers to the refined sentiments which result from education; is it, we ask, to be wondered at, that they are susceptible of error and delusion?

Fellow citizens of the southern states! we invite your calm and dispassionate attention to the subject; and, with the aid of that Being to whom we must look for instruction in this, as in all our other undertakings, we firmly trust that you will be enabled to devise such measures as may terminate in your own peace, and security, and the benefit of that unfortunate race whose miseries excite our sympathy, and the improvement of whose situation is the object of our anxious solicitude and care.

Another subject that required general attention, is the inhuman crime of kidnapping, which, in some parts of our country, has recently increased to an alarming degree. The friends of liberty view with horror the perpetuation of this abominable practice, and the holders of slaves have no security for them, as property, during its continuance. There is therefore a common interest in the removal of the grievance; and we confidently look for the assistance of the humane of all descriptions in detecting and bringing to punishment, these shameless violations of the rights of their fellow-men.

It is also a lamentable fact, that notwithstanding the general repugnance of all well disposed citizens to any further importation of Africans into this country, or concern in the infamous commerce in the persons of our fellow creatures, notwithstanding the prohibitions of the laws of most of the states on this subject, and the strict instructions of those of the general government, upwards of two hundred vessels, belonging to our own citizens, are employed in the purchase and transportation of slaves from Africa to the West-Indies, and the southern parts of this country.

The rage for this traffic is so far extended by avarice, that many persons have risqued their all in its pursuit; and it seems that nothing can stop the cruel and disgraceful enormities which are thus committed, in violation of the dictates of humanity, and the laws and policy of our country, but a more general activity and exertion on the part of good citizens, in the discovery and prosecution of the offenders. So large a number of vessels are fitted out for this trade, and sent to the coast of Africa from the eastern states, that we are induced earnestly to call on our brethren of those parts, to aid in its suppression; and surely as they have done away the evil of personal slavery among themselves, they cannot want inducements to enforce the laws against such of their citizens as set them at defiance, by pursuing a prohibited commerce, as shocking to the feelings of every benevolent mind, as it is offensive in the eyes of the Almighty Ruler of the universe.

Finally, fellow citizens! as you value your own peace

431

and that of your families; the quiet and security of our country; the obligations of our holy religion; and the favor of an over ruling Providence; let us entreat you to enter into the consideration of the subjects now submitted to you. Assist in mitigating the present ills of personal slavery, by an amelioration of the situation of slaves; lay the foundation for an eventual extinction of the mighty evil throughout our land; commence a determined opposition to the wicked infractions of justice and the laws of our country; and may the Divine blessing attend you, in every attempt that you may be encouraged to make, for the good of your fellow men.[22]

CIRCULAR ADDRESS

To the Abolition and Manumission Societies in the United
States of America.

At the close of the session of 1821, the American Convention deem it proper to address you on the important subjects which have occupied our attention.

In reviewing the labours of Abolition Societies in this country, we find much reason for congratulation. The cause of truth and humanity has regularly advanced, in the minds of an enlightened community; and nothing but perseverance, in presenting this subject to the public in its appropriate simplicity, is requisite to promote its triumphant march over the prejudice, hostility, and opposition of its enemies. To the perseverance of its advocates alone, may be imputed the great change in the public opinion, in favour of the Abolition of Slavery, that has already been effected in the Northern, Middle, and some of the Western States: and we confidently hope, that this will ultimately produce a similar change in the South. We therefore trust, that you will never relax your efforts to promote the emancipation of slaves, till every human being in the United States, shall equally enjoy all the blessings of our free constitution.

The best mode of effecting the abolition of slavery, so as to promote the interests and the happiness of the slave, and to be satisfactory to the master, is a subject of difficult solution; and one that has much engaged the attention of the Convention. However desirable a total emancipation might be to the philanthropist, we cannot expect the speedy accomplishment of that event.

Although the subject of colonizing the free blacks, has been repeatedly considered and disapproved by former Conventions; it has been revived, fully discussed, and, as we trust, definitively decided by this, that such a colony, either in Africa or in our own country, would be incompatible with the principles of our governments, and with the temporal and spiritual interests of the blacks.

How far voluntary emigration to Hayti should be encouraged, is a question which we do not possess sufficient information to decide; but which may receive much additional light from the correspondence already directed to be instituted for that purpose. We think it worthy of consideration, how far any measure should be recommended that may tend to draw from our country the most industrious, moral, and respectable of its coloured population, and thus deprive others, less improved, of the benefit of their example and advice.

Deeply injured as they have been by the whites, the coloured people certainly claim from us some degree of retributive justice. And if our efforts succeed in improving their intellectual and moral condition, and in

433

imparting to them a correct knowledge of the only true God, we shall do much towards compensating them for all the wrongs they have sustained. This object can be best attained by their permanent resident in a Christian country, and under suitable moral and religious instruction.

Influenced by a conviction of this truth, our attention has been directed to a gradual melioration of their condition, and to the adoption of such measures as will conduce to their elevation to a higher rank in society. We conceive that these objects may be promoted, by giving the slaves an interest in the soil they cultivate, by placing them in relation to their masters, in a situation somewhat similar to that in which the peasantry of Russia are placed in relation to their landlords.

This plan has been successfully executed by an extensive planter in Barbadoes; and it was found to conduce essentially to the promotion of his slaves. Should our southern planters be induced to adopt a similar course, there is doubt, that the result would be equally favourable.

We think it particularly desirable, that the legislatures of the slave-holding states, should be induced to fix a period after which all who are born of slaves shall be free. This is an object which we ought never to lost sight of, until it is attained. Although this period should be remote, and therefore no benefits be afforded to the present generation, yet an inestimable benefit would thus be assured to posterity.

Signed on behalf, and by order of the American Convention, held at New-York, the 29th of November, 1821.[23]

THE MEMORIAL OF THE AMERICAN CONVENTION FOR PROMOTING THE
ABOLITION OF SLAVERY, AND IMPROVING THE CONDITION OF THE AFRICAN RACE,

RESPECTFULLY SHEWETH,

That it has long been a source of deep regret to a large portion of the citizens of the United States, as well as to the friends of human rights and liberty throughout the world, that domestic Slavery, with all its odious features, continues to be tolerated by the national government in the small territory over which the Constitution invests it with exclusive jurisdiction. Your Memorialists are convinced, that a strong simultaneous effort of those who hold this sentiment in different sections of our country, would imperiously

435

engage the attention of Congress to this interesting subject; especially if that effort were sanctioned and directed by the authority of the different state legislatures. Impressed with this belief, we earnestly solicit your honourable body to use such means as your wisdom and the spirit of our admirable constitution will sanction, in order to remove this national reproach, and vindicate the purity and vigour of our republican institutions from the reproaches of their enemies.

We are only known to foreign states as one great nation, of which the Federal Government is the organ and representative; every state comprising the Union and all its inhabitants, are compelled to endure the *opprobium*, however they may abhor, the *guilt* of holding their fellow men in bondage. To permit the existence of slavery within the very sound of the voice of the orator and statesman, while he is pleading the cause of *Liberty*, or uttering his boast of *American Independence* upon the floor of Congress, is a flagrant inconsistency, which, in the view of foreign nations, attaches equally to Massachusetts and Virginia! We entreat you, therefore, by your regard for justice and the rights of man—by your religion, and the welfare of our common country—by your respect for yourselves and for the honour of your constituents, not to suffer the present session to elapse, without a recorded vote, which shall be *your* witness to posterity, that, if the exclusive territory of the national government remains to be polluted by the footsteps of a slave, it is because *your* exertions in the cause of liberty have been unavailing.

Respectfully, but most earnestly, do your memorialists request your honourable body, seriously to consider this subject; and if it shall appear to you advisable, let your senators be requested, to bring the subject into the view of the Congress of the United States, enforced with the commanding weight of your recommendation to an early and profound enquiry into the expediency of the measure.

W. RAWLE, PRESIDENT.[24]

THE FOLLOWING IS A CIRCULAR, PREPARED AND ISSUED BY THE ACTING COMMITTEE OF THE CONVENTION, AND SELECTED AND ORDERED TO BE PLACED UPON THE MINUTES OF THE CONVENTION:

RESPECTED FRIEND,

In inviting our fellow citizens to join in the great cause of justice, and humanity, it seems almost unnecessary to dwell upon the reasons which should influence their cordial co-operation. It would be an insult to their feelings and understanding, to suppose them unmindful of the rights of their fellow men, or indifferent to the honour of their country; yet it may be well to direct their attention to some of the calamities inseparably connected with slavery, and to strive to awaken the exertions requisite to effect its abolition.

By the Law of Nature, all men are entitled to equal privileges, and, although, the artificial distinctions of society may have abrogated it in practice, they are unable to justify the destruction of a right, which claims for the African that Freedom which the express and implied will of the Almighty has declared to be inherent in every individual of the human race.

The barbarous policy which sanctified the introduction of slaves into this country, sacrificed the injunctions of Revelation to mercenary ambition, and for temporary interest bestowed a lasting disgrace upon posterity. Time and perseverance may eradicate the

437

evil, which is increasing in importance, and which not only has brought obloquy upon our national character, but threatens to involve us in all disastrous results of civil discord.

There is nothing in our Republic so deeply calculated to promote sectional jealously as the existence of slavery. The conflicting policy of slave-holding and non-slave-holding states, will increase with its unhappy cause. We have already seen to what extent it may be carried, and it requires no effort to imagine consequences, from future excitement, the most dangerous to our political existence. There is also much to be feared, in many States, from the physical superiority of the Black population. The innate principle which so strongly impels to the acquisition of liberty, is, in itself, sufficient to arouse the energies of the slave; but, when the consciousness of numerical power unites with the desire of vengeance, arising from long oppression, the influence of example only, can be wanting to enkindle the exterminating rapacity that usually attends successful insurrection.

One of the strongest reasons that should induce us to exert every power for the suppression of slavery, is the indelible disgrace it brings upon our country. A people, enjoying the utmost limit of rational liberty, who proudly claim the name and rights of freemen, tolerate in their very bosom the most unnatural and cruel bondage. This glaring inconsistency, in part, justifies the sneers which the advocates of arbitrary power are continually casting on the boasted liberality of our political institutions.

We are trying the great experiment, whether liberal Government is best calculated for the happiness of man, and its opposers seize with readiness the argument, that one portion of our population is dependent for its luxuries, and even for its existence on the abject servitude of another. The power of example is lessened, and patriotism turns with disgust from our practical application of that splendid theory, which declares that all men should be free and equal.

The voice of humanity is loud in its appeal for the emancipation of the human race. The connection between slavery and cruelty, which results from the rigid discipline necessary to exact unnatural obedience, is alone sufficient inducement to excite the attention of the Philanthropist. It is degrading to behold the image of God bending under the brutality of imperious dictation, subject to the caprice of rude and ignorant authority, and liable to ignominious death for seeking that liberty which nature has declared to be equally due to all men.

Is the participation of natural right to be graduated by shades of complexion? Shall one man lead a life of thraldom, because his skin has darkened under a hotter sun? Shall he be the perpetual servant of his fellow man, because deficiency of intellectual power, naturally resulting from a want of education and opportunity, have given him less keenness of perception, disqualified him to stand forth the vindicator of the oppressed, to assert his rights, and demand redress for his injuries? No! We trust that there is a redeeming virtue in our fellow citizens, which will urge them to unite with us in abolishing Domestic Slavery. We invite them, because we believe it to be contradictory to the Law of Nature—in violation of the commands of Christianity—hostile to our political union—dangerous to a portion of our white population—inconsistent with our professed love of liberty—degrading to our national character— and in opposition to the feelings of humanity. Then let not this appalling injustice bring down the wrath of offended Heaven on our country—join with us in the endeavour to benefit mankind, and be determined

439

that your zeal shall not waver, nor your exertions diminish, while a single spot in our land is polluted by a slave.

We respectfully invite a correspondence on the subject of this address, and the communication of such facts as may, from time to time, come to your knowledge.

By order of the Acting Committee of the American Convention for promoting the Abolition of Slavery, and Improving the condition of the African Race.

OTIS AMMIDON, *Chairman*.[25]

Isaac Barton, *Secretary.*
Philadelphia, 22, 1825.

THE AMERICAN CONVENTION FOR PROMOTING THE ABOLITION
OF
SLAVERY, &C. TO THE CITIZENS OF THE UNITED STATES.

Among the various subjects which have obtained our attention at this time, that of the education of indigent colored children is considered one of primary importance. When we look around upon the one hand, and see the incalculable advantages which have accrued to the children of white persons in limited circumstances, from the instruction bestowed upon them by judicious benevolent provisions; and upon the other, to observe the deplorable effects of the want of instruction, in the case of the neglected children of colored parents, we feel a conviction that the period has arrived, when the Abolitionist and the Philanthropist ought to renew and redouble their efforts to remove the unpleasant contrast; and it is with much satisfaction we have learned that in some parts of our country, the attention of benevolent

440

individuals, and charitable institutions, has been attracted to this subject, and the success which attended their endeavours, furnishes a most powerful inducement to follow up so praiseworthy an undertaking by the united efforts of all those who are one in sentiment with us, in improving the condition of the African race. We trust it will be readily conceded, that whatever measures have the effect of enlightening any portion of the community, are a public good; and upon this maxim, the education of the children of what are called the lower classes, has often been recommended with a laudable zeal, by statesmen eminent for their wisdom and foresight; from hence, and the acts of some of the State Legislatures, much has been done to enlighten the minds of indigent children; unhappily, in some parts of our country, colored children are deprived of the benefits of education by ungenerous constructions of existing laws; in some, by the absence of all legal provision for their instruction, and in others by the existence of legal prohibitions; thus leaving a wide field open for the benevolent operations of those who feel an interest in raising the degraded African from a state of ignorance which is a reproach to the age and country in which we live.

As regards the capacity of colored children to acquire knowledge, when the opportunity is afforded them, many facts might be collected to shew that they are by no means deficient in intellect; that the minds of many of them are of quick perception, and capable of arriving at considerable degrees of eminence in scientific research; in short, that nothing but the means of instruction are wanting to the poor colored child, to elevate him to that station in society which he is entitled to upon every principle of justice and humanity; which his and our Creator, no doubt, designed he should occupy, and from which he is debarred by the cruel hand of injustice and oppression.

If these views are correct, it is much to be lamented that instruction has been so long withheld from thousands of these objects of pity, and our efforts ought to be so directed as to repair or remove the evil. Under these impressions, we earnestly recommend to the friends of emancipation and equal rights, that they give to this subject the solemn consideration which its importance so loudly demands, and adopt such measures as may appear best calculated to dissipate the cloud of ignorance by which the present colored generation is enveloped, and succeeding ones threatened. If those measures are pursued with a zeal worthy of such a cause, we trust your labors will be crowned with success, and the benevolent heart will expect no richer reward.[26]

To the Citizens of the United States.

The American Convention for Promoting the Abolition of Slavery, and improving the condition of the African race, now convened in the city of Baltimore, most respectfully takes the liberty of addressing you on the important subject of the gradual extinction of Slavery in the District of Columbia.

It is doubtless well understood, by our fellow citizens generally, that this District *is the property of the nation*—that the laws for the government thereof emanate from the representatives of the people, in Congress assembled, and that all who are entitled to the elective franchise in every State of the Union, have an equal right to express their sentiments, and urge the adoption of measures, relative to the abolition of the system of Slavery therein.

We are well aware that some will contend for the

legality of Slavery, as tolerated in some parts of the United States, and insist that the question of its abolition should be left to the decision of the people of the District, themselves. When we consider that slaves are, generally, viewed *as property*, this kind of reasoning assumes a specious appearance: yet it must be borne in mind, that the inhabitants of the District of Columbia *are not represented in any legislative body*; but that the sovereignty over that particular section of the country is vested in the people of the States—And when we reflect, that the question has long since been settled whether a legislative body possesses the right to enact laws for the prohibition or extinction of Slavery—that it has indeed been *acted on*, by several of the State Legislatures, and also by Congress—we think that no reasonable doubt can be entertained as to the expediency of the measure in the present case. It is well known that a very large proportion of the citizens of the United States are inimical to the system of Slavery; and it is believed by many intelligent persons, who are themselves residents of the District of Columbia, that a great majority of the inhabitants thereof are desirous for its total abolition. Viewing the subject in this light, we cannot, for a moment, hesitate in urging your attention to it.

The friends of Universal Emancipation, in several of the States, viz. North Carolina, Tennessee, Maryland, &c. have for several years memorialized Congress upon this important subject; but as a few, comparatively speaking, were thus heard to express their sentiments, little notice has yet been taken of their petitions. At the last session, a memorial, against the perpetuation of the cruel system, was presented to that body, by the people of the District, themselves. This memorial was signed by about one thousand of the most respectable portion of the inhabitants, among whom were several of the Judges

443

of the District Courts, and even some holders of slaves. Whatever may have been the doubts or scruples entertained by some of our citizens heretofore, respecting the propriety of urging this subject upon the attention of the National Legislature, we conceive that there is no longer cause for hesitation, since a very respectable number of the people of the District have themselves raised their voice in its favour; and, as we have before stated, it is also believed that by far the greater number are favourably disposed towards it.

That the discussion of this question may excite a lively interest, both in and out of Congress, and that whatever measures may be proposed, for promoting the object in view, will meet with violent opposition, from the advocates of Slavery, we are well aware. All past experience teaches us that this is to be expected. Not only the opponents of emancipation in the south may be expected to throw impediments in our way, but the prejudice against the unfortunate and degraded Africans, and the self-interest of many others will also be arrayed against us. Yet we would calmly and dispassionately appeal to the good sense of the people of this nation—to those who exercise the sovereign authority in this great republic—this boasted land of freedom and equal rights—and recommend the serious consideration of this very important subject. We most earnestly beseech them to weigh well the consequences of tolerating within the limits of this District, a system that has uniformly proved destructive to every nation that long permitted its continuance. But most especially, we would appeal to them as Christians and Philanthropists; and urge them by all the feelings of humanity and benevolence—by all the ties of social affection that binds man to his fellow man—by a due regard to the immutable principles of justice, mercy, and consistency—and by every desire for the perpetuation of our free institutions and the peace and happiness of our posterity,—to come forth in their might, and exert every moral energy to arrest the march of this gigantic evil, ere it overwhelms us, and precipitates us into the vortex of corruption and despotism.

Not only do we consider the honour of the nation as implicated by the toleration of Slavery in the District of Columbia; but the example has a most deleterious and pernicious effect even upon those whose education and habits have opposed it, when they come within the range of its influence. As a proof of the correctness of this opinion, we need only advert to the conduct of sundry persons who have acted in the capacity of representatives to Congress from non-slave holding states. We have reason to believe that they have thus in some instances become so insensible of the evils of the anti-christian practice as to disregard the will of their constituents, and join with its advocates in the adoption of measures for its extension and perpetuation. And we fear that this state of things cannot be remedied until the people of the United States in general turn their attention to the subject, and adopt measures for the extinction of the odious system, wheresoever it can be done, consistently with the Constitution of the Republic.

From statements submitted to this Convention, we are glad to find that this subject has already arrested the attention of a respectable portion of our fellow citizens, in different parts of the Union. Petitions and memorials, we learn, are preparing in many places for signatures, which will, in due season be laid before Congress. It is also understood that efforts will soon be made by some of the members of that body, to effect the great and desirable object. Let, then, all who are sincerely desirous to wipe from our moral escutcheon this crimson stain, come forward at this interesting crisis, and raise their voice in favour of the great principle of universal liberty, and the inalienable rights of man.

Signed by order, and on behalf of the Convention.[27]

To the Public

"The American Convention for promoting the abolition of slavery and improving the condition of the African race," having met for the first time at the city of Washington, deem it proper to address the public in general, relative to the objects and present prospects of the Institution.

We do not consider it necessary to enter into a detail of the history of our proceedings, in this address; neither shall we attempt to adduce any argument to prove the justice of our cause. The first is within the reach of those generally, who take an interest in the success of our undertaking; the last stands undenied and undeniable, among men of the least pretensions to virtue and candor. But having located this Convention at the seat of the National Government, many of our fellow citizens, who have never acquainted themselves with our proceedings, may be desirous to know the objects we have in view, as well as our prospects of success. A compliance with a wish so reasonable, we deem incumbent on us; and we shall frankly state our views and ultimate design.

The sole aim and end of this Convention ever has been, and now is, the abolition of slavery and improvement of the African race, (as its title imports,) in the United States, upon the principles of justice, equity and safety. The means by which it seeks to accomplish this great work, are:

446

1st. To enlighten the public mind, relative to the actual state of the slave system.

2nd. To concentrate the opinions and labors of philanthropists in every portion of the country, respecting the adoption of measure for its abolition.

3d. To give efficiency to the labors of individuals, and the various kindred associations in different parts of the Union, by petitions and memorials to the constituted authorities, accompanied by such information as may be useful to them.

4th. To point out the best and most practical modes of lessening the evils resulting from that system, during its existence in this republic.

With these views the Convention was originally organized, and upon these principles it has ever proceeded. It has been eminently successful in promoting the cause of emancipation in that portion of the Union, where it was at first located; and we consider it strictly within the bounds of reason to infer, from past experience, that it will exert a salutary influence where it is now established. As the light of liberty advances, and the bright luminary of truth shines through the mists of popular error, the labors of the advocates of emancipation will be duly appreciated and their laudable exertions crowned with success.

If we may be allowed to compare the exertions of philanthropists at the present day, with those of former periods in the history of our country, the most sanguine anticipations of future success may be indulged. Within little more than half a century, few, very few, and most of them possessed of comparatively little influence in the political circles, were known to advocate our cause. Now thousands are enlisted in it, some of whom are among the most influential characters in the nation. Then, the system of slavery was tolerated within the limits of the United States, from the Mississippi to the western confines of Massachusetts, and from the Atlantic to the farthest north-western frontier. Now, the vast extent of country, comprising the states of Rhode Island, Connecticut, New York, New Jersey, Pennsylvania, Ohio, Indiana, and Illinois, in the whole of which slavery was permitted to exist, is almost totally freed from the foul pollution. And further, a law has been enacted and enforced, positively prohibiting its extension beyond the line of thirty-six degrees and thirty minutes, north latitude, in all the territory belonging to the republic. This great and important work has unquestionably been accomplished by the active labors of those who have exerted themselves to show the impropriety of continuing to tolerate the system, and the feasibility of its total extinction.

From this view of the subject we draw the conclusion, that as "like causes produce like effects," we have sufficient ground for the belief, that by a faithful perseverance in the same course of benevolence, the same happy results will follow. We frankly admit that where the evil of slavery is felt to a greater extent than in the states to which we have adverted, not only must *greater exertions* be used, but even the plans of proceeding must be somewhat varied. Yet we contend that the same grand object must be kept constantly in view, and the same leading principles ever be acted on, to produce the desired result.

In locating this Convention at the city of Washington, we are actuated by the hope that influential men from different parts of the Union, may thereby become more ultimately acquainted with our proceedings, and so far as they may approve thereof, be induced to co-operate with us. From the very nature of the principles which we profess, it will be seen that our success depends wholly on the *united exertions* of the wise and virtuous. Our plans being entirely of a pacific character and having nothing in view but what is consistent with the welfare and happiness of all, we confidently rely on the wisdom of the patriot and philanthropist, and the good sense of our free, enlightened fellow-citizens, for the realization of our hopes, and the consummation of our important undertaking.[28]

FOOTNOTES:

[1] American Convention, Abolition Societies, Minutes, 1821-1829, pp. 42-48.

[2] Minutes of the Proceedings of the Fourth American Convention of Delegates from the Abolition Societies, 1797, pp. 37-43.

[3] American Convention Abolition Societies, Minutes, 1821, pp. 50-55.

[4] American Convention Abolition Societies, Minutes, 1828, pp. 21-24.

[5] American Convention Abolition Societies, Minutes, 1828, pp. 25-27.

[6] American Convention Abolition Societies, Minutes, 1829, pp. 16-18.

[7] American Convention Abolition Societies, Minutes, 1795-1804, pp. 24-29.

[8] Minutes of Proceedings of a Convention of Delegates, from the Abolition Societies, 1794, pp. 26-27.

[9] Minutes of Proceedings, Convention of Abolition Societies, Philadelphia, 1821, pp. 41-42.

[10] American Convention Abolition Societies, Minutes, 1821, pp. 46-48.

[11] American Convention Abolition Societies, Minutes, 1827, pp. 29-30.

[12] Minutes of Proceedings, Convention of Abolition Societies, Baltimore, 1827, pp. 30-31.

[13] American Convention Abolition Societies, Minutes, 1828, pp. 33-35.

[14] American Convention Abolition Societies, Minutes, 1829, pp. 21-24.

[15] "The holy fathers, monks and friars, had in their confessions and specially in their extreme and deadly sickness, convinced the laity how dangerous a practice it was, for one Christian man to hold another in bondage; so that temporal men by little and little, by reason of that terror in their consciences, were glad to manumit all their villeins."—Sir T. Smith His. Common, vide 2. Blackstone, p. 96.

[16] Two thousand slaves are said to be now offered to the Colonization Society for transportation.

[17] The slave population in 1810 was 1,191,364; in 1820, 1,531,436. Increasing in the same ratio, in 1830 it will be 1,948,587.

[18] The increase in ten years is about twenty-eight per centum, but as the increase of the latter portion of the period is much greater than that of the former portion, it will be evident that our estimate for a single year is correct.

[19] In 1828 it was $24,789,463. See Treasury Report for 1829.

[20] American Convention Abolition Societies, Minutes, 1821-1829, pp. 25-35.

[21] Minutes of Proceedings of a Convention of Delegates from the Abolition Societies, 1794, pp. 22-25.

[22] American Convention Abolition Societies, Minutes, 1801, pp. 37-41.

[23] American Convention Abolition Societies, Minutes, 1821, pp. 57-58.

[24] American Convention Abolition Societies, Minutes, 1825, pp. 31-32.

[25] American Convention Abolition Societies, Minutes, 1825, pp. 33-35.

[26] American Convention Abolition Societies, Minutes, 1827, p. 19.

[27] American Convention Abolition Societies,

Minutes, 1828, pp. 17-20.

[28] American Convention Abolition Societies, Minutes, 1829, pp. 37-40.

BOOK REVIEWS

The Bantu, Past and Present. By S. M. Molema. Edinburgh, W. Green and Son, Limited. Pp. 398. Price, 25/net.

This is an ethnographical and historical study of the native races of South Africa. The author of the work is a member of the race whose life he has described. To some extent, then, he has told here his own story, "relying somewhat on the life of the people in interpreting the psychological aspect which must be invaluable to a foreigner." As this book, however, is replete with quotations from various works of white men who have seen the country only from the outside, and the work contains no evidence that the writer has extensively traveled in his own native land, it drifts too much in the direction of a summary of what these various travelers have thought of Africa. The book, moreover, is not altogether scientific; and fraught with too many of the opinions of others who should know less about Africa than the native himself, it does not satisfy the need for a definitive account of the life and history of the various peoples of South Africa. On the whole, however, it is far in advance of most works bearing on the achievement of that continent and is certainly a step in the right direction, when the story of Africa will be told as it must be told by the native of Africa himself.

The book begins with an interesting introduction of that part of the work called *The Revelation*, which consists of an account of the antiquity of man in Africa, prehistoric Africa, the unveiling of South Africa and the distribution of the primitive races. In that portion of the work styled *The Past* there is a valuable summary of African ethnology, setting forth the various stocks of the southern part of the continent, their manners and customs, moral conduct, religious beliefs and language. This portion of the work is valuable, because it is a brief summary of valuable matter scattered through a large number of volumes.

In that part of the work styled *The Present* there is much matter which may be found in almost any history of Africa. What is said about missionaries, missions, the South African wars, and the like, may be found in various works, and in some more extensively treated. In those chapters bearing on the education of the Bantu, the relation of the races and the attitude of the government to the natives, there are adequately set forth the race problem in that part of the world and the effort toward its solution as expressed in such strivings of the natives as the Bantu National Congress and the Bantu Press. There is, moreover, the reaction of an intelligent native of Africa to the impressions made upon him by the European civilization there implanted.

The author does not seem to be very hopeful. On the whole, the ring of the book is rather pessimistic. Yet he mentions intellectual possibilities as well as impossibilities, bright prospects for religious developments as well as an unfavorable religious outlook, social and economic prospects favorable and unfavorable, and finally the hope that relations between the races may be amicably adjusted so as to secure to the black and white the privileges of a common government.

An American History. By Davis Saville Muzzey, Ph.D. Revised edition. New York, Ginn and Company, 1920. Pp. 537.

This new edition of the author's former work brings the narrative down to the spring months of the year 1920. The author has entirely recast that part of the book following the Spanish war and has made considerable changes in the preceding chapters to emphasize the social and economic factors in our history. Some illustrative material has been added, the maps have been improved and the bibliographical references brought down to date.

This book follows the line of the most recent writers of American history in giving less attention to the problems of the early periods to treat somewhat in detail movements culminating in our day. It does not contain so much about the discovery and exploration of the new world and gives only limited space to colonial history. The treatment of the birth of the nation, the development of the Constitution and the rise of political parties, is more interesting. The author is more elaborate in his discussion of the sectional struggle between the North and South, the crisis of disunion and the Civil War. The drama of reconstruction, however, is decidedly neglected; but the problems confronting the people thereafter are more extensively treated.

When a reader in quest of the truth has read this text-book of American History, however, he will be compelled to ask the question as to why there appears throughout this volume references to the achievements of all groups influencing the history of this country, and there is no mention whatever of what the Negroes, constituting a tenth of the population of the United States, have thought and felt and done. It is unreasonable to think that such a large element of the nation could be so closely connected with it without having decidedly influenced the shaping of its destiny, and history shows that the record of the Negro race in the western hemisphere is so creditable and far-reaching that it is impossible to write the history of the United States and omit the achievements of this group. Professor Muzzey's *American History*, therefore, is not a balanced and unprejudiced account of the rise and progress of the United States, but such a treatise as he believes that the American mind will absorb, and such a story as conforms with the biased minds of pseudo-American historians who do not desire to publish to posterity the achievements of all the people of this country.

The Annual Report of the American Historical Association for the Year 1918, Volume II. The Autobiography of Martin Van Buren. By JOHN C. FITZPATRICK. Washington, 1920. Pp. 808.

This autobiography of Martin Van Buren was presented to the Library of Congress by Mrs. Smith Thompson Van Buren in 1905, at the same time when the Van Buren papers were presented to the Library. It is a manuscript copy in seven folio volumes, made by Smith Thompson Van Buren, the son and literary executor of the President, from Van Buren's original draft. The editor reports that portions of Volumes VI and VII are in another hand and the last fifteen pages of the manuscript have many changes and corrections by Van Buren himself. A portion of the book was edited by Mr. Worthington C. Ford. The notes of Van Buren himself are distinguished by letters from the numbered notes of the editor of the work.

A study of this manuscript leads the editor of this work to the conclusion that it is written "with engaging frankness, and the insight it afforded to the mental processes of a master politician is deeply interesting." Van Buren's desire to be scrupulously fair in his estimates is evident, and if he did not always succeed, his failures are not discreditable. Mr. Fitzpatrick does not believe that the autobiography compels a revision of established historical judgments, although it "presents authority for much in our political history hitherto somewhat conjectural and records political motives and activities of the period in an illuminating and suggestive manner." On reading this work one must agree with its editor that, "in analyzing men and measures, Van Buren all unconsciously paints a picture of himself."

For students of Negro history certain parts of this work are both interesting and valuable. This is especially true of Chapter XI, in which Van Buren sets forth his own views on the slavery question and discusses the men and their measures proposed for dealing with it. This chapter not only gives a review of the history of slavery in the United States up to the time of the crisis of thirties, but brings out additional facts throwing light upon the situation at that time. In the beginning of Chapter XVIII, and on pages 528-529, Van Buren takes up the question of the concession of Great Britain by treaty stipulation of the right of search to prevent the prosecution of the slave trade under our flag, which he considered merely a pretense on the part of Great Britain for the impressment of our seamen. Near the end of Chapter XXX may be found other interesting comments and facts concerning the action of the leading statesmen of this country during the critical period of conflicting sectional interests. Much of the book has to do with slavery directly or indirectly, but those portions referred to may be of special interest to the reader.

———

Two Colored women with the American Expeditionary Forces. By ADDIE W. HUNTON and KATHERINE M. JOHNSON. New York, Brooklyn Eagle Press, 1920.

Pp. 256.

This is one of the first volumes published since the war to set forth the truth concerning the participation of the Negro troops in that struggle. While their achievements have evoked appreciative expressions from those who learned of the war from afar, this volume undertakes to present the observations of two women of culture who went forth with these black soldiers to war. The story is set forth in an interesting manner, under such topics as *The Call and the Answer, The First Days in France, Welfare Organizations, The Combatant Troops* in contradistinction to the *Non-Combatant Troops, Pioneer Infantries, Over the Canteen in France, The Leave Area, Relationship with the French and the Religious Life Among the Troops*. Many of these facts do not strike the reader as new, but the human touch given the story by these authors, who participated in the events themselves, makes the volume readable, interesting, and valuable.

The work is otherwise significant. From chapter to chapter there appear various documents giving unconsciously convincing evidence as to the part the Negro troops played in the war. While the authors make no pretense to scientific treatment, they have certainly facilitated the task of the historian who must undertake the writing of a definitive history of the Negroes' participation in the World War. The book, moreover, is well illustrated and well printed. It will be read with interest and profit by all persons who seek the truth and endeavor to record impartially the achievements of the various elements constituting the population of this country.

The greatest value of this work, however, lies not so much in the interesting facts set forth and the beautiful story told, as in the example set by these women of achievement. They are writing not only to convince the present generation as to the important service rendered by the Negro troops in France, but they would hand down these facts in printed form that coming generations may not be so biased as the present in estimating the character of the Negro and his worth to the nation. It is to be hoped that every Negro who, during his service at the front, received such impressions and had such experiences as to throw light upon the many phases of that world cataclysm will in the near future follow the example of these worthy women. The public will welcome history of divisions and regiments and will certainly be interested in the mere personal narrative presenting the experiences peculiar to those individuals placed in strategic positions to see at close range what was actually happening and had the time and availed themselves of the opportunity to record it.

NOTES

Answering a call to duty a number of persons, chief among whom are Carter G. Woodson, Washington, D. C., John W. Davis, Institute, West Virginia, Louis R. Mehlinger, Washington, D. C., D. S. S. Goodloe, Bowie, Maryland, Mordecai W. Johnson, Charleston, West Virginia, Byrd Prillerman and C. E. Mitchell, Institute, West Virginia, incorporated under the laws of the District of Columbia on the third of June, a firm to be known as THE ASSOCIATED PUBLISHERS, INCORPORATED, with a capital stock of $25,000. This firm will publish books of all kinds, but will direct its attention primarily to works bearing on Negroes so as to supply all kinds of information concerning the Negro race and those who have been interested in its uplift. Carter G. Woodson is President; John W. Davis, Treasurer; and Louis R. Mehlinger, Secretary.

The idea in the minds of the incorporators is to meet a long-felt need of supplanting exploiting publishers sending out book agents, who since the emancipation of the Negroes have gone from door to door filling their homes with literature which is neither informing nor elevating. Inasmuch as these publishing houses find it profitable to sell literature which in this advanced age of civilization of the race must be less attractive than it was years ago, it is to be expected that success will come to an enterprise like THE ASSOCIATED PUBLISHERS, INCORPORATED, bringing out more valuable works for which there is an increasing demand.

During the recent years the Negro race has been seeking to learn more about itself and especially since the social upheaval of the World War. The Negro reading public has been largely increased and the number of persons interested in the Negro have so multiplied that any creditable publication giving important facts about the race now finds a ready market throughout the United States and even abroad. To supply this demand these gentlemen have launched the enterprise, THE ASSOCIATED PUBLISHERS, INCORPORATED.

Africa Slave or Free, by John H. Harris, has been published by E. P. Dutton and Company, New York City.

Unsung Heroes: by Elizabeth Ross Haynes is being advertised as a forthcoming publication of DuBois and Dill, Publishers, New York City. This work consists largely of biographical material for average readers.

The following interesting articles have recently appeared: *West African Religion*, by R. E. Dennett (The Church Quarterly Review, January, 1921); *Christian Missions and African Labor*, by J. H. Oldham (International Review of Missions, April, 1921); *Unreached Fields of Central Africa*, by H. K. W. Kumm (The Missionary Review of the World, June, 1921); *A Doctor's Experience in West Africa*, by H. L. Weber (The Missionary Review of the World, June, 1921); *South Africa and its Native Problem*, by Earl Buxton (Journal of the African Society, April, 1921); *Semi-Bantu Languages of East Nigeria*, by Sir Harry H. Johnston (Journal of the African Society, April, 1921); *The Fulas and their Language*, by Sir Harry H.

Johnston (Journal of the African Society, April, 1921); *Race Legislation in South Carolina since 1865*, by F. B. Simkins (South Atlantic Quarterly, January, 1921); *Santo Domingo: A Study in Benevolent Imperialism*, by R. G. Adams (South Atlantic Quarterly, January, 1921).

THE JOURNAL
OF
NEGRO HISTORY

Vol. VI—October, 1921—No. 4

THE NEGRO MIGRATION OF 1916-1918[1]

CHAPTER I

INTRODUCTION

In accordance with its title, this essay is intended to be an interpretation of the recent Negro migration in the United States. Its object is to sift out from the mass of writings the most salient facts pertaining to this movement and to present them in such a manner as to give a correct impression of it in its entirety. In this regard, however, it is not a mere narration of events, but, as far as possible, a sort of scientific analysis of the facts therein contained. Thus, it aims to treat in a systematic and logical manner the various aspects of the movement, to show the relationship between them, and to try to understand and account for the economic and social forces involved. In pursuance of this it has, therefore, seemed fitting to include in this study a brief survey of migration in general, the origin, nature, and scope of the recent movement, its relation to previous movements, its causes and effects, and some conclusions regarding its meaning and significance.

In the preparation of this essay, moreover, the writer has drawn very freely from the material contained in a report of the United States Department of Labor. Accurately described, this source is rather a compilation of reports based on investigations of this movement during the summer of 1917. These inquiries were authorized by the Secretary of Labor and were supervised by Dr. James H. Dillard, formerly a professor and a dean of the faculty at Tulane

University, New Orleans, Louisiana, and, at present, Director of the Jeanes and Slater Funds for Negro education in the South. The actual investigations were made and reported on by the following: Mr. T. J. Woofter, Mr. R. H. Leavell, Mr. T. R. Snavely, Mr. W. T. B. Williams and Professor F. D. Tyson of the University of Pittsburgh.

This essay, however, views this movement as the Negro Migration of 1916-18 instead of the "Negro Migration of 1916-17," as some have termed it. This position is taken on the following grounds: The Negroes were attracted to the North largely through the great demand for labor which had been made a fact by the departure of thousands of aliens to serve their respective countries in the Great War. The Negro migration stream began flowing in the spring of 1916, reached its highest mark in 1917, and, even though much diminished, coursed on through 1918 up to the signing of the armistice. With the occurrence of this event the need for Negro labor became considerably less acute, thus causing a decided dwindling of the movement, but not a sudden stoppage of it. It drifted on, however, but with an ever-decreasing volume. Even during the latter part of the summer of 1919 signs that this movement was still in progress were evident, as Negroes were found moving North, though in very small numbers.

A study of the movement of any group of mankind almost of necessity reverts to the consideration of the relation of man to his environment, both natural and human. In the first place, it is known that man, like the plant or the animal, is greatly influenced by his natural surroundings. It is the policy of nature to allow an unlimited number of individuals to be born, while at the same time the amount of food and space upon the earth is limited. This results in a perpetual struggle for survival, or existence. In this struggle, through the process of natural selection, the individuals possessing those qualities suitable for life in their environment are allowed to survive and to transmit these favorable qualities to their offspring, whereas those having the less fit traits are weeded out. In a word, the battle is to the strong, the race is to the swift.[3] The chances of survival of all organisms, therefore, depend on adaptation or adjustment to external conditions.[4]

Besides adaptation, however, nature also presents to the plant or animal other alternatives whenever any fundamental change occurs in the environment which affects the life of these individuals. These alternatives are death, degeneration, and flight. These have all had their effects upon man as well as upon plants and animals. "It is well known that men die when natural conditions become favorable enough; famines recurrently sweep many from the earth. Again, they degenerate when they are forced to live a life that it is possible to live but only in a miserable way. Some of the lowest tribes of men, like the South African Bushmen, or the Digger Indians, have been forced by stronger tribes to withdraw into the desert and to exist upon a lower plane of life. The physique of such peoples betrays the hardships which they have suffered. Men also flee from an unfavorable environment, thus escaping death or degeneracy, if the way into a more favorable locality lies open to them. Much of migration and colonization comes under this alternative."[5] This topic is well illustrated by those farms of New England which have been abandoned by their former owners, and have been occupied by immigrants from Europe.[6]

As man is compelled to adapt himself to his natural surroundings in order to survive, so he must do in regard to his human or social environment. This external situation is due to the fact that man lives his life in a group, or a society, composed of numerous individuals like himself. In this society are laws or conventions which are imposed on all by the group, and which all are required to obey.[7] Often, however, it happens that in various ways the acts of large numbers of the group come into conflict with these laws, and the result is the maladjustment of those who have behaved thus. Society then takes steps to compel these individuals to bring themselves back into harmony with the life of the rest of the group. During this period of compulsion, however, all do not comply with the commands of society, for many avail themselves of the alternative of flight or migration to another place where conditions of life seem more favorable. The numerous historical accounts of men and women leaving their native lands in order to escape discomforts, dissatisfactions, punishment or persecution for various reasons, are examples of this state of affairs.

Migration then is an important element in man's environmental relations. It is the means by which he is enabled to escape the pain of an unfavorable environment and to find the pleasure which might result from adaptation in more favorable surroundings. Through flight or migration man simply adopts the course on which his efforts meet with the least resistance, because, instead of remaining in the unfavorable locality to struggle against the most adverse circumstances, or to run the risk of suffering death or degeneracy, he moves elsewhere, where the obstacles appear to be fewer, and where adaptation seems a matter of easier accomplishment. Now, should this same principle be applied to this specific subject under discussion, it would, perhaps, be demonstrated that the Negroes, likewise, simply used migration as a means of escaping the intolerable conditions in their home environment and of making their way into another accessible locality, where the chances of winning out in the struggle for existence seemed more certain.

In this view of migration as a means of escape from unfavorable environmental conditions we must distinguish it, however, from those earliest movements of primitive men. These were, perhaps, instinctive and differed little from the movements of animals. They were mere "wanderings"; but they were the necessary forerunners of the more recent movements.[8] Migration, in its truest sense, is a reasoned movement which arose after man had progressed far enough in the scale of civilization to have a fixed abiding place. It is a definite movement from one place to another. It involves an actual and permanent change of residence. Migration, therefore, occurred only in the most rudimentary form among people in the hunting stage; more developed forms of it occurred among pastoral peoples, when they, for instance, changed their base of operation; but in its most complete form migration occurred only after man had reached the stage of agriculture.

If migration is a reasoned affair, it then follows that for every migration there must be some definable cause. This cause must be a very powerful one, because man is inclined to become attached to the locality in which he finds himself placed. There are formed ties of various kinds which tend to hold him to his home. These are the ties of family, friendly associations, customs and habits of the community, politics, religion, business, property, and superstitious reverence for graves. His life is, therefore, closely bound up with his surroundings, and the changing of it for that of another locality is a matter of serious concern. Thus, "there is a marked inertia, a resistance to pressure among human beings, and the presumption is that people will stay where they are unless some positive force causes them to move."

Furthermore, the force which operates in causing men to move generally presents one of two aspects, viz., attractive and repellent. "Men are either drawn or driven to break the ties which bind them to their native locality." Again, the causes of migration are classified as positive advantages and satisfactions, and negative discomforts and compulsions. The causes of the repellent or negative type exist in the environment of the locality to which man is already attached. They, therefore, are much more important than the others, because, despite the inducements of another locality which may be opened to him, it is the tendency of man to remain where he is, if he is contented. These forces must produce dissatisfaction with existing conditions in order to induce man to move. The causes of the attractive or positive type, on the other hand, are in a foreign environment, and operate often by stimulating dissatisfactions through comparison. They must, before movement can be induced, show that conditions in the new locality are superior to those in the home environment. "Thus, in almost every case of migration one is justified in looking for some cause of a repellent nature, some dissatisfaction, disability, discontent, hardship, or other disturbing condition;" and, likewise, some positive advantage, satisfaction, prospect of contentment, or other favorable condition. Therefore, it goes almost without saying that the study of this subject of Negro migration will show that these two types of forces or causes were also present in this recent movement.

Again, these repellent or negative conditions which cause men to move may arise in any of the various interests of human life, and may be classified as economic, political, social, and religious. Of these "the economic causes of migration are the earliest and by far the most important. They arise in connection with man's effort to make his living and concern all

469

interests which are connected with his productive efforts. They are disabilities or handicaps which affect his pursuit of food, clothing and shelter, as well as the less necessary comforts of life. These are vital interests and any dissatisfaction connected with them is of great weight to men."

Inasmuch as the economic causes of migration are primal and most important, and since like causes played such a large part in giving rise to this recent movement, it might be well to pause here to enumerate some of these causes, and to note briefly the nature of the same. In the first place, a migration may occur because of permanent infertility of the soil, harsh climate, or a dearth of natural resources which may perpetually intensify man's struggle for existence. In the next place, it may be due to temporary natural calamities such as drought, famine, flood, extreme seasons and so on. This latter set of causes, as will be seen later on, were prominent factors in the recent Negro movement from the South to the North. Again, people may be forced to move because of serious underdevelopment of the industrial arts which may make living hard by limiting the productive power of the people or by retarding them in the struggle for trade. Finally, migration may be due to overpopulation—a condition in which the population of a country has increased to such a degree that there are too many people in proportion to the supporting power of the environment.

As has just been intimated, the causes of migration are fourfold, namely, economic, political, social, and religious. Because of this it must not be thought, however, that these causes are separate and distinct; but it should be understood that they overlap each other and exist almost always in conjunction. In any migration two or more of them will be found present. For example, it is very difficult to find cases in which social causes alone account for a migration. They often, nevertheless, act as a contributory factor to a movement. The economic causes are by far the most important and universal; but behind them are frequently other causes. "Political maladjustments often express themselves through economic or social disabilities, religious differences through economic and social limitations, etc." In short, it may be said that the motives of migration may be due to a complication of causes. This may be well illustrated by the study of the recent Negro migration in which it will be found that this movement was occasioned by a number of interacting economic, social, and, to a small extent, political forces.

As there are types of forces or causes giving rise to migration, there are likewise types of migration. These are the following four: invasion, conquest, colonization and immigration. Besides these four main types of movement there are other less important forms which deserve notice. They are of two kinds, namely, forced forms of migration, and internal or intra-state migration of peoples. The former occurs (1) when people are expelled from a country because of non-conformity to the established religion; (2) when they are compelled by actual force to leave one place and go to another, as in the case of the importation of Negroes from Africa to the United States to become slaves; and (3) when people are subjected to banishment from a country as a form of punishment for crime. The internal or intra-state movement is that which is going on all the time in most civilized countries, and which is usually a phenomenon of non-importance; but when it involves large masses of people, moving in certain well-defined directions, with a community of motives and purposes, it becomes of great interest and significance and deserves to be classed with the other great movements of peoples. One good example of this is the westward movement of the people of the United States during the early decades of the past century. Another which might be rightly classed as such is the recent large Negro migration which is under consideration in this essay.

The subject of migration in general is capable of very lengthy treatment, but as this is not our purpose here we shall terminate this discussion at this juncture. In this preliminary survey the aim has been to try to show, though in an exceedingly brief manner, the meaning and significance of migration as a factor in the human struggle for existence; the distinction between migration and the earliest movements of primitive man; the types of forces which figure in any migration; and the various forms in which a migration may occur. This has been done with the further intention of endeavoring to imbue the mind at the outset with the idea that this Negro migration is not very radically different from the past movements of civilized man, and that, like them, it occurred in obedience to certain laws which were operating in the environment of the migrants. If this object can be accomplished, little doubt is entertained that it will do much toward affording a clearer and more comprehensive view of the movement than could be otherwise obtained.

FOOTNOTES:

[1] This dissertation was presented by Henderson H. Donald to the Faculty of the Graduate School of Yale University in candidacy for the degree of Master of Arts, May, 1920. Since then it has been considerably revised and augmented.

In the preparation of this work the following books were used: James Bryce, *The American Commonwealth*, Volume II; F. S. Chapin, *Introduction to the Study of Human Evolution*; H. P. Fairchild, *Immigration*; H. E. Gregory, A. G. Keller, and A. L. Bishop, *Physical and Commercial Geography*; A. G.

Keller, *Societal Evolution*; R. F. Hoxie, *Trade Unionism in the United States*; E. J. Scott, *Negro Migration during the War*; W. G. Sumner, *Folkways*; F. J. Warne, *The Immigration Invasion*; C. G. Woodson, *A Century of Negro Migration*.

The following magazine articles were also helpful: Ray S. Baker, "The Negro Goes Forth" (*World's Work*, 34: 314-17, July, 1917); W. E. B. DuBois, "The Migration of Negroes" (*The Crisis*, 14: 63-66, June, 1917); B. M. Edens, "When Labor is Cheap" (*Survey*, 38: 511, September 8, 1917); H. A. Hoyer, "Migration of Colored Workers" (*Survey*, 45: 930, March 26, 1921); G. E. Haynes, "Negroes Move North" (*Survey*, 40: 115-22, May 4, 1917) and "Effect of War Conditions on Negro Labor" (*Academy of Political Science*, 8: 299-312, February, 1919); T. A. Hill, "Why Southern Negroes Don't go South" (*Survey*, 43: 183-85, November 29, 1919); H. W. Horwill, "A Negro Exodus" (*Contemporary Review*, 114: 299-305, September, 1918; *Literary Digest*, 54: 1914, January 23, 1917); "The South Calling Negroes Back; An Exodus in America" (*Living Age*, 295: 57-60, October 6, 1917); "The Negro Migration" (*New Republic*, 7: 213-14, January 1, 1916; *New York Times*, November 12, 1916, 11, 12: 1; September 4, 1917, 3: 6; October 7, 1917, 111, 10: 1; January 21, 1919, 3: 6; June 14, 1919, 3: 6; June 16, 1919, 12: 5; June 11, 1920, 18: 1; December 12, 1921, 14: 1); H. B. Pendleton, "Cotton Pickers in Northern Cities" (*Survey*, 37: 569-71, February 17, 1917); W. O. Scroggs, "Interstate Migration of Negroes" (*Journal of Political Economy*, 25: 1034-43, December, 1917); "The Lure of the North for Negroes" (*Survey*, 38: 27-28, April 7, 1917); "Reasons why Negroes go North" (*Survey*, 38: 226-7, June 2, 1917); "Negro Migration as the South sees It" (*Survey*, 38: 428, August 11, 1917); "Health of the Negro" (*Survey*, 42: 596-7, June 19, 1919); "Negroes in Industry" (*Survey*, 42: 900, September 27, 1919); "A New Migration" (*Survey*, 45: 752, February 26, 1921); F. B. Washington, "The Detroit New Comers' Greeting" (*Survey*, 38: 333-5, July 14, 1917); W. F. White, "The Success of Negro Migration" (*The Crisis*, 19: 112-15, January, 1920); T. J. Woofter, Jr., "The Negro and Industrial Peace" (*Survey*, 45: 420-421, December 17, 1921); J. A. Wright, "Conditions among Negro Migrants in Hartford, Connecticut" (a letter).

The following pamphlets and reports were also valuable: Branson and others, *Migration, Minutes of University Commission on Southern Race Questions*,

473

pp. 48-49, 1917; Bureau of the United States Census, *Negro Population in the United States, 1790-1916*, and *Negroes in the United States*, Bulletin 129: A. Epstein, *The Negro Migrant in Pittsburg*; G. E. Haynes, *Negro New-comers in Detroit, Michigan*; Home Mission Council, *The Negro Migration*; E. K. Jones, *The Negro in Industry, Proceedings of the National Conference of Social Work*, pp. 494-503, June, 1917; United States Department of Labor, *Negro Migration in 1916-17*, and *The Negro at Work during the War and Reconstruction*.

[2] A full list of these occurs in the bibliographical section of this essay.

[3] Chapin, F. S., *Introduction to the Study of Human Evolution*, pp. 30-31.

[4] This law, of course, does not fully operate among men in a highly civilized state of living, for in this state its force is much diminished by various uplift, or counter-selective, agencies.

[5] Gregory, Keller, and Bishop, *Physical and Commercial Geography*, pt. II, p. 126.

[6] Gregory, Keller, and Bishop, *Physical and Commercial Geography*, pt. II, p. 126.

[7] Keller, A. G., *Societal Evolution*, pp. 24-37.

[8] What is said here, and also in the remaining pages of this chapter, are for the most part reproductions of parts of Chapter I of *Immigration*, by H. P. Fairchild. In some cases quotations and paraphrases from this source are also given. The acknowledgment here, however, is once and for all.

Chapter II

PREVIOUS NEGRO MOVEMENTS

Among the many who have written concerning this exodus one finds that not a few of them have been prone to emphasize the fact that in this recent movement the Negroes suddenly developed within themselves a desire to move, thus implying that migration is not controlled by certain economic and social laws, and that this movement was an entirely new social phenomenon. Disregarding for the present the first assumption, and directing attention to the second, the writer holds that the latter must have sprung from the fact that no account was taken of the past economic and social history of the Negroes; for a study in that direction would have shown that ever since the time of their emancipation the Negroes have shown a tendency to migrate.[9] That this has been the case a number of instances will demonstrate.

Shortly after emancipation there occurred slow and confused movements of the Negro population which covered a period of several years. During his enslavement the Negro could hardly do anything without the will and consent of his master; he had not the liberty to order and direct his life as he chose. When, therefore, he was suddenly transformed from this state to that of freedom, the first thing he did was to put this freedom to test by moving about. Consequently he drifted from place to place and at the same time changed his name, employment, and even his wife. Many also devoted much of their time to hunting while they were awaiting Federal Government assistance in the form of land and mules. Emancipation meant to them not only freedom from slavery but freedom from responsibility as well. Thus during their early years of liberty large numbers of Negroes moved about almost aimlessly and thoughtlessly and made their way especially to the towns, cities and Federal military camps.[10]

There was, moreover, a considerable movement of the Negro population toward the southwestern part of the United States. It was very slow and was in operation between 1865 and 1875, when the expansion of the numerous railway systems gave rise to a great number of land speculators who did much to induce men to go West and settle on the land. Their appeals greatly aroused the Negroes who had reasons for a change of abode. This movement was at first composed of individuals; but later on it became a group movement. In this migratory stream which flowed southwestward were 35,000 Negroes, who came largely from South Carolina, Georgia, Alabama, and Mississippi.[11]

Again, in 1879, a large number of Negroes made a rush to Kansas.[12] This movement was due for the most part to agricultural depression in parts of the South, but was precipitated greatly by the activities of a host of petty Negro leaders who had sprung up in all parts of the South during the Reconstruction period. This exodus began early in March and continued till May. The estimated number of migrants was between 5,000 and 10,000; but there were thousands of others who had planned to migrate, but were deterred from doing so because of the news of the misfortunes which befell those who actually moved. The majority of those who left the South were from Louisiana and Mississippi. In this migration the Negroes left their homes when the weather was growing warm, but on reaching their destination found that spring had not yet arrived, the country being still bleak and desolate. Most of them were poorly clad and without funds. Consequently, many suffered from want and disease and consequently became public charges. As soon as it was convenient for them, however, large numbers returned to their homes where they scattered such discouraging reports that others who had planned to move declined to do so. Nevertheless, about a third of them remained in Kansas and of this portion a fairly large number attained a creditable degree of prosperity.

The years of the later eighties and the early nineties also witnessed a few small interstate movements of Negroes.[13] For a long time it was the custom of employers in the mineral districts of the Appalachian Mountains to hire only foreign labor to do their work, but during the time just referred to this labor failed to satisfy the demand. In order to meet this emergency the employers at once dispatched their agents to different parts of the South to appeal to the Negroes for their labor. The efforts of these agents were not without effect, because many Negroes soon flocked to the mining districts of Birmingham, Alabama, to those of East Tennessee, and to those of West Virginia. Also, large numbers went to southern Ohio, where they were employed in the places of white laborers, who were on a strike, demanding higher wages.

As is evident in the preceding citations, the Negroes of the South are inclined not only to move to the North and West, but are also prone to move about freely within the South. This can be further substantiated by a brief study of the interdivisional movements of the Negro population of the South. In 1910, according to the Federal Census, it was found that 1.4 per cent of the Negroes living in the South Atlantic Division, 5.8 per cent of those residing in the East South Central Division, and 13.1 per cent of those in the West South Central Division, were born in places outside these respective sections. On the other hand, it was shown that the South Atlantic Division registered a loss of 392,927 from its Negro population, the East South Central a loss of 200,876, whereas the West South Central Division revealed a net gain of 194,658 in its Negro population. Thus, while two divisions lost, the third gained heavily by interdivisional Negro migration.[14] This tendency toward interdivisional migration on the part of Negroes is, however, exhibited in a less degree than is the case on the part of whites. In 1910, 16.6 per cent of the Negroes had moved to other States than those in which they were born, whereas 22.4 per cent of the whites were found in States other than those in which they were born.[15]

Likewise, the Negroes are inclined to move about freely from section to section within the bounds of the North and West. In 1910, 47 per cent of the Negroes living in the New England Division, 52.3 per cent of those in the Middle Atlantic Division, 50.4 per cent of those in the East North Central Division, 32.1 per cent of those in the West North Central Division, and 80 per cent of those living in the Mountain Division and 77.7 per cent of those living in the Pacific Division, were born, in each case, in places outside of these sections.[16] Each section showed also a loss of a certain per cent of its total native Negro population through migration to some other division. In this respect, New England showed a loss of 18.5 per cent, the Middle Atlantic States a loss of 10.5 per cent, the East North Central 16.2 per cent, the West North Central 18.2 per cent, the Mountain 43.9 per cent, and the Pacific 26.4 per cent.[17] While this was the case, each division, nevertheless, received in turn, through migration from other places, enough newcomers to show a decided gain in its total Negro population. These gains in numbers were as follows: [18]

```
New England            20,310
Middle Atlantic       186,384
```

East North Central	119,649
West North Central	40,479
Mountain	13,229
Pacific	18,976

While much of the Negro migration has been interdivisional movements within the three major sections of this country, yet a very considerable amount of it has been directed from the South to the North and West. Between 1870 and 1910, a period of forty years, there was a marked increase in the number of Negroes who were born in the South but who had migrated to the North. In 1870 the number was 149,000, but in 1910 it had increased to 440,534.[19] This latter estimate is undoubtedly much less than the actual number of migrants, for it does not account for those who might have died or returned to the South or elsewhere before the taking of the Federal Census. Moreover, it is a fact that since the Civil War the Negro population of the North has been increasing faster than that of the South. In 1860 there were 344,719 Negroes in the North; in 1910 there were 1,078,336, an increase of 212.8 per cent for the fifty years' period. In 1920 there were 1,472,448 Negroes in the North, an increase of 43.8 per cent in ten years. In the West there were 78,591 in 1920. In the South, on the other hand, during the period from 1870 to 1910, the rate of increase was only 111.1 per cent. From 1910 to 1920 there was an increase of only 1.9 per cent whereas there was between 1900 and 1915 an increase of 10.4 per cent in that section in the Negro population in the South. During the past fifty years, therefore, the relative increase of Negroes in the North has been more than double that of the Negro population in the South. Before 1860 every census, except that of 1840, showed a greater relative increase in the Negro population of the South than in that of the North. Since that time, however, this condition has been reversed.[20] This increase of the Negro population in the North is undoubtedly due to migration from the South, and not to natural increase, because the vital statistics of Northern communities show that the Negro birth-rate is barely sufficient to balance the death-rate.[21]

Not only have Negroes been moving from the South to the North and West, but they have also been migrating from these latter sections to the South. Immediately after the Civil War a small number of Negroes left the North and made their way to the South.[22] This movement was composed of intelligent Negroes who had been fortunate enough to enjoy some of the educational opportunities of the North and who, because of this equipment, felt that they might be of service to the race during the Reconstruction period in the South. They were the ones who became the antagonists of the Carpet-baggers—the arch-corrupters of the governments of the Southern States. There were, however, other reasons why these men went South. In the first place, some had found northern communities so hostile to them that their progress was impeded; in the next place, many desired to reunite with their relatives from whom they had been separated by their flight from slavery; finally, others moved in response to a spirit of adventure to enter a new field which offered opportunities of all sorts.

The Federal Census of 1910, moreover, furnishes evidence of Negro movement from the North and West to the South.[23] This report shows that during that decade 41,489 Negroes who were born in the North and West were living in the South. This migration from these former sections to the South, though less considerable in volume than the migration from the South, is, nevertheless, proportionately greater when considered in relation to the Negro population born in these two sections than the

480

migration from the South when the latter movement is, likewise, considered in its relation to the total Negro population born in the South. Thus the 41,489 Negroes born in the North and West but living in the South in 1910 constituted 6.5 per cent of the total Negro population born in the North and West, whereas the 440,534 Negroes born in the South but residing in the North formed only 4.8 per cent of the total Negro population born in the South.

The fact that this recent Negro migration, as has been stated, was a movement to the large cities and industrial centers of the North and West should give no occasion for surprise, because this has been in progress for more than three decades. During this period the Negroes have shown a decided tendency to flock to the large cities of the North and West, and also to those of the South. This is verified by the discovery that since 1880 nine cities of the North and West have shown considerable increase in their Negro population. These attractive cities thus popularized are as follows: Boston, Greater New York, Philadelphia, Chicago, Cincinnati, Evansville, Indianapolis, Pittsburgh, and St. Louis. The increase for these nine cities between 1880 and 1890 was about 36.2 per cent; between 1890 and 1900 it was about 74.4 per cent; from 1900 to 1910 about 37.4 per cent; and from 1910 to 1920 about 50 per cent. In the first decade the increase was more than three times the increase of the total Negro population; in the second it was more than four times as large; in the third the increase was nearly three times larger; and in the fourth nearly five times as large as the increase of the same population. Likewise, during the same period there was a great Negro influx to the larger cities of the South, but the rate of increase was less than that of the Northern cities. In fifteen Southern cities the percentage of increase was about 38.7 per cent during the first decade; during the second about 20.6 per cent; and from 1900 to 1916 the increase (based on figures for sixteen cities) was about the same as that of the preceding decades.[24]

These numerous instances of previous Negro movements show that the recent migration is no new and strange phenomenon, that Negroes, like other elements of the population of the United States, have shown a tendency since their emancipation to move from place to place. This recent exodus was simply a part of a long series of movements which have been in progress for more than half a century. It is, therefore, much like the others and differs from them only in its immense volume. In the course of this migration, as we observed, the number of Negroes who moved to the North and West was probably a half million—a number which perhaps exceeds or certainly equals that which resulted from all other movements from the South to the North during a period of forty years. Herein alone, if such a view of it can be held at all, lies its strangeness and remarkability as a social phenomenon.

FOOTNOTES:

[9] Scroggs, W. O., *Jour. Pol. Econ.*, 25: 1034, Dec., 1917.

[10] Woodson, C. G., *A Century of Negro Migration*, pp. 117-20.

[11] *Ibid.*, pp. 120-21.

[12] Scroggs, W. O., *Jour. Pol. Econ.*, 25: 1035-37, Dec., 1917.

[13] Woodson, C. G., *A Century of Negro Migration*, p. 146.

[14] *Negro Population in U. S., 1790-1915*, Bureau of Census, pp. 69-70.

[15] *Journal of Pol. Econ.*, 25: 1040, D. '17.

[16] *Negro Population in U. S., 1790-1915*, Bureau of

Census, pp. 69-70.

[17] *Negroes in the U. S.*, Bulletin 129, p. 17. Census Bureau.

[18] *Negro Population in U. S., 1790-1915*, Bureau of Census, pp. 69-70.

[19] *Negro Population in U. S., 1790-1915*, Bureau of Census, p. 65.

[20] Scroggs, W. D., *Jour. Pol. Econ.*, 25: 1038, D. '17.

[21] *Ibid.*, D. '17.

[22] Woodson, C. G., *A Century of Negro Migration*, pp. 123-4.

[23] *Negro Population in the U. S., 1790-1915*, p. 65.

[24] Haynes, G. E., *New York Times*, Nov. 12, 1916, II, 12: 1.

Chapter III

SOURCE, VOLUME, DESTINATION, AND COMPOSITION

The exodus of the Negroes during the years from 1916 to 1918 occurred with such suddenness and attained such an immense volume that for a time it appeared to many observers that the whole "Black Belt" was shifting itself northward. Inasmuch as at the very time this migration reached its zenith this country had just entered into a state of war with Germany, it attracted almost nation-wide attention, and from some quarters the fear was that it would have the effect, either directly or indirectly, of obstructing the National Government in its prosecution of the war. Numerous also were the apprehensions of the economic, political, and social problems that might follow in the wake of this movement. On almost every hand, therefore, the discussions concerning this migration became legion, and varying were the opinions expressed regarding its causes and its probable effects upon the sections of the country involved and upon the migrants themselves.

It is uncertain as to the exact time when this movement began, because it was going on some time before any notice was taken of it. It is known, however, that conditions favorable to its beginning were manifest shortly after the outbreak of the European War, when, on account of this catastrophe, immigration practically ceased and thousands of alien laborers departed for their native lands. This caused a serious labor shortage in the Northern industries, and in order to obviate this employers, during the spring of 1915, sent agents into the South to seek Negro

484

laborers. If, as a result of the efforts of these agents, Negroes were induced to go North, then the number of those who moved was so small and in such scattered instances as to make it unworthy of being called a migration. This view is taken because it was not until nearly a year afterward that Negroes began to move in numbers sufficiently large to attract public notice.

The Negro migration in its truest sense, therefore, had its beginning in 1916 and was precipitated as follows: "A national philanthropic organization arranged with some Northern tobacco growers to import Negro students from some of the Southern private institutions for summer work and early in May, 1916, brought the first two trainloads from Georgia. Then the agent of a large Northern railroad, taking advantage of the publicity given this venture, used the name of this organization to get migrants to come North."[25] Other railroads and steel mills were also in great need for laborers and thus sent their agents in the South to solicit labor. These agents moved about through the States of the South and offered at first free transportation to the prospective laborers and pictured to them in very glowing terms the high wages and advantages of the North. This they did not have to do very long, "for the news spread like wild-fire. It was like the gold fever in '49. Negroes sold their simple belongings and in some instances valuable land and property and flocked to the Northern cities, even though they had no objective work in sight."[26] Regarding this same point, Mr. Ray Stannard Baker holds that during the spring of 1916 "trains were backed into Southern cities and hundreds of Negroes were gathered up in a day, loaded into the cars and whirled away to the North. Instances are given showing that Negro teamsters left their horses standing in the streets or deserted their jobs and went to the trains without notifying their employers or even going home."[27]

The next question which seems in order is whence came these migrants. As far as is known up to now they came largely from thirteen of the Southern States and from those lying mainly east of the Mississippi River. These States are as follows: Alabama, Arkansas, Florida, Georgia, Kentucky, Louisiana, Mississippi, North Carolina, Oklahoma, South Carolina, Tennessee, and Virginia—the cotton, tobacco, and sugar cane regions of the South.[28] Of these the States which paid the heaviest toll in the number of migrants are Virginia, North Carolina, South Carolina, Georgia, Alabama, Mississippi, Arkansas and Tennessee. In this respect Mississippi stands first, Alabama second, and Georgia third.[29]

When we come to the consideration of the number of Negroes who left the South during the course of this movement we find here much uncertainty. This state of affairs is due partly to the fact that the very beginning of the movement was unknown to those who might have been interested in taking a census of those departing and partly to the fact that perhaps after the movement was known to be in operation no counting was resorted to because no one believed that the exodus would amount to anything of importance. When, however, the exodus reached such proportions as to demand serious attention, steps were at once taken to ascertain its volume.

Numerical estimates regarding the size of this migration have been made in different ways.[30] In one case they have been based upon the statements of observers who have watched trainloads leave the South, in another they have been based upon the growth of numbers in different Northern cities, in still another upon records of insurance companies, and finally upon the number of railway tickets sold to Negroes. On these bases estimates have ranged from

486

150,000 to upwards of 750,000. To illustrate this, a few examples will be cited. Dr. W. E. B. Du Bois estimated that 250,000 Negroes had migrated to the North during 1916-17.[31] The estimate of the Colored Citizens' Patriotic League was 300,000,[32] and that of the Chairman of the National League on Urban Conditions Among Negroes was 350,000.[33] Dr. James H. Dillard set the minimum at 150,000 and the maximum at 350,000,[34] and Mr. Ray Stannard Baker put the number up to 400,000.[35] From these various estimates given it is at once obvious that no accurate statement as to the number of Negroes who left the South can be made. It is known, however, that a very large number must have moved, because in many instances the Negro population in villages, towns and counties in some of the Southern States was greatly depleted, while the same population of Northern urban communities increased from one to four-fold. The census shows that in 1920 there were in the North and West only 472,418 more Negroes than there were in those sections in 1910. It is clear that a smaller number went North, for there was some natural increase, and we have the fact that many have returned[36] to warrant the conclusion.

In this discussion of the volume of the migration it may not be out of place to show how the various States of the South furnished their quota toward making up this total number of migrants. In this regard our data are incomplete in that they were compiled some time before the movement was checked. The following table,[37] however, will give one some notion as to the number of Negroes who left each State affected by this movement:

Alabama	90,000	Tennessee	22,632
Virginia	49,000	Kentucky	21,855
North Carolina	35,576	Louisiana	16,912
Mississippi	35,291	Florida	10,291
South Carolina	27,560	Texas	10,870
Arkansas	23,628	Oklahoma	5,836
Georgia	48,897		

It has already been indicated that this movement was directed northward, but for the sake of accuracy it is better to say that it was directed toward points in the North and West. The movement was on the whole a great rush on the part of the Negroes to the large cities and industrial centers of these two sections of the country. Within these two divisions the Negroes widely distributed themselves, going as far north as Minnesota and as far west as the Pacific Coast States. In general the destination points of the migrants were found in the following States:[41]

California	Missouri
Connecticut	Nebraska
Delaware	New Jersey
Illinois	New York
Indiana	Ohio
Iowa	Oregon
Kansas	Pennsylvania
Massachusetts	Washington
Minnesota	Wisconsin

In this connection there might be raised the question as to the distribution of these thousands of migrants in these States of the North and West; and here again it must be stated that complete and accurate data are lacking, because no thorough study in this regard has yet been made. We have, however, some partial estimates which will go to show something of this distribution of the migrants in the various States. These estimates are for Pennsylvania, Ohio, Indiana, Illinois, Michigan and Connecticut.

The number of Negroes who migrated to Pennsylvania is estimated at 84,000. Of this number 33,500 were

488

in Philadelphia and 18,500 in Pittsburgh. The other 32,000 migrants were scattered in various numbers in Steelton, Harrisburg, Coatesville, Chester, Johnstown, Altoona, Scranton, Wilkes-Barre, Easton, Reading, Erie, Oil City, Franklin and Stoneboro.[42] As many of these returned home or migrated to some other point in the North, even the census of 1920 does not enable one to make an accurate estimate.

The estimated number of migrants in Ohio was 37,000, 10,000 of whom were in Cleveland and 6,000 in Cincinnati. The other 21,500 were located in the following cities and towns: Columbus, Dayton, Toledo, Canton, Akron, Middletown, Chillicothe and Portsmouth. More than 3,000 of them were settled in camps of the Baltimore and Ohio and Pennsylvania railroads, and with contractors and traction companies in different places.[43]

The total number of migrants received by New Jersey was 25,000. Of this number 7,000 were in Newark. Jersey City, Trenton, Wrightstown, and South Jersey had each 3,000. Bayonne, Paterson and Perth Amboy together received 4,000. The rest were scattered in Camden, Carney's Point, and in the railroad camps in Jersey City and Weehawken.[44]

Indiana, Illinois, Michigan, and Connecticut have the following estimates: Between 1916 and 1918, 23,320 migrants went to Indiana, most of whom stopped in Indianapolis and Evansville;[45] 24,390 found their way to Michigan and settled for the most part in Detroit;[46] in Illinois, 24,000 were in Chicago alone; [47] and in Connecticut the city of Hartford reported 3,200 newcomers among its Negro population.[48]

In order to obtain a comprehensive view of any migration something should be known about its composition as well as its volume. As regards this particular movement it can be said that first of all it was a mass movement and not a movement of Negro leaders. It was composed of the large numbers of Negro laborers and artisans who, being very sorely pressed by adverse economic and social conditions, as will be shown later on, refused to seek the advice of their leaders, but pushed forward of their own accord with a determination to find the way for themselves.[49] This great mass, from the standpoint of habitation, was made up of two separate and distinct classes,[50] namely, rural and urban. The rural class was by far the most ignorant, owing to the lack of educational advantages in the rural districts of the South. They were for the most reared upon farms and their occupation was that of farm labor. It is said also that from this class came the majority of the Negroes who migrated from the South.[51]

On the basis of the economic, social and moral status, moreover, the members of this movement were composed of three types.[52] The first type consisted of the less responsible characters, the younger men, mostly single, who immediately responded to the promises of high wages and of free transportation made by labor agents. It was undoubtedly the presence of this type in such large numbers in the North that led Professor F. D. Tyson, of the University of Pittsburgh, to the conclusion that the outstanding fact of the Negro migration from the South was that it was preponderately a movement of single men; and certainly 70 or 80 per cent of the migrants in the Northern States were without family ties, as is evidenced by the advanced reports of the Bureau of the Census showing a change of sexual ratio of the population of some Southern States.[53] Thousands of this type were imported by the railroads to the North, but they proved to be very unreliable workers. They did not stick to their work but moved from place to place, thus furnishing in industry what some have termed the "floaters" or "birds of passage."

490

The second type was composed of industrious, thrifty, unskilled workers.[54] These for the most part were men with families or other dependents. It was the custom for the men to go ahead first, earn money, and at the same time observe conditions to ascertain whether they were favorable enough to warrant their sending for their families to join them in the North. If things were favorable, their families soon followed. Many of these, because of hard working and living conditions in the South, were forced to accept, ready, free transportation and promises of work and of high wages just as did the members of the first type. A good many of them, however, had small savings which they used to pay their travelling expenses. In some cases, in leaving their homes, the migrants departed from the usual custom of the men going ahead and leaving the families behind, by taking their wives and children to the North with them in the beginning; in others, only the wives accompanied their husbands, while the children were left behind with relatives or friends to be sent for at some future time.

In the next place, the third type of migrants consisted of a rather small group of skilled artisans, business and professional men who shared the dissatisfaction and restlessness of the common laborers.[55] For this group, moving from the South became a necessity because the migration had deprived it of the patronage of the rank and file from which its means of subsistence had been derived. Many of these, however, were in good circumstances, having been in possession of good positions, cash money and considerable property. That this was the case the following citations will show: In regard to the economic condition of the Negroes leaving Alabama, the Birmingham *Age-Herald* said, "It is not the riff-raff of the race, the worthless Negroes, who are leaving in such large numbers. There are, to be sure, many poor Negroes among them who have little more than the clothes on their backs, but others have property and good positions which they are sacrificing in order to get away at the first opportunity."[56] It is also reported that highly skilled Negro workmen went to Michigan, Ohio, and Massachusetts with fairly large sums of money from the sale of their possessions in the South.[57] A study of the financial conditions of 2,500 Negro migrants upon their arrival in Coatesville, near Philadelphia, Pennsylvania, furthermore, revealed that many had brought with them sums ranging from $50 to $150, realized from selling their homes in the South. Their desire was to purchase new homes in Philadelphia, but in this they were disappointed, because very few houses were available for sale or rent.[58] Migrants of this type gladly sacrificed their means and earnings to leave the South, feeling that by so doing they were making an advance to a life of greater freedom.

FOOTNOTES:

[25] Tyson, F. D., *Negro Migration in 1916-17*, Rep. U. S. Dept. of Labor, p. 121.

[26] Pendleton, H. B., *Survey*, 37: 569, Feb. 17, 1917.

[27] Baker, Ray S., *World's Work*, 34: 315, July, 1917.

[28] *Lit. Digest*, 54: 1914, Jn. 23, 1917.

[29] Dillard, James H., *Negro Migration in 1916-17*, Rep. U. S. Dept. Lab., p. 11.

[30] Haynes, G. E., *Survey*, 40: 116, May 4, 1918.

[31] *The Crisis*, 14: 63-66, June, 1917.

[32] Horwill, H. W., *Contemp. Rev.*, 114: 299, Sept., 1918.

[33] *Ibid.*, p. 299.

[34] *Negro Migration in 1916-17*, Rep. U. S. Dept. Lab., p. 11.

[35] Baker, R. S., *World's Work*, 34: 315, July, 1917.

[36] Haynes, G. E., *Survey*, 40: 116, May 4, 1918

[37] *Lit. Digest*, 54: 1914, June 23, 1917.

[38] Dillard, J. H., *Negro Migration in 1916-17*, U. S. Rep. Dept. Lab., p. 11.

[39] *Ibid.*, p. 11.

[40] *Ibid.*, p. 11.

[41] Scott, E. J., *Negro Migration During The War*, p. 71.

[42] Tyson, F. D., *Negro Migration in 1916-17*, U. S. Dept. Lab., p. 157.

[43] *Ibid.*, pp. 157-8.

[44] *Ibid.*, pp. 157-8.

[45] *Negro Migration*, Rep. Home Missions Council, Jan., 1919.

[46] *Ibid.*

[47] Tyson, F. D., *Negro Migration in 1916-17*, U. S. Dept. Lab., p. 117.

[48] Wright, J. A., *Letter on Conditions Among Negro Migrants in Hartford*.

[49] Du Bois, W. E. B., *Survey*, 38: 227, June 2, 1917.

[50] Edens, B. M., *Survey*, 38: 511, Sept. 8, 1917.

[51] *Ibid.*

[52] Haynes, G. E., *Survey*, 40: 116, May 4, 1918.

[53] *Negro Migration in 1916-17*, Rep. U. S. Dept. of Lab., p. 145.

[54] Haynes, G. E., *Survey*, 40: 116, May 4, 1918.

[55] *Ibid.*, May 4, 1918.

[56] *Survey*, 38: 227, Je. 2, 1917.

[57] *Ibid.*, 40: 116, May 4, 1918.

[58] *Ibid.*, 38: 28, April 7, 1917.

CHAPTER IV

CAUSES OF THE RECENT NEGRO MIGRATION

In the study of the migration of any group or groups of mankind a consideration of its causes is highly important, because it seems that therein largely lies much of the significance of the movement. It has already been seen that for every migration there must be some definite cause, since man always moves in response to a rational impulse. Moreover, we saw that the cause must be a very powerful one, because it is the tendency of men to become attached to the locality in which they find themselves. In the investigation of this particular movement under consideration, we are, therefore, justified in seeking to know its causes; and this seems the more legitimate because we desire greatly to know why it was that at this particular time, perhaps more, or, at least, as many Negroes left their Southern homes for points in the North and West than did through a series of migrations which had been in progress for forty years.

The fundamental and immediate cause of this Negro exodus is economic, the basic and predominant cause of most of the movements of modern times. Its sudden occasion had its origin in the great labor shortage at the North, which was due to conditions growing out of the European War. This great war had the effect of cutting off the large and accustomed immigration stream from Europe and of withdrawing from this country thousands of foreign-born residents who were needed in the service of their respective native lands. Northern employers who had been dependent on them for their labor soon faced a serious shortage of labor, on the one hand, while, on the other, they saw their contracts with European concerns for war supplies increase tremendously. Being hard pressed for labor, these owners and operators of the various industrial enterprises, as a last resort, turned to the South and began to solicit Negro labor in order to meet their demands. Thus a Negro exodus from the South was started, and we say that the cause of it was economic. This statement, however, does not adequately cover the ground, because, as has already been seen, a migration is usually the result of the operation of a complexity of causes and not the result of any one cause. Therefore, we shall say that this Negro movement was due to the workings of a complication of economic and social causes, but that of these causes the economic were overwhelmingly predominant.

In studying the forces or causes which were behind this movement, we find that they group themselves under two categories, namely, attractive and repellent. In this migration the Negroes were to a large extent both drawn and driven to break the ties which bound them to their respective localities. One has said that these causes may be grouped as beckoning and driving causes, the former arising from conditions in the North and the latter from conditions in the South. [59] The beckoning causes are as follows: high wages, little or no employment, a shorter working day than on the farm, less political and social discrimination than in the South, better educational facilities, and the lure of the city.[60] On the other hand, we have these given as the driving causes: "General dissatisfaction with conditions, ravages of boll-weevil, floods, change of crop system, low wages, poor houses on plantations, inadequate school facilities, unsatisfactory crop settlements, rough treatment, cruelty of the law officers, unfairness in courts,

496

lynching, the desire for travel, labor agents, the Negro press, letters from friends in the North, and finally advice of white friends in the South, where crops had failed."[61] At this juncture a specific consideration of these latter causes as they were operative in three of the Southern States will now be made. These States referred to are those which were foremost in contributing to the movement and are, namely, Alabama, Georgia and Mississippi.

The causes of migration from Alabama[62] were in the main economic. In the first place the opportunities afforded Negroes to earn their subsistence were greatly curtailed by the boll-weevil pest which swept over the State a few years ago. In the black belt counties cotton had been for several generations the sole crop, and its cultivation wholly dependent upon Negro labor. On the other hand, the Negroes were dependent upon the landowners or overseers for money for their subsistence. In the meantime the Negro farmers and laborers were never taught or encouraged to raise any crop other than cotton. When the boll-weevil pest came and made the raising of cotton an impossibility, it became necessary to shift from the cotton crop to another which was not liable to be troubled by the weevil pests. While the transition was being made, however, the prices of cotton fell considerably and thus made it very difficult for landowners and Negro farmers to borrow money at a reasonable rate of interest. The outcome was that the Negroes suffered much in their struggle to maintain themselves.

Secondly, in 1916 there was a serious crop shortage due to floods. During the spring and summer of that year the rivers overflowed their banks and the water therefrom destroyed the crops throughout a large portion of the state. This made it necessary for both farmers and tenants to find other means of livelihood.

The customary advances in money and provisions to the Negro tenants were cut off and in many cases the owners of large plantations were compelled to advise their Negro laborers to move away. In other cases Negroes were so deeply in debt for provisions furnished them during the past winter, for rent and other causes that they were forced to forfeit their mules and other property in payment of these debts. These conditions brought on so much suffering among the Negroes that some sunk to the depths of starvation and had to be given food by the Federal Government, through the Department of Agriculture, and also by the Red Cross organization.

In the next place, shortage of railroad cars was another prominent factor in causing migration from this State. Officials of railroad companies reported that fully half the miners who left the Birmingham districts did so because the companies were unable to obtain cars. In June, 1917, the chairman of the Birmingham District Subcommittee on Car Service stated that more than 7,000 cars of manufactured products had accumulated for shipment in the district. [63] Also, certain lumber companies were forced to reduce the number of their employees on account of the impossibility of getting their lumber products removed from the yards. The shortage of cars, therefore, necessitated the discharge of many men and at the same time prevented the employment of additional laborers.

There was, moreover, a great demand for labor in the North, rendered effective by offers of higher wages than those paid in Alabama. There was at this time too a great surplus of labor throughout those sections affected by the boll-weevil, floods, and shortage of cars, which was ready to respond to this demand. This demand was made known to the migrants by Northern labor agents who played the part of middlemen in this exodus. The migration, through them, was made easy by the furnishing of free transportation and by the making of glowing promises to the Negro migrants.

Another potent influence was that of the persuasion of friends and relatives already in the North. In 1917, when an investigation of the movement was made, it was found that this was the principal influence operating to move the Negroes to the North. Former residents of some of the rural districts of the South who had gone North and secured a foothold wrote letters back to their friends and relatives telling them of their success in the new environment. They depicted in these missives wages which seemed fabulous sums when compared with those received in the South, told of the good conditions of their surroundings, and of numerous advantages and opportunities which they were enjoying, but which had been impossible for them to enjoy while in the South. Negro men, moreover, frequently sent large sums of money to transport their families to the North, and frequently sons in the North sent neat sums back to their parents in the South. These letters containing glowing reports concerning Northern conditions, and the large remittances to relatives and friends, played no small part in inducing thousands to move to try their fortunes in the new environment.

In Georgia[64] we find that the migration was due to a complex of economic and social causes in the form of low wages, poor conditions of labor, lynching, minor injustices in the courts and dissatisfaction with educational facilities. In regard to the first cause, it is known that at the time of the migration wages in this State were extremely low. In 1916 some counties paid only $10 and $12 a month for farm labor; others paid $13 and $15 a month for the same kind of labor.

After the movement got well started, however, there was a tendency on the part of most of the farmers to advance wages a little, so that some counties showed an average of $14, others $17, and not a few others as much as $20 a month. It should be added that these wages were in most cases supplemented by free housing and sometimes by food.

In another instance it was found that many Negroes left the farming districts because of unsatisfactory labor conditions due to failure on the part of the planters to keep in close touch with their laborers. There was utter neglect on their part to look after certain details of plantation life as they particularly affected the single men. For example, in many cases, no provision was made to have their food properly cooked, their clothes mended, to keep them supplied with fresh meat, to repair the houses in which they lived, and to furnish them with gardens. On the other hand, it was noted that those planters who carefully looked after these details had no difficulty in holding their laborers.

In regard to lynching as a cause of migration from Georgia, it is not easy to state exactly its effect on the movement, because the lynchings which occurred immediately before and during the migration were in the boll-weevil section where the economic conditions were also at their worst. Nevertheless, several planters whose premises were crossed by lynching parties held that their losses in regard to labor were heavier than those of the surrounding plantations because of the state of terror into which their tenants had been thrown by these lawless bands. In two instances occurring respectively in 1915 and 1916, in the boll-weevil section of this State, moreover, lynching parties killed not only the guilty Negroes but also others who were innocent. In another instance the mob, after murdering the criminal and terribly beating and terrorizing many others not implicated in the crime, proceeded across the county and killed the mother and another relative of the accused. These bloody deeds had the effect of developing in the Negroes a feeling of insecurity of life and thus caused them to seek the North as a place of refuge.

Another reason why Negroes left Georgia was the resentment of the minor injustices done to them in the courts. In this State, and in a number of others as well, there prevails a system whereby the county and police officials are compensated by a fee for their services, that is, they are paid so much a head for every man they arrest. The effect of this system is to render these officials overzealous in rounding up Negroes for gambling, drinking and other petty infractions of the law. As punishment for these small violations of the law Negroes are usually sentenced to work on the county roads for certain periods of time. In the rural districts where recreational facilities are wretchedly poor, Negroes feel themselves justified in indulging in these things as means of amusement and, therefore, when they are arbitrarily arrested and severely punished therefor, they feel that gross injustice has been done to them.

The poor educational facilities in Georgia, furthermore, were a source of dissatisfaction which caused many to leave. A recent report on the educational conditions in the State showed that the per capita expenditure in public school teachers' salaries for each white child between six and fourteen years of age is about six times the per capita expenditure for each Negro child between the same ages. It is also a fact that up to 1917 the only provision made by the State for agricultural, industrial, high and normal schools was an appropriation of $8,000 as an aid to the Georgia State Agricultural and Mechanical School, which is largely supported by Federal funds. The Negro teachers, moreover, are poorly trained and their salaries are unusually small.[65]

The causes for Negro migration from Mississippi[66] are significant. In the first place, there was in southeast and east Mississippi a lack of capital for carrying labor through the fall and early winter until time to start a new crop. This lack of capital was brought about by one or more of three causes, namely, a succession of short crops, the more recent advent of the boll-weevil, and a destructive storm in the summer of 1916. In the second place, there was a reorganization of agriculture behind the boll-weevil ravage, which required a smaller number of laborers a hundred acres. In the next place, migration was due to the hunger wages paid in this State. The wages ranged from seventy-five cents on farms in the southwest to one dollar or one dollar and a quarter a day in northern counties. These were wholly inadequate to maintain the Negro laborers in a high state of physical efficiency. The attractions of the Northern urban and industrial centers too were also causes of the movement from Mississippi. These attractions were of two kinds, namely, (1) decidedly higher wages for unskilled labor, and (2) better living conditions, such as housing, which seemed superior to the rough cabins of Southern plantations, better chances of obtaining justice in the courts in cases where both whites and Negroes were involved, better schools than Mississippi afforded, and equality of treatment in public conveyances such as street cars and railway trains.

In the foregoing pages we have noted the causes of the migration from three of the Southern States. Here we desire to pursue this line of thought a bit farther, though, we hope, not at the risk of monotony, in order to emphasize these causes in such a manner as to give an impression of what was in general back of this movement from all the states involved. In this regard we are to be guided by the testimonies of Mr. W. T. B. Williams, who, under the direction of the U. S. Department of Labor, made a general survey of the conditions which gave rise to this Negro exodus.

One cause of the migration which seemed to have been general was low wages. Small pay was indeed one of the leading grievances of the Negroes. Up to 1917 on Southern farms common laborers received from fifty cents to seventy-five cents, and rarely a dollar, a day. The wages for women and children were thirty-five and forty cents a day. It is true, in some instances, meals were given with these wages, but oftener this was not the case. The following examples are typical of the wages for common laborers in such industries as saw-mills and cotton oil mills:

Newbern, N. C.	$1.00 to $1.50.[67]
Americus, Ga.	1.25
Jackson, Miss.	1.25 to 1.75.
Laurel, Miss.	1.65 to 2.00.
Hattiesburg, Miss.	1.40 to 1.65.

There were, moreover, serious unsatisfactory farming conditions which did much to drive the Negroes from the South.[68] One of these was the injustice done to tenants by their landlords. The custom was for the tenant to furnish the stock, plant, cultivate and gather the crop, and to receive in return one-half of everything, except the cotton seed, which was by far the most important part of the crop, and of which he received nothing. When the crop was made the tenant could not sell it, because the law of the State gave only the landlord a clear title to any cotton which was sold. In order to hold the Negro to the land the landlord often employed this legal advantage by selling the whole crop and refusing to settle with the Negro till late in the spring, when the next crop had

503

been well started. Then, the Negro was well attached to the farm and was forced to accept anything or any terms which the landlord chose to offer. In some cases Negroes dared not ask any settlement for fear of bringing down upon them the wrath of their landlords. In other instances often the landlords made no settlement and arbitrarily dismissed the whole matter by telling the Negroes that they were in debt.

Another general grievance growing out of unsatisfactory farming conditions was the exorbitant rates of interest charged Negro farmers by merchants and planters for money borrowed to aid them in raising their crops. The system of lending sums of money was thus: The tenant would contract for a money loan from the first of January, but he received no money till the first of March and none after the first of August. Notwithstanding this, the Negro tenant was compelled to pay interest on the whole amount borrowed for the entire year and sometimes even for the extra months up to the time of the deferred settlement. This practice became so common and so obnoxious that the Comptroller of the Treasury of the United States declared to the Southern banks that it was usury and threatened the closing of these banks if this practice was continued. That this practice was a fact and had been long-standing the words of a prominent Southern man will show. "There is money in farming," says he, "lots of it, but the Negro farmer has been systematically robbed by the white man since the close of the Civil War. If the Negro farmers were to be returned all the interest in excess of 8 per cent charged them for money advanced them they would to-day be living in brownstone mansions, just as the rich white advancers do."[69]

Rough and cruel treatment of Negroes by whites, moreover, was also an important driving cause behind the recent exodus from the South. It is reported that this sort of treatment was meted out to Negroes in many of the small towns and villages; but it was more prevalent and worse on the farms and plantations. On the latter, especially in the lower part of the South, the beating or flogging of laborers was such a common occurrence that these places came to be considered veritable peon camps. Besides, in many of the saw-mill establishments overseers and bosses were accustomed to knock Negroes around with pieces of timber or anything else that happened to be within their reach at the needy time. This brought on much dissatisfaction and caused the Negroes to become determined to leave at their first opportunity.

Furthermore, the Negro press was a very influential factor in aiding the movement. This, however, was not a general thing, because most of the Negro publications, for various reasons, either remained silent or spoke only in a very feeble manner concerning the exodus. Two of these publications, nevertheless, were very outspoken on the whole matter, in that they urged the Negroes to leave the South by all means. The principal one of these was edited in Chicago and its appeal was made to the most lowly class of Negroes. During 1916 its circulation increased manifold, and in some sections its work in stimulating the movement, perhaps, had more effect than that of all the labor agents put together. Knowing well the mental outfit of this class of Negroes, it pursued the policy of summing up the troubles and grievances of the Negroes, of constantly keeping them in the forefront, and of pointing out the way of escape from this unpleasant state of affairs. It continually emphasized in the most convincing ways the great advantages and opportunities which were awaiting the Negroes who would go North, and consistently omitted to mention any of the possible disadvantages that might be encountered in the new environment.

It must be noted, moreover, that a good deal of mere sentimentalism or irrational selection had much to do with the movement of many Negroes from the South. "The unusual amounts of money coming in," says an observer, "the glowing accounts from the North, and the excitement and stir of great crowds leaving, work upon the feelings of many Negroes. They pull up and follow the crowd almost without a reason. They are stampeded into action. This accounts in large part for the apparently unreasonable doings of many who give up good positions or sacrifice valuable property and good business to go North. There are also Negroes of all classes who profoundly believe that God has opened the way for them out of the restrictions and oppressions that beset them on every hand in the South; moving out is an expression of their faith."[70]

In addition to these causes already given, we could enter into a discussion of the certain unsatisfactory conditions which undoubtedly had some effect on the migration. These are poor housing, inadequate street improvement, poor sewerage, water, and light facilities, exclusion from public parks, and segregating regulations.

FOOTNOTES:

[59] Scroggs, W. O., *Jour. Pol. Econ.*, 25: 1040-41, Dec., 1917.

[60] *Ibid.*, pp. 1040-41.

[61] Dillard, J. H., Rep. U. S. Dept. of Lab., *Negro Migration*, pp. 11-12.

[62] Dillard, J. H., Rep. U. S. Dept of Lab., *Negro Migration*, pp. 58-66, Snavety, T. R.

[63] Snavely, T. R., *Negro Migration in 1916-17*, Rep. U. S. Dept. Lab., pp. 58-66.

[64] Woofter, T. J., Jr., *Negro Migration in 1916-17*, U.

S. Dept. Lab., pp. 86-89.

[65] Woofter, T. J., Jr., *Negro Migration in 1916-17*, U. S. Dept. Lab., pp. 86-89.

[66] Leavell, R. H., *Ibid.*, pp. 21-22.

[67] Williams, W. T. B., *Negro Migration in 1916-17*, Rep. U. S. Dept Lab., p. 103.

[68] What will be said from this point on through the remainder of this chapter will be based largely on information taken from the preceding reference, pp. 100-111.

[69] Robertson, W. T., Mayor of Montgomery, Ala., *Contemp. Rev.*, 114: 300, Sept., 1918.

[70] Williams, W. T. B., *Negro Migration in 1916-17*, Rep. U. S. Dept. Lab., p. 101.

CHAPTER V

THE EFFECTS OF THE NEGRO MIGRATION ON THE SOUTH

As we have noted the immensity, the make-up, and the causes of this movement, we are now justified in seeking to know something concerning its effects upon the South. If this movement had any effects upon the South, these undoubtedly must have been felt first and most in its economic interests; for, as we have seen, the majority of the migrants were laborers who left the farms and industries of this section in response to the great demand for labor in the North. That the South is almost wholly dependent on Negro labor is a truism, because for various reasons it has been unable to obtain any considerable amount of any other kind of labor. Its native white labor supply that is available to perform the menial work is considerably small, and very little of its labor force is drawn from the foreign-born element, which has been coming to this country in such large numbers during the years immediately preceding the beginning of the Great War. In 1910, when a study was made of the distribution of the immigrants to this country, it was found that 84 per cent of them were in the North, 9.7 per cent in the West, whereas only 5.4 per cent of them were in the South.[71] In 1920, 82.9 per cent of the foreign born were in the North, 10.8 per cent in the West, and only 6.3 per cent in the South. We are aware of the fact also that previous to this Negro movement there existed a surplus of Negro labor due to adverse natural conditions in certain parts of the South, and that in order to remove this excess the migration was gladly welcomed. It happened, however, that when this superfluous labor was removed, the migration

508

stream did not stop, but flowed on, and thus swept off a very large part of the labor that was necessary to carry on production on the farms and in the various other industries. We may set down labor shortage, then, as the first effect of the movement upon the South.

Although the South was in direst need of labor as a result of this movement, yet the danger therefrom was not as extensive and serious as it was once thought to be. This labor shortage did not have the effect of plunging the whole section into disaster. For the most part, real hardships were experienced only in certain sections, especially those that had contributed heavily to the movement. From the farming and industrial interests of those States struck hardest by this exodus came many objections to the movement, and these were taken as indications of losses and interruptions in these enterprises. It is said that in every State from the Carolinas to Mississippi there lay idle thousands of acres of land, which would have been put to use had labor been available. Even where good crops had been grown, in many places, there was question as to whether or not sufficient labor could be secured to harvest them.[72] Again, in some instances, industries like farming had been completely paralyzed; in others they had been greatly retarded, owing to the necessity of breaking in new men to occupy the places of experienced workers who had left for the North. The lumber mills, mines, docks, and cotton oil mills all suffered from the effects of labor shortage.[73]

As far as this lack of labor affected the South, these facts indicate what was true in a general way; but in order to obtain a better view of the situation let us refer to labor shortage as it existed in a few of the States that were struck exceedingly hard by the migration. A study of the labor situation in

Mississippi[74] showed that while the supply of labor was considerably diminished by the migration, the demand for labor was altered. In some parts of the State the demand was decreased, in others it was increased. In those sections where agriculture had had time since the invasion of the boll-weevil to reorganize itself on a mixed farming basis, with the emphasis placed on the raising of livestock, the demand for labor was decreased, and the wages were lowest, because this type of farming required less laborers a hundred acres than did the old type which emphasized mainly the raising of cotton. In East Mississippi much land lay idle, but it seemed that the shortage of labor there was due to lack of capital. A heavy migration stream flowed also from South Mississippi and resulted in cutting short the labor supply of the lumber mills and docks. On the whole, labor shortage in this State was quite general, inasmuch as after the movement started employers throughout the State were forced to advance wages from 10 per cent to 25 per cent.

Shortage of labor was a serious problem in Alabama, [75] especially in those sections of the State designated the "black-belt counties." Throughout these sections during 1917 much land lay idle, partly because of the scarcity of tenants and laborers, and partly because of the reluctance of landowners, merchants, and bankers to supply the capital necessary for cultivating it. The farm demonstration agent of Dallas County reported in 1917 a reduction of 3,000 in the number of plows usually operated. In these same counties farms owned and managed by lumber companies were for the most part deserted and in many cases the crops were given very feeble attention. In all parts of the State the lumber companies complained of a serious labor shortage.

In 1917 it was reported that no acute shortage of

510

labor existed in either the rural or urban districts of Georgia, but that there could be found many instances of individual employers who needed more Negro labor. "If such labor were available," said an investigator, "from 700 to 1,200 (men) could be placed in the saw-mill and turpentine industries at $1.50 and probably $2.00 per day; perhaps 2,000 at $1.75 and $2.00 per day could be placed in shipbuilding industries; (and) from 1,500 to 2,000 could be utilized from September to December in picking cotton at $1.00, $1.50 and $1.75 per hundred pounds."[76]

In North Carolina there was a scarcity of labor before the movement got well under way. In 1916 eighty-seven counties out of a total of one hundred counties reported a shortage of labor, and in many parts of the State farmers adopted the plan of raising live-stock instead of agricultural crops. Much land lay idle, and where this was not the case there was a noted increase in the use of farm machinery to supplement the meager labor supply. Especially acute was the demand for cotton pickers. On the whole, the labor situation became so serious that average wages for Negro labor were rapidly advanced beyond those of former times.[77]

What then was the attitude of the South toward that movement? As has been seen, this Negro exodus, by causing a shortage of labor, threatened the economic well-being of many parts of the South. This being so, it is readily seen that those regions so affected could not ignore the movement. In fact, when the pressure was felt, keen interest in the whole matter was aroused and in some cases even much anxiety and apprehension were manifested. In this mood the South directed its attention to this unusual situation and resolved to meet the emergency by stopping the migration itself instead of first trying to remove its causes. In order to accomplish this it was necessary to use force, which was of two kinds, namely, (1) force in the form of moral suasion, and (2) certain devices which rest on physical strength.[78] The former weapon employed to check the movement took the form of strong and persuasive appeals on the part of Southern newspapers and Southern leaders to Negroes who were either leaving or who anticipated leaving the South. In these appeals the Negroes were told that they were better off in the South, that the southern white man was their friend and that living conditions in the North were far more difficult than those in the South. They cited as examples of this the cold climate of the North, the hard and heavy work, and asserted that even though wages in the North were high the cost of living was still higher. The Negroes, therefore, would do well to remain where they were.[79] In the employment of this weapon to check the movement the newspapers took the lead and carried on a well-organized campaign to frighten the Negroes out of the notion of leaving the South. Some papers carefully circulated false reports to the effect that many Negroes were returning to their homes because of unexpected hardships in the North. Others told of thousands of Negro men dying of cold and hunger in Northern cities, where the climate was so severe that icicles hung from one's nose and ears and one's breath actually turned to snow as it was exhaled.[80] These appeals and false reports, however, had no effect in checking the movement, and the South, therefore, was compelled to resort to more drastic means in order to achieve its end.

The first repressive move made by the South to check the movement was that against the labor agents of the North, who undoubtedly were the chief instrumentalities through which the migration was kept in operation. The method of procedure was to

512

pass laws which either regulated or prohibited the exodus of laborers through the activity of labor agents. Many States already had such laws on their statute books, and where this was the case these laws were revised or were substituted by new ones. [81] These laws usually took one of two forms, either excessive labor agents' license or requirements of State residence. These were the chief qualifications of any who desired to solicit labor to be employed outside the State so concerned. For the violation of these laws anyone was subject to arrest and upon conviction was either heavily fined or sentenced to terms of imprisonment with hard labor.

A few examples will show how these laws operated against labor agents or against any suspected of enticing labor away from the state. In Alabama, when the labor problem became very acute, laws were passed imposing heavy license fees upon labor agents. Any agent desiring to operate in that State was compelled to pay a license of $500 to the State and $250 to each county concerned. In addition, each city required of him a license of from $300 to $500. Thus the cost of soliciting labor in Alabama for each agent was upwards of $1,000. In the "black belt" counties of this state a number of labor agents caught operating in violation of these laws were convicted and heavily fined, and upon failure to pay the same were sentenced to labor on the public roads. The cities and towns of the State of Florida enacted measures requiring a very high license of labor agents and providing the penalty of imprisonment in case of failure to comply with these regulations. In Jacksonville, Florida, for instance, there was passed an ordinance which stipulated that labor agents each should pay $1,000 license fees for the privilege of recruiting labor to be sent outside of the State. The penalty for violation of this law was $600 fine and sixty days in jail.[83] Georgia also passed

513

severe laws to check the operations of labor agents. In Macon[84] the City Council set the license fee of a labor agent at $25,000, and required in addition a recommendation of said agent by ten local ministers, ten manufacturers, and twenty-five business men. In several counties of this State labor agents were arrested for violating these laws.[85] Four Southern cities and as many States brought lawsuits against a great Northern railroad for violation of the laws and ordinances regarding the soliciting of labor to be sent outside the boundaries of these respective cities and States.[86] In some instances also Negro assistants of railroad labor agents were maltreated, arrested, and heavily fined.[87] For example, at Thomasville, Georgia, a Negro and a white man were arrested on the charge of being labor agents.[88] In another case, at Sumter, South Carolina, a popular Negro minister who was found at the railroad station bidding farewell to some of his parishioners, who were leaving for the North, was arrested as a labor agent.[89]

Besides these tirades against the labor agents, drastic methods were adopted to prevent the Negroes from going North. These were resorted to mainly by the police and were so executed as to discourage movement from the South. In some cities police officers visited railroad stations, rounded up Negroes by hundreds, and took them to prison on the flimsiest sort of accusations. On the days following such arrests, however, all the Negroes who had been thus imprisoned were released.[90] An example of this is the occurrence at Savannah, Georgia, where on one occasion the police arrested and jailed every Negro who happened to be in the station regardless of where he might have been going. Sometimes, as was done once at Albany, Georgia, they destroyed the tickets of migrants who were waiting to board trains for the North.[91] At Greenville, Mississippi, it was the custom to stop

514

trains, drag Negroes therefrom, and prevent others from boarding them. Strangers were subjected to search in order to secure evidence which might prove them to be labor agents.[92] The ticket agent at Hattiesburg, Mississippi, until restrained by the general superintendent, attempted to interfere with the movement by refusing to sell tickets to Negroes desiring to leave for the North.[93] Also, the Mayor of the city of New Orleans, Louisiana, tried to check the movement by requesting the President of the Illinois Central Railroad to use his influence to stop this road from carrying Negroes to the North. To this request the President replied that, while he was opposed to the Negro migration, his road, as a common carrier, could not either refuse to sell tickets to the Negroes or fail to provide them the necessary means of transportation.[94] Moreover, many Negroes who were not migrants were subjected on every hand to arbitrary arrests on mere petty charges in order to intimidate and terrorize them.

These repressive measures apparently had no effect in checking the movement, for Negroes continued to move to the North in large numbers. When this was realized, a changed state of affairs followed. The better portion of the public opinion of those States affected by the migration condemned this policy of force as a means of stopping the exodus, on the one hand, and on the other suggested the adoption of measures which would conciliate the Negroes, and thereby remove those conditions causing them to leave the South. This was urged by some of the editors of leading newspapers, and by leaders of other social agencies interested in problems regarding the relations between the races in the South. These editors were for the most part very frank about the whole matter, and, therefore, did not hesitate to make it known that in order to check the movement there was need of a square deal for the Negro, higher

515

wages, and a more sympathetic attitude toward the aspirations and general improvement of the Negro race.[95]

The following excerpts from the editorials of a few of these papers will show what this opinion was. *The Charlotte Observer* said:

"The real thing that started the exodus lies at the door of the farmer and is easily within his power to remedy. The Negro must be given better homes and better surroundings. Fifty years after the Civil War he should not be expected to be content with the same conditions which existed at the close of the War. We cannot blame him for no longer countenancing life in the windowless cabin, nor with being discontented with the same scale of remuneration for his labor that prevailed when farmers were unable to do anything better for him."[96]

The Daily News of Jackson, Mississippi, moreover, had this to say:

"The Negro exodus is the most serious economic matter that confronts the people of Mississippi today. And it isn't worth while to sit around and cuss the labor agents either. That won't help us the least bit in getting to a proper solution. We may as well face the facts, even when the facts are very ugly and very much against us. The plain truth of the matter is the white people of Mississippi are not giving the Negro a square deal. And this applies not merely to Mississippi, but to all the other states in the South. How can we expect to hold our Negro labor when we are not paying decent living wages? Have we any right to abuse the Negro for moving to the Northern states where he is tempted by high wages when we are not paying him his worth at home?... Then, too, the Negro is not being given a square deal in the matter of education. In a majority of our rural districts especially the schools for Negro children are miserable makeshifts, the teacher often more ignorant than the pupils, little or nothing allowed for their support, and the children derive no benefits whatever.... The ugly fact remains that we have not been doing our duty by the Negro, and until we do there is no reason to hope for a better settlement of our industrial conditions."[97]

The Progressive Farmer, too, another Southern organ, was of this opinion:

"Farm labor has always commanded smaller wages in the South than in other parts of the country. In 1910, the average monthly wage of male farm laborers in the South Atlantic States was only $18.76, and in the South Central States, $20.27, while in the North Atlantic and North Central States the average exceeded $30, and in the Western States reached $44.35.... We ought to face the competition of other sections, not by taxing and mobbing labor agents, but by treating our own labor so fairly that it will be willing to stay with us."[98]

Besides these we have the opinions of two other social agencies that were also in favor of the remedy of conciliation as a means of checking the exodus. These are the University Commission on Southern Race Questions and the Southern Sociological Congress. The former advocated as a check on the movement the giving to the Negroes a larger measure of those things which human beings hold dearer than material goods.[99] In its judgment some of these things were as follows: fair treatment, opportunity to labor and enjoy the legitimate fruits of labor, assurance of even-handed justice in the courts, good educational facilities, sanitary living conditions, tolerance, and sympathy. At its annual meeting in 1917 the Southern Sociological Congress expressed the belief that the movement could be stopped, not by repression, but by cooperation between peoples of both races.[100] Most of the speakers at this gathering recommended a getting together of the leaders of the whites and the blacks so that they might discuss the situation very frankly and thereby work out plans to ensure the Negro a square deal and a man's chance in the South.

These preceding views, however, were not at all the general opinion regarding the remedies to check the migration, for there was another element, representing the old South, which did not consider them with any degree of favor. It viewed the movement as a specific and temporary thing, and held that had there been no floods during 1916, and if the boll-weevil had not ravaged the cotton plantations, there would have been no migration, for the Negroes

517

never would have been induced to go North. It alleged that the Negroes did not want more money, if the getting of it meant harder work; and that what the Negro needed was a soft climate. It also asserted that the relations between the two races were never so good as they were then. Hence this element favored standing aloof and allowing the movement to stop of its own accord.[101]

Notwithstanding this view of the situation, there prevailed the opinion that the remedy for checking the exodus lay in the adoption of those measures promotive of sympathy and kindness, and forthwith plans were effected with the aim of inducing the Negroes to remain and of inviting others who had departed to return to the South. The following are some of the chief measures which were adopted to achieve this end: (1) A general and substantial increase in wages; (2) movement on the part of the farmers to deal more fairly in business matters with the Negro tenants by making clear at the outset the terms of all contracts, and by keeping strict accounts and making prompt settlements with them; (3) the correcting of certain former abuses such as short weighing of coal, discounting of store checks, and unfair prices in the commissaries; (4) instituting of crop diversification in order to keep the laborers supplied with work the year round; (5) better housing; (6) better school conditions; and (7) the drawing closer together of the two races through the medium of county meetings for the study of problems growing out of racial relations. A typical example of this last-named policy is the "Community Congress" plan in Bolivar County, Mississippi. The essential feature of this body is a representative general committee composed of twenty-five white planters and business men, and five Negro leaders from the five supervisors' districts within the county. The function of this organization is to consider and offer solutions of any and all important problems pertaining to the community. There is, moreover, the Farm Extension Bureau of the Chamber of Commerce of Memphis, Tennessee, which was organized for the purpose of conducting educational campaigns to improve agricultural and rural conditions. This organization has extended its work from Tennessee into Mississippi and Arkansas, and has adopted the policy of employing Negroes to act as demonstrators among farmers of their own race in order to furnish the Negro farmers with greater incentive to become more skilful and industrious in their vocation.[102]

Since we have seen the attitude of the white leaders of the South toward this movement, it might also be of interest to know what was the view of the Negro leaders in regard to this exodus of their race. In the first place, many of the local leaders in the South were much opposed to this movement, but hesitated to give outward expression to this for fear of rebuke from members of their race. Hence, their policy was that of maintaining silence about the whole matter. On the other hand, the editors of some of the leading Negro papers of the South were somewhat outspoken and were more or less inclined to be in sympathy with the movement. They nevertheless expressed regrets that the Negroes were leaving the South, but this did not in the least move them to do anything to help check the movement. They took the position that the migrants had not been given justice in economic, political, and social affairs, and that, therefore, they had no just grounds on which to base appeals to them to remain in the South. In fact, in view of these adverse circumstances, they felt that the Negroes could not be blamed for moving to the North.[103]

Other leaders, however, especially those in the North, were more positive and frank as regards their attitude toward the movement. These may be roughly divided into two distinct classes, namely, the conservative and the radical. Those of the former class adhered largely to the view of Tuskegee Institute, which fosters the traditions of Booker T. Washington.[104] They advised the Negroes to remain in the South on the ground that it was there only that the Negro could become a landholder, and that there were chances for him to become a real estate owner almost at his own will. Some in this class felt also that the Great War would soon end and that after that the country would be flooded by immigrants from Europe, who would doubtless deprive thousands of Negroes of work in the North. They therefore counseled the Negroes to stay at home and to keep possession of their property, especially their property in land.

The radicals, on the other hand, who insist on equal rights for the race, boldly advised and urged the Negroes to come North. When this exodus was well under way one of the members of this class, Dr. W. E. B. Du Bois, spoke as follows: "There are not jobs for everybody; there is no demand for the lazy and casual; but trained, honest Negro laborers are welcome in the North at good wages just as they are lynched in the South for impudence. Take your choice."[105] Furthermore, others of this class, believing that immigration would not be a factor in the labor situation for a long time to come, likewise urged the Negroes to continue moving to the North. Their desire was to see the Negro population increase its size in such great proportions through this migration as to afford it the opportunity to exercise in the North economic and political power hitherto unknown. [106]

FOOTNOTES:

[71] Fairchild, H. P., *Immigration*, p. 226.

[72] Williams, W. T. B., *Negro Migration in 1916-17*, Rep. U. S. Dept. Lab., p. 98.

[73] *Ibid.*, pages 98-99.

[74] Leavell, R. H., *Negro Migration in 1916-17*, Rep. U. S. Dept. Lab., pp. 17-19.

[75] Snavely, T. R., *Negro Migration in 1916-17*, Rep. U. S. Dept. Lab., pp. 70-73.

[76] Woofter, T. J., Jr., *Negro Migration in 1916-17*,

Rep. U. S. Dept. Lab., p. 90.

[77] Snavely, T. R., *Negro Migration in 1916-17*, Rep. U. S. Dept. Lab., pp. 73-74.

[78] Baker, R. S., *World's Work*, 34: 315-16, Je., 1917.

[79] Baker, R. S., *World's Work*, 34: 315-16, Je., 1917.

[80] Horwill, H. W., *Contemp. Rev.*, 114: 302, Sept., 1918.

[81] Haynes, G. E., *Survey*, 40: 120, May 4, 1918.

[82] Snavely, T. R., *Negro Migration in 1916-17*, Rep. U. S. Dept. Lab., pp. 64-64.

[83] Scott, E. J., *Negro Migration During The War*, pp. 72-73.

[84] *Ibid.*, p. 73.

[85] Woofter, T. J., Jr., *Negro Migration in 1916-17*, Rep. U. S. Dept. Lab., p. 86.

[86] Tyson, F. D., *Negro Migration in 1916-17*, Rep. U. S. Dept. Lab., p. 121.

[87] *Ibid.*, pp. 121-23.

[88] Scott, E. J., *Negro Migration During The War*, p. 74.

[89] Williams, W. T. B., *Negro Migration in 1916-17*, Rep. U. S. Dept. Lab., p. 110.

[90] Horwill, H. W., *Contemp. Rev.*, 114: 301-302, Sept., 1918.

[91] Williams, W. T. B., *Negro Migration in 1916-17*, Rep. U. S. Dept. Lab., p. 110.

[92] Scott, E. J., *Negro Migration During The War*, p. 77.

[93] Scott, E. J., *Negro Migration During The War*, p. 77.

[94] *Ibid.*, p. 78.

[95] Dillard, J. H., *Negro Migration in 1916-17*, Rep. U. S. Dept. Lab., p. 13.

[96] Williams, W. T. B., *Negro Migration in 1916-17*, Rep. U. S. Dept. Lab., p. 104.

[97] *Ibid., pp.* 111-112.

[98] Williams, W. T. B., *Negro Migration in 1916-17*, Rep. U. S. Dept. Lab., p. 110.

[99] Min. Univ. Com. on Southern Race Questions, pp. 48-48, 1917.

[100] *Survey*, 38: 428, Aug. 11, 1917.

[101] *Living Age*, 295: 58-59, Oct. 6, 1917.

[102] *Negro Migration in 1916-17*, Rep. U. S. Dept. Lab., pp. 15-113. See topics titled as follows: "Constructive Adjustments," "Means of Checking the Exodus," "Constructive Possibilities," and "Initial Remedies."

[103] Baker, R. S., *World's Work*, 34: 316, July, 1919.

[104] *Living Age*, 295: 59, Oct. 6, 1917.

[105] *Ibid.*, p. 59.

[106] Woodson, C. G., *A Century of Negro Migration*, p. 176.

Chapter VI

THE EFFECTS OF THE NEGRO MIGRATION ON THE NORTH

As the migration had its effects upon the South, it likewise influenced conditions in the North and West; but in the latter cases these effects were somewhat different from those produced upon the former section. It is almost obvious that these two sections could hardly escape without being affected, since they were suddenly invaded by a multitude of newcomers who belonged to a race different from that of the dominant elements in their respective populations. In these places, moreover, these migrants were seeking for the most part better opportunities in order to enhance their progress in the struggle for existence, and in so doing created new situations which undoubtedly had decided effects upon these sections.

The first noted effect was a tremendous increase in the Negro population of some of the large cities and industrial centers of these sections. It is estimated that this increase in some cases ranged from one to four-fold. For example, the Negro population of Detroit, Michigan, jumped from 5,751 to 41,532 by 1920. In 1917 Pittsburgh, Pennsylvania, showed an increase of 47.1 per cent in its Negro population. During the same decade Philadelphia added 49,632 to its black population; and it is reported that 25,000 Negro migrants went to Cincinnati, Ohio,[107] and 52,000 to Chicago, Illinois.[108] The census of 1920 shows that the increase in the Negro population of Cincinnati during the preceding decade was 9,987 and that of Chicago 65,491.

Notwithstanding this, these sections were certainly

much gratified at this influx of Negroes, because it was meeting the unprecedented demand for labor. At this time the Negroes were sorely needed for economic purposes, and nothing was done to obstruct their coming in. That this was the case the following statement will show: "To-day the shutting down of immigration, due to the war," said *The New Republic*, "has created just such a demand for the Negroes. Colored men who formerly loafed on street corners are now regularly employed. Negro girls who found it once difficult to obtain good jobs at domestic service have leaped into popularity. The market for labor has taken up all the slack. There is a demand for all, for skilled workers, unskilled, semi-employables, Negroes. The employment agencies cannot meet the demand. Construction camps which formerly relied on Italian or Polish laborers now seek to secure an alternative supply of Negroes. Formerly the big contractor in the North could pick a few hunkies from a long line of eager applicants for work. He could get Poles, Italians, Greeks, in any number.... To-day he is willing to take black men, and finds it hard to get even them."[109]

This most unusual demand for labor, coupled with the necessity of having to be met wholly by thousands of Negroes from the South, wrought a considerable change in the labor mores of the North. In its employment of these laborers the North was compelled to adopt a policy hitherto unknown. On this point let us proceed by referring to the following testimony. "Until recently," said a contributor to *The Living Age*, "the Negro in the northern cities was restricted to certain occupations that are unskilled and outside the range of organized labor. To-day he is being welcomed on the farms of New England and the Middle West and in the industrial centers, where hitherto the employer has not wanted him and the white workman has regarded him as a dangerous intruder. In Chicago, Cincinnati, Pittsburgh and many other cities large numbers of Negroes are found in factories and workshops where until lately the Negro laborer was never admitted even as a visitor. This is especially true of the iron and steel works and the factories, while many thousands have been absorbed by the railroads and street railway companies."[110]

While the North was very desirous of the Negro migrants in order to utilize their labor, moreover, it was, nevertheless, ill-prepared to provide them proper dwelling places. The rush of the Negro laborers to this section suddenly overtaxed the capacity of the habitations alloted to Negroes, thus causing a demand for houses which far exceeded the supply. The result of this was the bringing on the hands of the North a serious housing problem which required immediate solution. The railroads were the first to attempt to meet the situation by adopting the method of erecting camps to house the large number of single men who had been imported from the South. These roads were the Pennsylvania, Baltimore and Ohio, New York Central, and Erie. The camps constructed by the Pennsylvania were wooden sheds covered with tar paper and equipped with sanitary cots, heat, bath, toilet and wash-room facilities, separate eating room and commissary. This road built thirty-five such camps, each capable of accommodating forty men. The camps of the other railroads consisted of freight cars and passenger coaches converted into sleeping and eating quarters for the men. In some cases old houses were renovated and used for the same purposes. Camps were also used by the large steel companies of Pennsylvania to house their workers. These were largely old barns and old houses which were transformed into living quarters. They were reported to be inferior to the railroads' camps in matters of equipment and sanitation.[111]

The most difficult part of this housing question, however, was that of community housing, the problem of supplying men with families with adequate living quarters. An investigation of the housing conditions among migrants of this type in twenty cities of the North and West showed that everywhere this problem was very acute. In few cities, where the Negro migrants were mixed in with the whites, the former were provided with fairly satisfactory housing conditions, but were compelled to pay comparatively high rents for least desirable quarters. Exceptions, nevertheless, were found in these places where the invasion of white districts by Negro families had resulted in the moving out of the white residents. Here, very desirable houses for Negroes were available, but at rental rates far in advance of those formerly paid by the whites.[112] The small number of available houses and the high rents asked for the same, moreover, caused the Negroes to locate themselves within restricted bounds of habitation which resulted in a great deal of overcrowding among them. There were found numerous cases in which there were too many persons for each room and too many for each bed. Instances in this regard will be cited farther on in this dissertation.

Another effect of the Negro migration was that of increasing the friction between races in certain parts of the North and West. This effect, however, was not as extensive as it was once thought to be; for in many instances Negroes worked and lived peaceably side by side with the whites. Nevertheless, there were found numerous cases in which racial friction operated to bring about strained relations between the two social groups. These manifested themselves in the form of refusals on the part of some employers to hire Negroes, because white laborers objected to working with black men, and in the form of emphatic protests of white residents of certain industrial towns

527

—especially in the steel districts of Pennsylvania—against the bringing in of Negroes to live among them. This neighborhood prejudice existed also in a number of the cities of the North and West, and was, no doubt, the source of much of the trouble between the races.[113] The most bitter form of racial friction occasioned through the migration was that which grew out of economic rivalry and competition for jobs. This competition was brought about by a policy pursued by Northern employers, the practice of deliberately importing Negro laborers from the South to replace white workers who went on strike. This naturally served to fan the flames of hatred of the white workers against the Negroes, and actual expressions of this were seen in the serious race riots which followed.

An example of a race riot which grew out of this economic competition was that which occurred in Philadelphia, during the early part of 1917.[114] There the white workers in a large sugar refinery went on strike, whereupon the owners of the plant attempted to break the strike by the use of Negro laborers. The latter were attacked violently by the displaced white laborers, and the result was a race riot in the course of which one Negro was killed, and several others were wounded. It is said that the whites resented this substitution of Negro labor for theirs, because the former was being used to keep down wages and thus destroy unionism.

Another typical example of such a race riot is that which took place in East St. Louis, Illinois, in July, 1917, during which more than a hundred Negroes were shot or maimed. Many of them were fatally wounded, five thousand of them were driven from their homes, and several hundred thousand dollars worth of property was destroyed. The origin and cause of this little racial war seemed to have been this: In 1916, 4,000 white men employed in the packing plants went on strike and, in retaliation, the employers of these plants brought in Negroes to work in the places of the strikers. When the strike ended, during the following year, Negroes were still retained as employees in these plants, whereas many whites, who struck, were refused their former jobs. The trade unions then realized the power in this vast resource of imported labor, and, therefore, took steps to check it by appealing to the city authorities to restrain employers from transporting Negroes from the South. In their appeal they threatened to take action themselves if the city officials did not do so. It happened that the latter failed to act, and, therefore, the unionists and their sympathizers, true to their threat, took complete control of the situation and resorted to mob law as a means of solving the problem.[115]

Besides these preceding cases, other riots occurred, but these were due to causes other than economic competition. One of these, which took place in Chester, Pennsylvania, in 1917, seemed to have been due to natural friction and conflicts between the worst elements of both groups in the community.[116] During the same year, Homestead, Pennsylvania, barely escaped a race riot due to ill feeling between the two groups which had been brewing for some time.[117] In Newark, New Jersey, there was a race riot in which four men were wounded, probably fatally, while thirty-three others received slight wounds. This outbreak was of such magnitude that 150 police reserves were required to quell it. It has been reported that it was precipitated by a fight which resulted from a dispute over the amount of money wagered in a dice game conducted by men of both races.[118] There were riots during the summer of 1919, in Washington, D. C., Chicago, Illinois, and Omaha, Nebraska; but it is difficult to say to what extent the recent exodus was responsible for these outbreaks. It seems highly probable, however, that the great increase in the white population of Washington and in the Negro population in Chicago, respectively, as a result of movements of our population, contributed much towards intensifying the ill feelings already existing between the two groups.

Furthermore, the coming of the Negroes to the North in such large numbers and their employment in trades and industries hitherto closed to them brought to the front the old problem of the Negro and the labor unions. With few exceptions, the Negroes have generally been barred from membership in the unions on account of race prejudice; and this has especially been the case in the North where the unions are oldest and most powerful and influential in labor affairs. Here white union laborers have manifested their prejudice by repeatedly refusing to work with Negro employés. This naturally prevented employers from utilizing Negro labor, and the outcome of this policy was to exclude the Negroes from the better paying positions and to push them almost wholly into those avocations which are unskilled or unsettled.[119] The Negroes have thus been forced into positions where generally they must work for less pay than the unionists, and because of this the latter have branded Negro laborers as "scabs," notwithstanding the fact that the doors of the unions were closed to them. Unwilling to bear this stigma, which made them an object of contempt in the eyes of trades unionists, Negro workers made efforts to organize themselves and drew up petitions requesting admission into the unions. These efforts, however, have been again and again made fruitless by the local labor unions which discriminate against men on account of race and color. When this matter has been referred to the national and international councils these latter bodies have held that their constitutions recognize no such discriminations, but at the same time acknowledged their inability to control these local unions. These locals, therefore, have been a great obstacle to the unionization of Negroes.[120]

Evidently this decree of the American Federation of Labor was not obeyed by all its affiliated internationals, because at its next annual meeting, held in Montreal, Canada, June, 1920, the question of Negro admittance to membership in unions figured as a conspicuous part of its proceedings. On this occasion the discussion of this question arose out of allegations made by delegates, mainly Negroes from Northern States, which accused the Brotherhood of Railway Clerks (whose constitution provides for white membership only) of having refused membership to Negro freight handlers, express and station employees. At the same time, demands were made to the effect that the Federation should change this state of affairs. The tense moments of the convention were reached when the Organization Committee, to whom the matter had been referred, submitted a non-concurrence report, taking the position that the Federation had no authority over the constitution of an affiliated union. This report naturally evoked a very heated controversy between the Negro delegates and their white sympathizers and those whites who were opposed to giving Negroes membership in the labor unions. The Federation, however, rejected this report, and for the first time in its history threatened the autonomy of an affiliated union by first demanding, by several motions, that the Brotherhood of Railway Clerks abolish the color line in its constitution or forfeit its charter in the Federation. None of these drastic motions prevailed. Finally, a modified motion, requesting, rather than demanding, this brotherhood to eliminate from its constitution the words "white only" and give the Negro freight handlers, express and station employees full membership, was carried.

Following the adoption of this motion, Chairman Duncan spoke thus, "This, I believe, will settle the Negro problem in our organization for all time. Our affiliated unions must now understand that the color line is abolished."[121]

This second act of the American Federation of Labor is, indeed, another step forward in its efforts to settle the problem of the Negro and the unions; but that it will settle this problem for all time is very doubtful. Certainly, there are great obstacles in the way of an early solution of it. Chief of all these obstructions is the force of racial prejudice, which has demonstrated again and again that in spite of laws to the contrary it is powerful enough to devise and put into effect plans whereby its desires may be accomplished. Furthermore, when one considers the structure and foundation of the American Federation of Labor he wonders whether it has authority over its affiliated unions sufficient to compel them to abide by its decrees. The American Federation of Labor is a loose federation of national and international unions—a federation of independent unions. Each national or international, though it receives its charter from the federation, is autonomous, free to withdraw from the federation, and it possesses all the machinery necessary for an independent existence. To this end, it is self-governing, having its own constitution which grants it vast powers. Local unions and other subordinate organizations are created by it. By means of charters and constitutional provisions it actually determines membership and membership conditions and privileges, the functions of locals, their officers and duties, the discipline of the members, and the general conduct of the affairs of the local. Thus, while theoretically the local union is the economic unit of unionism, practically the national or international is the unit, for it and not the local is of primal importance in the American Federation of Labor.

On the other hand, the powers of the American Federation of Labor, though very broad and potent, do not seem to have scope and force enough to permit this body to interfere with much effect in the local affairs of the national or international unions, because of the large degree of sovereignty possessed by these organizations. These bodies, therefore, are at liberty to do things which often are detrimental to the best interests of trades unionism. Here, then, it is seen that the great obstructions to Negro membership in the unions are not the locals but rather the national or international unions, because the locals are entirely responsible to the latter bodies, which are in turn accountable to the Federation. The American Federation of Labor is, therefore, confronted with the difficult task of compelling its nationals or internationals which discriminate against Negroes to change their constitutions and grant Negro laborers full membership in their unions. Can it or will it exert sufficient pressure on these organizations to bring this to pass? Its most potent coercive measure is the revoking of a union's charter, and the question is will it have the courage to employ this weapon to secure economic justice for the Negro, or will it hesitate to do so? By its action at its last annual meeting, when it preferred to request the Brotherhood of Railway Clerks to eliminate racial discrimination from its constitution and give the Negroes membership in its unions, rather than demand it to do so or forfeit its charter, the American Federation of Labor indicated that either it was doubtful of the extent of its authority over its affiliated international unions or that it is as yet unwilling to deal sternly with them.

Despite these difficulties, the Negro laborers are not giving up the fight for their admittance into the unions. In various ways they are still opposing these forces which are barring them from these organizations. In the meantime they are availing themselves of the aid of certain Negro social agencies which have undertaken to supply the Negro workers with that industrial leadership which they lack by being outside the labor unions. These agencies are the Young Men's Christian Association, Young Women's Christian Association, and the National Urban League. These bodies function through their respective industrial secretaries in cities of the North and West. These agencies aim to serve the Negro laborers by investigating and cultivating new avenues of employment, to stand as a buffer between them and the white unions and furnish the leadership usually exercised by trades unionism by taking up the Negro's grievances directly with the management. That these objects may be accomplished these organizations have adopted certain methods of procedure. Most of them operate free employment offices through which from several hundred to two thousand laborers are placed per month. The Chicago, Detroit, Cleveland, and Pittsburgh branches of the National Urban League, and the Indianapolis, Cincinnati, and Columbus Y. M. C. A. branches render still broader service by studying the demand for labor and by endeavoring to persuade employers to use Negroes in new capacities. They try also to aid men to make good on the job by appealing to race pride, by holding noon shop-meetings, and by stimulating the companies to cultivate friendly relationship between labor and the management. These bodies, by acting as mediators in labor disputes, moreover, have been successful in averting or settling a number of minor strikes.[122]

Finally, if by some means the American Federation of Labor should succeed in compelling its affiliated unions to abolish the color line in their respective constitutions and admit the Negro to full membership in their unions, the Negro will be granted a right long denied him, the right of working on terms of equality with the other race, if he can demonstrate his competence to do so. It will give him a chance to enter all of the skilled and therefore better paid trades and the opportunity to be judged on his merits in them. If this barrier of race discrimination is thoroughly broken down, moreover, there will be open to the Negro paths long closed to him, the effect of which cannot fail to elevate to an appreciable degree his status in the industrial world. Then, by enjoyment of this right, the Negro will no longer in effect be excluded from the higher type of occupations and pushed into those commonly regarded as menial and held in disdain.[123]

FOOTNOTES:

[107] Haynes, G. E., *Survey*, 40: 116, May 4, 1918.

[108] White, W. F., *The Crisis*, 19: 113, Jan., 1920.

[109] *New Republic*, 7: 213, July 1, 1916.

[110] *Living Age*, 295: 58, Oct. 6, 1917.

[111] Tyson, F. D., *Negro Migration in 1916-17*, Rep. U. S. Dept. Lab., pp. 145-48.

[112] Kingsley, H. M., *The Negro Migration*, Rep. Home Missions Council, Jan., 1919.

[113] Tyson, F. D., *Negro Migration in 1916-17*, Rep. U. S. Dept. Lab., p. 129.

[114] Tyson, F. D., *Negro Migration in 1916-17*, Rep. U. S. Dept. Lab., pp. 129-30.

[115] Tyson, F. D., *Negro Migration in 1916-17*, Rep. U. S. Dept. Lab., pp. 130-31.

[116] *Ibid.*, pp. 131-32.

[117] *Ibid.*, p. 133.

[118] *New York Times*, Sept. 4, 1917, 7: 1.

[119] Bryce, James, *The American Commonwealth*, 1916 ed., p. 549.

[120] Jones, E. K., *The Negro in Industry*, pp. 2-3.

[121] Hoxie, R. F., *Trade Unionism in the U. S.*, pp. 112-135.

[122] Woofter, T. J., Jr., "The Negro and Industrial Peace," *Survey*, 45: 491, Dec. 18, 1920.

[123] *New York Times*, June 16, 1919, 12: 5.

Chapter VII

THE EFFECTS OF THE MIGRATION UPON THE MIGRANTS THEMSELVES

We pass on now to the study of the effects of the movement upon the migrants themselves, or to a consideration of the behavior of the Negroes under the existing economic and social conditions in the new environment. This obviously involves an examination into the results of the efforts exerted by the newcomers in order to become adjusted to their new surroundings. In this regard the thing that was primal and most fundamental was the economic interest, or the interest of self-maintenance, which, as has been shown, was the most powerful force operating to draw the Negroes to the North. This interest was satisfied by the admittance of the Negroes in large numbers into lines of work hitherto closed to them; but these were for the most part unskilled occupations. It is estimated that of the thousands of Negroes who moved North about 90 per cent of them were engaged in unskilled work and that the other 10 per cent performed either semi-skilled or skilled labor. [124] This was especially true of the Negro workers who were employed in the large steel plants in the State of Pennsylvania. In the larger establishments of this sort almost fully 100 per cent of them did common labor, while in some of the smaller plants a few were sometimes found doing labor which required some skill. When employers were asked why this was the case they generally replied in a two-fold manner: first, the Negro migrants were inefficient and unstable; and secondly, the opposition on the part of white laborers to work with Negroes prohibited their employment of them to do skilled work.[125]

What has just been said sums up very briefly the whole situation regarding the efforts of Negroes to maintain themselves in the North. We wish, however, to continue this in a more specific way by making a little survey of the occupations and wages of Negro migrants in a few of the cities of the North and West. Although accurate information in this respect is meagre, yet that which will be given is undoubtedly authoritative, being based on specific studies of the labor and wage conditions of the newcomers in the cities named and which, therefore, may also be regarded as typical of the same conditions in most of the other cities not herein considered. The advanced reports of the Federal census of 1920 contain as yet no information of this sort and there were so many changes between 1918 and 1920 that it is still difficult to describe these conditions accurately.

The occupations and wages of these migrants throw further light on the situation. In Pittsburgh it was found that of 493 migrants who stated their occupations, 95 per cent were engaged in unskilled labor in the steel mills, the building trades, on the railroads, or were acting as servants, porters, janitors, cooks, and cleaners. Of this same number only 4 per cent were employed at what might be called semi-skilled or skilled work such as puddlers, mold-setters, painters, and carpenters. A further study revealed that out of 529 laborers only 59 had been doing skilled work in the South, and that of the rest a very large number had been rural workers.[126] While most of the workers were engaged in unskilled labor, their wages nevertheless were much in advance of those they had received in the South. These wages were as follows: 62 per cent of the workers received from $2 to $3 per day; 28 per cent received from $3 to $3.60 per day; and 5 per cent over $3.60 per day. The other 5 per cent of them received less than $2 per day, which was the same wage they had worked

538

for before coming North.[127]

This same investigation also brought out the fact that many of these migrants were exercising a good deal of economy and thrift. For example, 15 per cent of 162 families had savings, 80 per cent of 139 married men with their families elsewhere were sending money home, and nearly 100, or 46 per cent of 219 single men interviewed were contributing to the support of parents, sisters or other relatives. Most of these contributions amounted each to about $5 per week. Fifty-two persons were remitting from $5 to $10 per week, while seven were sending home over $10 per week.[128]

In Detroit where Negroes were hired largely by automobile firms or by firms making parts or accessories of automobiles, some interesting conditions were observed. The large majority of those so engaged did unskilled work, whereas only a very small number were found in the skilled or semi-skilled work. Also a very large number of men and women obtained employment as domestic and personal servants. For example, during a period of one year, ending November 15, 1917, one Negro employment office in this city secured jobs for 10,000 Negro workers, both men and women. In addition, the wages paid these laborers were found to be very satisfactory. A careful study of 194 workers showed that their monthly wages ran thus: One received between $30 and $39, three between $40 and $49, six between $60 and 69, twenty-nine between $70 and $79, and ninety-six between $80 and $89, six between $90 and $99, and twenty-seven between $100 and $119, twenty-one between $120 and $129, and four $140 or more, a month. The other one of this number received a wage of $6 per day. Hence the prevailing wages of colored male workers in Detroit were from $70 to about $119 per month, since the wages of 159 of the 194 interviewed ranged between these two amounts. The prevailing wage for women was $2 per day.[129]

In 1917 a study was made of the living conditions of seventy-five families who had moved North to Chicago and who had been in this city one year. The investigation discovered that the heads of these families were employed in stockyards, Pullman service, loading cars, fertilizer plants, railroad shops, cleaning of cars and taxis, junk business, box and dye factories, foundries and hotels, steel mills, as porters, in wrecking companies, in bakeries, and in the making of sacks. Inquiry into the wage conditions of sixty-six of these workers showed that four were earning less than $12 per week, twenty-two from $12 to $14.99 per week; twenty-seven were receiving $15 per week, and five between $15 and $20 per week. Of the remaining number three were ill and five were unemployed.[130]

Shortly after the Negro migration had begun, The Associated Colored Employees of America, with headquarters in New York City, came into existence for the purpose of helping Negro misfits in Northern industries, and also to secure a proper distribution of Negro labor both in the South and in the North. This organization discovered that 2,083 Negro men and women in New York City were engaged in twelve different occupations, but that only one was employed at his calling. The rest of them were rendering menial service as porters, elevator operators, chauffeurs, waiters, common laborers, and so on. The females were employed as chambermaids, waitresses, and as workers in other unskilled occupations. Many of these workers were graduates of Hampton, Tuskegee and other industrial schools of the South, and most of them had been attracted to the North by promises of better wages, better

540

schools and better living conditions than could be obtained in the South. Although no statement was made regarding the wages they were receiving, it is at once obvious that by being in these unskilled positions these migrants were not earning what they would have earned had they been employed at jobs of the higher type.[131]

Because of the varied and extensive industrial activities and the great demands for labor, many migrants were attracted to the State of New Jersey, and especially to the city of Newark. It is estimated that 6,000 male and 1,000 female workers were employed in the several industries of this city.[132] The male laborers were largely engaged in the ammunition plants where they received an average wage of $2.60 per day.[133] They were also employed to a great extent in the unskilled work in chemical plants, transportation, trucking, shipyard work, leather factories, iron molding, foundries, construction and team driving.[134] The females found employment in toy factories, shirt factories, clothing factories, and glue factories at an average wage of about $8 per week. In the shell-loading plants and piecework occupations, however, their wages were much higher. Besides, work was supplied them in tobacco factories, celluloid manufacturing plants, food production, leather-bag making and trunk manufacture, and in assorting cores in foundries.[135]

A survey of the labor and wage conditions among the migrants in the city of Hartford indicated that the males were employed in the factories and foundries and that most of them were doing unskilled work, although here and there a few were doing skilled work. Some had shown, moreover, that they possessed the capacity and energy sufficient to establish enterprises of their own as means of self-maintenance, for there were found among them a first-class restaurant, fine barber shops, first-class shoe shop, six grocery stores and three tailor shops for cleaning, pressing and repairing; and each enterprise was doing a thriving business. The wages of those working in the factories and foundries were $4 per day. The females, on the other hand, were employed mostly in domestic service, and their average wage was $9 or $10 per week. The girls and a few of the women were employed in the department stores as helpers and cleaners at wages ranging from $7 to $9 per week. About 250 of them were employed also as tobacco strippers and received wages of from $10 to $12 per week. Besides, the working conditions, on the whole, were reported to be very satisfactory.[138]

Most of the Negroes who were employed in the foregoing instances had been former employees in the cotton, tobacco, rice, sugar cane, turpentine and lumber industries of the South. Their coming to the North in search of work suddenly forced them into factories, foundries, ammunition plants, automobile establishments, packing industries, and into various other forms of work which were entirely different from those to which they had been accustomed at home. Attached to these occupations was a set of mores, wholly new to the Negroes, and with which they had, first of all, to make themselves familiar. It goes almost without saying, therefore, that at the beginning the Negroes experienced much difficulty in trying to adjust themselves to these new labor conditions. Among these newcomers, moreover, there were two types of laborers, namely, those who were intelligent, industrious, and thrifty. In this class were many students and men with responsibilities, who had been carefully selected by the labor agents. The second type was composed of men who had been picked up promiscuously and transported to the North. These were for the most part single men and in habits were shiftless and undependable; and in numbers this class far exceeded the former type. It will, therefore, be of interest to know what was the behavior of the Negroes in the various industries in which they were employed.

The performance of the Negroes in this regard is well seen in the railroad and steel industries which employed many thousands of them. In these we find that the deportment of the Negro workers was such as to cause a great deal of labor turn-over. This was due largely to the fact that these concerns hired mostly single men who were shiftless and given to wandering from place to place. For example, the Pennsylvania Railroad, in 1917, after a year of importation of thousands of Negroes from the South had less than 2,000 in its employ. The Baltimore and Ohio and New York Central roads, after having done likewise, had less than 1,000 Negroes occupied. Each of these roads experienced a demand for labor and was trying to fill the depleted ranks by further importations from the South. Again, in 1917, the Erie Railroad reported that among 9,000 Negroes brought from the South during a period of six or seven months a full labor turn-over occurred every eleven days. Of this number only the first two thousand remained long enough to work out the transportation that had been furnished them. In most of these cases the Negroes, after reaching the North, remained in the railroad camps only long enough to draw a first pay or until they learned of the opportunity for higher wages in other fields. Sometimes they would not wait even long enough to try the work and quarters after their transportation had been paid, but would start at once for other places.[139]

The steel mills in Pennsylvania, like the railroads, also found it difficult to keep a stable Negro labor force. At the Coatesville Midvale plant it was necessary to bring

543

in 150 new workers each week in order to keep the labor force up to the normal standard. This same plant was compelled to hire from 2,500 to 2,800 men a month to keep a steady force of 5,500 employed, and the turn-over was twice as great among the Negro as among the white workers. The Carnegie steel plant at Youngstown reported that 9,000 or 10,000 Negroes had been hired and that in the meantime it was necessary to keep hiring five men to have every two jobs filled. Even other plants paying the highest wages, moreover, were compelled to hire 200 or more per month in order to keep up a force of 600 men.[140] They would not stay in one place any length of time, but continued to move in search of better wages and accommodations. They could not be persuaded in many cases to wait until pay-day for their earnings, but would not be content if they could not get some of it in advance according to their custom in this regard in the South. In behalf of this they offered the most flimsy pretexts, and often spent this money for very unwholesome things.[141]

Thus, in 1917, it was concluded that the Negroes were not as yet adapted to the heavy and pace-set work in the steel mills, that they were accustomed to the easy-going plantation and farm work of the South, and that it would take them some time to become adjusted. It seemed that the roar and clangor of the mills made the Negroes a little dazed and confused.

In the city of Detroit the actions of the Negroes in the industries were highly pleasing to some of the employers, whereas to others they were just the reverse. The employers held two lines of adverse criticism against the Negro as a workman. In the first place, they complained that the Negro was too slow; that he did not have the speed which the routine of efficient industry demands; and that he lacked that regularity demanded by the routine of industry day by day. In the second place, the Negro was disinclined to work out-of-doors when the cold weather set in; and, in this respect, he was considered unsatisfactory, because his labor could be depended upon only at certain seasons of the year.[142]

Reports from Newark, New Jersey, likewise showed that the Negroes were having trouble in adjusting themselves to the new conditions. The female migrants manifested an unadaptability to housework, being accustomed to outdoor work on the farms. In factories and freight-yards men and boys when overheated would throw off their outer clothing just as they would in the mild South, with the consequence that they were often attacked by grip and pneumonia. The unaccustomed roads and pavements and long hours of toil caused the migrants to lose many days' work. In fact, outdoor work was attended with so many hardships that the Negroes began to apply only for indoor work. Again, it is said that the fumes in munition factories made many of them temporarily ill, thus necessitating their seeking other work even at lower wages. Explosions in ammunition plants, moreover, threw many out of work and frightened away many more to other occupations which seemed more secure. Thus, these difficulties and hardships attached to their new jobs together with the strangeness of their surroundings caused the Negroes to be very irregular in the performance of their work.[143]

Mr. Eugene K. Jones, the executive secretary of an organization interested in the economic and social welfare of the Negroes in Northern cities, affirms that the testimony of many of the employers was to the effect that the Negroes were rather inexperienced, frequently undependable, and were of a roaming nature, being easily tempted to change their places of

545

employment on account of such inducements as small increases in wages, shorter hours, and easier work. Nevertheless, he takes the position that enough testimony is available to show conclusively that Negro labor in the North, on the whole, was extremely promising. This position is taken on the following grounds: (1) That the Negroes were loyal to their employers; (2) that they took a proprietary interest in their employers' plants; (3) they did not either strike or become easily inflamed against their employers; (4) they were tractable; and (5), above all, most of the Negroes who proved unreliable did so because they had no hope on the job, or because they had been chosen from a group of idle loafers in some Southern city or community where real opportunity for training for the Negro is unknown.[144]

Next in importance among the efforts of the migrants to adjust themselves to the Northern environment was that of securing shelter. It has already been shown that the housing of the newcomers developed into a very serious problem and that unusual steps had to be taken in order to meet the emergency. It was indicated also that this unprecedented housing situation gave rise to high rents and caused much congestion or overcrowding among the Negroes. Our aim here, therefore, is simply to expand this further by means of specific examples in order to furnish a more complete picture of this housing problem, especially as it concerned the migrants themselves.

According to a report on housing conditions in Newark, New Jersey, we are informed that old dilapidated buildings, long closed as undesirable for habitation, were opened and rented to Negroes. These houses were rented out as housekeeping apartments regardless of the fact that there were no facilities for such purposes. Kitchen ranges, lavatories, baths, and toilets were either altogether

546

absent or inadequate. In a majority of these houses no heat facilities were supplied, and the consequence was that whole families were accustomed to crowd around a small kerosene stove in stuffy rooms with no ventilation, where all the housekeeping was done, and where frequently the whole family slept together to keep warm. Furthermore, a study of fifty-three families, consisting of three hundred persons—one hundred and sixty-six of whom were adults, and one hundred and thirty-four children—showed that all were crowded into unsanitary, dark quarters averaging 4-2/7 persons per room. These families paid a total rent of $415.50, an average of $7.86 per family for these very poor quarters in the worst sections of the city.[145]

As to housing conditions in Pittsburgh, it is reported that of four hundred and sixty-five migrants interviewed, 35 per cent lived in tenement houses, 50 per cent in rooming houses, about 12 per cent in camps and churches, and only 2.5 per cent in what may be called single private family residences.[146] It was further shown that of 157 families investigated to ascertain the number of rooms per family, 77, or 49 per cent, lived in one room each, 33, or 21 per cent, lived in two-room apartments and only 47 families, or 30 per cent, lived in apartments of three or more rooms each.[147] It was discovered, moreover, that sleeping quarters were not only in bed-rooms, but also in attics, basements, dining-rooms, and kitchens. In many cases the houses in which rooms were located were dilapidated dwellings with the paper torn off, the plaster sagging from the naked lath, windows broken, ceiling low and damp, and the whole room dark, stuffy and unsanitary. In a great number of cases, also, the houses had very poor water facilities and filthy toilet conditions, because of the total absence of sewerage connections. In spite of these conditions, however, rent charges for these quarters were comparatively high.[148] "As to housing conditions among the single men in this city, it was discovered that only 22 out of more than three hundred of them had individual bed-rooms. Twenty-five per cent of these lived four in a room, and twenty-five per cent lived in rooms used by more than four people. Thirty-seven per cent of them, moreover, slept in separate beds, 50 per cent slept two in a bed, and 13 per cent slept three or more in a bed."[149]

Still further, when the designated Negro quarters in Pittsburgh became congested, there grew up new colonies in various places elsewhere.[150] In many instances the houses in these colonies were those which had been abandoned by foreign whites at the outbreak of the European War. Some of these structures had been formerly condemned by the City Bureau of Sanitation, but were opened again to accommodate the migrants from the South. For these inadequate dwelling places Negro occupants were compelled to pay comparatively high rents, which ranged from $10 to upwards of $25 per month.

An investigation made in Cleveland in 1917 revealed the fact that Negroes were living in cramped unsanitary quarters two or three families per suite, and that in this regard there was very little relief in sight. Rents had increased far out of proportion, ranging from 50 per cent to 75 per cent higher for Negro than for white tenants. There were instances in which rents had jumped from $25 to $45, from $16 to $35 and the like.[151] An examination into conditions of housing in Detroit indicated that a majority of the houses were in very bad repair, many of them being actual shanties. Less than one-half of these houses were equipped with bath-rooms or inside toilets. Rents were also exceedingly high. The average rent a room of houses occupied by Negroes was $5.90, whereas the average rent a room for the city at large was only $4.25. The prevailing rent a Negro family ranged between $20 and $44 per month. It was estimated that the increase in rent of houses occupied by Negroes during eighteen months was all the way from 50 per cent to 350 per cent.[152]

A study of 407 families in Detroit, moreover, showed that 209 of them kept lodgers as a means of procuring money to pay the high rents. One hundred of these kept no lodgers; the other 98 were doubtful or unknown. The prevalent size of each family was from two to four persons, exclusive of lodgers; and 146 families were found living each in two or more rooms. Thus when the size of the families, consisting each of two or three persons, including lodgers, and the number of rooms occupied per family were considered, it was found that there was much overcrowding, which meant a serious hindrance to healthy and decent family life.[153]

In regard to the housing situation in Chicago, the Secretary of the National Urban League reported that the Negroes were living in a limited area similar to that of the most Negroes in Harlem, New York City. In the former place, the houses occupied by the migrants were the old one-family type, were unsanitary, and in a serious state of disrepair. Two years previous to the exodus 300 or more of these houses were vacant; but during the migration of the Negroes they all became occupied, many of them having been converted so as to house two or more families. The report further states that the Negro newcomers had pushed over into the white residential section and were occupying houses, vacated by the whites, at an increase of 20 per cent or more in rent. No new houses were being built, in spite of the serious demand for them. The result of this, therefore, was further excessive increases in rental rates, which greatly enhanced the tendency to overcrowd.[154]

Finally, we are informed that the housing conditions among Negro migrants in Hartford were very poor. These people were for the most part settled on the east side of the city and lived in tenements formerly used by the foreigners. These dwellings were without modern conveniences and comforts, and were, therefore, very unsanitary. Some of the migrants, however, were more fortunately situated; but were paying exceedingly high rents. The rents averaged from $20 and $25 for three rooms to $30 for four or five rooms. These high rents caused the Negroes to overcrowd in order to be able to pay the same. The owners of these houses, moreover, took advantage of the tenants by doing very little repairing; sometimes just enough to comply with the law.[155]

FOOTNOTES:

[124] Woodson, C. G., *A Century of Negro Migration*, p. 190.

[125] Tyson, F. D., *Negro Migration in 1916-17*, Rep. U. S. Dept. Lab., pp. 126-27.

[126] Epstein, A., *The Negro Migrant in Pittsburgh*, p. 22.

[127] *Ibid.*, p. 23.

[128] Epstein, A., *The Negro Migrant in Pittsburgh*, p. 24.

[129] Haynes, G. E., *Negro New-Comers in Detroit, Mich.*, pp. 12-20.

[130] Leavell, R. H., *Negro Migration in 1916-17*, Rep. U. S. Dept. Lab., pp. 22-23.

[131] Ross, J. A., "New Organization Helps Negro Misfits," *New York Times*, Oct. 7, 1917, III, 10: 1.

[132] *The Negro at Work During the War and During Reconstruction*, Rep. U. S. Dept. Lab., p. 89.

[133] Pendleton, H. B., *Survey*, 37: 570-71, Feb. 17, 1917.

[134] *The Negro at Work During the War and During Reconstruction*, Rep. U. S. Dept. Lab., p. 89.

[135] *Ibid.*, p. 89.

[136] Ross, J. A., "New Organization Helps Negro Misfits," *New York Times*, Oct. 7, 1917, III, 10: 1.

[137] Pendleton, H. B., *Survey*, 37: 570-71, Feb., 1917.

[138] Wright, James A., *Letter on Conditions of Negro Migrants in Hartford*, Dec. 1, 1919.

[139] Tyson, F. D., *Negro Migration in 1916-17*, Rep. U. S. Dept. Lab., pp. 122-24.

[140] Tyson, F. D., *Negro Migration in 1916-17*, Rep. U. S. Dept. Lab., p. 124.

[141] *Ibid.*, p. 127.

[142] Hayes, G. E., *Negro New-Comers in Detroit, Mich.*, pp. 12-20.

[143] Pendleton, H. B., *Survey*, 37: 570, Feb., 1917.

[144] *The Negro in Industry*, p. 2.

[145] Pendleton, H. B., *Survey*, 37: 570-71, Feb., 1917.

[146] Epstein, A., *The Negro Migrant in Pittsburgh*, p. 11.

[147] *Ibid.*, p. 15.

[148] *Ibid.*, pp. 12-13.

[149] *Ibid.*, p. 12.

[150] *Ibid.*, p. 16.

[151] Tyson, F. D., *Negro Migration in 1916-17*, Rep. U. S. Dept. Lab., p. 149.

[152] Haynes, G. E., *Negro New-Comers in Detroit, Mich.*, pp. 25-26.

[153] Haynes, G. E., *Negro New-Comers in Detroit, Mich.*, pp. 23, 26.

[154] Tyson, F. D., *Negro Migration in 1916-17*, Rep. U. S. Dept. Lab., p. 149.

[155] Wright, J. A., *Letter on Conditions Among Negro Migrants in Hartford*, December, 1919.

Chapter VIII

DEPENDENTS AND DELINQUENTS

Another way in which the migration affected the Negroes may be seen in a brief study of their health in the North. To any people moving into new surroundings health is an extremely important concern, because on it largely depends their success in adjusting themselves to the new situations, especially if hard daily toil is their sole means of subsistence. As regards the health of the Negro migrants in the North it is reported that from the start they became, to a great extent, victims of disease. Such a consequence, however, was inevitable because of the sudden change of the Negroes from the comparatively mild climate of the South to the severe climate of the North, their inadequate clothing for the cold weather of this section, the hardships of the unrelenting toil, and the congested and unsanitary living conditions, in the Northern cities and industrial centers. These forces all operated heavily against the bodies of the Negroes and thus rendered them susceptible to pneumonia, bronchitis, tuberculosis, and other deadly maladies. The following studies of health conditions among Negroes in a few Northern cities will demonstrate the extent to which the newcomers were menaced by disease.

According to accounts given by Mr. Abraham Epstein, the health problem of the Negro migrants in Pittsburgh was a serious concern. An investigation into the causes of Negro mortality, based on comparison between a seven-month period in 1915 and a like period in 1917, showed that pneumonia cases during the latter year had increased 200 per cent over those of the former year. The same period in 1917 indicated also a marked increase in acute bronchitis and meningitis, and almost twice as many deaths from heart disease. The seven-month period in 1917, when the migration was in operation, registered, moreover, a total Negro death rate of 527, whereas the same period in 1915, before the movement began, showed a death list of only 295. During the first seven months of 1917, furthermore, the death rate among Negroes in this city was 48 per cent greater than the birth rate. In other words, while in the general city population the number of deaths was 30 per cent less than the number of births, the number of deaths among the Negroes greatly exceeded the diminished number of births; "thus for every one hundred persons born in Pittsburgh in 1917, there were 70 deaths, whereas among the Negro population for every one hundred children born, one hundred and forty-eight died."[156]

The report of the Health Department of Newark stated that during the month of December, 1917, there were 975 cases of diseases, and that this number was 287 in excess of the number of cases of sickness reported during the preceding month. These cases were largely bronchial pneumonia, and the deaths resulting from this malady numbered ninety-four. The report attributed the cause of this increase in pneumonia to the severe weather and to the increasing number of Negro laborers from the South, who, unaccustomed to the harsh climate of the North, easily became victims to this disease.[157] In Philadelphia, in the early spring of 1917, the lack of housing accommodations for the Negro influx caused women and children to be stranded in railroad stations overnight; and this soon brought on a public health problem. As was the case in Newark, in this place, too, there was an increase in pneumonia cases due to the sudden rush of Negroes to the North before the cold period was passed.[158]

The health conditions were so serious in Cincinnati that the city health officer suggested the establishment of a community health center in order to improve the health of the Negroes. He pointed out that their general death rate was about double that of the whites, their pneumonia rates more than three times as high, and their syphilis rate more than five times as high as the whites. In proportion to the population, he affirmed also that three times as many Negro children died before birth as whites, and that three times as many of the babies born alive died before their first birthday anniversary; and that the excess in deaths of Negroes from preventable causes alone was so great that it accounts for more than one point in the general death rate of the city.[159]

This rush of the Negroes to the North, moreover, was accompanied by smallpox and venereal diseases. Philadelphia and Pittsburgh, for example, faced a danger of epidemic from the former and were compelled to undertake wholesale vaccination of laborers in camps and mills. In one year the city of Cleveland also reported 330 cases of this malady. As to venereal diseases these became so rife that some industries adopted the physical examination system as a part of application for work. One large sugar refinery found after three weeks of this experiment that three in every ten Negro applicants had to be rejected because of syphilis or gonorrhea. An examination of 800 Negroes at a large railroad camp showed that 70 per cent of them were infected with tuberculosis, syphilis, or gonorrhea, and that nearly 80 per cent of the total were infected with the latter disease. This, however, was the case for the most part only among the shiftless, the casuals and floaters, for the examinations of the better type of Negroes showed that the percentage of those affected by those diseases was exceedingly small.

The recent movement brought to the cities of the North a multitude of ignorant Negroes mostly from the farms and plantations of the South, where opportunities for education are almost unknown. To the majority of them city life was an entirely new thing, and especially strange to them was the extremely complex life of the large cities of the North. Theirs, therefore, was an extremely difficult task to adapt themselves to the mores of these places, and in their efforts to do so, it is very obvious that they could not avoid committing errors. Furthermore, there were among these migrants many who, having been freed from the influence of the strict moral and religious checks of the southern communities, lost complete control of themselves, and were thus led into the committing of criminal acts. These circumstances, however, do not warrant the conclusion that with the coming of the Negroes to the North there arose a wave of crime of various kinds. This was not at all the case. The truth of the matter is that there was an increase in certain cities in both minor and major offenses committed by Negroes, but in this regard the increase in minor offenses was far greater than that in major offenses.

What has just been said is well illustrated by the results of an investigation of Negro crime in Pittsburgh. This was done by comparing the police court records for a period of seven months during 1916-17 with those for the same period during 1914-15, before the migration occurred. This comparison showed that the arrests of Negroes for petty offenses during the former period greatly exceeded those of the latter. During 1914-15 the total number of arrests was 1,681, whereas during 1916-17 the total number was 2,998. There was also a disproportionate increase in arrests for such offenses as suspicious characters, disorderly conduct, drunkenness, keeping and visiting disorderly houses, and violations of city ordinances. Increase in arrests for major offenses was very small. In 1914-15 the number of Negroes arrested for grave offenses was 93, while the number arrested for same in 1916-17 was only 94.[160]

The report on Negro crime and delinquency in the city of Harrisburg, Pennsylvania, showed that the Negro population had served more than to double the number of prisoners of color during a period of one year ending 1917. During the spring and summer of that year more than half the average number of inmates of the county jail, 200 in all, had been Negroes, although the Negro population of the county was estimated to be about 10 per cent of the total population. Most of the Negroes had been sentenced to serve short terms for stabbing, carrying deadly weapons, or for fighting.[161] Likewise, in Steelton, Pennsylvania, there was much disturbance among the Negroes which manifested itself in the form of fighting and cutting one another. From the first there had been a general carrying of weapons, promiscuous shooting, and dangers of trouble with the white population. Many arrests of Negroes were reported to have been made on the especial charges of drunkenness, gambling and disorderly conduct.[162] The Census of 1920 shows, however, that very few Negroes remained in Harrisburg during this preceding decade as the increase was only 721 or 15.9 per cent.

In Cleveland, Ohio, it was found that the Negro population of the jail had increased from 13 per cent of the total jail population in September, 1916, to 87 per cent in September, 1917. During the month of August of the latter year the Negro population of the jail was 60 per cent of the total jail population. The superintendent of prisons, however, expressed the belief that these Negroes were not of the criminal type, and affirmed that they had been sent to jail for such minor offenses as loafing on street corners, drunkenness, and as suspicious characters. He declared, further, that in many instances, because they were inadequately housed, deprived of opportunities for decent recreation, poorly clad, and often hatless on the streets, Negroes were summarily picked up by the police and sent to prison on the mere charge of suspicion.[163] This accounts for much of the so-called "Negro crime" in the United States.

Without further investigation, and relying solely on the facts already presented concerning conditions among the migrants in the North, one would, no doubt, at once suppose that a great many Negroes at first failed in the struggle, fell by the wayside, and finally became public charges. Strange as it may seem to relate, however, the contrary was rather the case. Few, indeed, were those among the migrants who became so overwhelmed by poverty as to necessitate their calling for public aid. The only account of Negroes appealing for help is that given by the Society for Organizing Charity in the city of Philadelphia. In this statement we are informed that during one year, ending early in 1917, this society received twenty-eight applications from Negro families who had recently come from the South. This same report states also that the Juvenile Court had received relatively few applications; that the Children's Bureau had not removed any children from newly arrived families; and that the House of Detention had handled only twenty-eight children arrested on one charge or another.[164]

This surprisingly small number of Negroes who became public charges must not, however, convey the impression that the migrants were altogether self-supporting. Numerous instances could be cited in which it would be shown that many of the older Negro residents of the North came to the rescue of stranded

559

migrants from the South. Churches and missions did much to help the newcomers to settle themselves in the new environment. When the Negroes began to come in very large numbers, moreover, and when the public realized the many obstacles which were in the way of their adjustment, numerous uplift organizations or counter-selective agencies sprang up, having as their specific function the assisting of the migrants to adapt themselves to the new conditions. Foremost among these was the National League on Urban Conditions among Negroes. This organization, however, had been in existence for several years, and had been making itself interested in the welfare of Negro migrants who were flocking to the cities of the North and West before the recent Negro movement. When this exodus was in full operation, this organization greatly expanded its work by establishing branches in most of the cities where the migrants were located. In order to perform its work more effectively it adopted a program which was executed in most of these cities. The program was (1) the establishment of an employment bureau to secure jobs for all newcomers who had no promise of any before their arrival; (2) the opening of a bureau to locate suitable houses at reasonable rates for the migrants; (3) the organization of a department to provide various kinds of wholesome recreation for the newcomers; (4) the maintenance of a department to aid in suppressing and preventing delinquency and crime among the Negro migrants; and (5) the putting forth of systematic efforts to help the Negroes to become industrially efficient. Thus, it can readily be seen that this organization and the smaller uplift agencies played a large part in the adjustment of the Negroes to the Northern environment; and it is no doubt due largely to their efforts that so very few of the migrants became objects of public charity.

Very recent inquiries, however, show that in certain

centers large numbers of the Negro migrants are in distress and are, therefore, compelled to seek public relief. These are single men and in many cases men with families who have been deprived of work because of the great industrial depression now in existence for nearly a year. They are moving from the industrial centers where they were formerly employed into the larger cities either in search of work or on their way back to their homes in the South. Usually, in these places they become stranded and are thus forced to seek aid. Conditions due to the influx of Negro families into the city of Pittsburgh are described by Mr. Charles C. Cooper, head of the Kingsley House, as follows: "The great number of idle colored men and women in any part of the great cities is difficult to estimate; there is no method of computing those who have come into the city after being laid off in surrounding territory. During some twelve days in January, 1921, 2,100 colored men, who had come from surrounding districts, and none of whom had been working in Pittsburgh, applied at the little Providence Rescue Mission in Pittsburgh for assistance and work. In one week 1,027 applied to the Urban League of this City for work, and 8 received it." He states, further, that the usual uplift or philanthropic agencies were overburdened in their efforts to help these unfortunates. Two prominent Negro churches volunteered their services and rendered valuable assistance to the regular relief organizations in the matter of feeding and housing these migrants. The situation, moreover, was all the more aggravated because of the attitude of the police department toward these newcomers and the acute housing conditions. With its usual lack of understanding, it permitted the police officers to arrest hundreds of these Negroes, many of whom were sent to the workhouse. On account of the scarcity of dwelling places rents were very high, and even where money was available for the purpose, the purchasing of houses was an impossibility. When a large group of these distressed men were asked if they were going to return to the South on account of their misfortunes they firmly replied: "Like Hell we are!"[165]

A small movement of some unemployed Negroes endeavoring to reach their original homes in the South, however, greatly augmented the number of homeless Negroes in the city of Louisville, Kentucky, during December, 1920. As this city has never made provision to care for homeless men, these wanderers at first received a very cold reception. The workhouse became the lodging-place of a large number of them, because they were arbitrarily arrested by the police, and on the charge of vagrancy were sentenced by the court to this institution for a period of ninety days. Efforts of the State Employment Bureau and the local branch of the Urban League to find jobs for these men were of no avail. Finally, through the instrumentality of the Community Council of this city a meeting of representatives of a number of organizations devised a plan of action for the purpose of aiding these homeless men. To supply them with sleeping quarters the Young Men's Christian Association furnished the use of its basement wherein thirty beds with bedding, loaned by the Associated Charities, were placed. Blankets were provided by the Salvation Army Industrial Home. Funds to defray the expenses of a night man and for breakfasts for the men were pledged by the Urban League and the National Association for the Advancement of Colored People. The Director of the Board of Public Safety promised the cooperation of the police by requesting the latter to refer homeless men to the Young Men's Christian Association instead of arresting them with the view of having them sent to the workhouse. The Associated Charities agreed to see to it that every man who actually could be taken care of in another community would be given the necessary transportation, and the city promised to assist in meeting this item of expense. In the meantime the State Employment Bureau and the Urban League gave assurance that they would renew their efforts to secure jobs for those in need of work.[166]

The extent to which these conditions exist is not yet definitely known; but owing to unemployment there are many more cases of Negroes undergoing hardships such as those to which reference has just been made. Mr. E. K. Jones, the Executive Secretary of the National Urban League, states that in the city of Detroit a very large number of Negroes are unemployed and in consequence have had to appeal to the city for relief. He is of the opinion that proportionally the Negroes are receiving more aid than any other group, for while they constitute a small percentage of the population of the city, they receive 37 per cent of the total relief given. In Chicago and its vicinity, owing to decreased production, not long ago, 70,000 Negro laborers agreed to accept a cut in wages rather than lose their jobs. The agreement was that they would accept a 10 per cent reduction in wages for unskilled laborers and a 15 per cent reduction for skilled workers. Mr. Parker, President of the American Unity Labor Union, declared then that there were 100,000 unemployed men in Chicago and its environs.[167] Thus here too a large number of Negroes are undoubtedly undergoing some hardships or are being placed in positions where these will certainly overtake them.

The fact that so many Negroes are out of work and on this account have fallen into poverty raises the question as to whether their unemployment is due to a general policy of employers to deprive Negroes of work simply because of their color. It is known that during this industrial depression production is exceedingly small and that correspondingly there is an infinitely small demand for the very large available supply of labor. The result is that there is an almost universal state of unemployment which presumably affects all groups alike. However, Mr. Charles C. Cooper, head of the Kingsley House in Pittsburgh, does not think that this is the case, for he is of the opinion that discrimination has been made against Negro workers. He holds that unskilled Negroes, the latest to be employed in industrial plants, have been among the first to be discharged and that only in exceptional instances is this untrue. These exceptions exist where the percentage of Negroes discharged is no larger than that of white workers because of the efforts of Negro social workers who were employed to act as spokesmen for the Negro laborers.[168] Opposed to this is the view of the Executive Secretary of the National Urban League. He does not believe that the percentage of Negroes discharged from work is larger than that of whites. In many plants, where Negroes have made good, when the necessity of cutting down the labor force arose, the proportion of Negroes who were dropped was no greater than that of any other group. In fact, in a few cases, employers have actually retained, proportionally, more Negro than white laborers. Be that as it may, the fact, nevertheless, is that unemployment is largely responsible for the distressed conditions of many of the Negro migrants; and the hope is that when this industrial crisis is passed and they are again given the opportunity to work, they will lift themselves once more to the level of self-help and independence.

In any migration of peoples in modern times there are usually those who either intend to remain in the new locality temporarily or who, because of the least dissatisfaction with conditions, are willing to return home at the earliest possible time. This gives rise to an outflow as well as an inflow of migrants. Perhaps the immigration from Europe to this country may

564

illustrate this. For several years previous to the Great War, while thousands of immigrants arrived in this country, on the one hand, on the other, thousands departed for their respective native lands.[170] To some extent this principle likewise applies to this intra-State movement of the Negro population. From our study of conditions among the migrants in the North it is obvious that many of them found conditions very different from what they had been represented to be by labor agents and others. This undoubtedly brought on much dissatisfaction and disappointment, and thus caused many to seek their way back to the South. The number of those acting thus is very uncertain, because no accurate study in this regard has been made. Nevertheless, some have estimated that only about 10 per cent of the total number of those who left the South returned there; others have estimated it as high as 30 per cent.[171] Both of these percentages, however, are mere guesses, with the likelihood perhaps of the former being approximately nearer the truth. The only attempt which has been made to investigate this phase of the movement was that on the part of the Chicago branch of the National League on Urban Conditions among Negroes shortly after the Washington and Chicago riots in July, 1919. This study was made mainly to verify the reports to the effect that because of these outbreaks the Negroes had become terrified and were on the move back to the South. This investigation was very limited in that it took cognizance of conditions as they pertained to Chicago only. The method of procedure was the study of Negro arrivals and departures during the week following the riot in that city. The interesting result was that during that period 261 Negroes arrived in the city while 219 departed. Of those leaving 83 gave some southern State as their destination. They were for the most part persons returning from vacations, visiting the South, going on business, or returning to join their families. Only 14 gave the riot as a cause for their leaving the city.[172]

It is reported, moreover, that the South, still feeling the effects of migration in the form of a serious labor shortage in its main industries, has been trying to induce the Negroes to return. As a means of accomplishing this it resorted to a scheme of using certain newspapers in the North to make persuasive appeals to the Negroes. In these the South's needs were made known, its kind treatment of Negroes was extolled, its opportunities were enumerated, and its growing change of heart on the question of race relations was affirmed. After rumor went broadcast that after the Washington and Chicago riots the Negroes, in terror, were leaving the North, moreover, more positive efforts were made, especially on the part of two Southern States, to obtain Negro laborers. These took the form of sending agents to the North to solicit labor and of empowering them to offer the Negroes free transportation and to make them promises of increased wages and better living conditions. These inducements, however, were ineffective because the Negroes doubted the sincerity of the Southern agents. Indeed, they were inclined all the more to be skeptical, for in the meantime news had reached them from various parts of the South to the effect that, except school conditions, things have not at all changed for the better; that, in many instances on the contrary, since the Great War living conditions of Negroes have become worse and that from a few places a small stream of Negroes was still moving northward.[173] The Federal census of 1920 justifies us, furthermore, in saying that for the most part the Negro migrants are satisfied with conditions in the North and are inclined to remain there; and that the number of those returning or who have returned to the South is, in comparison to the great number of those who came North, infinitely small.

566

FOOTNOTES:

[156] Epstein, A., *The Negro Migrant in Pittsburgh*, pp. 56-59.

[157] Pendleton, H. B., *Survey*, 37: 571, Feb. 17, 1917.

[158] *Survey*, 38: 28, April 7, 1917.

[159] *Survey*, 42: 579, July 19, 1917.

[160] Epstein, A., *The Negro Migrant in Pittsburgh*, pp. 47-48.

[161] Tyson, F. D., *Negro Migration in 1916-17*, Rep. U. S. Dept. Lab., p. 141.

[162] *Ibid.*, p. 142.

[163] *Ibid.*, p. 141.

[164] Bell, J. B., *Proc. Nat. Conf. Soc. Work.*, pp. 502-03, June, 1917.

[165] *Survey*, 45: 752, Feb. 26, 1021, "A New Negro Migration."

[166] Hoyer, R. A., "Migration of Colored Workers," *Survey*, 45: 930, March 26, 1921.

[167] *New York Times*, Dec. 12, 1920, 14: 1.

[168] *Survey*, 45: 752, Feb. 26, 1921.

[169] Washington, F. B., *Survey*, 38: 333-35, July 14, 1917.

[170] Fairchild, H. P., *Immigration*, pp. 348-52.

[171] Dillard, J. H., *Negro Migration in 1916-17*, Rep. U. S. Dept. Lab., p. 11.

[172] Hill, T. A., *Survey*, 43: 183-85, Nov. 29, 1919.

[173] Hill, T. A., *Survey*, 43: 183-85, Nov. 29, 1919.

Chapter IX

THE STATISTICS OF THE MIGRATION

The apparent effect of the migration in the light of the advanced reports of the census of 1920 has been the movement of the Negro population from the southern cities to northern industrial centers, while there was going on at the same time a movement of the rural Negro population from the rural districts in the South into the thus depleted southern cities to take the places of those migrating to the North. Statistics show, therefore, a small increase or stability in the cities of the South, whereas the Negro population of the State increased less, remained about the same, or decidedly decreased.

Delaware, for example, although a southern State, economically connected with the North, suffered a decrease in its population, having lost during the decade 846 Negroes, or 2.7 per cent, as against an increase from 1910 to 1920 of 484, or 1.6 per cent. Delaware had 492,614 whites and 30,341 Negroes in 1920. Wilmington, however, had 99,381 whites and 10,751 Negroes, showing an increase in the white population of 26.9 per cent and in Negro population of 18.4 per cent.

In Alabama, out of the total population of 2,248,174 there are 900,652 Negroes, whereas in 1910 the Negroes numbered 908,282, showing a decrease in numbers of 8,282, or a decrease of eight-tenths of one per cent. In 47 of the 60 counties there was also a decrease in its number of Negroes. Statistics further show that this decrease in the Negro population was largely among the males and accounts for the change in the sex ratio of the total population of Alabama.

The white population during this decade increased by 17.8 per cent. Yet the cities of Alabama did not thus fare. In Birmingham the increase in the white population during the decade between 1910 and 1920 was 28,193, or 35.1 per cent, while the corresponding increase in the Negro population was 17,912, or 34.2 per cent. In Mobile the white population increased during the same period 8,132, or 28.3 per cent, whereas the Negro population increased 1,130, or 5 per cent, as compared with an increase of 5,718, or 33.5 per cent, from 1900 to 1910. In Montgomery the increase in the white population was 4,828, or 25.7 per cent, while the Negro population increased 504, or 2.6 per cent.

In 1920 the population of the State of Mississippi included 853,962 whites and 935,184 Negroes. In 1910 there were 786,111 whites and 1,009,487 Negroes. The white population increased 8.6 per cent as compared with 22.6 per cent for the previous decade, while the Negro population showed a decrease of 7.4 per cent as against an increase of 11.2 per cent during the preceding decade. The proportion of Negroes in the total population declined from 56.2 per cent in 1910 to 52 per cent in 1920. In most counties of the State the percentage of Negroes decreased and in 68 of the 82 counties there was also a decrease in the number of Negroes.

The population of the State of Louisiana, according to the last census, is 61 per cent white and 38.9 per cent Negro. In 1910 the percentage of Negroes was 43.1 per cent. The Negro population, which was 713,874 in 1910, decreased to 700,257 in 1920, a decrease of 1.9 per cent. The white population during the same period increased from 941,086 to 1,096,911, or 16.5 per cent. In most of the parishes of the State the percentage of Negroes decreased and in 41 of the 64 parishes there was also a decrease in the number of Negroes. In the city of New Orleans, however, the development was the other way. In 1920 the city had 285,913 whites and 100,918 Negroes. The white population constituted 73.8 per cent of the total in 1920 and 73.6 per cent in 1910 while the Negro population constituted 26.1 per cent of the total in 1920 and 26.3 per cent in 1910. The increase in the white population since 1910 was 36,510, or 14.6 per cent, while the corresponding increase in the Negro population was 11,656, or 13.1 per cent.

Statistics place South Carolina in middle ground. In 1920 there were in that State 818,538 whites and 864,719 Negroes. The corresponding figures for 1910 were 679,161 whites and 835,843 Negroes. The rate of increase in the white population was 20.5 per cent as compared with 21.8 per cent for the period from 1900 to 1910. The percentage of increase between 1910 and 1920 in the Negro population was only 3.5 per cent, a rate slightly more than half as great as the corresponding one for the decade from 1900 to 1910, when it was 6.8 per cent. The proportion of Negroes in the total population declined from 55.2 per cent in 1910 to 51.4 per cent in 1920. In the city of Charleston there were 35,617 whites and 32,292 Negroes. The white population constituted 52.4 per cent of the total in 1920 and 47.2 per cent of the total in 1910 and 52.8 per cent in 1900. The increase in the white population since 1910 was 17,853, or 28.3 per cent, while the corresponding increase in the Negro population was 1,236, or 4 per cent.

Some other Southern States did not have the usual increase in the Negro population, but nevertheless did not report a loss in 1910. In 1920 there were found in Maryland 1,204,737 white persons and 244,479 Negroes. The white population increased by 13.4 per cent while the Negro population increased by 5.3 per

571

cent. In almost every county in the State the percentage of Negroes decreased and in 19 of the 24 counties there was also a decrease in the number of the Negroes. In Baltimore, on the other hand, the tendency was the other way. The white population was 625,074 and the Negro population 108,390, whereas in 1910 there were 473,387 whites and 84,749 Negroes. Both the white and Negro populations, therefore, had increased since 1910, that of the whites being 32 per cent as compared with 10 per cent of the previous decade, and that of the Negro being 27.9 per cent as compared with 6.9 per cent of the previous decade.

The population of Virginia was 1,617,909 whites and 690,017 Negroes. In 1910 there were 1,389,809 whites and 671,096 Negroes. The white population increased 16.4 per cent while the Negro population increased only 2.8 per cent. Lynchburg had 21,714 whites and 8,355 Negroes. In 1910 there were 20,023 whites and 9,456 Negroes. The white population showed an increase since 1910 of 1,691, or 8.4 per cent, while the Negro population showed a decrease of 1,111, or 11.7 per cent. In 1920 Norfolk had 72,243 whites and 43,377 Negroes. In 1910 the figures were 42,353 whites and 25,039 Negroes. The increase of the white population since 1910 was 29,890, or 70.6 per cent, while the corresponding increase in the Negro population was 18,338, or 73.2 per cent. In 1920 Portsmouth had a white population of 31,104 and 23,242 Negroes. In 1910 this city had 21,560 whites and 11,617 Negroes. The increase in the white population since 1910 was 9,544, or 44.3 per cent, while the corresponding increase in the Negro population was 11,625, or 101 per cent. Richmond had 117,565 whites and 54,057 Negroes in 1920. In 1910 the city had 80,879 whites and 46,733 Negroes. The increase in the white population since 1910 was 36,686, or 45.4 per cent, while the corresponding increase in the Negro population was 7,314, or 15.7 per cent. Roanoke had 41,530 whites and 9,300 Negroes while in 1910 the figures were 26,945 whites and 7,924 Negroes. The increase in the white population since 1910 was 14,585, or 54.1 per cent, while the corresponding increase in the Negro population was 1,376, or 17.6 per cent.

North Carolina had some increase in its Negro population. The total population of 2,559,123 included 1,783,779 whites and 763,407 Negroes. In 1910 there were 1,500,511 whites and 697,843 Negroes. The increase in the white population was at the rate of 18.9 per cent, while that of the Negro population was 9.4 per cent. In most counties of the State the percentage of Negroes decreased and in 37 of the 100 counties there was also a decrease in the number of Negroes.

In Georgia the total population of the State comprised 2,895,832, having 1,689,114 white persons and 1,206,365 Negroes. The white population increased by 18 per cent and the Negro by 2.5 per cent. Augusta had a white population of 29,894 whites and 22,576 Negroes, showing an increase during the decade of 32 per cent for the white population as compared with an increase of 8.3 per cent during the previous decade, while the Negro population showed an increase of 23.1 per cent as against a decrease of less than 1 per cent from 1900 to 1910. The white population of Macon increased 32.8 per cent, while the Negro population increased 27.2 per cent. In Rome there was an increase of 19 per cent for the white population as compared with 87.1 per cent of the period before but a decrease in the Negro population of 11.5 per cent against an increase of 32.8 per cent from 1900 to 1910. In Savannah while the white population increased 38.5 per cent, the Negro population increased 17.9 per cent. The

573

statistics of the counties of Georgia show that the percentage of Negroes decreased and that in 82 of 155 counties there was also a decrease in the number of Negroes.

The total population of Florida in 1920 was 968,470. 638,153 of these were white and 329,487 were Negroes, whereas corresponding figures for 1910 showed 443,634 whites and 308,669 Negroes. This indicates that the white population increased by 43.8 per cent and the Negro population by 6.7 per cent. Jacksonville then had 50,031 whites and 41,479 Negroes. The increase in the white population since 1910 was 21,702, or 76.6 per cent, while the corresponding increase in the Negro population was 12,186, or 41.6 per cent. The city of Tampa had a population of 40,057 whites and 11,520 Negroes. The increase in the white population since 1910 was 11,267, or 39.1 per cent, while the corresponding increase in the Negro population was 2,569, or 28.7 per cent. In almost every county of the State the percentage of Negroes decreased, and in 28 of the 54 counties there was also a decrease in the number of Negroes.

The border States suffered much from the migration. Kentucky, according to the census of 1920, had 2,416,630 persons. Of these 2,180,560 were whites and 235,938 were Negroes. The corresponding figures for 1910 were 2,027,000 whites and 261,656 Negroes. The white population increased 7.5 per cent and the Negro population decreased 9.8 per cent. There was a decrease in the number of Negroes in 104 of the 120 counties. The city of Covington, however, showed that while the white population was increasing 7.4 per cent, that of the Negro increased 4.9 per cent in contradistinction to what took place in the State as a whole. In Louisville the increase of the white population since 1910 was lower than that for the preceding decade, and the Negro population increased only one-tenth of one per cent during that period, having been 40,522 in 1910 and 40,118 in 1920.

Tennessee belongs to the declining class so far as the Negro population is concerned. In 1920 the State had 1,885,993 whites and 451,758 Negroes. The corresponding figures for 1910 were 1,711,432 whites and 473,088 Negroes. The white population increased by 10.2 per cent while the Negro population decreased by 4.5 per cent. In most of the counties of the State the percentage of Negroes decreased and in 75 of the 95 counties there was also a decrease in the number of Negroes. In Chattanooga there were 39,024 whites and 18,856 Negroes. The figures for 1910 were 26,660 whites and 17,942 Negroes. The increase in the white population during the decade was 12,364, or 46.4 per cent, while the corresponding increase in the Negro population was 924, or 5.1 per cent. In Knoxville there was a white population of 66,508 and a Negro population of 11,303. The figures for 1910 were 28,760 whites and 7,638 Negroes. The increase in the white population was at a much higher rate than during the preceding decade, the increase from 1910 to 1920 being 37,802, or 131.7 per cent, as compared with 3,428, or 13.6 per cent, from 1900 to 1910. The increase of the Negro population was also greater from 1910 to 1920 than from 1900 to 1910, the increase being 3,665, or 48 per cent, from 1910 to 1920 as compared with 279, or 3.8 per cent, from 1900 to 1910.

The population of Memphis included 101,117 whites and 61,173 Negroes. The figures for 1910 were 78,590 whites and 52,441 Negroes. The increase in the white population since 1910 was much lower than that for the preceding decade, the increase from 1910

575

to 1920 being 22,527, or 28.7 per cent, as compared with 26,210, or 50 per cent, from 1900 to 1910. The increase in the Negro population was greater from 1910 to 1920 than from 1900 to 1910, the increase being 8,732, or 16.7 per cent, from 1910 to 1920 as against 2,531, or 51 per cent, from 1900 to 1910. In 1920 Nashville had 82,699 whites and 35,634 Negroes. In 1910 the corresponding numbers were 73,831 whites and 36,523 Negroes. While the increase in the white population since 1910 was lower than that of the preceding decade, there was a decrease in the Negro population from 1910 to 1920, the decrease being 889, or 2.4 per cent, from 1910 to 1920, as against an increase of 6,479, or 21.6 per cent, from 1900 to 1910.

Missouri, however, forming a part of the industrial West, did not follow the fortunes of Kentucky and Tennessee. In 1920 there were in Missouri 3,225,044 whites and 178,241 Negroes, whereas the figures for 1910 were 3,134,932 whites and 157,452 Negroes. During the decade the white population increased by 2.9 per cent. The population of Kansas City was 293,532 whites and 30,706 Negroes. The white population constituted 90.5 per cent of the total population and the Negro 9.5 per cent. The increase in the white population since 1910 was 30.6 per cent, while the corresponding increase of the Negro population was 7,140, or 30.3 per cent. In St. Louis there were 702,764 whites and 69,603 Negroes. The increase in the white population since 1910 was 60,276, or 9.4 per cent, while the corresponding increase in the Negro population was 25,643, or 58.3 per cent.

The more favorable condition in Missouri obtained throughout the Southwest. In 1920 there were in Oklahoma 1,821,194 white persons and 149,408 Negroes. The corresponding figures for 1910 were

1,144,531 white persons and 137,612 Negroes. During the decade the white population increased by 26.1 per cent, while the Negro population increased only 8.6 per cent. The white population of Oklahoma City was 82,847 and that of the Negroes 8,269. The increase in the white population since 1910 was 25,354, or 44.1 per cent, while the corresponding increase in the Negro population was 1,723, or 26.3 per cent. There were in Okmulgee 13,967 whites and 3,372 Negroes. The white population increased since 1910 11,241, or 412.4 per cent, while the increase in the Negro population during the same period was 1,996, or 145.1 per cent. In Tulsa there were 63,430 whites and 8,442 Negroes. The white population constituted 88 per cent of the total in 1920 and 88.1 per cent in 1910, while the Negro population constituted 11.7 per cent of the total in 1920 and 10.8 per cent in 1910. The increase in the white population since 1910 was 47,212, or 296 per cent, while the corresponding increase in the Negro population was 6,483, or 330.9 per cent.

In Arkansas the situation seemed to be somewhat the same. The total population of that state in 1920 was 1,752,204. Of this number 1,279,757 were whites and 472,220 were Negroes. The white population increased by 13.2 per cent and the Negro population by 6.6 per cent. During this period the city of Little Rock in that State increased its white population to 47,658 and 17,474 Negroes. The increase in the white population during the decade was 16,273, or 51.8 per cent, while the corresponding increase in the Negro population was only 2,935, or 20.2 per cent. The statistics as to counties show a decrease in a percentage in the Negro population and 43 of 75 counties reported a decrease in numbers.

The white population of Texas in 1920 was 3,918,165 and that of the Negro 741,694. The corresponding figures for the previous decade were 3,204,848 whites and 690,049 Negroes. During the decade the white population increased by 22.3 per cent while the Negro population increased by only 7.5 per cent. Dallas had a white population of 134,888 and 24,023 Negroes, whereas in 1910 there were 74,043 whites and 18,024 Negroes. The increase in the white population since 1910 was 60,845, or 82.2 per cent, while the corresponding increase in the Negro population was 5,999, or 33.3 per cent. El Paso had 75,843 whites and 1,373 Negroes. In 1910 the corresponding figures were 37,586 whites and 1,452 Negroes. While the white population showed an increase in 1920 of 38,257, or 101.8 per cent, the Negro population showed a decrease of 121, or 8.3 per cent. Fort Worth had a white population of 90,466 and 15,876 Negroes. The figures for 1910 were 59,960 whites and 13,280 Negroes. The increase in the white population since 1910 was 30,506, or 50.9 per cent, while the corresponding increase in the Negro population was 2,616, or 19.7 per cent. In Houston there were 104,367 whites and 33,843 Negroes. In 1910 there were 54,832 whites and 23,929 Negroes. The increase in the white population since 1910 was 49,535, or 90.3 per cent, while the corresponding increase of the Negro population was 9,914, or 41.4 per cent. In San Antonio there were 146,795 whites and 14,355 Negroes. In 1910 there were 85,801 whites and 10,716 Negroes. The increase in the white population since 1910 was 60,924, or 71.1 per cent, while the corresponding increase in the Negro population was 3,639, or 34 per cent.

West Virginia, economically a part of the North or West rather than of the South, showed tendencies directly opposite to those of that section to which it is historically connected. In 1920 the State had 1,377,235 whites and 86,345 Negroes. The corresponding figures for 1910 were 1,156,817 whites and 64,173 Negroes. The white population increased by 19.1 per cent while the Negro population increased by 34.6 per cent. The city of Huntington had 47,279 whites and 2,890 Negroes, whereas in 1910 the figures were 29,009 whites and 2,140 Negroes. The increase in the white population since 1910 was 18,270, or 63 per cent, while the corresponding increase in the Negro population was 750, or 35 per cent. Wheeling had 54,579 whites and 1,619 Negroes. In 1910 the figures were 40,433 whites and 1,201 Negroes. The increase in the white population since 1910 was 14,146, or 35 per cent, while the corresponding increase in the Negro population was 418, or 34.8 per cent.

The effect of the migration in the North and West will be interesting also. The census showed a decidedly large increase in the population in the important industrial States just beyond the line of the North and South. In the North and West there were 1,550,754 Negroes, whereas there were only 1,078,336 in 1910, the increase being 472,448, or at the rate of 43.8 per cent. In the extremely northern and north-western portions of the country the Negro population was not affected otherwise than normally. New England had 66,306 Negroes in 1910 and 79,051 in 1920. The increase was 12,745. The increase and the decrease in the Negro population of these States does not mean very much in percentage because of the very small number of Negroes in that section. For example, the increase in the Negro population of Connecticut, the State most affected thereby, was 5,872, which in the form of a percentage would mean 38.7 per cent. The state had only 21,046 Negroes in 1920 as compared with 15,174 in 1910. The Negro population of New Hampshire, moreover, increased from 564 in 1910 to 621 in 1920, meaning an increase of 10.1 per cent. Vermont had only 572 Negroes in 1920 as against 1,621 in 1910, showing thereby a decrease of 64.7 per cent. Rhode Island had 10,056 Negroes in 1920 and 9,529 in 1910. Massachusetts had 45,466 Negroes in 1920 as compared with 38,055 in 1910. While the white population was increasing 14.4 per cent, the Negro population increased 19.5 per cent. Boston had 16,350 Negroes in 1920 and 13,564 in 1910, showing an increase of 20.5 per cent, while the white population was increasing 11.4 per cent. Maine had 1,310 Negroes in 1910 and 1,363 in 1920, showing an increase of 3.9 per cent in the Negro population, while the white population was increasing only 3.5 per cent.

New York increased its Negro population 47.9 per cent. This State had 134,191 Negroes in 1910 and 198,423 in 1920. The migration did not materially affect any cities in the State except New York City, Buffalo and Rochester. The Negro population of New York City increased from 91,709 in 1910 to 153,088 in 1920, an increase of 66.9 per cent. In Buffalo, an industrial center, the Negro population increased 154.8 per cent, that is, from 1,773 in 1910 to 4,517 in 1920. The Negro population of Rochester increased from 879 in 1910 to 1,599 in 1920, an increase of 720, or 81.9 per cent.

In New Jersey there was an increase of 30.5 per cent in the Negro population during this period, that is, from 89,760 Negroes in 1910 to 117,132 in 1920. The cities much affected thereby were Camden, East Orange, Jersey City, Atlantic City, and Newark. The Negro population in Atlantic City increased 11.3 per cent, that is, from 9,834 in 1910 to 10,948 in 1920. That of Camden increased 40.1 per cent, that is, from 6,076 Negroes in 1910 to 8,513 in 1920; that of East Orange 24.6 per cent, that is, from 1,907 Negroes in 1910 to 2,377 in 1920; that of Jersey City 33.3 per cent, that is, from 5,960 Negroes in 1910 to 7,947 in

1920; that of Newark increased 79.5 per cent, that is, from 9,475 in 1910 to 17,010 Negroes in 1920.

The Negro population of Pennsylvania increased 46.7 per cent. This State had 193,919 Negroes in 1910 and 284,568 in 1920, the increase being 46.7 per cent. The cities which were materially affected by the migration were Philadelphia, Pittsburgh, Harrisburg and Chester. The Negro population of Philadelphia increased from 84,459 in 1910 to 134,098 in 1920, showing an increase of 49,632, or 48.8 per cent. The Negro population of Pittsburgh increased 47.1 per cent, that is, from 25,623 in 1910 to 37,688 in 1920. The Negro population of Harrisburg increased from 4,535 in 1910 to 5,256 in 1920. The Negro population of Chester increased 48.5 per cent, that is, from 4,795 in 1910 to 7,119 in 1920. The Negro population of such cities as Altoona, York, Washington, Harrisburg, Johnstown and Lancaster was considerably increased, in some cases more than doubled; but not sufficiently to make any material change in the complexion of the city.

Ohio had an increase in the Negro population of 67.1 per cent. This State had 111,452 Negroes in 1910 and 186,187 in 1920. The cities much affected thereby were Cincinnati with an increase of 35.6 per cent, that is, from 19,639 in 1910 to 29,636 in 1920; Columbus with an increase of 73.4 per cent, that is, from 12,739 in 1910 to 22,091 in 1920; Dayton with an increase of 43 per cent, that is, from 4,842 in 1910 to 9,029 in 1920. Toledo had an increase of 203.1 per cent, that is, from 1,877 in 1910 to 5,690 in 1920; Youngstown had an increase of 244 per cent, that is, from 1,936 in 1910 to 6,660 in 1920; and Cleveland had the largest percentage of all, showing an increase of 308.1 per cent, that is, from 8,448 in 1910 to 34,374 in 1920.

The Negro population of Indiana increased 34 per

cent, that is, from 60,320 in 1910 to 80,810 in 1920. The cities most affected by this migration were Gary with an increase from 383 in 1910 to 5,299 in 1920; Indianapolis with an increase of 59 per cent, that is, from 21,816 in 1910 to 34,690 in 1920, and Terre Haute with an increase of 40.6 per cent, that is, from 2,593 in 1910 to 3,646 in 1920. Fort Wayne was not materially affected. Evansville had 6,400 in 1920, only 134 more than it had in 1910. South Bend had practically no Negroes at first but received 691 during this decade in addition to the 604 which it had in 1910.

The Negro population of Illinois increased 67.1 per cent, that is, from 109,049 in 1910 to 182,274 in 1920. The two urban centers chiefly affected in that State were East St. Louis and Chicago. The Negro population of Chicago increased 148.5 per cent, that is, from 44,103 in 1910 to 109,594 Negroes in 1920. The Negro population of East St. Louis increased from 5,882 in 1910 to 7,433 in 1920, the percentage being 26.5 per cent. The change in the complexion of the population of Peoria, Rockford, and Springfield is not interesting.

Michigan showed an increase in the Negro population of 251 per cent, that is, from 17,115 in 1910 to 60,082 in 1920. Detroit was most affected thereby, its population having increased 623.4 per cent, that is, from 5,751 Negroes in 1910 to 41,532 in 1920.

Kansas showed an increase in its Negro population from 54,030 in 1910 to 57,925 in 1920, or an increase of 7.2 per cent. Kansas City, an urban center of importance influenced by Kansas City, Missouri, was most affected thereby. Its Negro population was increased 55.1 per cent during this period, that is, from 9,285 in 1910 to 14,405 in 1920. The population of Topeka decreased 5.3 per cent, that is, from 4,538 Negroes in 1910 to 4,297 in 1920, while in Wichita there was an increase of 44.2 per cent, that is, from 2,457 in 1910 to 3,543 in 1920.

Iowa showed an increase of only 26.9 per cent in its Negro population, that is, from 14,973 in 1910 to 19,005 in 1920. Nebraska had 7,689 Negroes in 1910 and 13,242 in 1920. Omaha showed an increase in its population of 133 per cent, that is, from 4,426 in 1910 to 10,314 in 1920. Wisconsin increased its Negro population from 2,900 in 1910 to 5,201 in 1920, an increase of 79.3 per cent. Milwaukee received most of these, having 908 Negroes in 1910 and 2,234 in 1920, an increase of 128 per cent.

The statistics of the States of the Far West, such as Idaho, North and South Dakota are not very interesting. North Dakota had a decrease in its Negro population of 24.3 per cent and South Dakota increased its 1.8 per cent. Utah increased its Negro population 26.4 per cent; Idaho 41.3 per cent; Minnesota 24.4 per cent; Nevada decreased 32.6 per cent; and New Mexico increased 252.1 per cent. That of Colorado decreased from 11,423 in 1910 to 11,318 in 1920, that of Montana decreased from 1,834 in 1910 to 1,658 in 1920; and that of Wyoming decreased from 2,235 in 1910 to 1,375 in 1920. Oregon's Negro population increased 43.7 per cent, that is, from 1,492 in 1910 to 2,144 in 1920. Washington increased its Negro population 13.6 per cent, that is, from 6,058 Negroes in 1910 to 6,883 in 1920. The Negro population increased 79.1 per cent in California, that is, from 21,645 in 1910 to 38,763 in 1920.

Chapter X

SOME CONCLUSIONS

If now we put together here much of what we have learned from the study of this movement, we perceive first of all that it was a social phenomenon representing the maladjustment of almost 500,000 Negroes to their present environment and their escape from this situation by flight to another locality. This maladaptation was the result of defeat of the migrants by natural forces operating in the struggle for existence, and of their failure to overcome the powerful economic and social adversities due to racial prejudice in the Southern society. The floods and boll-weevil pests had, in many cases, either destroyed crops, or rendered the raising of them totally impossible, and in consequence had practically destroyed the very means of subsistence of the Negroes. Added to this were numerous economic and social disadvantages in the form of unjust farming conditions, wretchedly low wages, lynchings, segregation, injustice in the courts, poor housing, poor schools, and so on, all of which tended to make life in the home environment more and more unendurable. While these driving forces were at work, there suddenly loomed up in the North a most unusually large demand for labor, and in this the Negroes saw the possibility of gaining access to an environment where conditions of life seemed much more favorable than those in the present surroundings. Consequently, as a means of escaping the pain of maladaptation and of seeking the pleasure which results from proper adjustment to external conditions, the Negroes simply chose the line of least resistance; that is, flight or migration to the North.

In the next place, we see that the migration was merely one of many such movements which have been in progress for more than fifty years, and that it differs from these only in volume. Its uniqueness, as we said,[174] lies in the fact that it alone brought from the South to the North and West a number of Negroes which exceeds that which resulted from all the combined movements in this direction during a period of forty years. While this is the case, it should not be overlooked, however, that this was due largely to the then existing extraordinary economic and social conditions. At the time of the occurrence of this movement conditions causing the Negroes to desire to leave the South, and opportunities for their employment in Northern industries, were never so favorable and widespread as then. The forces of push and pull, both economic and social, were present and were operating on a scale larger than any hitherto known. It is, therefore, very evident that without these most unusual and favorable conditions this migration either never would have occurred when it did, or if it would have, it would not have acquired such an immense volume.

It has been seen, moreover, that this recent exodus was a sort of spontaneous movement of the masses of the Negro population and not one composed of its leading elements. This fact has been marveled at, because in this migration the rank and file of Negroes, accustomed to being led, showed some initiative by acting of their own accord, and thereby abandoned the old policy of seeking and awaiting the advice of their leaders.[175] While this is true, and is, indeed, a very commendable performance, yet a careful view of the situation will show that it is hardly a phenomenon to be considered a marvelous affair. As we saw in Chapter IV of this dissertation, this movement was largely precipitated and stimulated by the labor agents who were seeking a supply of labor to satisfy the demand of northern industries. The Negroes, then suffering from the pangs of maladaptation, were seeking an avenue of escape, and this was pointed out to them by these agents. The latter offered the Negroes free transportation, and promised them higher wages, better working conditions, better social advantages, and on the whole better things than the southern environment could afford them. In many instances, for a time all the Negroes needed to do was to decide to leave the South, and, thereafter, they had very little to worry about until they had reached their destination places. In this whole matter it seems that the Negroes were confronted with what Professor Sumner calls the first task of life, which is the task of living, not thinking. Conditions in the environment had brought to them necessities which had to be satisfied at once. Need then was their experience and was followed immediately by efforts to satisfy it. This was the impelling force.[176] Through the efforts of the northern labor agents the Negroes obtained instruction as to the means whereby this need might be satisfied. They, therefore, were the actual leaders of the movement, and thus rendered it unnecessary for the Negroes to turn to seek and await the counsels of their customary leaders.

While this movement was in operation, furthermore, the opinion of a few was to the effect that this migration would act as a means of so distributing the Negro population throughout the country as to bring on an equalization of the racial problem. This, it was alleged, would be a good thing, first, because it would remove the fear of race domination in the Southern States and thus deprive them of many of their peculiar characteristics which they have developed in the course of their efforts to keep the Negroes in the background; and, secondly, because it would be of benefit to Negroes, in that it would mean for them better education, more wealth, and greater political

587

power.[177] It is evident that had this movement wrought such results it would have been a social occurrence of extraordinary importance, because it would have, perhaps, accomplished much in the way of lessening the tense friction between the two races; but it produced no such results. The Census of 1920 shows that the North and West had a very large increase in its Negro population during the preceding decade, the number being 472,448, but the Negro population in the Southern States decreased in only a few and remained almost normal in others while actually increasing in some of these commonwealths. In fact, when we consider the effects of past movements upon the distribution of the Negro population in this country, we are forced to the conclusion that such a dissemination of this population can hardly be accomplished through migration. According to the Federal census of 1910, in 1870 the total Negro population of the United States was 4,880,009. Of this number 4,420,811 lived in the South, and 459,198 lived in the North and West.[178] In 1910, forty years later, this same population was 9,827,763, and of this number 8,749,427 resided in the South, whereas only 1,078,336 dwelled in the North and West.[179] Looking at this distribution of population from the standpoint of percentage estimates, we find that in 1870 90.6 per cent of the Negro population lived in the South, whereas only 9.4 per cent lived in the North and West. In 1910, 89 per cent of the total Negro population of the United States was living in the South, while only 11 per cent was living in the other two sections.[180] In 1870, moreover, the number of Negroes born in the South and living in the North and West was 149,100; in 1910 this number had increased to only 440,534.[181] This number, however, was exclusive of that of the migrants who might have died or returned to the South or elsewhere before the taking of the Federal census.

588

Owing to a number of small and unimportant movements, and this great movement of 1916-18, the Federal census of 1920 shows, on the one hand, a decrease in the percentage of the total Negro population living in some of the Southern States and, on the other, a considerable increase both in the number of Negroes born in the South and living in the North and West, and in the percentage of the total Negro population of the United States residing in these two sections. The point here, however, is that notwithstanding the numerous movements of Negroes from the South since their emancipation, in 1910 nearly nine-tenths of the total Negro population of this country was still living in that section, whereas only a little more than ten per cent was residing in the North and West. This shows that the Negroes in proportion to their numbers are leaving the South very slowly, and that the tendency is for the greater bulk of the Negro population of the United States to remain in that section. This, therefore, seems to preclude the notion of a general dissemination of the Negro population in the United States, unless those conditions which gave rise to the recent large Negro exodus should repeat themselves in such rapid successions as to cause numerous similar movements; but the occurrence of such phenomena, while not altogether impossible, is, to say the least, very highly improbable.

During this movement also migration was suggested as a weapon which the Negroes might use against the South. In this regard the opinion was expressed that since the Negroes cannot defend themselves by the ballot or armed revolt they have in their possession an effective weapon in the form of migration, because it can be used quietly, without open threats, and with telling results. All they need do, when conditions in the South become intolerable, is to move away, provided, however, there are economic opportunities for them in the North. By so doing they will render the South decidedly hard up for labor, and thus force it to make concessions to them or face economic stagnation.[182] While there might be a possibility of putting this suggestion into effect, yet a little inquiry into the nature of migration will show that its use as an economic weapon is greatly limited. For the occurrence of a migration, as has been seen, there must always be both a repellent cause and an attractive cause. These causes, however, do not always occur simultaneously, for while the repellent or drawing cause may be existent, the attractive or beckoning cause may be non-existent and vice versa. Hence, in either case there will be no migration, because it is the tendency of man to prefer to remain in the environment to which he has become accustomed, even under most adverse conditions, or to leave it only when he feels certain that another environment offers him advantages superior to those afforded him by his home surroundings.

According to this principle, then, there might occur repeated instances in which conditions in the South may become very distressing, but unattended by signs of better things in the North. This would, no doubt, result in compelling the Negroes, for the most part, to remain where they are. In a word, a migration, in the true sense of the word, is not a phenomenon brought about by the mere whims or fancies of the individuals or groups participating, but is rather brought into being by a sort of rational response to certain economic and social laws. A movement engendered otherwise is almost certain to bring disaster to the migrants, as was the case in the Negro exodus to Kansas in 1879.[183] The occasion for a Negro migration of sufficient volume to affect the industries of the South, moreover, as did this recent one, might require such a long time for its occurrence as to render the force of the migration as a weapon almost nihil. On account of the peculiar position in which the Negroes find themselves placed, therefore, it might be well if they had in their possession some economic instrument by which they might peaceably force concessions from the South, and thereby remove many of the obstacles in the way of their progress; for it is hardly possible that they will accomplish this through the agency of migration.

Another thing in regard to this movement is that it has undoubtedly taught the South a few lessons. First of all, it must have brought home the fact that the Negroes, to a very large extent, are dissatisfied with conditions in the South; that they resent the economic and social injustices done to them; that they are not wholly anchored to this section; and that large numbers are ready to leave whenever there are signs of favorable opportunities for them in the North and West. As never before, perhaps, moreover, the South has been made to realize the economic value of the Negroes. It has been brought to see the valuable asset it possesses in having at hand this almost illimitable supply of labor so well adapted to its climate and industries, and that there are possibilities of its losing it to such an extent as to endanger very seriously its economic interests. The migration, moreover, has, on the whole, demonstrated to a large part of the better elements of the South that the Negro has not been getting a square deal; that in dealing with him rough methods will not work; and that if the South would have the Negro remain there, "the conditions under which he lives must be kindlier, the collective attitude of the white people toward him friendlier, and that equal opportunities with the whites for his prosperity, enjoyment of life, and the education of his children, must be assured him, not grudgingly, but gladly and abundantly."[184] In a word, the realization is that in order to allay his discontent with conditions in the South, the Negro must in every

591

way be given a man's chance.

The migration likewise is not without its lessons to the Negroes themselves. In the first place, it must be evident to many that moving from the South to the North is no mere trifling affair, but rather a matter of serious concern. It causes the migrants to change suddenly from a mild climate, comparatively easy and slow-moving types of occupations, and relatively simple living conditions to a climate that is for the most part severe, to hard, relentless, and pace-set work of various kinds, and to very complex living conditions. This sudden shift from the old to the new locality brings many hardships and misfortunes to the migrants, because it means for them the putting forth of strenuous efforts for a long period of time in order to make themselves fit for the new occupations, crowded and unsanitary conditions of living, grave problems of health, and much delinquency and crime among them. It brings, also, additional burdens upon the communities of the North and West, because they are compelled to expend much energy, time and money in creating and maintaining social agencies for the purpose of helping the newcomers to adjust themselves to the new surroundings. It means, again, the increasing of the friction between the two races which frequently results in horrible race riots like those of Chicago and East St. Louis.

In the next place, the migration must have made it obvious to the Negroes that the North's interest in them is predominantly economic. The North wants the Negro, but to a limited extent only. It is glad to have him, but only so far as he can be of use to it in its industries. It is not at all disposed to invite and welcome him within its confines merely for the sake of enabling him to escape his unfortunate situation in the South. This is seen, to some extent, in the somewhat changed attitude on the part of certain employers toward Negro labor. It is reported that with the signing of the Armistice the barriers of race were again setup in industry. During the war Negro workers were used widely in the place of white workers to turn out war supplies, but with the ending of hostilities, making these products unnecessary, this policy came to an end. Employers are less willing now to hire Negroes than before, race riots are making it difficult for Negroes to get jobs, and firms which never employed Negro workers are loath to begin the experiment at this time.[185]

This movement perhaps has furthermore indicated very clearly another factor besides racial prejudice which has been a great obstacle in the way of the Negroes' admission into northern industries, and that with its removal there is a possibility of the Negroes becoming greater participants in them. This is foreign labor. This factor has worked along with that of racial antipathy, and has been the latter's most efficient ally in rendering insecure the interests of Negro labor in the North. As we saw, white workers for the most part have long objected to working with Negroes, and where this was the case, employers usually adopted the policy of non-employment of Negro laborers. With the coming of the hordes of immigrants from southern and south-eastern Europe this policy assumed a more rigid permanency, because from these foreign groups the employers could recruit all the labor they needed, and at the same time that sort of labor to which little or no objection could be made on the ground of race and color. Consequently, the Negro was pushed farther and farther back in industry, his opportunities for obtaining situations in the better paid occupations were considerably lessened, and he was thus forced almost wholly into those lines of work which are very menial, often irregular, and poorly remunerative. Even many of these were invaded by the foreigners to such an extent as to drive the Negroes almost completely out of them. This has been especially true of those occupations in which Negroes exclusively formerly served as cooks, waiters, butlers, footmen, coachmen, barbers, porters, janitors, bootblacks, and the like.[186]

When, however, the Great War came and suddenly removed thousands of the aliens from the industries of the North, employers experienced such an urgent need that they were only too glad to draw freely from the Negro population of the South to meet their demands. As the economic interests here were paramount, racial prejudice was apparently swept aside, and Negroes by the thousands were admitted into industries hitherto closed to them. In these they worked beside white men, and, where they measured up to the efficiency of the latter, they received the same pay. Hence, it is to a great extent the foreign labor element that has been a formidable barrier to the Negro in the industrial field, for it was seen that on its removal from this place Negro labor was employed in its stead, notwithstanding the force of racial antipathy. Though this force is capable of accomplishing much, the probability is that in the face of economic stress it would have been rendered impotent by the action of employers just as it was in the recent emergency, and Negroes would have been hired freely according to the exigencies of industries, if foreigners had not been available in such large numbers.

In view of the fact that Negro laborers have now been given a chance in these industries from which they were formerly barred, and the fact that the American Federation of Labor has consented to admit them into the international unions, and is endeavoring to urge these bodies to carry out this policy, the outlook for Negro labor begins to brighten; for there is a possibility of its becoming a potent factor in industrial affairs: but this outcome is conditioned by three things. These are the volume of post-war immigration from Europe, the extent to which Negroes are actually given effective membership in the unions, and the ability of industrial establishments, operating under normal conditions, to absorb fully the available supply of Negro labor. Already, immigration has attained such a height as to cause grave concern in that it threatens, if left unchecked, to surpass its pre-war records even at a time when an almost unprecedented industrial depression is in existence. So serious is the situation that Congress has passed a bill, which has been approved by the President, and thus will soon become a law, providing for a restriction of the number of immigrants from Europe, for a period of one year, to less than half a million. Judging from the past, one can hardly escape taking the view that, if foreigners should come here in numbers sufficient to meet the demands for labor as they were doing before the European War, the Negro's position as a laborer will be greatly endangered, for by this supply of alien labor it may again be pushed back to its old pre-war status. On the other hand, on account of racial prejudices, the international unions are still defying the American Federation of Labor by being unwilling to change their constitutions in order to grant the Negroes membership in their unions, and unless the Federation succeeds in coercing these bodies to execute its will, the withholding of this right will stand as another barrier in the way of the Negro workers.

It should be recalled, moreover, that most of the migrants were attracted North to work for great manufacturing concerns which were engaged in turning out supplies to carry on the European War. The ending of this war rendered, on the one hand, many of these establishments unnecessary because they had been erected for emergency purposes, and, on the other, it brought about a great curtailment of production in those plants of a permanent nature. The question now, therefore, is will production in those industries operating under peace conditions, barring industrial crises, be of such a magnitude as to occasion a demand for the full utilization of the very large available supply of Negro labor?

Here, it might not be amiss to give attention to the question as to whether or not the migration has, on the whole, been a success; or, in other words, have the Negroes in general given a good account of themselves in the new environment? A thoroughly satisfactory answer to this question at this point would be impossible, because such an attempt would lead us beyond the intended scope of this essays. A partially satisfactory reply may be had, however, by taking cognizance of the results of the efforts of the migrants in the various occupations in which they were engaged. On the basis of much that has been said concerning the migrants in this regard, one would at once be in serious doubt as to the success of this movement; but this viewpoint would not be altogether correct, because it would be based on facts which reflect conditions existing at the time when the Negroes had recently arrived North and were struggling to adjust themselves to the new life conditions. Under these circumstances it was almost impossible for them to make a record that could be considered creditable. Despite the hardships which many of the migrants have undergone, and those which numbers of them are undergoing at present because of unemployment, since sufficient time for adjustment has elapsed, the migrants have so wrought in industrial affairs as to furnish ground for reason to believe that the migration has, at least from that standpoint, been a success. This view is firmly taken by a representative of the National Association for the Advancement of Colored People. His conclusion in this regard is based on the discoveries of a recent study of the progress of Negro migrants in certain industrial centers in the North and West. These localities are Chicago, Pittsburgh, Detroit, Cleveland, and the shipbuilding plants on the Atlantic Coast. This investigation showed that the Negroes were rapidly becoming adjusted to the new industrial and social conditions, that they were still being hired as laborers, that they were casting off the habits of tardiness, of indolence and of unreliability, were developing skill and efficiency, and were in every way giving satisfaction to their employers.[187]

More recently many employers of large numbers of Negroes were interviewed and the majority of them indicated that they were satisfied with Negro labor. Several steel mill superintendents said that they were agreeably surprised by the results of that sort of labor. The employment manager of a string of large foundries stated that Negro laborers are making good with him and that they can have their jobs as long as the foundries are operating. It was found also that the Pullman shops in Chicago, which hire 15,000 Negroes, were very well satisfied with Negro labor. A superintendent of one of the largest automobile plants in Detroit said that he knows that Negroes are good workers, and that he is trying to make his shop one which they will be eager to enter. In this same city an inquiry into the status of the Negroes in various industries showed that 60 per cent of the manufacturers employing Negro workmen were fully satisfied with their labor, 20 per cent were neutral, and 20 per cent expressed themselves as being dissatisfied.[188] A short while past, information from questionnaires sent out by the United States Department of Labor to thirty-eight employers of 6,757 Negro employees showed that the majority of these employers were promoting Negro workmen to the skilled ranks; that they were giving the Negroes the same opportunity as the whites to learn semi-skilled or skilled processes; that they were of the opinion that the Negro workmen show ambition for advancement; that there was no difference in the conduct and behavior of Negro and white workers in the plant; that there was no difference between white and Negro employees in the loss of materials due to defective workmanship; and that the time required to break in employees to the work was the same for Negroes as for whites.[189]

Besides, as evidence of their being satisfied with Negro labor, some employers are manifesting personal interest in the affairs of Negro workers by adopting plans of aid and conciliation which tend to encourage laborers and thereby render them more efficient. Accordingly, in a number of plants there exist industrial relations or "mutual interest" departments. The lines of activity of these departments vary from plant to plant. Some establishments merely offer bonus and insurance schemes, emphasize safety, and take steps that lead to the cultivation of cordial group relationship between labor and the management as a substitute for the old cordial individual relationship between the laborer and the boss. Others go beyond this. They see to it that absentee employees are visited, and when the latter are ill they have them provided with medical treatment and free nursing. They also supply their workers with better housing, lectures, clubrooms, playgrounds and cheap homes. In this welfare work an Ohio steel mill has gone to the extent of erecting a $75,000 school building and presenting it to the city for the purpose of educating Negro children. Few employers, moreover, have given Negro labor a voice in determining some of the policies of management through a shop council. Many plants, furthermore, have men of color on the staff of their employment office to see that these various programs adopted by the industrial relations departments be made effective among the Negro workers.[190]

Thus the foregoing examples of favorable opinions of employers regarding Negro labor and their acts of good will toward it are indications that the Negro migrants are giving a good account of themselves in the various occupations in which they are engaged. They are signs, too, that Northern employers are beginning to give more recognition to Negro labor and that they are learning that this labor is capable of becoming as profitable as any other labor when it is given a fair chance to demonstrate this. These instances also show that the Negro laborers themselves are awaking to the fact that indolence, irregularity, unreliability, and slothfulness will yield them nothing, and that if they would be successful in the great economic struggle they must make of themselves industrious, prompt, reliable, skilful and alert workers. In short, they are being made to see that they must be efficient. Finally, these favorable expressions and acts of employers in regard to Negro labor point to the fact that the Negroes are gradually approaching their due place in industry, and that they are likely in time to obtain it, provided they do not perpetually encounter effective obstruction by the prejudice of labor unions, by the force of foreign labor and by the failure of peace-time industry to utilize his labor to its fullest extent.

HENDERSON H. DONALD

FOOTNOTES:

[174] See Chapter III of this Essay.

[175] *Survey*, 38: 227, June 2, 1917; and 38: 428, Aug. 11, 1917.

[176] *Folkways*, p. 2.

[177] Woodson, C. G., *A Century of Negro Migration*, pp. 183-84; *New Rep.*, 7: 214, July 1, 1916.

[178] *Negro Population in the U. S.*, 1790-1915, p. 33.

[179] *Ibid.*

[180] *Ibid.*

[181] *Ibid.*

[182] *New Republic*, 7: 214, July 1, 1916.

[183] See Chapter III of this Essay.

[184] *New York Times*, Jan. 21, 1918, 10: 4.

[185] *Survey*, 42: 900, Sept. 27, 1919.

[186] Warne, F. J., *The Immigrant Invasion*, p. 174.

[187] White, W. F., "The Success of Negro Migration," *The Crisis*, 19: 112-15, Jan., 1920.

[188] Woofter, T. J., Jr., "The Negro and Industrial Peace," *Survey*, 45: 420, Dec. 18, '20.

[189] *The Negro at Work During The World War and During Reconstruction*, Rep. U. S. Dept. Lab., pp. 50-51.

[190] Woofter, T. J., Jr., "The Negro and Industrial Peace," *Survey*, 45: 420, Dec. 18, '20.

BOOK REVIEWS

The Life of Charles T. Walker. By Sᴉʟᴀs Xᴀᴠᴉᴇʀ Fʟᴏʏᴅ. National Baptist Publishing Board, Nashville, Tennessee, 1902. Pp. 193.

This is a brief biography of a distinguished Negro churchman who for more than forty years rendered valuable service in the church in the United States. It begins with the usual account of the parentage, birth, and early childhood of the man and his preparation for his task, as is customary in biographical treatment. This part of the book brings out nothing particularly striking, except an appreciation of the valuable experiences of the subject of the sketch in his struggles to acquire an education and to establish himself in his chosen field. The more interesting part of the work is found in chapter V devoted to a discussion of his call to the Central Baptist Church of Augusta, Georgia. Here we read of a busy life devoted to the settlement of church troubles, the raising of funds for a new edifice, and the expansion of the work under more favorable conditions. Some of the most interesting efforts mentioned here are the management of the *Augusta Sentinel* and the establishment of the Walker Baptist Institute. His work was immediately productive of great good and his influence became a force throughout the State.

The author shows how Dr. Walker, emerging as a more useful man, served as a chaplain of the United States volunteers during the Spanish-American War. He is then presented as an important figure cooperating with the National Baptist Convention and the International Sunday School Convention. As an evangelist, he showed unusual power with an influence so great that he was asked to accept the pastorate of the Mt. Olivet Baptist Church in New York City, where he served five years in spite of the persistent efforts of his former church in Augusta to have him return to that field. In New York, as in Augusta, according to this account, he was interested in all matters pertaining to the social uplift of Negroes and, therefore, started the movement to establish for young men of his own race a branch of the Young Men's Christian Association, a plan which was finally adopted and supported by the city management.

Called back to Augusta so urgently, at the expiration of five years' service in New York, he resumed his work in that city, preaching with more power than ever. The press gave him favorable comment and persons of distinction like John D. Rockefeller, William Howard Taft, Lyman B. Goff, and General Rush C. Hawkins came to hear him expound the gospel, so great was his power of analysis and his ability to impress the thought of his discourses upon the minds of his hearers. The book, therefore, as whole, is a eulogistic treatment; but, on the other hand, it is an interesting account of the career of a man both useful and popular, a worker who connected with so many social forces in our life and engaged in so many different enterprises for the advancement of humanity that every one having an intelligent interest in the Negro may profitably read this volume.

———

A Short History of the American Labor Movement. By MARY BEARD. Harcourt, Brace and Howe, New York, 1920. Pp. 174.

This book is intended as a brief and simple story of the labor movement in the United States in a single comprehensive volume of moderate size for the busy citizen. It undertakes to emphasize the nature and significance of the labor movement and the rise of trade unions. There follows a discussion of the old tactics of labor, its first political experience, and its final return to direct industrial action. Some attention is given to the industrial panics, political utopias, trade unionism, politics, schemes, and plans, which have engaged the attention of the labor element during and since the Civil War.

Discussing the situation during the Civil War, the author brings out valuable information bearing on the history of the Negro in the United States. According to the author, labor was forced to take a stand against slavery because of the advanced opposition taken by the South. Up to that time there had been no uniformity but a necessity for such thereafter existed. This was especially true of the mill workers in Massachusetts, among whom there were many abolitionists, while the molders of Kentucky and Pennsylvania struggled for a compromise to avoid bloodshed between the two sections by limiting slavery to the area it then occupied. When manifesting opposition to the extension of slavery into new territory however, the labor leaders were generally opposed to the aggressive policy of the anti-slavery groups. They, therefore, endeavored to take the question out of Congress. The war finally became inevitable; but some of the labor leaders refused even then to grow excited about slavery, believing that many of the bondmen were better off than the starving wage workers of the free States. Thus, indirectly they supported the institution in that they were advancing the argument set forth by slaveholders during that great crisis. The slave had his food, clothing, and shelter provided by his master who took care of him in his old age, while under the factory system workers earned hardly enough sometimes to eke out an existence. In the end, however, organized labor abandoned its opposition or

603

neutral position and gave its support to save the Union.

———————

The United States and Latin America. By JOHN HOLLADAY LATANÉ, Ph.D., Professor of American History and Dean of the College Faculty in the Johns Hopkins University. Doubleday, Page and Company, New York, 1920. Pp. 346.

This book is a study in modern diplomacy based upon the former work of the author entitled *The Diplomatic Relations of the United States and Spanish America.* In response to the demand for this work which is out of print, the author has herein set forth the same facts in a revised and an enlarged volume. There is added to this work much new matter relating to the events of the last twenty years.

The book begins with a discussion of the revolt of the Spanish-American colonies, followed by an account of the recognition of the Spanish-American republics by the leading nations of the world. It becomes more interesting in that portion dealing with the diplomacy of the United States in regard to Cuba, although the author does not frankly state the case from an impartial point of view. He does not bluntly express the truth that the diplomacy centering around the relations between Cuba and the United States resulted from a systematic effort at the expansion of slavery on the part of the slaveholding class controlling this country from 1800 to 1860. The discussion of the history of the Panama Canal is interesting in view of its subsequent development as is also the chapters on French intervention in Mexico. The two Venezuelan episodes, the difficulties of the United States in the Caribbean, tendencies toward Pan-Americanism and the Monroe Doctrine are

604

extensively treated.

The work as a whole, moreover, does not give important facts with regard to Cuba and Haiti. There is no effort on the part of the author to show the imperialistic tendencies of the United States in extending its authority over weak republics at the time that it is professing to be laboring in the interest of the self-determination of smaller nations. The inside cover of the foreign policy of the United States toward Cuba, therefore, cannot be seen in reading this book. There does not appear in this work sufficient treatment of our relations with the Spanish American Republics to show that because of serious tilts in our diplomacy, the relations between the United States and Latin America have become strained.

No better example of the shortcomings of this book can be cited than the very meager reference to the Haitian Republic, which, contrary to international law and the principles of government which we profess to foster in the United States, has been occupied by United States marines, who according to official reports have instituted a regime of murder supported by the Wilson and Harding administrations. Professor Latané should have treated this phase of the question with the same detail with which he treated other aspects of it and his failure to do so identifies his book with that of many others written in the interest of a special class or to promote a special cause.

***

Creole Families of New Orleans. By GRACE KING. Macmillan Company, New York, 1921. Pp. 465.

This book, according to the author, "comes in response to a long-felt wish of an humble student of Louisiana history to know more about the early actors in it, to go back of the printed names in the pages of Gayarré and Martin, and peep, if possible, into the personality of the men who followed Bienville to found a city upon the Mississippi, and who, remaining on the spot, continued their good work by founding families that have carried on their work and their good names." The families chosen are such as Marigny de Mandeville, the Dreux family, De Pontalba, Rouer De Villeray, De la Chaise, Lafrénière, Labedoyère, Huchet de Kernion and a score or more of others. The work is well illustrated with scenes bearing on the life of the pioneer aristocracy of that commonwealth. The aim of the author evidently is to publish those records bearing witness to their good blood, their "maintenances de noblesse," which they considered as much a family necessity as a house and furniture. From the records of their baptisms, marriages and deaths, from bits of old furniture, jewelry, glass, old miniatures, portraits, scraps of silk and brocade, flimsy fragments and the like, the author has made an interesting story and well illustrated it. There is a regret that some of these achievements of the past are so deeply hidden for the lack of records to throw light thereupon that a definitive account of some of these families cannot be obtained.

There is evidence, however, that certain records of families equally as noble and aristocratic as some of those recorded in this work were not mentioned therein for the reason that they had mingled too freely with the blacks during the early period and had, therefore, been classed as persons of color. One does not find, therefore, in this work so much about these distinguished families of color as may be discovered in the author's earlier work entitled *New Orleans, the Place and People* (pages 346 to 349). Referring therein to this *gens de couleur*, she mentions in the former work a number of musicians, merchants, money and real estate brokers, as the ambitious element of this class, which monopolized the trade of shoemakers, barbers, tailors, carpenters, and upholsterers. Some of these in the course of time attained positions of distinction in the commercial world, acquiring large fortunes in the form of shares of stock in business enterprises and large landed estates like the plantations of Louisiana. One of these families, we know, had a large plantation of about 4,000 acres and owned hundreds of slaves. The head of the family lived in luxurious style in keeping with that of the planters of the South.

In other cases in which the color of the quadroon or octoroon did not brand him as far removed from the white race, the social distinctions existing between whites and such Negroes were not observed. If they were enforced against some of these aristocratic persons of color fortunate in having sufficient of the world's goods to secure the comforts of this life in spite of their social position, they usually sent their children to northern institutions and even to Paris where they were well educated. Thousands of these on their return to this country easily passed to the other race and mingled their blood with some of the most aristocratic families mentioned in this recent treatise of Grace King.

NOTES

On the first of October Mr. Victor R. Daly, who has recently been the Industrial Secretary of the New York Urban League, became the Business Manager of the JOURNAL OF NEGRO HISTORY. For some time his work will be largely in the field in an effort to extend the circulation of this publication and to find friends for this cause. It is earnestly hoped that the public will receive him as a coworker and give him the most hearty support.

The Association for the Study of Negro life and History will hold its next annual meeting at Lynchburg, Virginia, on the 14th and 15th of November. The morning sessions will be held at the Virginia Theological Seminary and College and the evening sessions at the Eighth street Baptist Church and at the Court street Baptist Church.

Men of national prominence will address this meeting. President R. C. Woods, of Virginia Theological Seminary and College, will deliver the welcome address, to which Professor John R. Hawkins will respond. Other addresses will be made by Dr. I. E. McDougle, Dr. W. H. Stokes, Professor Bernard W. Tyrrell, Professor Charles H. Wesley, and Dr. C. G. Woodson.

The April number of the *Monthly Labor Review* contains a discussion of various features of the labor situation of interest to all students of social sciences.

608

It embraces among other things the treatment of the trend of child labor in the United States from 1913 to 1920, the average union scale of wage rates during the same period, Federal labor legislation, and Negro labor during and after the war. The treatment of the last topic centers around the work of Dr. George E. Haynes, who during the World War and for some time thereafter was the head of the Bureau of Negro Economics in the Department of Labor.

The article briefly discusses the formation of the division of Negro economics, showing the difficulties of finding a person competent to do the work and the handicap preventing the Department from carrying out its chief objective, that of bringing the two races together. The article shows, moreover, how the beginning was made in North Carolina among citizens of both, races, how they directed their attention seriously to the economic problems, and how many of the obstacles which at first were encountered were finally removed by hearty cooperation. There is a discussion of the industrial employment of Negroes during the scarcity of labor and the depression which followed after the war. In this case valuable statistics are given to set forth the writer's point of view. The article finally closes with a discussion of Negro women in industry. Here are given valuable facts as to how these workers were employed, the problems which they faced, and what this Department did to meet the exigencies of the situation. This short but valuable article may be read with interest and profit.

www.ingramcontent.com/pod-product-compliance
Lightning Source LLC
Chambersburg PA
CBHW021933110726
47901CB00003B/817